W9-AMP-108

Deception and Desire

BY THE SAME AUTHOR

Oriental Hotel
The Emerald Valley
Women and War
The Black Mountains
The Hills and the Valley
Folly's Child
Daughter of Riches

DECEPTION AND DESIRE

Janet Tanner

St. Martin's Press
New York

Library of Congress Cataloging-in-Publication Data

Tanner, Janet.
Deception and desire / Janet Tanner.
p. cm.
ISBN 0-312-11261-0
1. Missing person—Fiction. I. Title.
PR6070.A545D4 1994
823'.914—dc20 94-31318 CIP

First published in Great Britain by Century Limited

First U.S. Edition: March 1995
10 9 8 7 6 5 4 3 2 1

Acknowledgments

My grateful thanks are due to Bill Head, who, as a former deep sea diver, was able to answer all my queries on North Sea oil rigs and diving in general as well as helping me with suitable locations and underwater mishaps. Also to Warwick Newton, for sharing with me his extensive knowledge of the boot and shoe industry both past and present. And to everyone else on whom I pressed questions about various topics – Thank you!

'Things and actions are what they are, and the consequences of them will be what they will be; why then should we desire to be deceived?'

Bishop Butler, 1692–1752

Deception and Desire

Prologue

The story was front-page news in every one of the tabloids.

VANDINA BOSS DIES IN FLYING ACCIDENT, the headlines screamed in inch-high capitals. DINAH MARSHALL WIDOWED BY AIR CRASH.

The young man saw them when he went to pick up his mail.

The newspapers were brought to the oil rig off the Aberdeen coast by the helicopter which made the thirty-minute journey twice daily, and they were always seized upon eagerly by the men who lived and worked there. There was a loneliness about the life, a feeling of being isolated from the rest of humanity, that the comradeship and closeness that existed between them could never quite eradicate, a sense of being cut off by the elements and buried alive in the danger and the boredom and the exhaustion that came from the sheer hard work that made them long for news of the outside world with a hunger that no amount of television-watching could satisfy.

But the young man had not even seen the television news the night before – he had been in recompression following a dive – and now the headlines that leapt up at him started an interest that was more than mere curiosity. A jolt like an electric shock ran through him and he felt his pulses change gear the way they did just before a dive. He put down his money on the counter and picked up the paper, forcing himself to jam it in the pocket of his windcheater. Eager as he was, he did not want to read it here, with others watching him. That had to wait until he was alone.

Back in his cabin he yanked the newspaper out of his pocket and spread it out on the table, bending over it avidly without even stopping to take off his jacket. Not that he wanted to take off his jacket – it was always so damned cold out here in the North Sea, a bone-chilling cold that seemed to invade every pore and devour his flesh so that it was hard to remember what it felt like to be completely, comfortably warm.

The headline leapt at him again.

He absorbed it automatically and moved swiftly on to read the report.

Van Kendrick, head of the Vandina leather goods fashion empire, died yesterday when the light aircraft he was piloting crashed into a hillside in Gloucestershire. Van Kendrick, 54, was alone in the Cessna at the time of the accident, the cause of which is a complete mystery. Witnesses said the aircraft, which had only recently undergone a complete overhaul, seemed to go into a steep dive before ploughing into the hillside and bursting into flames.

'I saw it come down from the field where I was working,' farmworker Melvin Tucker, 25, said. 'I ran to the scene but there was nothing I could do. The heat was so intense I couldn't get anywhere near it.'

Experts sifting the wreckage agreed that the devastation was such that in all likelihood Van Kendrick died instantly, but even if this were not the case he would have stood no chance of escaping the inferno that followed. Weather conditions at the time of the accident were fine and clear and wind speeds were normal. But friends said that Van Kendrick had been complaining of chest pains recently and speculation is rife that he might have suffered a heart attack.

The Vandina fashion empire, the brainchild of Van Kendrick and his wife, Dinah Marshall, was born twenty-five years ago in a tiny workshop in Somerset. Dinah Marshall's talent for anticipating trends and designing quality products to capture the imagination of the fashion- and quality-conscious rich the world over, coupled with Van Kendrick's legendary business acumen produced a phenomenon that outstripped its humble beginnings and swept like a bushfire through the once staid accessories scene to challenge the great houses such as Hermes. It was Van Kendrick who was responsible for the slogan that epitomised Vandina's appeal – 'A Touch of the Country' – which was to become synonymous with quality, style and understated elegance.

The question being asked today – along with the inevitable ones as to how Van Kendrick died – is: Will Vandina survive without him?

'Of course it is business as usual,' a spokeswoman for the company told our reporter. 'Dinah was always the inspiration and guiding light. At the moment, naturally, she is in deep shock, but she has no intention of letting Vandina fail.'

But the fact remains that the company will sadly miss its dynamic and innovative boss. And Dinah, his wife of twenty-five years, will be fighting an uphill battle without him at her side. The couple have no children and have always been known to be inseparable. 'They complement one another absolutely,' this paper once declared after an exclusive interview. 'They are the perfect partnership.'

Now Dinah, a glamorous but somewhat reclusive figure, has lost her perfect partner. Somehow she must carry the flag of Vandina alone.

The young man straightened up, rasping at the week-old stubble on his chin with fingers that shook slightly. The adrenaline was flowing fast now; every inch of his skin seemed to be crawling with it.

So – the man behind one of the most successful and innovative designers in England was dead. Dinah Marshall had lost the husband who had so often been described as her Svengali, and she was totally alone.

Or so she, and the world, believed.

Only he knew different.

Barely able to contain his excitement he crossed to the small chest where he kept his personal possessions, getting out a manila envelope, extracting the strip of official-looking paper and spreading it out.

A birth certificate. Everyone has one and thinks nothing of it, but to him this one was special; not an original but a copy of an original, obtained from the registers of St Catherine's House as a result of the Act of Parliament which allows adopted children to discover the truth of their origins.

Thoughtfully the young man allowed his eye to run along the line from left to right.

He knew it by heart, of course, but he still wanted to look at it again.

Date of birth: 2 September 1961.

Sex: Male.

Name: Stephen John.

District of registration: Watchet, Somerset.

There was a dash in the space where the father's name should have been, and the word: Unknown.

But there was a name on the certificate, as both informant and mother.

Dinah Elizabeth Marshall.

The young man straightened again, smiling slightly.

The papers did not know it but Dinah Marshall had a son. He had known it for more than two years but he had not told another living soul. He had kept his own counsel, waiting for the right moment to present itself.

Now he rather thought that moment had come.

Chapter One

Mike Thompson crawled his silver Citroen ZX through the early evening rush-hour traffic that congested the Bristol city-centre streets with an endless slow-moving stream, keeping a sharp look-out for somewhere to park. As he passed a side road close to the Central Police Station he saw a car move out from a meter and grabbed his chance. That was a piece of luck – the first he'd had all day. Mike reversed into the space, jumped out slamming the door impatiently behind him and fished in his pocket for change to feed the meter. Then he sprinted along the street in the direction of the police station.

Rain was falling from an overcast sky, a thick, unseasonal downpour that was also surprisingly cold. Flaming June, Mike thought, and wondered briefly what had happened to the summers of his youth, when the sun had seemed to shine endlessly from a sky of unbroken blue on to the 'rec' where he and his friends had played cricket every evening when homework was done until it was too dark to see the ball. There had not been much cricket so far this year for anyone. Most of the matches he'd arranged for the First and Second XIs of the comprehensive school where he was head of PE had been rained off, and so had the practices. He had had to spend almost every day in the gym with his classes of eleven- to sixteen-year-olds, organising basketball and volleyball instead and hoping vainly to work off some of their unquenchable and often destructive energy.

Today had been no exception. Six periods of one lot after the other, all yelling and shouting, jostling and fighting amongst themselves – because most of the lads in the part of the city his school catered for were handy with their fists – and Mike had thought he'd go crazy. Had they been worse than usual? Probably not. It was just that today, unusually for him, he had not wanted to be bothered with them. He'd had other things on his mind. Perhaps they had sensed that, with that infallible instinct students have for a chink in the armour of a teacher, and thought they could get away with the sort of behaviour he usually came down on like a ton of bricks.

They had been wrong, of course. Whatever his personal worries Mike was not the man to let them get the better of him. He had meted out exactly the same treatment he always did – a stinging reprimand for run-of-the-mill obstreperousness, a clip around the ear for the worst offenders. Some vengeful parent could have him taken to court and charged with assault for that, he knew, but he had never let it worry him and, oddly, they respected him for it, those tough cases from the most deprived areas. In their world the law of the jungle applied, they understood it and made an icon of the powerfully-built PE teacher who had played rugby for a hugely successful club side and been capped twice for England before a serious knee injury had put an end to his glory days.

Mike crossed the road, dodging between the almost stationary traffic, and ran up the flight of steps and into the police station foyer. It was surprisingly busy. At the desk a middle-aged woman in a headscarf and mackintosh was reporting a lost handbag, her plump, paunchy face flushed and crumpled with anxiety; behind her a young man in the city office uniform of dark suit and trenchcoat, and two girls who might have been students waited their turn.

Mike joined the queue, loosening the zip of the waxed jacket he was wearing over his dark-blue tracksuit and dripping rainwater on to the tiled floor. One of the two girls turned round and glanced at him, her eyes brightening with interest as she became aware of the ruggedly good-looking face beneath the short cropped hair, already shot at the temples with more than a sprinkling of premature grey. Those first specks of silver had appeared when Mike was only twenty-two and he had been horrified. Though not in the least vain they had given him a stomach-churning sensation of time racing by and youth slipping away. 'Don't worry about it, darling,' Judy, Mike's ex-wife, had said. 'Men who go grey don't usually go bald too.' And for once she had been right. No – not for once. Judy's indisputable habit of always being right had been, he thought, her most irritating trait, infuriating him even as he reluctantly admired her for it. But in this instance he was glad that, so far at least, it seemed her reputation for being right had not been sullied. He was thirty-three years old now, and unlike so many rugby players he still had a full head of hair.

The girl's eyes lingered now, noticing the slightly irregular jawline and the nose that had taken a battering in numerous scrums, the hazel eyes, green-flecked, the mouth with its deep, well-defined lower lip. Becoming aware of her scrutiny Mike returned her gaze and she looked away hastily, embarrassed by her own wishful thoughts. Mike saw the pink flush rise in her cheeks before it was hidden behind a curtain of hair, and instantly forgot it. Teaching in a comprehensive he had become used to being ogled by pubescent Lolitas and their seductive older sisters, girls who combined the freshness of youth with the alarming knowingness of modern teenagers. Their attentions had been a part of his life for so long now that he had come to accept it without much thought – except for keeping a sharp eye out for the traps that lay in wait for the unwary male teacher. And in any case, today he was too preoccupied to give any one of them a second thought.

The queue moved forward and Mike glanced at his watch, hoping he had put enough time on the parking meter. With the police station so close by the area would probably be crawling with traffic wardens returning to base at the end of their shift and he did not want the hassle – or the expense – of a parking ticket. As a teacher his salary wasn't so great that he could pay it and not notice. But if he got a ticket he got one. It was the least of his worries just now, barely of any importance set against the reason he was here.

Another policeman appeared and spoke to the girls, and Mike found himself at the counter where the original duty policeman made a note on a form and looked up at him. 'Yes, sir?'

Mike cleared his throat, feeling slightly foolish.

'I want to report a missing person.'

The policeman's expression remained implacable.

'Oh yes, sir, and who is that?'

'My girlfriend.' That, too, sounded stupid, he thought, like one of his sixteen-year-olds talking about his current date. But then how else did one describe someone who was as Ros was to him? They had been together for a good long while now but there was no formal relationship. She wasn't his wife or his fiancée, she wasn't even his live-in lover. Ros hadn't wanted to give up her independence. Like him she had a broken marriage behind her, like him she had been wary of committing herself again. Theirs was an adult relationship between two highly individual people, and it had worked well enough. Until now . . .

'Your girlfriend.' There was a hint of a sneer on the policeman's almost expressionless face now, indicating that the ludicrousness of the term had occurred to him too. 'How old is she?'

'How old?' Even given his earlier thoughts Mike was surprised by the question. 'Twenty-seven. No, twenty-eight. She had a birthday last month.'

'I see. And when did you last see her?'

'Just over a week ago. Before I went off to camp.' Mike ran his fingers through his wet hair which was threatening to drip into his eyes. 'Perhaps I should explain. I'm a teacher at St Clement's Comprehensive. We run a school camp every summer and I usually get talked into being one of the members of staff to go. We left last Friday week.'

'Hardly camping weather,' the policeman observed. 'Where did you go?'

'The Isle of Wight. It rained practically all the time. Anyway, I saw Ros on the Wednesday before I left – I was too busy packing and so on to see her on the Thursday night. I tried to telephone her once or twice whilst I was away but got no reply, just her answering machine. I didn't think too much of it – she's a busy lady and out quite a lot. But when I got home and still couldn't get hold of her I began to wonder what the hell was going on. I drove over to her place on Saturday and she wasn't there. It looked as though she hadn't been there all week.'

'What exactly do you mean by that, sir?'

'Well – how do you usually tell someone hasn't been at home? Papers and post lying on the mat, milk gone sour in the fridge, dead flowers in the vases . . . you know the sort of thing. I have a key . . . when she didn't answer the door I let myself in.'

'So the place was all locked up.'

'Yes. Obviously. I told you – she wasn't there.'

'Perhaps she'd decided to take a holiday – like you, sir.'

'Without telling me – or anyone – she was going?'

'Why not? She is twenty-eight years old, you say. At that age she doesn't have to answer to anyone.'

'Well I know that!' Mike said, annoyed by the policeman's

patronising manner. 'But it's totally unlike her to just take off like that. Ros is a very organised lady. If she was going on holiday she would have cancelled the papers, thrown away any milk that might go sour and made sure everything was in order. She'd hate to come back to vases of dead sweet peas and tubs of mouldy yoghurt. And besides, there's her job. Ros has a very high-powered position as personal assistant to Dinah Marshall.'

'Dinah Marshall.' The policeman looked up, eyes narrowing. 'You mean . . .?'

'Yes – *the* Dinah Marshall. Vandina – you know?'

The policeman nodded, looking interested for the first time, and Mike experienced a moment's grim satisfaction. Even he would have heard of Vandina – worldwide fashion leaders in quality leather accessories and beautiful silkscreen-printed scarves, whose headquarters was just a few miles from the heart of the city, yet set in the open countryside that was its inspiration. Twenty-five years ago Dinah, together with her husband and mentor, Van Kendrick, had opened the first little factory in a barn at the rear of their farmhouse home and in a success story that might have rivalled a fairytale they had gone on to take the world by storm. Vandina bags, belts and wallets were sold now in exclusive stores from London to New York, Paris to Hong Kong (only the most exclusive stores were allowed to market them – a deliberate policy of Van's which had undoubtedly paid handsome dividends in terms of desirability). Vandina scarves graced the necks of the rich, the titled and the famous wherever they gathered at races or horse trials or point-to-point meetings. The Vandina slogan, 'A Touch of the Country', appeared on double-page-spread advertisements in *Vogue* and *Harpers* as well as commercial publications such as the prestigeous Peninsula Group magazine, distributed to those who patronised the most famous and luxurious hotel chain in the Far East, and fashion editors fell over themselves to get a scoop on details of the new season's collections or some fresh avenue Vandina planned to branch into.

'Ros has been with Vandina ever since she left college and she takes her responsibilities as Dinah's assistant very seriously,' Mike said. 'I contacted the company on Monday after I got home, and found her missing. They don't know where she is either. It seems she phoned the office first thing in the morning on Tuesday of last week and said she wouldn't be in. She wanted to take some emergency leave. They haven't heard from her since.'

The smirk was back on the policeman's face but it was a smirk of weariness rather than humour.

'Well there you are then, sir. She decided she wanted a bit of a break and took it. There's no law against that, you know.'

Mike felt his exasperation growing.

'You're not hearing a word I'm saying, are you? That's not like Ros either. She lives for her job, thinks she's indispensable, and knowing what she puts into it she probably damn near is. When she takes her holiday, twice a year, she makes certain everything is set to run smoothly and she still frets about it while she's away. She'd never just leave them in the lurch unless something pretty catastrophic had happened. But she gave no word of explanation, no reason for wanting leave, no indication of where she was going. Nothing. That phone call, as I say, was on the Tuesday morning. They haven't heard from her since. Frankly I'm extremely worried about her. There is something very odd about all this. That's why I've come to report her missing.'

The policeman sighed. He still looked unconvinced but he nodded resignedly and lifted a flap in the counter.

'All right, sir, you'd better come through to the interview room and we'll take a few details.'

Mike followed him along a corridor to a small interview room furnished only with a bare table and two or three chairs. A clock on the wall showed 5.10, but the grey light filtering in through the small high-up window made it feel, somehow, much later. The constable flicked a wall switch and the room flooded with harsh white light.

He fetched a form and sat down, indicating Mike should sit opposite him.

'Name?'

'Rosalie Newman. Rosalie Patricia Newman.'

'Address?'

'Woodbine Cottage, Stoke-sub-Mendip.'

The policeman stopped writing.

'Stoke-sub-Mendip. That's not our patch.'

'What do you mean?'

'It comes under the jurisdiction of another division. This is the city. You should be reporting this to your local police station.'

'This is my local police station, damn it! *I* don't live in Stoke-sub-Mendip. And what the hell difference does it make anyway?'

'There's no need to take that tone, sir. I'm pointing out that if the lady lives in Stoke-sub-Mendip this should be reported to her local police station.'

'But since I am here . . .'

'Since you are here I'll take the details and pass them on. Now, do you have a photograph?'

Mike reached into his jacket pocket and extracted his wallet. This, at least, he had anticipated. The photograph was the best one he had been able to find of Ros, taken by a commercial photographer at the Vandina dinner-dance last Christmas. He looked at it for a moment, at Ros's wide-set blue-green eyes and lovely clear-featured face framed by sharply bobbed dark-brown hair, and the smooth shapely line of her shoulders bare above the line of her strapless emerald-green evening gown. She was half smiling in that typically enigmatic way of hers, looking straight at the camera with a hint of challenge in her eyes. It was almost, he felt suddenly, as if she was reaching out to tease him. Abruptly he pushed the photograph across the desk and saw the policeman's mouth twist in wry appreciation.

'This is her?'

'Yes. It was taken about six months ago. It's a good likeness.'

'Hmm.' The policeman eyed Mike, taking in his waxed jacket and tracksuit, and Mike imagined he could read his thoughts: What's a girl like that doing with a bloke like him? No wonder she's disappeared!

With an effort he controlled his irritation as the policemen fired off a seemingly endless list of questions. What sort of car did Ros drive, what was its number and was it also missing? Mike confirmed it was and the questions continued. What family did Ros have? Who were her friends? Names? Addresses? Was there anywhere she might have gone? Had she ever gone missing before? Any known problems? Debts? Family crises? Disagreements or even outright quarrels?

Perhaps amongst this plethora of information there was something relevant, Mike thought. And what had he expected anyway?

He had been annoyed at not being taken seriously, then annoyed because they were doing their job. What had got into him?

At last it was over. The policeman put down his ballpoint pen.

'Right, sir, I'll pass this on for enquiries to be instigated. But I think I should explain – if we do find Miss Newman there's no guarantee we shall be able to tell you where she is.'

'What the hell do you mean?' Mike exploded.

'It could be, sir, that Miss Newman doesn't want you to know,' the policeman said darkly. 'Often when people disappear it's for the very good reason that they want to cut contact with someone. And that, of course, is their right. We have to respect that in the case of adult persons.'

Suddenly Mike had had enough. He could see the way the policeman's mind was working and in a way he could almost understand the way it must look to him. An independent young woman, a divorcee, who had suddenly decided she had had enough of the pressures of her job, had perhaps grown tired of the man with whom she shared a relationship, and had decided to cut loose, temporarily at least. It was all too feasible. Probably all too common. Small wonder they were scarcely interested. To this rather jaded policeman it was all a routine domestic matter – fill in a form, find the lady, establish her right to her privacy, close the file.

Only they didn't know Ros the way he did. They didn't know how out of character it would have been for her to simply disappear of her own volition for no reason with no word to anyone.

Mike scraped back his chair and stood up.

'Thank you for your time, Officer. I only hope someone will take this more seriously than you appear to be doing. And I have to tell you, in the meantime I shall be making a few enquiries of my own.'

He strode along the corridor. The foyer was still busy, milling with members of the general public all convinced their problem was the most important in the world at this precise moment. Easy to see how the officers dealing with them became complacent. He threaded his way between them and out into the street. It was still raining.

*

There was a parking ticket in a plastic envelope on the windscreen of his car. Mike swore and tore it off. That was all he needed. He stuffed it into his pocket without bothering to read it and got into the car, leaning back against the leather headrest and letting out his breath in a long sigh.

The feeling of frustration that had overcome him in the police station was still pressing in on him and he closed his eyes, rerunning the interview in his mind and wondering exactly how far the police would go in trying to find out what had happened to Ros. Presumably they'd get in touch with her mother, who lived in Wiltshire, but Mike knew they'd draw a blank there – he had already spoken to Dulcie on the telephone, asking, in a roundabout way so as not to alarm her, if she knew where Ros was. She hadn't and he had not been surprised. Ros was not close to her mother, who had married for the second time when Ros was in her late teens. According to Ros her stepfather resented both her and her younger sister Maggie and demanded total devotion from their mother. Maggie herself was married to a Greek and lived in Corfu so it was doubtful she would know anything and he found it almost impossible to believe Ros would have flown out to visit Maggie without telling anyone. Similarly he couldn't imagine her absenting herself to visit friends but he had been given the police some names and addresses anyway – old college chums in London and a best friend named Annie who lived in Scarborough.

The police would make some enquiries at Vandina, too, he assumed, in the hope that she had said something which might give a clue to her whereabouts. But he thought it unlikely that she had. Ros was such a self-sufficient and private person he could not imagine her indulging in girlie chats or confidences with her colleagues, even Dinah, for whom she had worked for six years and to whom she was fiercely loyal. That loyalty was such that Mike had sometimes seen it almost as a threat to their relationship; though he was not by nature a jealous man he had felt that there was little doubt that he did not come first in Ros's scale of priorities. He had known from the beginning, of course, how important Ros's job was to her, but her protectiveness of Dinah, which now seemed almost an obsession with her, had stemmed from the death of Dinah's husband, Van Kendrick, who was also head of the company, in a light plane crash a little over a year earlier. From that moment on Ros seemed to have assumed responsibility for Dinah, in her own mind at least, and it was this fierce sense of loyalty that Mike found one of the most worrying things about her disappearance.

Little as he liked to admit it, he could almost believe Ros might have walked out on him as the policeman had suggested. Life had taught him that women were not always to be trusted, and recently things had been a little strained between him and Ros. There had been times when Ros had snapped at him impatiently, times when she had put off a planned meeting on the flimsiest excuse, times when something had seemed to hang unsaid in the air between them, and Mike feared it might indeed be possible that she had taken the easy way out and simply left without bothering to tell him. But that she should have done so without telling Dinah was inconceivable.

Unless . . . Mike sat up suddenly, drumming his fingers on the steering wheel thoughtfully as it occurred to him to wonder if certain recent changes at Vandina might have had any bearing on Ros's sudden decision. He recalled the story of what had happened as Ros had related it to him.

Dinah had, it seemed, had an illegitimate son who had been adopted as a baby. About six months ago he had turned up, having obtained his original birth certificate and discovered that Dinah was his natural mother. Dinah had welcomed him with open arms, Ros had said, and the fact that she had found her long-lost son had gone some way towards making up for the fact that she had lost the Svengali-like figure of her husband. Was it possible he had upset Ros in some way, treading on her toes where Dinah was concerned? But even given her single-minded devotion to Dinah he would have thought she was too professional to allow something like that to drive her away without even a fight.

Mike sighed in exasperation. The visit to the police station had not, in spite of the constable's obvious scepticism, done anything to make him less worried. If anything it had strengthened his anxiety. He was so damned sure the policeman was wrong in blithely assuming she had simply taken off. Yet he had chickened out of actually putting his worst fears into words – that in fact there was something sinister about Ros's disappearance.

The hollow sickness that had been there in his gut to a greater or lesser degree ever since he had arrived home from camp and found her missing reasserted itself. He was not an imaginative man, but neither was he a stupid one. Less stable characters than Ros might walk out on a home, a relationship and a career because of pressures of one kind or another, and she had seemed a little preoccupied during the last weeks. But if she had intended to cut loose she would never have done it this way, leaving so many untidy ends. It just wasn't Ros. There was the telephone call to Vandina, of course, but he couldn't help wondering if she had made it under duress and that someone was perhaps holding her against her will – or worse.

The windscreen of his car had misted up against the rain. He wiped it with the back of his hand – and saw a traffic warden turn the corner of the street. Irritation momentarily displaced anxiety. Couldn't they leave him alone for five minutes? But he did not want to tangle with the law again today. He switched on the engine and pulled hastily away from the meter.

But the dark cloud of foreboding came with him.

Halfway home Mike thought again of Maggie.

Would the police get in touch with her in the course of their enquiries? he wondered. They might, and if so she should be forewarned. Mike could not imagine Dulcie would have taken the trouble to put her in the picture and it would be too dreadful to hear from official strangers that her sister was missing.

Mike had met Maggie only briefly on her infrequent visits home, when she usually stayed with her mother in Wiltshire. But he knew Ros had written her telephone number in the book beside his own phone when she had called Maggie once from his flat.

'Just in case I should ever lose my Filofax,' she had said, doodling a little picture of a man in Greek national costume beside the number – doodles were a habit of Ros's, a throwback to her art school days.

'I should think if you lost your Filofax you'd have a good deal more to worry about than your sister's telephone number!' he had teased her. Ros carried everything in her Filofax, from credit cards and passport to addresses of friends and business contacts and her all-important engagement diary.

Well, it wasn't only her Filofax that was lost now, Mike thought grimly. It was Ros herself too.

He put his foot down hard on the accelerator and manoeuvred skilfully through the now thinning rush-hour traffic and the rain.

He would ring Maggie as soon as he got home.

Chapter Two

Maggie Veritos was drinking iced coffee on the patio of her home in Kassiopi, Corfu, when the telephone began to ring. She wriggled her feet back into her flip-flops, rose from her white plastic patio chair and went into the house, screwing up her eyes in an effort to adjust to the dim light after the brightness of the evening outside.

The telephone was on the farthest wall of the inner room. She unhooked it and pushed aside her thick fall of light-brown hair to put it to her ear.

'Hello. Maggie Veritos.'

Nothing but a series of crackles came down the line.

'Hello?' she repeated. Still nothing.

Maggie sighed. It wasn't unusual. The telephone system in Corfu was unreliable, to say the least. More often than not it was impossible to get through and conversations, carried on over a background of static, tended to fade or even get cut off altogether. But at least the telephone was in working order now, theoretically. For a year after it had first been installed it had remained unconnected, nothing more or less than an ornament. Maggie had accepted the fact with good grace – she had learned that the Corfiote workman couldn't be hurried. '*Mañana*' might be a word of Spanish origin but it also applied to the attitude of most natives of Corfu. She had almost given up hope of ever having the use of her own telephone when one day the engineers had arrived and to her amazement remained long enough to do the job. Now all that was needed was for someone to improve the lines.

'Hello!' she said again, without much hope, and when the crackles continued unabated she replaced the telephone and shrugged.

If someone wanted her they would try again. It could be a wrong number, of course – very common – or it could be a friend inviting her round for the evening.

Or it could be Ari, telephoning from his office in Kerkira to say he'd be late home again . . .

Maggie's mouth tightened a shade. On balance that was probably who it was. Ari often telephoned these days to say he'd be late, and Maggie was all too horribly sure what lay behind the constant stream of excuses. For a long while she'd tried to talk herself out of her growing suspicion. Ari was kept very busy – as an architect on an island where development was springing up all over the place there was plenty of work, and with his own practice to sustain he took on every offer that came his way. Besides this, he was in many ways typically Greek. Though his sense of 'family' was very strong his attitude towards women tended to be macho. Maggie had realised early on that he had no intention of allowing himself to be tied down in the role of dutiful husband. After a long session at the office he liked to have a drink with 'the boys' – friends from his old crowd and new business acquaintances.

Maggie had tried not to be hurt that he no longer rushed home to her as he had done when they were first married, tried to tell herself that as long as she didn't nag, as long as she let him have his freedom, he'd get over this restlessness. But it was cold comfort. She might have her own friends in the English community, and she certainly had Ari's family – close-knit and almost claustrophobic in the way the unit was constructed, with Ari's mother, the matriarch, ruling them all with a rod of iron – but it was *Ari* she wanted. It was for him, after all, that she had moved to a foreign land, a different culture. It was him she loved, him she wanted to be with.

And then she had found out it wasn't just 'the boys' that Ari was seeing when he stayed late in Kerkira. There was a woman too. Her name was Melina. And Maggie did not know what she was going to do about her.

She stood for a moment with her head bowed. The knowledge that Ari had a lover was a constant weight on her heart; even when she was not actually thinking about it it was still there, an ache that refused to go away.

Perhaps, she thought sometimes, she should confront him with it – tell him straight out that she knew. If this had been England, if Ari had been English, she felt quite certain she would have done just that. But it wasn't England, it was Corfu, and Ari wasn't

English; in spite of having been educated and trained in England he was Corfiote through and through. It was four years now since she had first met him, almost three since he had married her and brought her home to Corfu, yet sometimes his foreignness made her feel she scarcely knew him at all.

In spite of the temperature in the room, still pleasantly warm from the heat of the day, Maggie shivered. They had warned her, of course, everyone who knew anything about mixed marriages and a great many who knew nothing besides. They had pointed out the difficulties of the culture divide, drawn attention to the pitifully high failure-rate of marriages that tried to bridge it. She would be terribly homesick, they said. She would hate being part of a family unit so tight that they lived, if not all in the same house, then next door and next door and next door again, brothers and uncles and cousins, and all ruled over by the matriarch who would expect to have the last word on every aspect of family life, from the upbringing of the children to the menus for the traditional shared Sunday meals. And leaving all that aside, looking just at the man, he would be different to any man she had ever known, the way he thought and spoke and acted determined by a heritage that was totally, absolutely foreign to her. Oh yes, they had tried their hardest to dissuade her, those prophets of doom. And her mother had been the most gloomy of all.

'I'm sure it all *seems* very romantic, darling. Ari is incredibly handsome and Corfu is a beautiful island – so long as you keep away from the dreadful touristy places. But what will happen when the gilt comes off the gingerbread? And it will . . . it will!'

She had said it all in that infuriatingly high-handed way of hers, her light and musical tone concealing her strong desire to domineer. It was as if she was so certain she was right that she simply could not believe that anyone, least of all one of her daughters, would go against her wishes. Maggie sometimes thought that if it had not been for her mother's opposition she might not have rushed into marriage with Ari quite so speedily.

The fact that she had gone against all advice, however, was one of the reasons she was so reluctant to admit defeat now, or, indeed, do or say anything that might bring matters to crisis point. She had married Ari and come to Corfu determined to make it work; her fierce pride refused to allow her even to consider the possibility of admitting that the prophets of doom had been right and she had been wrong.

Maggie shivered again. She went through into the bedroom, dominated by the bed, with its headboard of dark wood and coverlet of woven cotton, which she shared with Ari, and fetched a light silk wrap, slipping it on over the swimsuit she practically lived in at this time of year. From the mirror in the heavy old wardrobe her reflection looked back at her – a tall, slender girl, her skin tanned to a warm golden-brown by the almost constant sunshine, her hair falling in soft and unstyled waves on to the peacock-blue and scarlet of the wrap.

Ari had given it to her for her birthday last year. She had seen it in one of the dozens of fashionable shops in Kerkira that catered mainly for the tourists and had fallen in love with it.

'Go and buy it for yourself,' Ari had said when she told him.

'But it's horribly expensive . . .'

'Don't worry, it's no problem. I have some nice fat fees coming in. And besides, it's been a good year for the olives.'

Ari's family owned a number of extensive olive groves and the harvest this year had been exceptional. Not only had the weather been right but also the trees had been in their 'full crop' mode – although they bore fruit annually the rhythm of the trees meant that they produced good and poor returns in alternate years.

Though these days many landowners found it difficult to get pickers to harvest their crops and had to resort to spreading acres of nylon net beneath the trees to catch the olives as they fell or simply let them rot on the ground, Ari's family had no such problem. The old women still came to the Veritos groves, loosing their donkeys to graze under the trees and singing in tuneless unison as they picked. But they were not well paid and thinking of the hours of backbreaking work they put in for such a pittance whilst the Veritos family sat back and took the profits made Maggie feel vaguely guilty.

'I don't think I should spend so much on one little wrap,' she had protested.

Ari's good-looking face had darkened.

'What's the matter with you? I said have it, didn't I? It's your birthday soon anyway.' He pulled a handful of notes from his wallet and put them down on the table in front of her. 'That should be enough. And get yourself some perfume or something with the change.'

Oh Ari, Maggie thought sadly, fingering the soft silk. Whatever else he might be there was no doubt he was generous. But she couldn't help wishing that he had gone out and bought her a birthday present himself rather than just giving her the money. And there was also the sneaking suspicion that such generosity might be the result of a guilty conscience . . .

Maggie helped herself to a cigarette from the pack on the dressing table, lit it and went back out outside. Dusk was beginning to fall now, soft and warm. She drank what was left of her iced coffee and walked to the edge of the patio to sit on the low wall that separated it from the beach where the water, dark, mysterious purple now, lapped against the shingle. On the horizon sea merged with sky in a faint blue haze which was, she knew, the coast of Albania, and the peace was broken only by the barking of a dog somewhere along the shoreline and the first mournful cry of a skops owl in an olive grove above the house.

This, she thought, was what she loved best about Corfu, the sense of timelessness and peace, the feeling that civilisation had gone so far and no further, achieving that perfect balance before deteriorating into modern chaos. Here the old values still had meaning; crime, in the country areas at least, was almost non-existent, and children could be allowed out to wander and play in perfect safety.

Children.

As she thought of them a small, sharp pain spiralled deep within Maggie, a little thread of primal longing that tugged at the very core of her being. Sometimes she wanted a child so much that it was like a fever, sometimes, as now, it was a sweet sadness mixed with all those other longings for the fulfilment that somehow seemed to have eluded her.

Perhaps if there was a child things would be different. Perhaps if he had a son Ari would have a reason to come home. Maggie drew impatiently on her cigarette, realising that the supposition that a child of their own might keep Ari true when she herself had been unable to was an admission of defeat, yet at the same time accepting how much store Corfiotes set by their children and knowing how much Ari longed for a son.

In the early days they had often talked about it, lying in that big bed with its wooden headboard during the long, lazy afternoons when Ari returned from his office for lunch and the traditional siesta.

It had been something that had amused her, the way he split his working day into two, mornings and evenings, with the afternoons, after the midday meal, reserved for rest. In winter, when the rains came and the roads were sometimes impassable, he insisted they move into their town flat, but throughout the long summer months he made the half-hour journey between Kassiopi and Kerkira four times a day instead of twice as a commuting Englishman would, and thought nothing of it. Siesta in Mediterranean countries was, after all, a way of life.

Maggie had come to enjoy those hours that had seemed, somehow, stolen out of time, when they lay in each other's arms with only a soft sheen of perspiration to cover their bodies, he drowsy after an enormous meal of fish or moussaka or octopus casserole, she not sleepy because afternoon naps had not yet become a habit with her. They would make love – in those early days hadn't it seemed they made love constantly? – Ari would sleep a little and they would talk, hopes and plans and dreams whispered in the softly cloying heat of the afternoon when the whole world outside their shuttered room seemed to have fallen still and silent but for the gentle tug of the waves on the shingle and the occasional whisper of warm breeze.

'When we have our first son he will be called Iannou after his grandfather. You know that, don't you?' Ari had said. He was lying a little apart from her but with his hand resting on her belly as if already a little life was beginning to grow there.

'Yes, I know. It's the custom, isn't it?'

'It has always been. We believe, you see – the old people believe – that the soul lives on through a name.'

She said nothing. She knew better than to mock. Corfiotes were very religious – mostly Greek Orthodox. In any case she thought it was a beautiful idea.

'So our first son will be named Iannou but you can call him Yanny for short. He will be very sturdy and very bright and we shall put his name down to go to a good school in England. You'd like that, wouldn't you?'

Her heart had lurched a little with a tug of homesickness, both for herself and also for her unborn, unconceived son who would have to leave Corfu and everything familiar to him to get a good English education.

'Yes,' she had said, 'yes, I think so. But not until he's much older. I should miss him too much.'

'Of course, darling. First he will go to the little nursery school here, and then the junior school. After that . . . we will see.'

'Ari!' she had said, laughing suddenly. 'We are talking as if he were here! I'm not even pregnant yet!'

'Then we must see what we can do to rectify that. Starting perhaps . . . now!' He reached for her, pulling her close, and she felt the warmth of his body suffuse her own.

Making love had, in those days, been perfect pleasure, soft English sensuousness crossed with Mediterranean passion. But although they had done it so often – she had teased him that they would wear out in six months flat the bed that had so far survived a century – she had not become pregnant. And what, in the beginning, had seemed like something to be treated lightly, because it would be the inevitable next stepping-stone in their lives together, began to assume greater and greater importance.

Maggie learned to live with the sidelong questioning glances of her mother-in-law. She learned to live with the twin senses of inadequacy and longing which overtook her when she watched Ari's sister's children playing in the shingle or running about in the lane behind the four houses that made up the family commune. Ari's sister, Christina, had been married at eighteen taking with her a fine prika – a dowry – of olive trees. Maggie knew she was already slightly inferior in her mother-in-law's eyes because she had had no dowry. But the fact that she had so far produced no offspring, no child to carry on the Veritos family name was, she knew, an even more heinous offence in their eyes.

'Perhaps we should seek medical advice,' she had ventured tentatively after more than a year and a half had gone by with no sign of the much longed for baby. But Ari had scowled, his dark brows lowering and almost meeting, his black eyes gone suddenly small and hard beneath them.

'What the hell for?'

'Well, to find out why I haven't got pregnant.'

'Are you suggesting there is something wrong with me?'

'Ari – of course not! But surely it would be sensible to make sure everything is . . .'

'I don't want to see some interfering doctor and I don't want you to either!' he interrupted her. 'Our private life is our own.'

'But if they could help us to get a baby . . .'

'No! Veritos men don't need any help in fathering strong sons. Be quiet about it, can't you? I don't want to hear any more.'

He had turned away angrily and Maggie was left fighting a sudden desire to burst into tears. She was both upset and surprised by his outburst but she also felt hopeless and defeated. The fierce pride of the Greek male was at stake here – Ari felt she had insulted his manhood, though that was the last thing she had intended to do. She had not for one moment thought he might be infertile; if anything it was her own ability to conceive that was worrying her. She had always suffered from painful and irregular periods, and she was beginning to think she might need medical help of some kind. But Ari had been so adamant, so totally unwilling even to discuss the matter, she did not know how she could persuade him to see things in a different light.

It was the first time Maggie had been brought face to face with the yawning void between the Greek and the English way of thinking, and the clash disturbed her. In how many other vital areas would they be totally unable to see each other's point of view? But for the moment she knew there was nothing to be done. Perhaps eventually Ari would come to see the sense of her suggestion that she, at least, should seek medical help. She hoped and prayed it would not be necessary, but the months went by and still nothing happened. And although the subject was not raised between them again Maggie knew that Ari minded dreadfully that she had not yet been able to present his mother with another grandchild or his father with a boy to carry on the Veritos name.

Now, sitting on the low wall in the fading light, Maggie felt the desperation creep over her like a bank of the low cloud that sometimes swept in from the sea. She had come to Corfu with such high hopes, a girl very much in love and determined to make this enchanted island, as it was sometimes called, her home. She had tried, she really had tried, but somehow it all seemed to be falling apart. And sometimes she began to doubt her ability to put it back together again.

She sighed, getting up from the wall and starting back towards the house. There was an ache inside her that might have been the ache of unshed tears, for Maggie seldom cried. What was the point? Crying was such a self-indulgent thing to do and it did not solve anything.

Halfway across the patio she heard the telephone shrilling again. Obviously down by the beach she had been out of earshot. She ran into the house, willing it not to stop before she reached it, and snatched up the receiver.

'Hello?'

The crackles of static were distorting the line again, but this time, above them, she could hear a man's voice. Not Ari – an English voice.

'Am I speaking to Maggie Veritos?'

'Yes,' she said. 'This is Maggie Veritos. Who is that?'

'Mike Thompson.'

'Mike . . .' For a moment her mind was a blank. Then she said uncertainly: 'Ros's Mike?'

'Yes. I wasn't sure you'd remember me.'

She remembered very well. 'Lucky old you – he's an absolute dish,' she had said after her sister had introduced them last time she had been in England, and Ros had smiled, a little ruefully. 'Perhaps it's time I had some luck. To make up for Brendan, my ever-loving ex.' Maggie had not replied to that. Neither of them seemed to have had much luck in the husband department, she had been thinking, for already she had known things were going dreadfully wrong betwen her and Ari.

'Of course I remember you,' she said now. 'I was just really surprised, that's all. Where are you ringing from? Are you in Corfu?'

'No – I'm in England.'

Maggie experienced the first twinge of foreboding. Why the hell should Mike Thompson be ringing her from England?

'Is something wrong?' she asked anxiously. 'Is it Mum? She's not ill, is she?'

'No, it's nothing to do with your mother. It's Ros.'

'Ros!' Maggie's fingers tightened on the receiver and little prickles of tension ran up her arm. 'What's wrong with Ros?'

'She's not with you by any chance, is she?'

'With *me*? No. Why?'

There was a little pause, then Mike said: 'I was just hoping she might be. I'm . . . well, I'm rather concerned about her. She seems to have disappeared.'

Maggie brushed her hair away from her face with her free hand.

'What on earth do you mean – disappeared?'

'I don't know where she is.'

'You mean she's walked out on you?'

'No – I don't think so, anyway. I've been away on school camp with the kids I teach and when I got back she wasn't here. Her cottage is locked up, her colleagues at Vandina don't know where she is, and neither does your mother. I just hoped you might know.'

'No, I don't,' Maggie said. 'I haven't heard from her for several weeks now. She does ring me from time to time but the phone lines are so difficult here it's a pretty hit-and-miss affair, and neither of us have ever been letter-writers. Could she be visiting friends, perhaps? She has lots of friends in London.'

'Possible, I suppose. But it's not like her to go off without telling someone where she's going. I was away, it's true, but I would have thought she'd have left an address with Vandina where she could be contacted if she was needed. You know what she's like where her work is concerned.'

'Yes, she is pretty obsessed with it, isn't she?'

It had always been a joke between the two of them. 'I don't know how you can bear to stay home all day and do nothing,' Ros had said when she had last come to Corfu to visit Maggie. 'I'd go crazy! Sun, sea and sand is all very well, but after a week I'd be pining for my portable telephone, if not my desk!'

'She thinks she's indispensable at Vandina, and I shouldn't be surprised if she isn't right.' He said it lightly but Maggie heard the edge of anxiety which he was trying to conceal in order to avoid worrying her. 'Well, I'm sorry to have bothered you, Maggie. I just thought you might be able to shed some light on it.'

'I'm afraid I can't. What will you do, Mike?'

'I honestly don't know what I can do, apart from keep trying to think of where she might be.'

'Try her friends in London.'
'Perhaps I will. Though I imagine the police will do that.'
'The police! What do you mean – the police?'
There was a small silence. The line crackled ominously as if it was about to break up. Then he said a trifle awkwardly: 'I reported her missing this afternoon.'
'To the police?'
'Yes.'
'The police!' Maggie repeated, the enormity of it beginning to sink in. 'You mean – you really think something might have happened to her?'
'I sincerely hope not. But I thought maybe I ought to, just to be on the safe side. Look, Maggie, I'm sorry if I've worried you. I didn't mean to. I'm sure there's a perfectly reasonable explanation.' But he didn't sound very sure, she thought. 'I'll let you know as soon as there's any news.'
'Mike . . .' Crackles. Silence, followed by a loud buzzing. 'Mike!' she said again urgently. But the line had finally broken up.
Maggie replaced the receiver and stood, her fingers pressed against her mouth, thinking furiously.
Ros missing? It was crazy – it made no sense at all. But there was no doubt Mike had been worried. From what Maggie could remember of him he had certainly not seemed the sort to panic. And everything he had said was true. Ros wasn't a fly-by-night. She wasn't the type just to drop everything and go off without a word to anyone, and certainly it was totally unlike her to let her employers down.
Again Maggie thought of the last time Ros had come out to Corfu to visit her. She had been here only a week, and she had worked overtime before she had left to make sure everything was in order, she'd told Maggie. Yet still she had been gnawing her nails fretting about what might be happening in her absence. Either she had undergone a complete change of character or else there was a very good reason for her disappearance. A very good reason . . . or a sinister one.
Brendan, Maggie thought, going cold. Oh God, has Brendan got anything to do with it?
Brendan was Ros's ex-husband. Once upon a time he had had a promising career in the media. For a while he'd had his own

programme on a local radio station, and had even made TV appearances. Maggie could remember how impossibly glamorous he had seemed to her, an impressionable teenager, when Ros had first started going out with him. But he'd blown it all because of a fondness for the good times – and the bottle – and he'd blown his marriage to Ros too.

Ros had been through a terrible time with him, Maggie knew, though her sister had done her best to keep the worst of it from her. She had covered up for him, pretending to her mother and to Maggie that everything was all right, making up stories about falling downstairs and walking into doors to explain away the bruises that frequently disfigured her face and arms. But in the end she could take no more and she had admitted it: Brendan was impossibly jealous, he had a violent temper, he drank – and when he was drunk he let his imagination run riot and lost control of his fists. She had left him, but it had not ended there. He had refused to accept it, pestered her, threatened her, lain in wait for her. Maggie remembered one terrible night when Brendan had come to the cottage when she had been there, banging on the door and demanding to be let in, roaring abuse, even ramming Ros's car with his. In the end they had had to call the police to have him removed and the sisters had sat up half the night after everything was quiet again, talking and talking because there was no way they could sleep. Maggie could never remember seeing Ros more shaken, and with her emotional defences down it had all come out.

'I'm scared to death of him,' Ros had confessed. 'He's so jealous it's crazy. He's always been the same.'

'You never gave him any cause for it, did you?' Maggie had asked.

Ros had shaken her head. 'Brendan doesn't need cause. Not real cause, anyway. It was all in his mind. We could be fine, having a really nice evening out together, and he'd suddenly turn, just like that, because he imagined someone was looking at me or trying to chat me up. He'd whisk me out, take me home – and then more often than not take it out on me because he said I must have been encouraging them. He can be really violent, Maggie, and to be honest, I'm terrified of him.'

'But you've left him now,' Maggie had said. 'He doesn't own you any more.'

Ros had laughed a trifle bitterly.

'I'm not sure Brendan sees it like that. He threatened me once, you know. *If I can't have you, no one else will.*'

'That's just talk,' Maggie had comforted her. 'He'll get over it in time and leave you alone.'

'Will he? I'm not sure.'

'He'd never really harm you, Ros,' Maggie had said. 'If he loves you, he'd never do you any real harm.'

She had almost believed it then. Even with the thunder of Brendan's fists against the cottage door still ringing in her ears it had been almost impossible to imagine he could be really dangerous. Jealous, yes. Violent, when the drink was in him, yes. But as for really dangerous . . . that was the sort of thing that only happened in lurid newspaper stories. Not in real life . . . *their* lives . . .

Time had passed, Brendan seemed to accept that he had no option but to leave Ros alone, and Maggie had all but forgotten what had happened.

But now the cold place inside her spread and grew as she found herself remembering all too vividly.

Was it possible Brendan had had something to do with Ros's disappearance? Oh surely not! It was all so long ago now. But with a man as obsessively jealous as Brendan, who could tell? Who knew how his mind worked, who knew what fantasies had been festering away all this time? Who could say what would trigger him to suddenly take it into his head to do something about it? Maggie had not really talked to Ros for some time now. Suppose Brendan had started bothering her again, maddened by the knowledge that she had someone else? Suppose he'd just been biding his time? Mike had been away at school camp, he had said. Perhaps Brendan had known that and taken his chance . . .

Maggie realized suddenly that she was shaking all over. She reached for another cigarette, lighting it with hands that seemed unwilling to respond to the commands of her brain and drawing deeply on the smoke.

For goodness' sake, Ros, what has happened to you? Am I getting into a panic about nothing? Probably. It's just because I'm so far away I feel so helpless.

But Mike had been worried too. She had heard it in his voice, and if she hadn't it would have been self-evident. He would never have telephoned her here if he hadn't been very concerned indeed. And he certainly would not have reported Ros's disappearance to the police unless he too thought there was a possibility something terrible had happened to Ros.

Oh if only I were there! Maggie thought, and almost instantaneously knew what she wanted to do. She wanted to go home and help Mike search for Ros.

For a few minutes she sat pondering the idea. It seemed drastic, but at the same time she was able to justify it to herself. She might be able to suggest somewhere Ros might be that Mike hadn't thought of – once upon a time she and her sister had been close and that must count for something. And at least she would be on the spot. The thought of simply staying here and waiting for news was unbearable.

With a quick, decisive movement Maggie ground out her cigarette. She'd begin packing now and in the morning she'd find out about flights to England. There should be plenty at this time of year; she'd surely be able to get a seat on one of them at short notice.

Ari wouldn't like it of course – but the hell with it! Ros was her sister and she was now desperately worried about her. And besides, Ari did as he liked – why shouldn't she do the same?

Chapter Three

Dinah Marshall stared at the pile of papers and documents heaped on the desk in front of her and thought there was nothing in the world she hated quite as much as paperwork. Long wordy reports confused her – her attention was always wandering before she'd finished so much as the first few paragraphs – computer print-outs of stock, orders and sales were nothing but mumbo-jumbo, terrifyingly well organised, of course, but mumbo-jumbo all the same. As for forecasts, they were even worse, a combination of factors that seemed to have no relevance, and all put together with the primary intention of making her feel hopelessly inadequate – a kind of crackling black-and-white hell from which she could not escape.

It wasn't that she was stupid – far from it. It was just that her creative quicksilver brain didn't work this way. Dinah saw things in her imagination, felt them with a rush of excitement in her pores, created them with her nimble fingers. It was the smell of leather and the touch of soft pure silk that excited her. Acres of neatly typed print and columns of figures simply made her want to run away.

But she couldn't run away. She was imprisoned in her ultra-modern studio and Liz Christopher, her secretary, was the jailer, seated behind her typewriter in the outer office and waiting for Dinah's call to say that she had read her mail and was ready to dictate some replies, discuss the business of the day and check her appointment diary.

Dinah sighed, running her fingers through her short-cropped silver-blonde hair. She hated the office too, hated the ordered perfection of its layout and the highly polished pine woodwork, hated the smooth blue leather in which the chairs were upholstered and the ankle-deep blue carpet chosen to look luxurious but not to show scuff-marks. Wood should look as though it was able to breathe, she thought, leather ever so slightly worn. And the floor should be woodblocks with rugs, not this soulless wall-to-wall practicality. Often, looking at it, she longed with all her heart for the comfortable scruffiness of her little studio in the dilapidated building they had used in the old days. It might have been inconvenient, with nowhere really to put anything and know where to find it again, it might have been cold in winter, heated only by a portable gas fire and with draughts coming under the door and in at the old-fashioned, rather loose-fitting windows, it might have been lacking all the mod cons to impress visiting buyers, but it had been home! Dinah believed fervently that she had done most of her best work there. But of course that might have had more to do with the way things had been in those days, with an exciting future beckoning, than it had with her environment. Goodness knows, she could hardly complain about the surroundings here. The purpose-built factory and office block were set in miles of beautiful countryside – obtaining planning permission for them had been a major achievement in itself – and the view from Dinah's office window was as peaceful as it was spectacular, green fields with cows grazing, broken only by hedgerows and a little copse of trees, now in full summer leaf.

As for the fabric of the building, Van had employed only the very best architects and interior designers with a brief to produce a setting that was both functional and impressive. Vandina had an international reputation to uphold, he had maintained, it was important for them to project an image of elegance and material success. And perhaps he had been right – almost certainly he had been. When had Van's instincts ever been out of trim? From their impressive new headquarters Vandina had gone from strength to strength, a success story that had become a legend in the world of fashion accessories, and Dinah had been forced to concede that once again Van's drive and confidence had been well placed, even if it did not coincide with her own vision of how things should be done. She had been content to leave all the organisation to Van and concentrate on what she did best – watching the market, planning the new season's ranges and playing her hunches in setting new styles and trends.

But now Van was no longer here to supervise the day-to-day management of Vandina and mastermind long-term projects. It was over a year since he had been killed when his Cessna had crashed into a Gloucestershire hillside, and she still mourned him and missed him as sharply as if it had been just yesterday.

When the crash had happened Dinah had thought her world had come to an end. On a personal level she had felt as if her heart had been torn out, leaving a great gaping hole that refused to heal, and often in the beginning she had wished that she had been with him and had died at his side in the blazing wreck of the Cessna. She and Van had been together so long she could scarcely remember a time when she had not loved him, and the thought of a future without him was a desert waste too bleak to contemplate.

But for Dinah the loss was not only personal. There was also the business to think of – the business which Van had controlled and masterminded from its very inception.

How the hell could she keep going? she had wondered when the first numbing shock of his death had begun to wear off and she could think again. How the hell could Vandina survive without him? But the need to work had been strong – it was the only analgesic for the all-consuming pain of loss – and besides, she had known she had to keep going for Van's sake.

Vandina had been their dream. Together they had built it. Now it would be his memorial.

There were, of course, plenty of advisers Dinah could turn to. Vandina had not grown to its present size without collecting an army of accountants and lawyers, a strong middle-management team and a sales force second to none. Dinah had taken advice and promoted the best of them to take on increased responsibility in their own fields. But she had been unwilling to relinquish control to them, hopelessly inadequate though she sometimes felt. Instead she had hired a new and inspired designer, Jayne Peters-Browne, to take over some of the work she had previously done herself, and tried, in her own way, to assume the helm.

It was an uphill struggle and Dinah hated it. But at least with the help and advice of her team she was making it work – or so she had thought. The last few days she had not been so sure. Ros Newman, her personal assistant, had taken unexpected leave, and as she floundered among the mounds of paperwork that now came directly to her Dinah began to realise with a sinking heart just how vital a role Ros had assumed in the running of the company.

Sighing, Dinah reached for her spectacles and slipped them on. The metal frame cut uncomfortably into the narrow bridge of her nose, and she adjusted it carefully with a beautifully manicured finger. The spectacle frame wasn't the most sensible design, she knew, much too heavy for long periods of use, but she liked the way she looked in them – stylishly businesslike. So many of the frames had made her look, in her opinion, 'mumsy' – the very last impression she wanted to project.

This worry was, in fact, totally unfounded. Though Dinah was now almost fifty years old there was nothing even marginally 'mumsy' about her appearance. Her hair, highlighted to conceal the dull grey that had begun to appear in the natural silver-blonde, was cut short and feathered into a style that was both glamorous and flattering, and her face, with its minimal make-up, was clear-skinned and almost unlined. Dinah had gone on record as an advocate of hormone replacement therapy, and certainly her glow and vitality appeared to be a testament to it. Her figure, always slim and shapely, had been kept in trim by a rigorous diet and the use of health clubs and Van's home gym – though she had not been able to bring herself to use the gym since his death.

As might be expected of a woman in her position Dinah's dress sense was perfect if, surprisingly, a little unadventurous. She had always worn a great deal of black; since Van's death she had worn nothing else – little black dresses, short snappy black skirts with black satin opaque tights, black sweaters with either scoop or polo necks, black cigarette pants, oversized black jackets, masculine style. Today it was a tailored suit, obligatory short skirt and cropped jacket teamed with a perfectly cut black silk blouse. Dinah had some important meetings today, so she had felt the need to be a little more formal. But first there were the motions to go through – this stultifyingly boring pile of papers that had been put on her desk for her attention.

One by one she leafed through them, noting with relief the ones that could be passed on, trying to absorb information from the others so that she could discuss them intelligently with the relevant departmental heads. Amongst the pile was a report from the fabric design department with computerised sketches of how the new fabrics would look made up into the blouses she intended integrating into the range, and she put it to one side to study later. That, at least, would be a pleasant job.

Next in the pile was a newspaper cutting marked for her

attention. Dinah instantly recognised the layout of the women's page of a popular national daily in whose columns Vandina often figured.

Not today, however. The article headlined 'Bags of Glamour' seemed to be about Reubens, a new firm on the fashion accessory scene. The moment she realised it Dinah felt her hackles begin to rise, and as she read on her irritation grew, through disbelief to full-blown anger. When she had finished she read it again, trembling with fury. Then she reached for the intercom and buzzed for Liz. A moment later the blue leather-padded door opened and the secretary appeared, pad, pencil and engagement diary in her hands.

'You're ready for me now, Miss Marshall?'

'Have you seen this?' Dinah demanded, stubbing at the article with her pink-tipped finger.

Liz Christopher nodded. She was an excellent secretary, a pretty if rather plump girl, whose softly rounded face became almost beautiful when she smiled. She was not smiling now.

'Yes, Miss Marshall. It was in my morning paper. I thought you ought to know about it.'

'Frankly, I can hardly believe my eyes!' Dinah blazed. 'If this article is to be believed Reubens have come up with almost exactly the same idea for a range of bags as I had for my new line for next spring.'

'I know. It's odd, isn't it?'

'It's worse than odd – it's catastrophic. The idea should have been exclusive to Vandina. Absolutely right for our image but using totally different combinations of materials – natural fabrics, softwood handles, suede and leather trims. Now here are Reubens coming up with something very similar and releasing details of the range before we have. They've cut the ground right out from under our feet.'

'It is pretty devastating,' Liz agreed. 'But these things do happen.'

Dinah snorted angrily. It was true; in the constant search for something new it was not unheard of for two totally unrelated designers to hit on the same idea. Some claimed there was an almost psychic element at work, as if the designers were 'plugging in' to the same 'ideas pool', others that it was simply the law of inevitability, it had to happen sometimes that two or even more individuals or companies would come up with a supposedly innovative idea simply because they were all desperately searching for something new – or, at least, something that had not hit the headlines for a very long time. There was, they claimed, nothing new under the sun, only ways of making it *seem* new.

Dinah was not sure she subscribed to either theory. Her success had given her a slight edge of arrogance, and as someone who had always been a setter of trends she had in her time seen a great many imitators. None of them had done anything to damage Vandina. The quality of their products set them head and shoulders above the rest of the market, and the fact that they were first with the bright new ideas made them unassailable. What did it matter if High Street chain stores followed where they had led with cheap and cheerful copies? They weren't in competition for the same customers. But Reubens . . . that was a very different kettle of fish.

Reubens had erupted on to the scene just a couple of seasons ago and they clearly intended going after a slice of the Vandina market. At the time of their launch Van had still been alive and with his legendary business sense he had scented danger immediately.

'There's money behind this one,' he had warned darkly. 'I'm not sure yet who it is – they are keeping their heads down for some reason. It will come out eventually, of course – they can't remain anonymous for ever. There's always someone who will tittle-tattle. In the meantime we'd better watch out for them or we could find ourselves losing out.'

At the time Dinah had let it all wash over her. She didn't like getting too involved with the business side. It inhibited her creativity to worry about competitors and market shares and all the hundred and one things involved in running a successful company. She was the ideas side of the partnership, Van could cope with the administration. He would see that Reubens were not allowed to become a threat, just as he juggled budgets and investments, expenditure and forward planning.

Now it seemed Reubens was threatening Vandina just as Van had predicted they would – but he was no longer here to troubleshoot on her behalf.

Damn Reubens for coming up with an idea so similar to hers that it stole all her thunder, damn them for causing her trouble just when she wanted an easy ride. She'd have to have a major rethink now on the spring lines. Since Reubens had already gone public it would only look as if she was copying them if she went ahead now with her plans. But the omission from the range would leave a gap unless she could come up with something to replace it, and she had already placed orders for some of the materials to begin manufacture. The orders would either have to be cancelled, with all the attendant problems of possible penalties, or she would have to come up with an idea for a different way of using them.

Damn, damn, damn! And all this *would* happen when Ros, her personal assistant, was away. Even without the Reubens fiasco she had a full day ahead of her. She did not need to check her engagement diary to know what was in it – an appointment with one of the union representatives to discuss a bonus scheme, a progress meeting with a director of the firm Vandina subcontracted to make certain items for their limited range of costume jewellery, and lunch with the chief buyer of one of Vandina's most important customers. The lunch was unavoidable, of course – as a public relations exercise it was vital that she herself should take the buyer out to lunch and keep her champagne glass well filled – but Ros would have dealt with the jewellery company executive and sat in on the meeting with the union rep.

More than 'sat in', Dinah conceded. Though to all intents and purposes it was Dinah he was coming to see, it would have been Ros who would have stage-managed the interview, skilfully steering Dinah through the pitfalls of dealing with the union rep, who would at best be abrasive and disconcertingly disrespectful, at worst openly aggressive. Dinah hated confrontation. For her there was no excitement in the cut and thrust of fighting for the best possible deal, no satisfaction in the bluff and double bluff necessary to keep the workforce happy, or at least satisfied with their lot, and make the maximum profit for Vandina at the same time. Though thankfully George Pitman, the brash, hard-talking union man, didn't seem to have realised it yet, every brush with him left her shaking with tension, her nerves in shreds. In his lifetime Van had shielded her from any unpleasantness and since his death she had relied on Ros more and more to do the same.

Why on earth had she chosen this moment to take an unscheduled holiday? Dinah wondered distractedly. She had never done such a thing before in all the time she'd been with Vandina, which she had joined as a trainee buyer six years previously. From the very beginning she had been impressive, studying for extra qualifications in economics and business studies to add to her degree in fashion design, and it had not been long before Van had spotted her potential and promoted her to the prestigious position of Dinah's personal assistant. In all that time Dinah could never remember Ros not being there when she was needed and when Van had died so suddenly and shockingly she honestly did not know what she would have done without her. Ros was calm and efficient – Dinah could never once remember seeing her flustered or fazed – but she was also good at dealing with people. There was a confidence about her that inspired respect and she was wonderful at pouring oil on troubled waters. But most of all she was reliable. Unlike so many of the office staff Ros never seemed to be ill, and when she took holiday it was always planned well in advance and carefully scheduled to avoid the busy periods in Vandina's calendar. Before she left Ros always made certain everything was set to run smoothly in her absence. There were no loose ends but a sheaf of copious notes for whoever was taking over from her to cover every eventuality.

Under her jurisdiction the whole office ran so smoothly that it was only when she was not there that Dinah realised just how much she actually did. And without her this last week had been absolute hell.

Dinah sighed. A small frown furrowed her forehead and she smoothed it out with two fingers. She couldn't understand Ros taking time off like this. She had been utterly amazed when Liz had told her a week ago that Ros had rung in and said she needed to take some leave – amazed, and annoyed. Quite frankly it hadn't occurred to her to wonder or worry about what was behind this totally uncharacteristic behaviour. She had been too annoyed at being left in the lurch.

Now, a week later, with chaos piling up around her, she was even more annoyed. How could Ros do this to her? Hadn't she any sense of loyalty at all? She knew the suppliers had to be chased, she knew the union man was agitating. Surely there was no need for her to have absented herself so suddenly and for so long?

'There's no news of Ros, I suppose?' she said now to Liz.

'Not a word. I just can't understand it. It's not like Ros to go off like this. I'm beginning to be quite worried.'

'Yes. Well. What's worrying me at the moment is how on earth I'm going to cope today without her. And now, on top of everything else, this Reubens business! It really is too bad!'

'What is too bad?'

Liz jumped as the man's voice spoke from the doorway behind her, and a sweet smile of pure joy erased Dinah's frown.

'Steve! I didn't know you were coming in this morning!'

'You can always count on me to surprise you.' He grinned and the corners of his eyes crinkled engagingly. 'You sound pretty browned off. Is something wrong?'

'Everything. Just don't ask.'

'Anything I can do?' Though he was speaking to Dinah he managed a sideways glance at Liz so that it almost appeared the offer was directed at her. Liz turned a little pink as she always did when he looked at her that way. 'He is such a dish you wouldn't believe!' she had told her friends. 'Fantastically good-looking and a real man too – you know what I mean! He used to be a diver on an oil rig in the North Sea. It's hard to get more macho than that!'

'Just come and talk to me for five minutes, Steve,' Dinah said. 'That alone will do me the world of good.'

'You want me to come back later, Miss Marshall?' Liz asked, hovering.

'Yes. Organise us some coffee, would you?'

Liz left and Dinah looked at the young man with pleasure, taking pride in his tall, fair good looks and the easy way he had with clothes – dark blazer, striped shirt, light-beige chinos, stylish handmade moccasins. He was, she thought, everything she could have hoped for and more. His presence calmed her edgy mood, his very existence made everything worthwhile.

The warmth inside her grew and spread, a special feeling that had not dimmed one iota since the day he had walked back into her life.

Her son. When she had parted with him as a baby, forced by circumstances beyond her control to give him up for adoption, she had never expected to see him again. Over the years she had thought of him often, imagining him growing up, wondering what he looked like and what he was doing, aching for him with a terrible overwhelming longing that was sometimes so fierce it was a physical pain. Nothing had erased the memory of when they had first placed him in her arms; the smell of him was a faint but unforgettable aroma in her nostrils, the feel of his small firm body nestled against her breast had filled her with love, the image of his soft baby face with its pursed-up mouth and unwinking blue eyes was imprinted on her heart. Not a Christmas had gone by but she had imagined what it would have been like if he had been there, she had pictured his excitement and wept inwardly that she could not share it, and each year on his birthday she had spent some time alone, reliving the day he had been born and weeping for the desperately frightened girl she had been then, faced with an impossible decision.

But she had kept it all to herself. Van, she had known, would be angry if he guessed at the way her thoughts ran.

'If only I knew he was all right – that's all I want,' she had said once and seen Van's face grow dark with impatience.

'Of course he's all right! And that isn't all you want,' he had replied. 'If you had one bit of information you'd want more – and more. There would be no stopping it.'

She had known in her heart, even then, that he was right. What she really wanted was to have Stephen with her, to see him, to hear his voice, to hold him in her arms again. But it was a hopeless dream. She had no idea who had adopted him. Absolute confidentiality was part of the deal. She had no rights – none at all. In all likelihood she would go to her grave wondering about him.

She had accepted it, on a conscious level at least. She had given Stephen up, and as far as she was concerned that had to be the end of the matter. Yet the spark of hope had refused to die and she had continued to cherish the hope that one day, God willing, she would find him again.

And all the longing, all the silent prayers, had been answered.

Steve's letter had arrived shortly after Van had died. Dinah had been at her lowest ebb, stunned at the brutal way in which she had lost the man who had been so much more than husband and business partner for more than half her life. Grief was still raw, anger at the cruelty of fate and even a little anger at Van himself for leaving her so unceremoniously had just begun to manifest itself. Etched clearly in her memory was the way she had felt that morning, the morning that, though she had not known it at the time, was about to change her life.

She had been crying, she remembered, the sort of terrible tearing sobs that racked her body and turned her beautiful face haggard, and between the sobs she had railed at Van. Why hadn't he gone to see his doctor about those chest pains? Why had he been so ready to dismiss them as the result of an overindulgence of rich food and fine wine? And why, most of all, had he decided to fly his plane that day? There had been no need for him to. He could easily have taken the company Lear jet to the meeting he was to attend and asked the professional pilot he employed to fly it. But Van loved his Cessna. He flew it whenever he could, so that at times the Lear jet and the professional pilot seemed like unnecessarily expensive additions to the Vandina budget.

He shouldn't have done it! Dinah had wept. Any normal man would have realised his health was cracking up and allowed someone else to take some of the stresses and strains for him. But Van had not been any normal man. He was exceptional, his determination to remain in the driving seat as solid as the image his barrel-chested bulk portrayed. Van had made a success of himself and of her because of that determination; in the end he had died because of it.

At last Dinah's spasm of grief had passed and she had gone downstairs, still pale beneath the foundation she had applied, her eyes still a little red and puffy from weeping. The mail had arrived and she had taken it with her into the drawing room where she had steeled herself to begin to wade through it.

As always there were many letters of condolence, each one a fresh knife-wound in Dinah's heart. It was good of people to write, of course, and one day she felt sure the words of praise that they heaped on Van would be of some consolation to her. But at present reading them was painful, a terrible reminder of what she had lost.

One letter bore an Aberdeen postmark. She did not recognise the handwriting, but then plenty of the letters had come from people she had never even heard of, business acquaintances of

Van's, old school friends, even complete strangers who had simply read of the tragedy in the newspapers and felt moved to write to his widow. Mostly they were kind letters – the few spiteful ones she had quickly consigned to the wastepaper basket.

For some reason Dinah had hesitated over the letter with the Aberdeen postmark. Intuition, perhaps? No, that was putting it too strongly. But there *had* been some kind of knowledge hovering on the very edges of her consciousness before the cloak of grief had descended once more, dulling her senses. Then she had torn the envelope open and extracted the sheet of paper inside. Fairly cheap paper, written on with a ballpoint pen. She glanced at the address. Epsilon Rig, Forties Field. An oil rig? Who had Van known who worked on an oil rig?

She had begun to read the letter and suddenly she was shaking, the use gone out of her hands so that the paper almost fluttered and fell.

The letter was from a young man who said he was her son. He had always known he was adopted, he wrote, and a year earlier he had applied for his original birth certificate and discovered that she was his mother. At the time he had done nothing about it. He had been too afraid she would not want anything to do with him. But now he had read in the newspapers that Van had died and he wondered if there was anything he could do to help. Perhaps he was being presumptuous but he did so much want to meet her. Was there any possibility that she might feel the same way?

Was there a possibility? Never in all her life could Dinah remember having experienced such a rush of joy as she had felt then. It lifted her, catapulting her into a whirlpool of emotion that left her breathless. In that moment she was afraid as well as wildly elated – afraid of meeting the son she had not seen since he was just two weeks old, afraid she would be unable to cope with the situation, afraid of what he would be like, afraid she might not live up to his expectations, or he to hers.

But those fears had all been unfounded, she thought now, looking at Steve smiling at her across her paper-strewn desk. He was everything she had hoped for – and more. And thank God he had not simply visited her and then vanished again as she had been so afraid he might. She couldn't have borne to lose him twice.

'So – what's worrying you, Dinah?' he asked now, sitting down opposite her in one of the blue leather chairs she disliked so heartily and stretching his long legs. 'Is it business?'

'It's always business,' Dinah said. 'But just for now, don't let's talk about it.'

He raised an eyebrow in a lazy, quizzical gesture.

'Suit yourself. But remember, if there is anything I can do you only have to say the word.'

Dinah nodded. 'I know. And whether you realise it or not, that really is one of the most important things.'

He looked doubtful. She saw it in his startlingly clear light-blue eyes. Where had those eyes come from? She sometimes wondered.

'It's the truth,' she told him and knew that it was.

Ros's absence, the anxiety about the meetings that were scheduled for the coming day, even the Reubens business all paled into insignificance beside this one very important fact of life.

Steve was here. After almost thirty years of separation they were together again. And set against that yardstick nothing else mattered.

Chapter Four

The Inter-European Airways jet was approaching Bristol Airport, coming in low over the Somerset countryside. Maggie looked out of her window, peering down at the patchwork of fields dotted with houses and farms, the dark clumps of trees, the blue expanse of water that made up the Chew Valley lakes. They were valleys, she remembered, that had been artificially flooded to make reservoirs to provide water supplies for the city and the surrounding areas. Beneath one of them was an entire village, houses, pub, church. The people who had once lived there still felt bitter and sad about what had happened; in times of drought when the water receded they gathered at the edge of the lake and walked down on to the dry caked mudflats trying to make out the tower of the church and pointing out the spot where their house had been to anyone who would stop and take an interest.

Today, however, apart from the wildfowl and a few fishermen, the lakes looked deserted and the water, dark and mysterious, kept its secrets.

'Looks like we're back to the English weather!' the man sitting next to Maggie grumbled.

He was still wearing a singlet more suited to the sunshine of Corfu than this damp grey day. When he had moved in beside her Maggie had been unable to avoid noticing that his arms were scorched red from too much unwise sunbathing and the skin across his shoulders and back was peeling away in big flaky bubbles.

He was a holidaymaker, of course – herself excluded, holidaymakers made up the entire passenger list of the plane, she guessed, and she knew she had been lucky to get a seat at such short notice.

Lucky – and crazy, as Ari had maintained.

'You can't go to England just like that!' he had said when he had finally come home the previous night to find her packing. 'It's madness!'

'I have to go,' she had said, trying to make him understand. 'I'm really worried about Ros. And it's not as if I have anything to stop me. No one will even notice I've gone.'

'My mother will notice,' he said, deliberately misunderstanding her. 'It's the big family get-together next week and you know how she likes everyone to be there. Besides, aren't you supposed to be helping her to wash the carpet?'

Washing the great carpet squares that covered the living room floors in Corfiote houses was an important annual event. In a country where carpet shampooers were all but unheard of, the carpets had to be scrubbed and then spread out in the sun to dry, a job which needed at least two women to manage it.

The suggestion that Maggie should postpone her trip until the carpet wash had been done grated on her already frayed nerves.

'I should have thought finding my sister was just a little bit more important than washing the carpet!' she had retorted scathingly. 'It can be done any time between now and September and if I'm not here your sister will just have to chip in and help.'

Ari's mouth had tightened.

'You are being childish now, getting at my sister. She has her hands full with three small children. Anyway, I'm not very happy about this – you just deciding to pack up and go without consulting me.'

'If you'd been here I would have consulted you. But you weren't here. You never are. Where have you been until this time?'

'You know where I have been – working hard to put food on the table and clothes on your back.'

That had been the point when Maggie's temper had finally snapped, and now, looking out of the aircraft at the green sweep of countryside beneath her, she saw only Ari's arrogantly handsome face scowling at her with displeasure and heard only her own angry voice above the buzzing that always affected her ears when flying, or, more specifically, coming in to land.

'You haven't been working until this time of night, surely? What do you take me for, Ari – a fool?'

He had stared at her, his black eyes narrowing.

'What do you mean by that?'

'Just what I say. I don't believe you have been at your office all this time. You've been with *her*, haven't you? Melina Skripero. Your secretary or whatever it is she's supposed to be.'

For a moment she had thought Ari was going to strike her. An expression of fury contorted his features, an expression so thunderous that a cold hand of fear clutched at her stomach. But Ari was not a violent man. For all his hot Mediterranean temper he had never laid a finger on her and he did not do so now. After a moment his angry expression hardened into something very like guilty defiance.

'So? What if I have been?'

It was Maggie's turn to be shocked.

'Aren't you even going to deny it?'

'What's the point?' He shrugged and turned away. 'Obviously you have been spying on me.'

'No, I haven't! I just put two and two together. I'm not stupid. I've seen the way she looks at me when I come to your office, smirking like the cat that got the cream. I've seen the way she looks at you. And I've smelled her perfume on your clothes. You can't hide something like that. It clings, Ari.'

'You've never said anything before!'

'I didn't want to believe it. I didn't, really! I thought if I kept quiet it might all blow over . . .' She broke off, tears threatening suddenly. Oh yes, she'd known about Melina for weeks now, for all the reasons she'd enumerated and a dozen others besides, all the tiny pieces of evidence a wife gathers almost subconsciously until they come together to make a whole picture. But it was still a shock to hear him confirm it – and so nonchalantly too, as if he was admitting to having left a ring of scum around the bath instead of telling her that yes, it was true, he had another woman.

'How could you?' she asked miserably. 'How could you do it, Ari? What's happened to us?'

He shrugged. 'Nothing has happened to us. You're still my wife, aren't you? I'm here, aren't I?'

'Yes – but not because of me. You're here because this is your home – your *family* home. That's what matters to you – what they think – the family.'

She heard the bitterness in her voice and hated herself for it. She hadn't meant to drag his family into this, though sometimes she felt she hated them, hated the claustrophobic sway they held, whilst at the same time being oddly hurt because she felt excluded. It was like being gripped by the tentacles of an octopus, she thought, yet in her case it was a very cold fish indeed. She was tied down by tradition, prevented from taking a job, expected to conform and accord respect in every way, yet looked upon a little askance, the English girl with no dowry who had captured a heart she had no right to.

In better times she had tried to talk to Ari about the way she felt, but it was one area in which she had never been able to break through to him, never been able to explain how she felt. Where his family were concerned Ari was fiercely defensive – he could not, or would not, understand. Now he homed in on her implied criticism, turning the line of attack deftly back towards her.

'Why do you always have to bring my family into it?'

'Because they are the ones you really care about, not me. If your mother wants something you're there like a shot. She rules you as if you were still a little boy.'

'That's enough!' Ari said furiously. 'The trouble is you just don't understand the Corfiote way of life. I'm beginning to think you never will.'

'And that is why you are having an affair with Melina Skripero, I suppose.'

'Who said I am having an affair with her? We go for a drink and something to eat when we have finished work at the office. I like her, yes. I like her company. Is it so surprising? At least she understands. She does not go on forever about my mother, my sister, my father. She understands respect. Perhaps if you were to try a little harder then I might find it more pleasant to come home at the end of the day.'

'That's not fair, Ari!' she protested. 'I have tried, very hard indeed. Can't you understand how different all this is to what I'm used to?'

'I understand the family is of no importance in England. This is why you have problems with lager louts and football hooligans – they have no family pride to uphold. Their mothers and fathers feel no shame when they behave badly. And why? Because they do not care for their children either. They go to work, leave them to come home from school to an empty house, allow them to run wild. Here there is always a member of the family to keep an eye on them, comfort them if they fall down and hurt themselves, box their ears if they are bad. The family unit . . .'

'Do you know how pompous you sound?' she demanded. 'And how hypocritical too? You go on and on about the family, yet all this started because you object to me going home to find out what has happened to my sister. When you say "the family is important" what you really mean is *your* family. Mine can go to hell!'

She saw the uncertainty for a moment in his face and rushed on: 'What's more, it's hypocritical to go off and have an affair with your secretary behind your wife's back!'

Ari rolled his eyes. 'I told you, I am not having an affair. It's not like that. Don't you believe me?'

'No!' she said. 'No, I don't!'

He spread his hands in a little gesture that was typically Mediterranean. 'Then you understand me even less than I thought. Maggie . . . listen to me. I like women, yes. I like Melina. But you are my wife. One day we will be the ones to carry on the traditions. *We* will be the family to our children and our children's children.'

The change in his tone, the sudden realisation that yes, she did believe him, and most of all, the reference to the children he was still hoping she would give him in spite of all the disappointments and the slowly growing despair, made Maggie suddenly weak. Tears sprang to her eyes and she turned away.

'It upsets you?' he said more gently. 'You hate the idea of the family so much?'

She shook her head. 'No, of course not. Ari . . . are you honestly not having an affair with Melina?'

'I told you. How many times must I say it?'

'I don't know . . . I really thought . . .'

He came up behind her, putting his arms around her. She thought she caught a whiff of that perfume she had come to associate with Melina, strong and sexy, smelling of musk, and tried to ignore it.

She loved Ari. She wanted to believe him. She had to believe him. Particularly if she was going away.

'Come to bed,' Ari said in her ear, and her stomach twisted. It was always like this, in spite of all the frustration and despair, in spite of the rows that flared and died as suddenly as a summer storm; in the end he still had this animal magnetism for her. She would cross the world for him – she had! – and she would do so again. Her legs felt weak, her body, sensitised by all the emotional upheaval, responded urgently, almost treacherously quickly, to his touch.

She turned to him, feeling the cool cotton of his shirt against her bare skin as he eased the silk wrap from her shoulders, letting him part her lips with his mouth, arching her body so that her hips and thighs moulded to his. For a little while, as she let him guide her into the bedroom, peeling off her swimsuit and easing her back on to the big old bed, the anxieties and despair of the last hours became unimportant. She gave herself up to his lovemaking with a fervour heightened by the recent trauma of their differences. But afterwards, when it was over, the first thing she saw was her suitcase, half packed, on the old fashioned carved wood chest at the foot of the bed, and her dresses hanging on the outside of the wardrobe waiting to be folded, and reality began to creep in once more.

'Ari – I do still want to go to England,' she said, half afraid.

She felt him stiffen slightly but he only said: 'Yes, yes, I suppose it's a long time since you went home.'

'It's not just that. I wouldn't go off at such short notice if it was just a holiday. You know that. I have to find out what has happened to Ros – make sure she is all right.'

'Surely it is up to your English police force to do that?'

'But I'm her sister. We can almost get inside one another's minds. Please try to understand, Ari.'

He did not answer and she went on: 'And when I come back, let's try to make a fresh start. Remember how wonderful it used to be? It could be like that again, I know it could, if we both really tried.'

They had fallen asleep in one another's arms and Maggie had woken in the night from a good dream to nestle against him again, her body warmed through with twin senses of relief and purpose.

But in the morning he had already risen when she came drifting out of the layers of sweet refreshing sleep, and when she joined him on the patio where he was eating his usual breakfast of muesli, fruit and thick creamy yoghurt, she knew immediately that he had gone away from her again.

'There's nothing I can say, I suppose, to stop you going to

England?' he said, stirring sugar into his thick, aromatic black coffee.

You could say you love me and want me here, she thought. You could promise me that you won't stay out late with Melina again and tell me that however it might look I am more important to you than your mother and the rest of the family. But she knew it would only sound childish.

Aloud she said: 'I have to go. I thought I'd explained.'

'Yes. Well, if that's your decision I suppose I must abide by it.' His voice was cold; the closeness of the previous night's lovemaking might never have been. 'How long will you be gone?'

'I don't know . . . it depends. However long it takes to find Ros, I suppose.'

'Don't hurry back on my account. I'm going to be very busy the next few weeks. I have a big job on – a new hotel complex down in Kavos. If you're not going to be here I might decide to stay in the apartment in Kerkira. That would save me quite a bit of travelling time.'

And be very convenient for Melina, too, she had thought involuntarily, but she had not said anything. She did not want to raise the subject again now, just as she was leaving, did not want him to realize that she still did not know whether to believe him when he protested that theirs was nothing more than a friendship between employer and secretary. But it had been there in her mind as she kissed him goodbye and it was still there now, worrying at her as the plane approached Bristol Airport.

Even if it wasn't a full-blown affair yet she'd given them every opportunity to make it one by flying home to England and leaving Ari alone. If she had stayed in Corfu now that he knew she was suspicious he might have had second thoughts about what – if anything – he was doing, if he cared for her and their marriage at all, that was. With her out of the way it would be easy, so easy, for him to turn to beautiful Melina with her dark eyes and olive skin, clever Melina, who spoke perfect English and had more than a smattering of German as well, suitable Melina, whose father would no doubt present her future husband with a prika of a grove of olive trees, and who understood Ari perfectly because she was native-born Corfiote.

The plane descended a few hundred feet rather swiftly and Maggie's stomach went with it.

I had to come, she thought. I had to make my stand and I had to make sure Ros is all right. And if I can't trust my husband for a couple of weeks, then what point is there in any of it?

Wheels touched tarmac, the engines went into reverse and the jet slowed on the runway.

I am home, Maggie thought, and it never even occurred to her that the sentiment had betrayed her deepest feelings, nor that, after living there for almost three years, it was Corfu she should think of as home.

Mike Thompson stood in the waiting area beyond the customs hall. Maggie had telephoned him this morning asking if he could meet her at the airport, and naturally he had agreed.

'My plane is due in at eighteen-thirty your time,' she had said. 'I know it's an imposition to ask you to meet me and if you can't I'll quite understand. But I thought I could stay at Ros's cottage and I imagine you have a key.'

'Yes, of course,' he had said. 'But look – I didn't mean to worry you to this extent. I wouldn't like you to think I was implying you should come.'

'I want to,' she had said. 'You still haven't any news of her, I imagine?'

'No, nothing.' As usual the line had begun breaking up. 'I'll be at the airport,' he said hastily.

'Are you sure it's not inconvenient?'

'Not a bit. I'll see you.'

And so here he was, watching the passengers from the Corfu plane emerge. Most were obviously holidaymakers, sunburned, dressed in leisure suits and anoraks, pushing trolleys laden with suitcases and plastic carrier bags of duty-frees, and Maggie did not appear to be among them. Would he recognize her? he wondered – and felt sure he would. He'd met her only once but he remembered her very clearly indeed – a younger, softer version of Ros.

The flow thinned to a trickle and Mike began to wonder if perhaps she had changed her mind and decided not to come after all. Or perhaps she had got to Kerkira airport only to discover there were no spare seats on the plane. But wouldn't she have telephoned again to tell him so? He turned around, looking at the cars drawing up and pulling away outside the airport building, and when he turned back there she was, emerging from the customs corridor, a tall girl with shoulder-length brown hair, wearing navy-blue chinos and an expensive-looking T-shirt, logoed with a designer emblem, beneath an unstructured white linen jacket.

She saw him at precisely the same moment and smiled, a sweet, somewhat apologetic smile that lifted the corners of her wide mouth, as she hurried towards him.

'Mike! I'm sorry I've been so long getting through. My case was the very last on the carousel and then the customs officers decided they wanted to check me out. I don't look like a returning holidaymaker, I suppose – but I didn't think I looked like a drug-smuggler either!'

'You don't.' He returned her smile. He was thinking that the customs officers, bored with the endless routine, had probably fancied ten minutes with a very attractive woman. 'I must say I was beginning to wonder what had happened to you, though. I'd almost given you up.'

'Thank goodness you didn't. Look – it really is very good of you to meet me. Are you sure I haven't put you to any trouble?'

'Quite sure. *I*'m the one who's put *you* to trouble. I was going to say I hope I haven't dragged you over for no reason, but of course I don't mean that at all. I sincerely hope it is going to turn out to be a fool's errand.'

'You really think something may have happened to Ros?'

'I hope to God not. But I am worried, yes. Look, I'll go and get the car. We can't talk here.'

'Where is it?'

'In the short-stay car park.'

'Then I'll come with you. I could do with stretching my legs.'

He took her suitcase from her, noticing with some surprise how light it was. When Ros went anywhere she seemed to take her entire wardrobe with her. They went out through the swing doors. It was not raining today but the air was still damp and cold for June. Maggie shivered.

'After Corfu this feels like the Arctic! I should have brought some warmer clothes. But I suppose I can always borrow something of Ros's.'

They walked the short distance to the car park, where Mike

unlocked the boot of his Citroen and put Maggie's case inside. Then he let her into the passenger side, got in himself and turned on the heater.

'It shouldn't take too long to warm up. But you're right, the weather is pretty foul for midsummer.' He stopped to pay the parking fee and pulled away towards the airport exit. 'You still plan to stay at the cottage, do you?'

'Yes. It seems the sensible thing to do.'

'Do you want to go straight there or do you want to get something to eat?'

'No, it's all right, I ate on the plane.'

'Perhaps we ought to stop at a garage so you can buy milk and bread.'

'That might be an idea.' They swung out on to the main road. 'So,' Maggie said, still hugging herself with her arms to try to get warm, 'what is this all about, Mike?'

Mike changed gear smoothly, the car gathered speed.

'I wish I knew. But to be honest I don't think I can tell you any more than I told you on the telephone. When I left for my week at school camp Ros was here – everything seemed perfectly normal. When I came back, no Ros. And no messages, no phone calls, nothing. Not a single word from her.'

'And nobody else has heard from her either?'

'Not as far as I know. I've rung just about everybody I can think of, without any success, but of course there may be someone I've missed. Ros's address book is in her Filofax and she takes that everywhere with her, so there's no way I can check if I've missed anybody. That's one area I'm hoping you might be able to help with.'

'I can try,' Maggie said doubtfully. 'But I've been in Corfu for the last three years, remember. I knew all her old friends, of course, but I'm sure during that time she's made some new ones. And it's always possible that the ones I do know will have moved or married or something. Though I suppose if I could give them some starting points the police could take it from there.'

Mike snorted, executing a racing change to sneak through a bend in the narrow curving lane.

'The police aren't being exactly helpful. They seem to think Ros has simply gone walkabout and her whereabouts are none of their business – or mine, either.'

'You mean they aren't going to do anything?'

'They said they would institute enquiries but I got the distinct impression they would be low-key, low-priority. The policeman to whom I reported her missing was fart-assing on about it not being his area and I think he thought it was just a case of a broken romance – Ros running out on me and not wanting me to know where she'd gone.'

'It's not that, is it?' Maggie asked.

Mike glanced in her direction, eyes narrowing.

'I don't think so. Do you?'

'No. Ros isn't the run-out type. She's a girl who stays to fight her corner. And besides . . .' She broke off, not wanting to put into words the thought that had occurred to her – that Mike really did not look like the sort of man girls ran out on. With that profile, the crooked nose and strong jawline, with those narrow hazel eyes and wide sensuous mouth, with his powerful yet athletic physique and a smile to die for Mike was more likely to excite undying adoration than be run out on. He might be an utter heel, of course, beneath all the outward charm, but even that, in Maggie's experience, was unlikely to sway things much. Women didn't run out on devastatingly attractive heels as a rule. They ran out on ordinary nice guys who bought them flowers and chocolates and did everything in their power to please. Unfair, but true. And besides, unless Ros had had a massive change of heart she had been crazy about Mike. He was the best thing that had happened to her in a long time, she had said, and somehow Maggie could not believe she had fallen out of love with him so completely that she had gone to these lengths to avoid him, or that it would be in her nature to do so. She had not even run away from Brendan, and goodness knows, he'd given her cause. She had stayed and brazened it out, in spite of his jealousy, in spite of his violence. She hadn't run then and comfortable though it would be from Maggie's point of view to accept the explanation favoured by the police, she honestly did not think it was likely.

'I suppose one can't blame them in a way,' Mike was saying. 'I had a pal in the force once and he used to say more people went missing after domestic disputes than for any other reason – not just lovers' tiffs, of course, but problems between parents and children and husbands and wives as well. I expect the poor old overworked constable I saw thinks he's heard it all before.'

'Perhaps they'll take more notice of me,' Maggie said. 'I'll get on to them tomorrow and try to find out what progress they are making.'

'None I should think or they'd have got back to me, surely.'

'We'll see,' Maggie said. 'Oh – is that a garage there? Will they sell milk, do you suppose?'

'There's a good chance they might.' Mike pulled on to the forecourt, parking beside the little shop that housed the pay desk, and Maggie went inside, noticing with some surprise the range of goods on sale, from groceries to flowers and even some household plasticware. When she had lived in England garages had sold chocolate bars and cigarettes and de-icer for the car windscreen, and that was about all.

She selected a carton of milk, a loaf of bread, biscuits and coffee, paid for them and went back to where Mike was waiting. There would almost certainly be coffee in Ros's store cupboard, she imagined, but she wasn't prepared to chance it. Getting up tomorrow morning and finding herself without any didn't bear thinking about!

Ros's cottage was only a few miles further on, on the outskirts of the village of Stoke-sub-Mendip. As Mike turned the car into the lane leading to it Maggie noticed the hedgerows, burgeoning thick and green from all the recent rain, and the thick clumps of white cow parsley growing against them. The may was still in flower, too, overhanging the road in places, and through the gateways she glimpsed meadows with cows grazing placidly, interspersed with fields of bright yellow rapeseed.

A Somerset idyll, she thought. No wonder her sister loved it here and was unwilling to move, lonely though the spot was for a woman living alone.

There were just two houses in the lane and Ros's was the second, a tiny picture-book cottage which had once been the dwelling of farm labourers. The cottage was square with low eaves, but a single-storey extension which had at some time been built on to the side gave it a slightly lopsided look. One wall was covered with Virginia creeper, red-tinged leaves giving a warm glow to the grey stone, and honeysuckle grew around the little porch that shielded the front door. But as Mike pulled on to the gravelled hardstanding to the side of the gate Maggie noticed that the tiny front garden had a slightly uncared-for look about it, with roses that needed pruning and shrubs and herbaceous plants jostling for light and space around the lawn, which was at least ankle deep and thick with clover and even the odd dandelion.

Ros didn't have much time for gardening, she knew, though she pretended to enjoy 'pottering', and she used to employ a man from the village to come in for a few hours a week to keep the place tidy. It didn't look as though he'd been lately, and briefly Maggie wondered why. He might simply be ill or on holiday of course – it didn't take long for a garden to run riot at this time of year.

Mike got her case out of the boot and carried it to the front door, turning the keys on his key ring to select the appropriate one. As she waited Maggie breathed in the scent of the honeysuckle, heavy on the evening air, but when he pushed open the door and she stepped into the tiny hallway it was quickly overpowered by the airless smell of a house that had been shut up for more than a week.

It shocked her somehow, that smell, reminding her forcefully that Ros was not here. It had been so different last time she had visited. Ros was a superb cordon bleu cook who loved to entertain when she had time, and the kitchen had been full of the lingering aromas of frying garlic and fresh herbs, simmering wine sauces and fresh-brewed coffee. In winter Ros was in the habit of burning perfumed candles, in summer the scent of freesias and roses filled the house. Now what flowers there were were dead, their withered petals lying in sad, untidy drifts around the murky-looking vases.

Mike set down Maggie's case in the hall and followed her through to the kitchen where she was unloading the purchases she had made at the garage on to one of Ros's spotless formica worktops.

Apart from a cereal bowl and cup washed up and left upside down on the draining board the kitchen was reasonably tidy.

'It's not exactly the *Marie Celeste*, is it?' she said doubtfully. 'I mean – it doesn't look as though she left in a hurry.'

'No, but you know Ros. She likes to clear up even before going to work. And I have had a bit of a tidy round. I threw out the milk that had gone sour and some rotten fruit. And I stopped the newspapers and picked up the post – there's probably some more now in that wire basket thing under the letter box.'

'I'll sort it out later on.' Maggie leaned over to open a window and let in some fresh air, then emptied the water that had been standing in the kettle, swilled it out and refilled it from the cold tap.

'Let's have a cup of coffee. Or do you have to get off?'

'No rush.' Mike usually played squash on a Wednesday evening but he had cancelled tonight. 'The most important thing on the agenda is trying to find out what the hell has happened to Ros.' He paused, watching Maggie unhook beakers from Ros's wooden mug tree and spoon instant coffee into them. 'You don't think I've blown this up out of all proportion, do you?'

She bit her lip, a little-girl gesture which was at odds with her sophisticated appearance and made her look suddenly very vulnerable.

'I wish I did. I notice her car wasn't outside, Mike. Wherever she went she must have been driving it. And what about her clothes? Have you checked to see how much she has taken with her?'

'No.'

'Then let's do that while we're waiting for the kettle to boil. You'll have to help me. I haven't seen enough of her recently to know what's missing.'

'Her trenchcoat seems to be. That usually hangs behind the door. But that doesn't tell us anything. We've had so much rain recently she'd hardly be likely to go anywhere without it. But I'm not sure I'll know what else is missing. Ros seems to have an awful lot of clothes.'

Maggie smiled briefly. Mike was of course a typical man's man who had not the slightest interest in women's fashions. She imagined her very smart, very clothes-conscious sister going to a great deal of trouble to dress up for him and not realising for a moment that he hadn't a clue what she was wearing – beyond the fact that, as usual, she looked stunning. But she was determined to try to make him remember.

She led the way up the steep and narrow staircase. Ros's bedroom was on the right of the landing. The bed, with its designer duvet of pinks and mauves, was neatly made, a paper-back book, opened, was on a small octagonal table beside it, and on top of the book lay Ros's reading glasses. Maggie's stomach contracted. Ros couldn't read small print without glasses, she knew – would she have intentionally gone anywhere without them? It was possible she had another pair, of course – one pair for reading in bed, one pair kept in her handbag so that she could be sure of having them with her at all times . . . Yes, that sounded like businesslike, well-organised Ros.

Maggie looked around the bedroom feeling like an intruder. On the dressing table, which was covered with a thin layer of dust, a small family of china animals Maggie remembered from their shared childhood gave her a sharp whiff of nostalgia; beside them stood a bottle of Ros's favourite perfume, Coco, still in its cardboard carton to protect it from the light. Again Maggie wondered – would she have gone away for any length of time without her perfume? But she might have a small phial of it in her bag, and there were no pots of cream or tubes of foundation jostling for space in front of the mirror.

'Her make-up doesn't seem to be here,' she said hopefully.

'I think she keeps it in the bathroom,' Mike offered, and Maggie remembered that as the man in Ros's life he would be familiar with the intimate details of her routine – had often slept with her in this bed, in all probability. 'I'll see if it's there.'

A moment later he was back.

'It's there all right, at least, it looks to me as though it is.'

Maggie went into the bathroom to check. Sure enough, pots of moisturiser and night cream, cleansing lotion, foundation and a jar of face powder were lined up on a shelf above the basin, and her heart sank. Ominous, but still not conclusive. Ros could have miniature versions in a vanity bag. She was the sort who would organise her life that way.

'Where are her clothes?' she asked – there had been only a very small wardrobe in the bedroom, prettily carved but more ornamental than functional.

'Spare room.' He led the way past the room Maggie had used when she had stayed to a door at the end of the landing. 'She had it converted to a sort of walk-in wardrobe a couple of months ago. As I told you, she has rather a lot of clothes.'

That was, Maggie thought as he opened the door, the understatement of the year. The tiny room was full of clothes – row upon row of hangers, the garments all shielded by plastic dust bags, and in a corner a rack of shoes. This could take all night. But at least Ros had things organised. Her summer clothes were nearest the door, whilst her coats and winter suits had been packed away in the least accessible places.

'What has she been wearing recently?' Maggie asked.

Mike shrugged helplessly. 'Well – dresses, I suppose. Trousers sometimes. She has been wearing a pair of white denim jeans,' he added with a sudden flash of inspiration.

Maggie sighed, flipping through some of the clothes. Two or three linen suits, half a dozen cool but smart dresses, a casual pyjama-style pants suit, a raw-silk jacket and trousers . . . It was impossible to know whether Ros would have chosen to take them with her if she had planned a holiday. But there were only a few empty hangers – that must say something. Of the white denim jeans there was no sign. Perhaps she had been wearing them when she had gone . . . wherever she had gone. Maggie said as much to Mike and he nodded.

'She's got an emerald-green thing she wears with them,' he offered.

'An emerald-green thing?'

'A shirt. I can't see that here. But that . . .' he indicated the pants suit, 'I've seen her in that a lot. I'd have thought she'd have taken that. And that cream shirt-dress is another favourite. But I honestly wouldn't like to say for certain.'

'I know. It's impossible, isn't it?' Maggie was struck by another thought. 'Suitcase! Has her suitcase gone?'

'I don't know. She keeps it in the attic.'

Maggie was overcome by a feeling of utter weariness. Suddenly she thought she did not want to know for certain whether Ros's suitcase was missing. If it was there, in the attic, it would confirm all their worst fears and she did not think she could cope with that confirmation just at the moment.

'Let's go down and have that coffee first,' she said. 'The kettle will have boiled by now.'

They went back downstairs. Dusk had begun to fall, and though some of the staleness had gone out of the kitchen now, the dim light intensified the deserted feel of the place. Strange, Maggie thought. There were two of them here now, yet because Ros, whose home it was, was not here the aura of emptiness remained.

Disconcerted, she switched the lights on, thinking that at least here in England one did not have to worry about the light attracting the mosquitoes.

'I don't like it, Mike,' she said, pouring hot water on to the coffee and opening the carton of milk.

With easy familiarity he fetched a bowl of sugar from a cupboard and stirred some into the mug she pushed across the counter towards him.

'No,' he said quietly, 'neither do I. You see why I was worried, Maggie.'

'The police will have to do something. If we made a list of all the suspicious circumstances . . .'

He brought his fist down hard on the counter and the mug shook, spilling coffee on to the formica surface.

'Dammit, we shouldn't have to do that! Why won't they take our word for it? We *know* her, for God's sake. We know she wouldn't just go off like this without telling anyone. I'm going to talk to them again myself in the morning – try and shake them up, *insist* something is done. I mean suppose – just suppose – that something has happened to her. Suppose somebody is holding her against her will. I know it sounds bloody melodramatic but these things do happen. If it was something like that, the sooner the police start believing she hasn't just run off to avoid me the better.'

'You're right,' Maggie agreed. 'There's a limit to what we can do and how quickly we can do it. And as you say, time could be of the essence if she has been kidnapped . . .'

She broke off. Worried as she was, wild as her imaginings might be, to actually speak the word 'kidnapped' in connection with Ros sounded ridiculously lurid, like a story from one of the tabloids. As for anything else . . . Maggie was all too painfully aware that both she and Mike had referred to 'kidnapping' or 'being held against her will' because the other possibility – that something even worse had befallen Ros – was too dreadful to face. But it was there at the back of both their minds all the same, a looming fear they could not bring themselves to mention, yet very real for all that. If Ros was missing and not of her own volition there could be only two explanations – the one they had put into words and the other which they dared not . . .

'I can't help thinking that if someone had kidnapped her we

should have heard something by now,' Mike said after a moment. 'A ransom demand or something . . .'

'If she is being held for money.'

'What other reason . . .?' Mike stopped abruptly as he mentally answered his own question.

'Do you mind if I smoke?' Maggie already had the packet of cigarettes out.

Mike sipped his coffee. 'I don't mind. Ros would. She hates the smell of smoke in the house.'

'Tough.' Maggie lit her cigarette, feeling guilty about it but desperately needing the comforting feel of the cigarette between her fingers and the nicotine calming her nerves. She kept intending to give up the habit but not now . . . oh no, not now. 'You don't indulge, I suppose?'

'I don't. Never have. Sport and smoking don't go together.'

But Maggie's thoughts had already returned to Ros's disappearance.

'Has she seen Brendan lately, do you know?' she asked.

'Her ex-husband? I don't think so, but then she knows it's my opinion she should give him as wide a berth as possible, so she might not tell me even if she had. Why – you don't think he's involved, do you?'

Maggie sighed. 'I honestly don't know. I don't think we can rule him out. Ros was pretty scared of him, wasn't she?'

'Was she?' Mike looked genuinely surprised.

'She was, yes. Didn't she tell you about it?'

'No.'

'I wonder why not? Perhaps she was afraid of what you might do if you knew how he used to treat her.'

'How did he treat her?'

'Badly. He was excessively jealous, with a fertile imagination; he'd drink and then he'd knock her about.'

Mike's face had darkened. 'If I'd known that I certainly wouldn't have been responsible for my actions if our paths had crossed. But are you saying you think Brendan might have something to do with Ros's disappearance?'

'I don't know. I only know she was afraid of him.' Maggie hesitated, unwilling to add that Ros had told her Brendan had threatened that if he couldn't have her no one else would. 'I would have thought if he was going to do something stupid it would have been then, when they first broke up, not after all this time. But I suppose with a man as unpredictable as Brendan one can never be certain,' she went on. 'His career is well and truly on the rocks now, isn't it?'

Mike shrugged. 'I told you – we rarely discussed him. But I certainly haven't heard him on the radio for some time.'

'I'll try to see him tomorrow, suss out if he knows anything,' Maggie said.

Mike looked worried. 'Do you think you should? If he's the violent sort, mightn't he be dangerous?'

'He wouldn't harm me.'

'But if he was holding Ros . . .'

'If he is holding Ros he will have gone to ground. If he isn't I don't suppose I have anything to fear. Anyway, I can take care of myself.'

'You sound just like Ros,' Mike said ruefully. 'If ever there was a girl I would have said could take care of herself it would be Ros. But something has happened to her. You mustn't take any chances, Maggie.'

Maggie shivered. 'It's not very warm, is it?' she said irrelevantly. But she knew the shiver had more to do with thinking of what might have happened to Ros than with the cold. 'Don't worry, I'll be careful,' she went on. 'We've got to explore every avenue – if there is something suspicious and we can take it to the police they are more likely to take notice, aren't they?'

'I have to work tomorrow but I could come with you in the evening to see him,' Mike said. He was silent for a moment, drinking his coffee, then he went on reflectively: 'I've been racking my brains trying to remember anything Ros said that might give a clue. The only thing I can think of is something she said about Vandina.'

'Her job, you mean?'

'Not exactly. What she said was: "There's something odd going on at Vandina. I don't understand it." But we got sidetracked, something happened to interrupt the conversation, and she didn't mention it again. I just wonder, though, if it might be important. Perhaps it would be worth having a word with the people there to see if they have any ideas.'

'Yes, I was going to do that,' Maggie said. 'Ros might have said something to someone there about her plans. Has she got any special friends at work? Anyone she might confide in?'

'Ros doesn't seem to make many friends these days. She's too independent. She works mainly with Dinah Marshall herself. That by definition isolates her from the hoi-polloi.'

'Then I'll see Dinah Marshall.'

'That might not be altogether easy. Dinah is quite a difficult person to get at, from what I understand.'

'She'll see me.' Maggie's tone was determined. 'Well, I suppose there's not a lot more we can do tonight. Perhaps I ought to try to get some sleep – Corfu time is two hours ahead of here and I want to have my wits about me tomorrow.'

'In that case I'll leave you.' Mike drained his cup and got up, reaching for his waxed jacket which he had draped over the back of a chair. As he put it on he seemed to fill the kitchen, a big masculine man with a slightly rumpled air. 'Are you sure you'll be all right here on your own?'

'I'll be all right. I only wish I could be so sure about Ros. Oh Mike – where the hell is she? And if there's nothing wrong why doesn't she get in touch – phone you, phone me, contact *somebody*?'

Mike shook his head, looking suddenly almost helpless.

'I don't know. I suppose all we can hope for is that things have got on top of her and she's gone off somewhere to get away from it all.'

'Yes, that's what I'm hoping. Anyway, I'll start making some enquiries first thing tomorrow. Will I see you?'

'I'll ring you after school. Perhaps I can take you out for something to eat. There are some good pubs round here which do excellent bar food.'

She nodded. 'Right. I'll expect to hear from you.'

She watched him go down the path and reverse his Citroen off the parking space. When it had disappeared from view she went back inside. The cottage felt horribly empty now and all her doubts and fears crowded in on her, making her conscious suddenly of how alone she was. She'd told Mike she'd be all right and of course she would be. But all the same she wished he was still here, filling the kitchen with his comfortable presence.

Ros was very lucky to have someone like him, she thought. So why, unless there was something very wrong, should she disappear without telling him where she was going?

Tomorrow I'll begin to try to find out, Maggie promised herself. Tomorrow I'll see Brendan, and I'll go to Vandina . . .

She would need transport to do that of course. First thing in the morning she would ring one of the hire companies and fix herself up with a car. But for tonight there was nothing much she could do but go to bed and try to catch up on the sleep she had promised herself.

Maggie locked up, put out the lights and went upstairs. But when she saw her suitcase standing on the landing she remembered: she and Mike had forgotten to check the attic for Ros's case. She hesitated, wondering if she should leave it until morning but decided she would be unable to rest until she knew one way or the other.

The attic door was positioned over the landing, reached by means of a loft ladder. Maggie fetched a chair from the bedroom and stood on it to unfasten the hatch, then she unhooked the loft ladder and eased it down. Above her the attic was in total darkness. She looked in vain for a light switch – obviously the cottage was not sufficiently sophisticated to have an attic light.

She went back downstairs searching for a torch and found one on top of one of the cupboards in the kitchen, a big wide-angle-beam lantern. Then she climbed the ladder again, hoping against hope that she would not find Ros's suitcase. If it was not there – if it was not anywhere in the house – then the chances were that wherever Ros was, she had gone because she had planned to go. Whatever the reason for her leaving it could be sorted out – personal problems, trouble at work, health . . . nothing was so terrible it couldn't be dealt with, ironed out, put right in the end, however long it took.

But if the case was there . . . Maggie swallowed as she reached the top of the ladder and shone the torch into the dark attic.

There, in its place just to her left, within easy reach of the well, was Ros's suitcase. Maggie shone the torch directly on to it, not wanting to believe the evidence of her eyes but staring hard at it all the same.

The case, smooth pigskin and embossed with Ros's initials, seemed to stare right back at her.

Chapter Five

Next morning Maggie woke with the dawn. Though it had been hours before she had been able to get to sleep the previous night her body clock had not yet adjusted to British time.

For a moment she found herself wondering where on earth she was, then, as she took in the pink and mauve curtains which she had forgotten to draw last night, the mullioned window through which early sunshine was streaming, and the unfamiliar pale-green walls, she remembered.

She was in Ros's bed, in Ros's room. The spare bed had not been made up, its duvet covering bare mattress, and she had been too tired to begin searching for clean sheets. Now, however, she felt a little guilty at the liberty she had taken. *Who's been sleeping in my bed?* she thought, hearing, in her imagination, the voice of an aggrieved Mummy Bear as played in a pantomime she had seen as a child, and the ridiculousness of it seemed to heighten the feeling of nightmare closing in.

She pulled herself up against the pillows, wondering what Ari was doing at this moment. It would be half past seven in Corfu, he would be having his breakfast on the patio, might even have finished it by now and be getting ready for the drive to his office in Kerkira. Always supposing he had come home last night. Perhaps he had not. Perhaps he had stayed in the town apartment. And if he had – was Melina with him?

As the familiar wave of helpless jealousy engulfed her, Maggie pushed aside the duvet and got out of bed. Pointless to waste time and energy worrying about Ari now. There would be time enough to sort out her marital problems when Ros was found. Maggie crossed to the window and drew the curtains fully. The garden, lush and green from all the recent rain and now bathed in a golden glow of early-morning sunshine, looked wild and unspoiled, a little corner of the England she missed so much.

Corfu was a green island, of course – if it had been dry and dusty like Crete or some of the other Greek islands Maggie did not think she could have borne it. But there was a different intensity to the greenness of olive groves and tall cypress trees beneath a sky which was almost endlessly sapphire-blue, a shimmering shiningness that was a world apart from this heavy dew-wet foliage.

The birds, too, were different. Maggie was used to wheeling flights of swifts, swallows and house martins who sometimes built their nests in the overhang of the balcony of her home at Kassiopi, and the wagtails who loved to splash in the puddles on the patio after the autumn rains. She knew that in winter there were robins, blackbirds and thrushes, but she had rarely seen one; now, standing at the window, she listened to the tail end of the dawn chorus and watched a pair of blackbirds searching for worms in the long grass of the lawn, their heads cocked, whole bodies alert, as they tapped and listened for the sounds, indistinguishable to the human ear, that would announce the arrival of breakfast.

It was so beautiful, so peaceful, so typically English, that it was hard to imagine anything seriously amiss in this idyllic world. For a moment Maggie felt as though she must have fallen asleep and dreamed the whole worrying scenario of Ros's disappearance. But the fact that she was here at all made it all too indisputably real.

Ros's towelling robe was hanging behind the bedroom door. Maggie pulled it on over the oversized T-shirt she had worn to sleep in. Ari hated her wearing T-shirts to bed, he liked her in seductive silk and lace. But after the balmy Corfu nights Maggie had half expected to feel cold, and besides, the T-shirt was *comfortable*, much more comfortable than spaghetti shoulder straps and flowing floor-length skirts. If she couldn't be comfortable sleeping alone, when could she be? It was a small, self-indulgent luxury, but when the thought occurred to her that perhaps in future she was going to have a great deal more opportunity for such luxuries, Maggie quickly brushed it aside.

She drew a comb through her hair, splashed cold water on her face at the bathroom basin and then went downstairs, collecting the pile of mail from the wire basket beneath the letter box as she passed it. In the kitchen she leafed through the post whilst she waited for the kettle to boil – a couple of letters offering guaranteed prizes in return for a viewing of a timeshare, advertising from two mail-order houses and a club specialising in CDs and cassettes, and an envelope promising a free film for each one processed by the company. Maggie dumped the lot in the waste bin, angry to think that trees had been cut down to make the paper for such unsolicited rubbish, and turned to the only two envelopes that seemed even vaguely interesting.

The first – in an envelope printed with the name of Ros's bank – was disappointing; it was simply more advertising in a more sophisticated guise – this time an attempt to sell financial services. But as she tore it in two and dumped it in the bin with the other junk mail Maggie thought that perhaps the bank might offer another avenue of enquiry – they should be able to tell her whether cash had been drawn out of Ros's account in the last week or so.

The second envelope was handwritten and Maggie hesitated before opening it. But when she did, she discovered it was only a note from Ros's dentist advising her that an appointent had been made for her six-monthly check up for 19 July at 4.30 p.m. Would Ros be able to keep it? Maggie wondered uncomfortably.

So – there was nothing even vaguely illuminating amongst the mail. What about Ros's telephone answering machine? Would there be anything there? The display was showing nine messages; Maggie rewound it and punched the replay button.

Again she was disappointed. Three of the calls were from Mike, two from her mother, one from a man who must be an upholsterer telling her the chair she had been having re-covered was ready for collection, and one saying nothing at all – some callers' reaction to hearing a recorded message at the end of the line. But one call was from Ros's old friend in Scarborough asking her to get in touch – that must mean Ros was not with her, Maggie realised – and the other was evidently someone from Vandina.

'Ros, Liz here. I was just wondering if you were back yet. There are one or two queries that really only you can answer and Dinah is going spare without you. Oh – and I've got a little bit of information on you-know-what that I want to tell you about. I think you'll find it rather interesting. Please ring me as soon as you get back. Ciao.'

Maggie rewound the tape and listened to the message again. Clearly things at Vandina were floundering a little without Ros, clearly her departure had been unexpected and unexplained as Mike had said, clearly they didn't know when to expect her back.

But the *sotto voce* mention of something too sensitive to be discussed over the telephone was intriguing. Maggie found herself remembering what Mike had said about Ros's comment that there was something odd going on at Vandina. Might there be some connection?

There was a pad and pencil beside the answering machine; Maggie reached for it and wrote 'Liz – Vandina' in large letters. At least she now had the name of a contact at Vandina besides the reputedly elusive Dinah Marshall herself. And when she went to the office she would have a word with this Liz and find out exactly what she had meant.

The kettle had boiled by now and switched itself off. Feeling suddenly more purposeful, Maggie made herself toast and coffee. When she had finished it was still too early to set out on the calls she intended making and she decided to use the time to search the cottage for any other clues. It felt like prying – but wasn't that why she was here?

Maggie started methodically enough, checking the post Mike had taken in earlier in the week and left piled neatly on a kitchen worktop, and moving on to examine anything that would help her to build up a picture of her sister's life. Mike could tell her how Ros lived, of course, but it wasn't quite the same as finding out for herself, trying to see it through Ros's eyes, and in any case there might be things Mike did not know. He might be Ros's man, but Maggie suspected that after her disastrous marriage to Brendan, Ros would find it difficult to trust anyone totally, and in any case she had always had a slightly secretive side to her nature. It was quite likely she had kept certain things back from Mike, Brendan's violence being a case in point.

As she went from room to room examining the evidence Maggie felt her new-found optimism beginning to wane. Though Mike had thrown away the dairy foods that had gone sour or curdled there were other things in the fridge he had missed – a vacuum-sealed pack of peppered herring fillets, out of date by a week, and a piece of cooked chicken wrapped in foil, the smell of which made Maggie wrinkle her nose in disgust when she opened it. In the tiny scullery there was a pile of ironing waiting to be done, and in the Ali Baba basket in the bathroom some dirty linen. It was all negative, negative, negative – every single thing pointing to the conclusion that Ros had not intended to be absent for long, whilst giving no clue as to where she might be or what had happened to her.

The tour of the cottage completed, Maggie returned to the kitchen and checked the clock. Just after nine. She had better telephone her mother before she did anything else, she supposed – but it was not a call she was looking forward to making. She did not relish the prospect of having to explain that Ros was missing in much clearer terms than Mike had used when he had been trying not to worry her. And she was not looking forward either to to the personal questions that were bound to be asked – about Ari and Corfu and why she had seen fit to leave both and come dashing home to England. But there was no avoiding it. Maggie sighed, picked up the receiver and dialled her mother's number.

The phone seemed to ring interminably and Maggie was just about to give up when a man's voice answered.

'Hello. Colonel Ashby speaking.'

Maggie's heart sank. If there was one person she wanted to talk to less than her mother it was the Colonel. Ridiculous man, she thought. Why does he insist on still calling himself Colonel? He hasn't been one for at least twenty years.

'Harry? It's Maggie,' she said. 'Can I speak to Mummy, please?'

'Not sure where she is.'

I'm going mad! Maggie thought.

'You mean she's not there?' she said aloud.

'She's about somewhere – in the garden I think. Said something about going to cut roses.'

'Then do you think you could call her please?' Maggie said.

'Dare say. Dare say.' But he sounded grumpy. 'He resents having to do anything,' Ros had once said bitterly. 'He wishes he still had a batman to wait on him, I think. Instead, he's got Mummy.'

Maggie waited, mentally rehearsing what she was going to say. But when her mother's breathless silvery voice came down the line all the carefully thought-out phrases went straight out of her head.

'Margaret – is that you?'

'Yes, Mummy.'

'Good gracious, what a surprise! And how clear you sound! As if you werc in the next room, not in Corfu at all.'

'I'm not,' Maggie said.

'Not what?'

'Not in Corfu. I'm in Stoke-sub-Mendip.'

'Stoke – with Rosalie, you mean?'

'I – well, I'm not exactly with Ros . . .'

'Margaret!' There was an element of theatricality in Dulcie Ashby's voice, a rather contrived note of cautious shock. 'Margaret – you haven't left Ari, have you?'

Maggie felt herself begin to tighten up. How was it that just talking to her mother could do this to her? But it was always the same – at least it had been now for years and years. There was nothing calming or comforting about Dulcie's effect on her daughter. On the contrary, there was this irritation so intense it made her feel like a stretched wire coil just waiting to spring violently back to its original shape.

'No, Mummy, I haven't left Ari.'

'Then what are you doing in England? I didn't know you were coming over. Why didn't you let me know? When did you arrive?'

'Yesterday. Last night. I didn't know I was coming myself.'

'It was a spur-of-the-moment decision to take a holiday, you mean?'

'Mummy.' Maggie tried to take control of the conversation. 'I think Mike rang you a few days ago.'

'Mike? You mean Michael? Ros's Michael?'

'Of course.'

'Yes he did telephone. He wanted to know if I'd seen her. As if that were likely! I think I see Ros even more infrequently than I see you.'

'Look – Mike didn't want to worry you, but nobody seems to know where Ros is. He phoned me too, to see if she was with me. Of course she wasn't so I've come over to see if I can find out what's happened to her.'

'Whatever for?'

'Because she seems to be missing, Mummy.'

'Oh my goodness, not that again! What is the matter with the man, getting into such a panic? I had the police here yesterday. He's been to them about it. Quite ridiculous!'

'The police have been to see you?'

'Yes. A uniformed constable called here at a most inconvenient time – just as Harry and I were having lunch. I told them I hadn't the slightest idea where Ros was – why on earth should I? You girls have never been in the habit of telling me your movements – I am, after all, only your mother! I also told them I thought it was the most ridiculous fuss about nothing. Ros is a grown woman – she lives her own life. Not that I always agree with the *way* she lives it, of course, but that's neither here nor there. Everyone seems to have divorces these days. No staying power. Probably due to the ridiculous marriages they make in the first place.'

Maggie sensed the incipient criticism and bristled. But she had no intention of being drawn into an argument on the subject just now.

'You haven't seen Ros then, or heard from her?'

'I have not. But as I say, that is nothing new. And as for Michael Thompson, there's no earthly reason why Rosalie should tell him her every move. It's not as though he's her husband, is it?'

'Mummy . . .'

'Look, Margaret, this really isn't the best time for me. I'm having a coffee morning in aid of Help the Aged and I have a hundred and one things to do. I was just trying to cut some roses when you rang, but the poor things have been absolutely ruined by the rain. And it's been so cold! The buds just won't open properly and when they do they're spotted and stale-looking. Now, when are you coming over? I will be seeing you, I suppose, whilst you are in England?'

'Of course you'll see me,' Maggie said irritably. 'I'll ring again when you're not so busy.'

'Do that. After dinner tonight might be a good time. There's a programme Harry likes to watch on BBC2 – something to do with current affairs and between you and me it's dreadfully boring. We'll arrange something then. And for heaven's sake, darling, do stop fussing about Ros. I'm quite certain she is perfectly all right.'

'Yes, Mummy. 'Bye for now.'

Maggie replaced the receiver and stood for a moment feeling like a wrung-out dish rag. At least her mother was not worrying about Ros. How could she ever have imagined for one moment that she would?

She has the brain of a pea, Maggie thought viciously. How on earth had poor Dad put up with her? No wonder he'd gone to an early grave, disillusioned no doubt with the discovery that the beautiful young woman he'd fallen in love with had turned out to have no real substance beneath that decorative exterior and the excessively charming manner that made fools of sensible men.

'She's like a baked Alaska,' Ros had said once. 'It looks good but when you bite into it there's nothing there, just melted ice cream.'

Maggie, who had always admired what she thought of as Ros's sparkling wit, had laughed because it really was very funny, although she was not at all sure, then, that one should say such cutting things about one's own mother. Now, however, she felt she knew exactly what Ros had meant.

'Thank goodness we take after Daddy!' Ros had said on another occasion, and this was a sentiment Maggie had wholeheartedly agreed with. Just as long as they *did* take after the father they had both adored. Sometimes Maggie had nightmares thinking she had spotted one of her mother's infuriating traits in her own nature . . .

But at least the conversation had told her one thing, she thought, going back into the kitchen to make another cup of coffee. Whatever impression they had given Mike, the police *were* investigating. At least they had been to see Dulcie – though whether they would pursue their enquiries, now that she had told them she was of the opinion there was nothing whatever to worry about, was quite another matter.

As she drank her coffee Maggie's hand hovered over her cigarette packet. She shouldn't really . . . it was much too early in the day . . . but the circumstances were really exceptional. I really will give up when I go home, Maggie decided, then, her conscience pacified, took out a cigarette and lit it.

She'd been right first time, it was too early in the day. The tobacco tasted stale on her tongue but she smoked it anyway, thinking about what she should do next.

Book a hire car – that was a number-one priority. Without transport there was very little she could do. The thought reminded her that Ros's car too was missing – just about the only hopeful indication so far. Had the police circulated the number? she wondered. Would they be keeping a lookout for it? But she couldn't imagine it somehow, and it wasn't as if a Golf GTi would attract much attention. If Ros had had flashy taste in cars it might have been easier. But she didn't. She liked something fast, reliable and easy to park. Functional, like everything else in her life.

Maggie sighed. Perhaps she should take a leaf out of Ros's book and organise herself and her life methodically. She drew one of the envelopes she had opened earlier across the table towards her, scrabbled in the drawer for a pencil, and began to make a list of what she intended to do.

1. Book hire car
2. Phone for taxi, if necessary, to go and collect it
3. See Brendan
4. Go to Vandina
5. Take any information to police and try to shake them up
6. Confer with Mike
7. Ring Mummy again

She drew on her cigarette, daunted suddenly by the day that lay ahead of her. In Corfu she would have had nothing more taxing to do than helping her mother-in-law with washing the carpet, and then she would have had the rest of the day to sunbathe, swim, read, or anything that took her fancy.

I was right, she thought, to try and organise myself as Ros does. I've become so lazy that if I didn't nothing would get done.

And then the irony of the situation occurred to her. Ros might be the organised one but it was Ros who was missing, whilst she, Maggie, the wanderer, who had never had any particular ambition but to marry the man she loved, was here trying to rationalise a situation that was quite beyond her!

Chapter Six

At eleven o'clock Brendan Newman was still in bed. He rarely surfaced before midday and today was no exception. What, after all, was there to get up for? It wasn't as though he had a job to go to – not, of course, that he had been very keen to get up in the days when he *had* had a job.

Brendan was, he had always proudly maintained, a night owl, much at his best after dark. He never really came to life until he had had his first whisky of the day, but when everyone else was ready to fall into bed Brendan would still be going strong, still tipping the bottle and still yarning with anyone who would listen to him. In the old days there had been plenty. His name was familiar to everyone within a forty-mile radius, and the fact that he was a radio personality had given him star status. But even now, when newcomers to the area would ask 'Brendan *who*?', he could still command an audience at any club or party.

When Brendan was on form there was something almost magical about the way he could talk, the words spilling out in a torrent that could be amusing as well as informative – somehow he managed to sound like an expert on almost any subject that was raised – and to talk to him was to find the conversation hijacked at every turn, but people rarely minded. With his Irish ancestry Brendan was a superb raconteur – 'Sure an' I kissed the Blarney Stone. What else would a true son of Ireland do?' he would say, exaggerating the rolling lilt so that it sounded as if he had left County Cork just last week instead of when he was five years old.

In the beginning the powers that be at the local radio station where he had worked had been doubtful about employing someone with so marked a 'foreign' accent. It was their policy to use presenters with a faint local burr – quite the vogue since the demise of the ubiquitous 'BBC Oxford English' accent. But Brendan had blarneyed his way into the station and into the hearts and homes of the listeners. Without a doubt he would have gone far if he had had as much self-discipline as he had charm. His own programme quickly followed the first tentatively arranged fill-ins, he had acquired a cult following and national stations had begun to show an interest.

But Brendan had let vanity and licentiousness spoil it all for him. Instead of going home to his bed to be fresh for the next day's work he had chosen to hang out in the sort of places where everyone wanted to fête and admire him, buy him drinks and listen to his endless fund of stories. And before long his way of life had caught up with him. Jaded and hung-over he had begun turning in too late to do the proper and very necessary preparations for his programme. He missed interviews, he lost tapes, he was extremely rude on air to some of the people who called with answers for his jokey daily phone-in quiz. Several times he had failed to turn up at the studio at all, and one day when his producer and a reporter went to the bachelor flat in town, which he used during the working week, to find out what had happened to him they had discovered him still fast asleep – not in bed, but in the bath!

'What the hell are you doing there?' the producer, badly shaken because he had been momentarily convinced that Brendan was dead, of hypothermia, if not an overdose, had demanded.

'Sleeping! What do you think I'm bloody well doing?' Brendan, who had a thundering headache and cramp in both legs, had roared back.

'But why in the *bath*, for Chrissakes?'

'It's nearer the loo if I want to pee or be sick.'

The producer was beginning to realise that Brendan could be as disgusting as he could be charming.

'Don't you know we are trying to run a radio station and you are supposed to be on air in fifteen minutes?' he had yelled.

'Don't worry, I'll be there.'

'You bloody well won't! You're in no fit state. God alone knows what you'd say. Bruce is going to cover for you.'

'Bruce Stapleton? That spineless, boring little git . . .?'

'At least he's there! He's pleasant and he's polite and people like him. He reminds them of their favourite son.'

'You make me puke!'

'No, Brendan, the drink does that. And I promise you, if you don't cut it out and start taking your job seriously you'll be out of the station so fast your feet won't touch the ground.'

'You wouldn't do that to me. I'm Brendan Newman, remember?'

'I don't care who you are, pal. You can't get away with this sort of carry-on and you'd better start believing it.'

Brendan had sworn at him, using the most colourful and expressive words in his vocabulary, which, even in his present condition, was impressive. It did not impress his producer, however, or the board of directors called together to discuss his case.

It was a pity, they said – Brendan could have been a wonderful asset. He had talent, without a doubt. But the way he was going he was fast becoming a disaster area. Whatever the repercussions he would have to go.

Brendan, marginally more sober, had kicked and argued and threatened, without any success, to sue for wrongful dismissal. He had found himself out of a job and with the sort of reputation that did not bode well for getting another one.

During his glory days in the world of entertainment Brendan had acquired an Equity card and he used it now. At first, because his name was well known, he got a certain amount of work, mostly doing voice-overs for advertisements and trailers, and he had one foray into pantomime, playing the King in a small local professional production of Old King Cole. But as the legend of his unreliability grew and people began to forget his one-time celebrity status, even this work began to dry up and Brendan found he had got what he had always thought he prized most – plenty of time to do exactly what he wanted. If he drank and yarned the night away there was no longer any need to fall out of bed next day, shave the stubble from his increasingly raddled face, and turn in for a day's work.

It had not, however, made him happy. The morose side of his nature, previously well concealed beneath his personable jovial exterior, had begun to take over, and Brendan blamed the rest of the world for his slide into obscurity and the fact that he no longer had the ready money to live the life of luxury he had become accustomed to, wining and dining without a thought to the expense, taking extravagant foreign holidays and running his flashy sports car. He blamed the radio station, he blamed the fickle public, he blamed fate. But most of all he blamed Ros.

'I hate that bitch,' he would say when the drink was in him. 'She was nothing when I met her. I gave her everything. God knows I loved her. I set her up on a pedestal and worshipped her. And see what she's done to me!'

'What did she do?' newcomers to Brendan's circle would ask – old friends knew better than to lead him on.

'Lied to me, deceived me, cuckolded me and made me look a complete fool. I'd have done anything in the world for that woman – she used me up and when there was nothing left she didn't want me any more. I hate her for what she's done to me, but yet I love her still. Sometimes I think I'll kill her, just so no one else can have her. Sure an' it's the only way I'll ever have any peace of mind now, for the thought of her with another man drives me out of my mind!'

He was a tragic figure, the newcomers would think, his romantic heart broken, his whole life destroyed by his love for a faithless woman.

His old cronies, however, though they still enjoyed his company, took a more pragmatic view. Brendan had no one but himself to blame for losing Ros, they thought, just as he had no one but himself to blame for his ruined career and the mess that was his whole life.

This morning Brendan had woken a little earlier than usual. He came out of his heavy drink-induced slumber to find the sun streaming in, hurting his eyes when he opened them and making his head throb unbearably. He closed his eyes again and swore.

Why the hell did the sun have to be shining this morning just when he was feeling so bloody awful? It hadn't shone for the last week and he didn't suppose it would shine again for another. But this morning here it was, unrelentingly piercing, even with his eyes closed. Of course the worst of it was he hadn't bothered to draw the curtains last night. He couldn't even remember undressing, though he supposed he must have done since he was now clad in nothing but his underwear.

Funny, he thought, the way you could do things and not remember you'd done them. It was happening to him more and more often these days, whole chunks of memory simply disappearing, as if his mind had totally blanked out. It had happened for years, of course, when he'd had too much to drink, and he'd lose a whole evening, have no recollection of where he'd been or who he'd been with, but this was different and more disturbing because it was more far-reaching.

He'd be unable to find something – a book, his wallet, his watch – he'd spend ages looking for it, getting madder and madder, and then when it turned up it would be in a place that only he could have put it. Or he'd begin to say something only to discover he couldn't remember what it was. For a man who loved talking as much as Brendan did, that was infuriating. If he lost his thread in mid-speech he could usually blarney his way out of it but it wasn't funny, all the same, not to him. He forgot arrangements, he forgot that friends had called him, he forgot where he had been on a certain day at a certain time.

It's being inactive that's to blame, he thought. It's not having any work to do. I'm going to seed. Time to do something about it – time to pick myself up out of the gutter where those bloody so-and-sos have kicked me and show them they can't beat Brendan Newman so easily.

His resolve, for the short time it had lasted, had been high. Brendan with an idea could be as enthusiastic as anyone – more enthusiastic than most. No one could doubt his initial keenness – it was staying power Brendan lacked, along with self-discipline.

But he was not feeling enthusiastic this morning, far from it. This morning despair seemed to throb through his body in time with the pounding behind his temples. There was not a single positive thought in his head beyond closing the curtains and shutting out that God-awful bright sunlight.

He stumbled across the floor, stubbing his toe on a discarded shoe as he went and swearing at it. He jerked the heavy curtains across the window and visited the bathroom. The sun was there too, slanting in bars through the venetian blind and making bright sparkling patterns on the mirror. Trying not to open his eyes too wide he fumbled through the bathroom cabinet for the Alka-Seltzer. Several other items fell out on to the floor – a pack of plasters and a pouch that had once contained the cleaning kit for his contact lenses – but he did not bother to pick them up. Bending over would only make his head thump more than ever, he knew. He split the packet, put two Alka-Seltzers into a tumbler and filled it with water. God, why did they have to make such a noise? Why couldn't you get *silent* relief for hangover headaches? He started to drink the fizzy solution and was almost sick.

When he raised his head again his own image stared back at him from the mirror above the sink and his sense of utter depression deepened. Once he had been considered handsome. Now the face that not so long ago had been round and boyish looked bloated and raddled both at the same time, distorted by pouches and hollows. His eyes, red-rimmed and dull, seemed to have sunk into folds of flesh, his jawline, with its shadow of dark uneven stubble, was indistinct with the beginnings of a serious double chin. At least he still had all his hair, but it flopped unbecomingly over his forehead, and the jet blackness of it, which came out of a bottle since he had started to grey, very early, at the temples, emphasised the doughy pallor of his skin.

Brendan stared at his reflection in disgust. Would anyone really believe this was the same face that smiled winningly out of his publicity photographs? But at least no one need see him looking like this. He'd go back to bed for an hour and give the Alka-Seltzers time to work before he so much as poked his nose out from beneath the duvet again.

He had been back in bed for about twenty minutes and was dozing when his doorbell rang. He swore, burying himself deeper under the duvet and willing whoever it was to go away. But the bell only rang again, more insistently, as if his caller was keeping a finger on it. Brendan threw back the covers and stamped across to the intercom.

'Yes? Who is it?'

'Maggie Veritos. I need to talk to you, Brendan.'

A great flood of anger washed over him. Maggie, Ros's sister. The bitch. She'd encouraged Ros to dump him, he was sure of it. But along with the rage was something else – a cold prickle of something that might have been fear. Fear? Why should he be afraid of Ros's sister? She was only a woman, when all was said and done. Or was there a reason – a reason he had forgotten?

'Brendan? Will you let me in please?' He heard the determination in her voice. There was no way Maggie was going to go quietly away.

'All right. I'm opening the door now.' He depressed the button and heard the buzz as the door of the ground-floor lobby released.

Then he went back to the bedroom, pulled on a red silk dressing gown and opened his own front door.

Maggie was already running up the last flight of stairs. Dislike stirred in him again and with it a slight sense of surprise. Somehow in his mind's eye he always saw Maggie as the teenager she had been when he had first begun courting Ros, a tall, slightly gangly girl in blue denim jeans and oversized rugby shirts. Though he had seen her grow up, the image had remained with him, and when she had gone to Corfu and he rarely saw her any more it had somehow superseded the other, more recent, images so that it had become the way he remembered her. Now he realised with a shock that she and Ros were far more alike than he had allowed. They had the same clear-cut features, the same shade of blue-green eyes – 'like the sea when it catches the first light of morning' he had said once in lyrical mood – even the shape of their faces was similar. Maggie's hair, too, was long and luxuriant as Ros's had been before she had had it cut in that short, sharp bob that she considered more suitable for her image as a professional businesswoman in the fashion industry.

A nerve twisted somewhere deep within Brendan's solar plexus, exciting an unbearably sweet sensation that was half pleasure, half pain. It was like looking into the past and seeing Ros as she had once been, running up the stairs towards him, and he was consumed by longing for times lost and happiness which had slipped from his grasp.

How he had loved her – loved her with a fierce fire that had burned him up. But she had thrown it all back in his face. The Ros he had worshipped and placed on a pedestal had disappeared – maybe she had never existed at all – and the one who had taken her place was nothing more than a parody of his beloved, a cold, hard, ambitious woman who had lied to him, cheated on him, betrayed his trust. That Ros he hated with an intensity that was almost paranoid, that Ros . . . His mind closed over the thought that was forming, blanking it out. But he knew that it was there, all the same, that desire, that sometimes washed over him with the merciless rush of a flood tide, to take all that flawed beauty and destroy it.

All her bright golden hair
  Tarnished with rust
She that was young and fair
  Fallen to dust

He couldn't remember now where he had first heard the quotation but it had become a litany to him, anguished as he was by his destructive blind passion. Ros's hair wasn't golden, it was brown, but that did not matter. What mattered was the way the lines made him feel, powerful somehow, as if just speaking them gave him jurisdiction over her fate, condemned her to a condition that put her beyond the reach of other men.

If he couldn't have her he would make sure no one else did. He had said it often enough, and the poem did it for him. But it didn't stop there always. Sometimes he imagined killing her himself, putting his hands around her throat and squeezing the life out of her. Occasionally he dreamed he'd done just that. Recently the dream had come more often – the other night the aura of it had remained with him the whole of the next day, making him feel certain that Ros was dead and it was his doing.

So real had the impression been it had almost frightened him.

You are mad! he had thought. You really are going mad! Next thing, my boy, they'll have you in the funny farm. But still he couldn't rid himself of the pervading sense of guilt, coupled with something like euphoria, and now, as he looked at Maggie coming towards him, he thought for a moment he was seeing a ghost.

But the ghost was flesh and blood, breathing a little heavily from running up the stairs. The ghost was wearing a loose cotton sweater and tailored slacks, both in pale blue, that he had never seen before. He gripped the edge of the door, feeling his head spinning.

'Hello, Brendan.' The voice, too, was definitely not Ros's but Maggie's. It was missing that ring of briskness that Ros had acquired after she had begun to move up the ladder at Vandina.

'Maggie.' It came out sounding thick. He cleared his throat and the effort made his head pound again. He clung to the door, not daring to move.

'Aren't you going to ask me in, Brendan?' Maggie said.

He felt defensive suddenly, the fear was back, though he did not know why.

'What do you want?'

'To talk to you. About Ros.'

'What about Ros?'

'Brendan, I would really rather not have this conversation on the doorstep. Why won't you let me in?'

'You've just got me out of bed. What time of day do you call this?'

'Half past eleven. Hardly the crack of dawn.'

He threw open the door with a sudden impatient gesture.

'Oh, all right, come in if you must. But whatever you have to say, say it and get out again. I'm feeling bloody lousy.'

'You don't look very special,' Maggie said tartly, but the astringency did not quite cover the little tremble in her voice. She was nervous, he thought, surprised. Why the hell should she be nervous?

He shut the door after her and followed her into the kitchen, aware that it looked a complete tip and not caring. He saw Maggie's eyes moving over the litter of dirty coffee cups, overflowing ashtrays and discarded clothing and almost laughed. If she was as much like Ros as she appeared to be she'd hate it – Ros had been fanatical about everything being clean and tidy. He cleared a muddle of magazines, an empty loaf wrapper and an odd sock from a chair, throwing them into the corner behind him, and sat down. If he didn't he'd fall down, he thought. Maggie remained standing. He covered his eyes with his hand so as not to have to look at her.

'Brendan,' Maggie said. 'Did you know Ros is missing?'

The words penetrated the thick fog that was his brain this morning. He looked up sharply as if they had shocked him and pain like a white-hot needle shot through his temple. But it wasn't a shock really, of course. He did know. It was just hearing Maggie say it that was the shock.

'Yes,' he said. 'Well, at least a policeman came to see me. I told him I didn't know where she was.'

'When was this?' Maggie asked.

'Oh, I don't know – yesterday or the day before. What does it matter? And why the hell should they ask *me* where Ros is anyway? How would I know? I'm only her ex-husband. I'm not party to her plans nowadays.' There was a whine of bitterness and self-pity in his voice.

'When did you last see her?' Maggie asked.

'Not for months. It must have been before Christmas. No, wait, I tell a lie – I saw her a few weeks ago in a bar in Clifton. We didn't talk, though. She was with somebody.'

'Who?'

'A man, of course.' He got up, switching on the kettle and searching for a jar of coffee in an effort to divert himself, blot out the memory of seeing Ros with another man. He had known she had someone else, of course – hadn't she always? Ros was a queen bee where the men were concerned, letting them dance attendance on her and leading them a merry chase. He'd learned to live with it – hadn't he? But actually seeing them together was something else entirely. It had torn his guts out.

'It was Mike, I expect,' Maggie said.

'Mike? You mean that bloody PE teacher?' he said disparagingly. 'No. It wasn't him.'

'Who was it then?'

'How the hell should I know?' The truth was that the edges of his mind were closing in again but he wasn't about to admit it. Ros, with another man. That was the important thing. Who he was didn't matter. If he'd laid hands on him he'd have killed the bastard, whoever he was, as well as Ros. But Keith Buchanan, his one-time colleague and old friend, had been with him and he had kept him talking until Ros and the man left. There had been no confrontation that night at least.

He opened the cupboard to look for a mug but the shelf was empty. He took one of the used ones from where it had been dumped on the windowsill, emptying the dregs down the sink and swilling it out under the cold tap.

'Do you want one?' he asked Maggie.

'Are you offering?'

'Well of course I'm offering. What does it sound like?'

'I didn't think you felt like being hospitable.'

'I don't. But since the kettle's on . . . There aren't any clean cups though.'

'I can see that. I'll wash some up for you.' She moved round the kitchen, collecting mugs and taking them to stack on the draining board. 'Is there any hot water?'

'There should be some if you let the tap run. But you've no need to do it. I survive.'

'I can see that,' Maggie said drily, searching for washing-up liquid and finding only an old bottle, glued by stale spilled solution to the shelf. 'If I'm joining you for a coffee, however, I really would prefer a clean cup. One that I *know* is clean.'

'Suit yourself.' He poured boiling water on to the granules in his own mug. 'You'd rather make your own as well, I suppose.'

'Yes, I think I would. But whilst I'm about it I'll do all these cups for you. Are there any more anywhere else? It's a pity to waste this nice hot water.'

'Leave them . . .' he started to say, but it was too late. Maggie was already disappearing out through the door.

He stirred sugar into his coffee and sipped it, black. It seared his tongue and when it hit his stomach he felt sick again. He jettisoned the cup and made for the bathroom, but it was only another wave of nausea.

When he emerged Maggie was coming out of the bedroom.

'What the hell are you doing in there?' he demanded.

'Collecting dirty cups.'

'Well you won't find any in there!' he snapped, annoyed at the way she seemed to be making herself at home.

Maggie rattled a mug and a whisky tumbler under his nose.

'That's where you're wrong. These were under the bed. Plus three in the lounge. How can you live like this, Brendan? It's like a pigsty.'

Oh yes, he thought, bitterly sarcastic. Just as he'd expected – it was Ros all over again.

'Was there anything else you wanted?' he asked. All he could think of now was getting her out of the flat so he could get back to bed and try to ease this splitting head.

'Not if you don't know where Ros is,' Maggie said.

'I told you I don't know.'

'And she hasn't been here recently, you say?'

'She hasn't been here for bloody ages. I told you, when I see her I see her out. She doesn't like being alone with me – don't ask me why. I used to be her husband, after all – she was happy enough to be alone with me then. But times change, Maggie, times change.' He laughed suddenly. 'I think she was afraid of me.'

'I see.' Maggie's back was towards him, and again he was struck by the similarity to the old Ros, the girl he had married. He put out a hand, letting it hover over her hair where it fell in a soft sweep over her shoulders, then withdrew it again very quickly without having actually touched her as Maggie banged the last mug on to the draining board and turned to him.

'In that case I'll leave you in peace, Brendan. I was hoping you might be able to help but it seems you can't.'

'Aren't you going to have your coffee?' he asked.

'I don't think I'll bother. If you do hear anything from Ros you will let me know, won't you?'

'She wouldn't contact me. I'd be the last person,' Brendan said.

Maggie nodded and moved to the door. He followed her, undoing the catch. He stood for a moment, watching her go back down the stairs. Then he closed the door again, leaning heavily against it.

Thank God she'd gone! The relief was so enormous it made him dizzy. But why the hell had she come at all? Did she really think he might know what had happened to Ros? Or had she just come to gloat?

The thinking process was too much for his aching, fuddled brain. Brendan lumbered back to the bedroom, lay down on the bed without bothering to remove his dressing gown, and pulled the covers over his head.

Maggie let herself out of the main door and walked across the communal car park to where she had left her hired Metro. Her hands were shaking slightly as she retrieved the keys from her pocket, got in and started the engine. She pulled out of the car park a little too fast, bumping over the dip where drive met kerb, and turned along the road which was lined on either side by imposing Victorian mansions. Only when she reached the roundabout at the end and swung the car back in the direction of town did she slow down.

Her nerves were twanging, her mind seething. She'd been almost afraid to call on Brendan; in spite of her assurances to Mike that she could look after herself she had been well aware that it was not a very sensible thing to do – Brendan had always been a dangerous man and given her suspicions of him she had known she could be walking into danger.

But she had risked it – anything to try and find out what had happened to Ros. And the risk had been well worth taking. She had emerged unscathed and though she had not found Ros, and Brendan had insisted he knew nothing about her disappearance, she knew for a fact that he had lied to her.

She had asked him not once but twice whether he had seen Ros recently and he had denied it, specifically stating that she had not been to the flat since before Christmas. But Maggie knew different. She had used collecting the dirty mugs as an excuse to take a good look around, and in the bedroom she had found a piece of very telling evidence.

On the floor, amidst the general clutter, was a scarf Maggie had instantly recognised. It was a silk scarf, patterned blues and greens with a border of gold. Now she eased her foot off the accelerator and pulled it out of her pocket where she had thrust it out of sight.

She had bought this scarf herself for Ros in one of the fashionable boutiques in Kerkira. At the time she had wondered if it was taking coals to Newcastle to give a scarf to Ros, who worked for one of the world's most renowned producers of luxury neckwear, but she'd thought Ros would like the typically Grecian pattern, might even show it to Vandina's own designers for their inspiration. And she had sent it to Ros only last month as a present for her birthday.

Useless for Brendan to protest that Ros had not been at his flat since before Christmas – the scarf proved otherwise.

Oh my God, Ros, what has he done to you? Maggie wondered, and felt her stomach close with dread.

The very first public telephone booth she saw, Maggie stopped the car and put a call through to Mike's school.

Luckily it was the lunch hour, she knew he would not be teaching now, but it took some time for the secretary who answered the phone to locate him and Maggie had used up almost all her small change feeding the meter before he came on the line.

'Mike – thank goodness!' She was trembling with anxiety, the receiver sticking to her moist palm.

'Maggie! Is something wrong?'

'I'm not sure.' She forced her voice to sound reasonably normal. 'But I think it might be. I've just been to see Brendan.'

'What did he say?'

'Oh, he told me he hadn't seen Ros for months. But he was lying, Mike. Her scarf was there, in his flat.'

'Scarf? What scarf?'

'The one I sent her for her birthday last month. She's been there, and recently. I'm going to the police now, to tell them about it, but I wanted you to know first. And to ask you which police station I should report to. Who is dealing with the case?'

'The local divisional HQ. But to be frank, Maggie, I don't think they'll be interested.'

'What do you mean – not interested?'

The digital display on the telephone was flashing again. Maggie fed her last ten-pence piece into it.

'They rang me earlier on. There's been a development. They've found Ros's car.'

'Where?'

'That's just it. It was in the car park outside Bristol Temple Meads railway station. The car park attendants say it's been there for more than a week and the police seem to think that confirms their theory that Ros has simply gone off somewhere.'

'But she wouldn't!'

'Try telling them that. With her car sitting outside a main-line station it does seem to point to her having taken a train.'

'Yes, but . . .'

'Tell them about the scarf if you like but I think you'll be banging your head against a brick wall.'

'What are we to do then?' Maggie asked desperately.

'Have you been to Vandina?'

'No, not yet.'

'I think you should. I keep thinking about what she said about something odd going on there. It's possible it does have some bearing on her disappearance. And someone like Dinah Marshall might be able to throw some light on it.'

'But the scarf . . .'

'Could be leading us up a blind alley. There was no other sign of Ros being there?'

'No, but . . .'

'It's not much to go on then, is it? And if she's not there now we're no further on. I think you could be overreacting, Maggie. Go and see Dinah, see what you can find out there, and we'll talk again tonight.'

'But . . .'

But the display was showing zero again and before she could finish, the line disconnected. Maggie stood for a moment looking at the telephone as if it might reconnect her to Mike by magic, then she hung up and walked back to her car.

She felt a little calmer now. Just talking to Mike had made her feel better, and perhaps he was right. Perhaps she was overreacting. The fact that Brendan had lied to her didn't necessarily mean he was hiding something sinister. It could simply be that for some reason he didn't want her to know that Ros had been to see him. But still she was uneasy. All very well for Mike to take the sensible, unmelodramatic point of view. He didn't know Brendan as she did. And he seemed to have it in his head that they might find the reason behind Ros's disappearance at Vandina.

Was it possible he had something there? Had something happened that had upset her so much she had simply taken off for a few days? Her car had been found at the railway station, Mike had said, and that certainly pointed to her driving herself there and leaving by train. As for the suitcase – perhaps she had treated herself to a new one, or taken an overnight bag and then stayed away longer than she had intended, unable to bring herself to return and face . . . whatever it was that was troubling her.

But whatever it was, why hadn't she confided in Mike? He had been away when she left, it was true, but she had already mentioned 'something funny going on' – why hadn't she explained further? Mike was the easiest person in the world to talk to, Maggie thought, straightforward, easy-going, with plenty of sound common sense – the very opposite of her own explosive, impatient husband who was totally unsympathetic to anything which did not directly concern him. And surely whatever the reason for her going, Ros could have got in touch with Mike since his return –unless something was dreadfully wrong.

Maggie realised she had begun to tremble again.

She started the car, trying to subdue the feeling of rising panic.

She would drive over to Vandina now, she thought, and see

what she could find out there before going to the police with the evidence of the scarf.

Resolutely she pulled out from the kerb into the heavy traffic and concentrated on finding the right lane to take her out of town once more.

Chapter Seven

The Vandina factory and office block, architect-designed to be both functional and aesthetically pleasing, stood in open countryside on the outskirts of a small village. As Maggie pulled into the spacious car park the bright June sunshine seemed to be reflected from endless panes of glass, and from the landscaped gardens which surrounded the car park the scent of hundreds of rose bushes perfumed the air.

Maggie locked up her hired Metro and went in through the main entrance. A receptionist seated behind a polished wood desk looked up and smiled at her.

'Good afternoon. Can I help?'

'I'd like to see Dinah Marshall,' Maggie said.

The receptionist's smile became a little more fixed.

'Do you have an appointment?'

'No, I don't, but I was hoping to see her anyway. I'm Maggie Veritos, Ros Newman's sister.'

'Oh, I see.' Clearly she did not, but Ros's name carried weight anyway. 'I'm terribly sorry but I'm afraid Miss Marshall isn't in at the moment. She had a lunch appointment and she hasn't returned yet. And when she does I believe she will be tied up in meetings. Could her secretary help you, perhaps?'

Maggie hesitated. It wasn't what she wanted but if Dinah Marshall wasn't here it might be an option.

'Well, possibly . . .' she demurred.

The receptionist lifted the receiver of a dove-grey telephone and dialled a number.

'Liz – I have Ros Newman's sister here in reception. She wanted to see Miss Marshall but I have suggested perhaps you might be able to help.'

Liz – the person who had telephoned and left a message on Ros's answering machine. She could do worse, Maggie thought.

'Thank you, Liz.' The receptionist replaced the receiver and smiled at Maggie again. She was clearly either a very bright-natured girl or else she had been trained to do a lot of smiling, Maggie decided. 'If you'd like to go through, up the stairs, turn left and it's the third door on the right.'

Maggie followed the directions, her feet sinking into the pile of a luxurious carpet of deep blue. As she reached the head of the stairs a door away to her left opened and a pretty but rather plump girl wearing a smart navy-blue coat-dress came out.

'You must be Ros's sister. I can tell that just by looking at you.'

'I didn't know we were that much alike,' Maggie said.

'Well, perhaps you're not. But I can certainly see the likeness. Do come in.'

She led the way into a square office. Like the corridor it was carpeted in blue. The walls were lined with filing cabinets, pine-faced, not metal, and above them hung framed prints of some of the most successful Vandina advertisements and one or two original design sketches. The girl plumped down in her own swivel chair and indicated a blue-leather upholstered chair drawn up at right angles to the desk.

'Have a seat. I'm Liz Christopher.'

'Maggie Veritos.'

'Pleased to meet you, Maggie. What can I do for you?'

'It's Ros. No one seems to know where she is. I was wondering if you could help.'

Liz shook her head, dark hair bouncing about her round, pretty face.

'Sorry, I can't. She's not here. She called in and said she needed to take emergency leave.'

'She didn't say why?'

'No.'

'Are you sure?'

'Quite sure. I took the call myself. She didn't give any explanation at all.'

Maggie chewed at her lip. Liz must have been the last person to speak to Ros before she went . . . wherever she had gone.

'How did she sound?' she asked. 'I mean, was she upset?'

Liz considered. 'Not upset, exactly. A bit strained, perhaps. But then she had been strained for a few days.'

'Do you know why that was?'

'Not for sure. She had been under a certain amount of pressure.'

'What sort of pressure? You see the reason I ask is that she had told Mike Thompson, her boyfriend, that there was something odd going on here but she didn't say what it was. I was wondering if you might know.'

'Oh, I see.' Liz's plump cheeks turned a gentle shade of pink. 'Well, I don't know that I ought to talk about that . . . it's really very awkward –' She broke off suddenly as a door to an inner office opened and a young man emerged. Tall, fair, stunningly good-looking in a striped shirt and chinos, he seemed to dominate the office. Liz's flush deepened and she became overtly flustered.

'What is awkward, Liz?' he asked. There was a slight trans-atlantic twang to his voice, Maggie noticed. Then, without waiting for an answer, he swung his gaze to Maggie, piercing blue eyes offset by a smile that could almost take your breath away. 'I'm sorry to interrupt. I'm Steve Lomax, Dinah Marshall's son.'

Maggie was surprised. She hadn't known Dinah had a son. No reason why she should, of course, but she didn't think she could ever remember having heard Ros mention him.

'Maggie Veritos, Ros Newman's sister.'

'Yes, I gathered that.' His voice, his whole manner, was pleasant, but was there something guarded in those startlingly blue eyes? 'Do I understand you've come here looking for Ros?'

'Not looking for her in the way you mean. I realise she's not here. But I am trying to find out her whereabouts. I'm very concerned about her.'

'I'm sorry, I don't quite understand. Why are you concerned about Ros?'

Another disbeliever, Maggie thought wearily. Aloud, she said: 'No one seems to know where she is. I was hoping someone here might have some idea.'

Steve's eyes narrowed slightly. 'Who, exactly?'

'Well – anyone. Anyone Ros might have talked to or confided in.'

'I have already explained we are totally in the dark,' Liz put in. 'I took Ros's call and she didn't say anything by way of explanation to me.' She was still looking extremely hot and bothered, Maggie thought, and she clearly had no intention of finishing whatever she had been about to say when Steve Lomax had put in his appearance.

'I was rather hoping Ros might have mentioned something of her plans to your mother,' Maggie said. 'They are quite close, I imagine.'

A corner of Steve's mouth twisted. 'You imagine right. As a PA Ros is invaluable to my mother, who is not actually the most efficient person in the world. Ros organises her beautifully. But I don't think Dinah has any more idea where Ros is than the rest of us. She's pretty miffed with her at the moment, actually, for leaving her in the lurch, as she sees it.'

Maggie nodded. 'I'd still have liked to speak to her myself, though. There might be something . . . could I make an appointment, perhaps?'

'Her diary is very full . . .' Liz began defensively.

'I wouldn't take up much of her time. Surely if she's missing Ros it would be as much in her interests as anyone's to try and track her down.'

'Well this afternoon is right out, I'm afraid. And tomorrow . . .'

'I have a far better idea,' Steve said. 'We are having a small dinner party tomorrow evening. Why don't you come and meet my mother then?'

'A private dinner party? Oh no, thank you, but I couldn't possibly intrude.'

'You wouldn't be. It will only be my mother, Don Kennedy, her accountant, Jayne Peters-Browne, the new designer, and her husband, and myself. All Vandina people with the exception of Drew Peters-Browne – one of them might be able to shed some light on your problem.' He smiled, that smile that could turn the hardest-nosed female into a jelly of desire. 'Actually Ros should have been making up the six. Since she's not here I would be delighted if you would come in her place, and I know Dinah will agree with me.'

A slight rustle of papers made Maggie glance at Liz. The secretary was bending over her desk, fiddling conspicuously with a pile of documents and looking rather put out. Perhaps she would have liked to have been invited to dinner in Ros's place, Maggie thought.

'Well, can we make it a date?' The look in Steve's eyes might almost have been a challenge. 'Unless, of course, you have other arrangements . . .'

Maggie made up her mind.
'No – I don't. And thank you, I'd be very pleased to accept your invitation.'
'Good. Do you have your own transport or shall I send a car for you? In fact, that might be an idea in any case. Then you'll be able to have a drink without worrying about having to drive. Where are you staying?'
Maggie frowned slightly, wondering how Steve knew she was 'staying' anywhere. Unless of course Ros had talked about her sister in Corfu. That must be it.
'At Ros's cottage,' she said. 'You know where that is?'
'I do. I'll have the car pick you up at around seven. Now, if you'll excuse me I'm trying to wade through some of my mother's paperwork – one of the jobs Ros would normally do. And Liz – give me five minutes and then bring your notebook in, if you would. I'd like to dictate some letters.'
The dismissal was polite but firm. That young man knows what he wants and goes for it, Maggie thought.
'Thank you, Mr Lomax, I'll look forward to it,' she said.
In the doorway he turned, cool glance appraising.
'So will I. And please, do call me Steve.'
'Can you find your own way out?' Liz asked. 'Perhaps I'd better show you.'
'There's no need. I'm sure I can manage.'
'It's no trouble.'
She accompanied a rather bewildered Maggie down the stairs and out of the building into the car park, where it quickly became obvious that there was something she wanted to say.
'Mrs Veritos, you were asking me just now if I knew what Ros has been so screwed up about lately.' She hesitated. 'I couldn't talk then because Steve was in the next room and I'm not really sure I should say anything at all. But as you are Ros's sister I suppose it would be all right for me to trust you with it . . . and if it might help you to find Ros . . . though I can't honestly see what it could have to do with her disappearing . . .'
'What?' Maggie asked.
'Well . . .' Liz glanced around, as if to make sure no one was within earshot, then went on: 'Ros thought there might be a mole at Vandina.'

'A mole?'

'An industrial spy – checking out our sales figures and contacts on behalf of some third party, even making copies of designs and project sheets for new ideas and passing them back to whoever it is that really employs them. It sounds far-fetched, I know, like James Bond or something, but it does happen. Competition in any industry is very fierce; in the fashion world it can be absolutely cut-throat. It's so terribly important to be the first with original ideas, you see – anyone who can forecast a trend and get in ahead of the field is going to make a killing. Vandina have been leaders for so long now it's almost inevitable that they suffer from this kind of espionage from time to time. Ros believed it's happening now – and I think she may be right. This morning one of our competitors, a new firm called Reubens, broke cover with an idea for a range of bags to be launched in the spring that is practically an exact copy of Dinah's latest idea. It could be coincidence, of course, but I don't actually think that's the case. I think Ros was right – there is someone in a position of trust here at Vandina who is actually working for another company – probably Reubens.'

She stopped, flushed and breathless, and Maggie stared at her in frank amazement.

'Good heavens! That's creepy! But why should it have anything to do with Ros disappearing?'

Liz shook her head. 'I honestly don't know. But you asked me what she was worried about and I'm suggesting a reason. Look – I'll have to go. Steve wanted me for dictation and I'd rather he didn't know I'd been talking to you about this. It's terribly sensitive.' She hesitated, that ready flush deepening again. 'Oh, and Mrs Veritos, please – would you mind not mentioning this to Miss Marshall when you meet her tomorrow evening? I know for a fact Ros didn't want her to know anything about it until she was certain who the mole was. Dinah can get in a dreadful state about things – Ros tries to protect her as far as possible.'

'But surely she'll have to know?'

'Eventually, yes. She already knows Reubens have duplicated her idea. When it was in the newspaper this morning I was bound to bring it to her attention. Something like that creates a dreadful situation. There will have to be a major rethink on the whole spring launch, but I'd really rather she didn't hear the worst of it until Ros is here to break it to her herself.' She looked over her shoulder nervously. 'I'm sorry, but I have to go. And please, you will treat what I've said as absolutely confidential, won't you?'

Before Maggie could question her further she had gone, hurrying back across the car park, and Maggie stood for a moment looking after her and thinking about what she had said. If there really was an industrial spy at Vandina then perhaps it was possible that Ros had gone off to do some checking up. But why should she have been gone so long? It didn't explain anything – only posed more questions. And it had done nothing to dispel the underlying sense of apprehension for her sister's safety that had been with her from the moment she had first heard Ros was missing.

Oh Ros, where the hell *are* you? Maggie asked silently. And if you are all right, why, oh why, don't you get it touch?

Here, as at the cottage, it seemed there was no satisfactory answer.

She told Mike what had happened at Vandina that evening over a casual meal in a country pub – the type of place Maggie still missed desperately in spite of all the lovely alfresco tavernas she had become used to in Corfu. It was pleasant, of course, to eat at tables covered with neat checked cloths within sight and sound of the sea, pleasant to watch the sun dip towards the horizon so suddenly that it was there one moment, a ball of fire, and gone the next, leaving only a scarlet stain on the dark water, pleasant to listen to the strains of the balalaika while eating freshly-caught seafood and to see the taverna owner performing traditional Greek dances with one or more of his small sons, but enjoying these things did not stop Maggie from longing for the typically English atmosphere of a smoky crowded pub.

The Haywain was everything she could have wished for. The bare wood tables were set around the centrepiece of a great stone fireplace – though thankfully, poor as the weather had been, it was not so bad as to require a fire to be lit in midsummer – the walls were decorated with horse brasses and there was a shelf housing a collection of eccentric Toby jugs. From a varied menu and a blackboard announcing the day's specials Maggie had chosen home-made steak and kidney pie, that most English of dishes, but when it arrived, steam issuing invitingly from vents in the thick pastry crust, she found she had very little appetite. Ever since leaving Vandina the knot of anxiety in her stomach had been growing, and now the delicious aroma of the steak and gravy made her feel slightly queasy.

Mike, however, was not in the habit of letting worry affect his appetite. He too had chosen steak and kidney pie and within minutes both his dish and the one containing the extra chips – 'Real chips, not French fries,' he had said with satisfaction – were empty.

'Now tell me how you got on at Vandina,' he said, taking a long pull from his tall glass of lager.

Maggie told him. She had promised Liz Christopher confidentiality, of course, but in her book sharing it with Mike did not count.

'Well,' he said when she had finished. 'It's all good, fascinating stuff but I'm not sure how much further forward it takes us. Especially since Liz didn't tell you who she thought might be responsible for the leaks at Vandina.'

'I know. And not being able to mention it to Dinah is another bind. I can't imagine what I can find out from her tomorrow night without raising the subject.' She toyed with a forkful of meat. 'I spent the afternoon phoning everyone I could think of – all Ros's old friends – but I drew blanks there too. I feel as if I've run into a blind alley, Mike. I honestly don't know what to do next.'

He nodded thoughtfully.

'I feel the same. It's the way I felt before I got in touch with you – absolutely helpless. When I knew you were coming over at least I felt purposeful again, but I think that was just an illusion.'

'I'm sorry.' She gave up the attempt at eating, putting down her knife and fork. 'Somehow we've got to make the police take this seriously. I still have the feeling something is dreadfully wrong but I just don't know what to do about it. What did they say about her car?'

'I told you – it's parked outside the railway station. They maintain that is proof that she's gone off somewhere by train, and I suppose they could be right. It's all locked up and legally parked. Who else would have left it there but Ros? And why would she leave it there if she wasn't catching a train?'

'Have they checked it out?' Maggie asked.
'Checked it out?'
'Looked inside to see if there's anything that might give a clue.'
'I doubt it. They didn't say so. I would imagine they would take the view that they would need more evidence of something suspicious having happened to Ros before they break into a locked car legally parked. What sort of clue were you thinking of?'
'I don't know really. But all sorts of things get left in cars, don't they? I wonder if Ros had a spare set of keys? If she had, and I could find them, I'd go and have a look inside myself.'
'Could be an idea. But somehow I can't imagine Ros leaving anything of importance in her car.'
Maggie said nothing. He was right, of course, Ros wasn't the sort to leave things lying about. She was far too well organised. But that was exactly what was so disturbing about this whole thing – there was so much that simply did not fit in with Ros's character. Maggie had held back from voicing the thought that was in her mind; she did not want to add that what she really wanted to see was if there was any evidence of someone else having been in the car with Ros – Brendan perhaps?
'Do you want another drink?' Mike asked.
She shook her head. 'I don't think so.'
'Shall we go, then?'
'Don't you want another one? If you do, don't let me stop you.'
'I'd better not. I don't want to fall foul of the breathalyser.'
'We could always go back to the cottage and have a coffee.'
'Good idea. I shall be glad to get away from that racket anyway.'
He jerked his head in the direction of an electronic gaming machine which stood in a corner. When they had first arrived Maggie had not even noticed its presence, but whilst they were eating a small group of youths had come in and were feeding it with money. The steady whirr and the occasional clatter as a shower of coins cascaded into the metal tray was annoying. Maggie wondered why a pleasant country pub specialising in good food should have resorted to such a thing.
'There's money in it, I expect,' Mike said, reading her thoughts. 'Tenants have to make what they can where they can.'
The sun had set now. As they walked to the car Maggie pulled on her cardigan – a long, loose Professor Higgins style in white

cotton – but there was no real warmth in it and she shivered slightly as a cool breeze whipped across the car park.

'Cold?' Mike asked.

'I'm all right. It's just that English weather is a bit of a shock to the system after Corfu.'

'It must be.' Mike unlocked the car and reached across to open the passenger door for her. 'I don't think I've really thanked you properly, Maggie, for dropping everything at such short notice and coming over.'

'I don't need thanks,' Maggie said, fastening her seat belt. 'Ros is my sister after all. I'm worried about her too.'

'What did your husband have to say about you jetting off at the drop of a hat?'

'He wasn't very pleased,' Maggie admitted, deliberately understating Ari's reaction. 'But it won't make a great deal of difference to him, except that it might make life marginally easier. He'll stay in town, I expect, while I'm away, instead of having to drive from Kassiopi to Kerkira and back twice a day as he normally does in the summer. We have an apartment in Kerkira, for business purposes.'

'What exactly is it he does?'

'He's an architect. And Corfu is a growth island. Everyone who has a bit of suitable land wants to put up a hotel or apartment block on it. They have suddenly woken up to the fact that tourism means prosperity – and a much easier way of earning a living than harvesting olives. Most of the interesting little tavernas and cafés came about because the people who live on the main road or the seashore realised that all they needed to do was open their front doors and put up a sign announcing refreshments for sale and the visitors would flock in. Not so long ago many of them were incredibly poor; now, suddenly, they've found themselves with a licence to print money, so much they scarcely know what to do with it. They are simple people at heart, you see, very family and religion orientated. I only hope the influx of the Western world doesn't change them too much.'

'It sounds as though you like them.'

'I do. Basically they are good people. Take the family structure, for instance – it's terribly strong. As it was in this country maybe fifty years or more ago. Because of the extended family there is always someone with time for the children and they grow up with a strong respect for authority. They don't do anything dreadful, in the main, because it would bring shame on the family.'

'Sounds like a system that would be good for some of my pupils,' Mike said drily.

'It certainly helps to keep the wayward on the straight and narrow. I assure you, a Corfiote mama is a force to be reckoned with.'

'From your rueful tone I suspect you have some experience of Corfiote mamas.'

'You could say that. Oh, it's fine if you're born to it, I guess. I wasn't.'

'So how did you come to marry a Corfiote?' he asked, slowing for a crossroads and accelerating away again.

'I met him when he was in this country studying to qualify.'

'You were at college too?'

'Oh no, not me.' She laughed. 'Ros was always the clever one in our family. I was a secretary – well, typist, really. Ari came to the firm I was with for work experience.'

She broke off, remembering the way it had been. He had seemed so impossibly romantic to her, totally different from any of the other young men she knew. When he had asked her out she had been thrilled, the whole of their whirlwind romance had been conducted in a hot, heady haze, and when he had asked her to marry him she had hardly hesitated at all – she had been so afraid she would lose him when he returned to Corfu that she hadn't really stopped to examine any of the realities of what it would mean.

'I guess I was swept off my feet,' she said drily.

'Any regrets?' He glanced sideways at her, then added swiftly: 'I'm sorry, I shouldn't be asking that. I didn't mean to be personal.'

'It's all right.' She bit her lip. 'Well, yes, if I'm honest – a few, I suppose. But that's life, isn't it? Nothing ever turns out as you expect.'

They were back at the cottage. Mike pulled on to the hard standing but left the engine running.

'Aren't you coming in for that coffee?' she asked.

'I thought maybe you could use an early night.'

She could – but suddenly she didn't want him to go, didn't want to be alone with the emptiness and her anxiety. She realised with a shock that subconsciously she had been half expecting to see lights on in the cottage and Ros's car miraculously there in the drive. There was something so strangely unreal about this whole thing. Ros couldn't simply have disappeared. Yet she had . . .

'Do please come in for a coffee,' she said.

'All right, if you insist.' He switched off the engine, turned and smiled at her, and quite unexpectedly her tummy tipped, a strange little spiral not unlike G-force deep inside her. It shocked her, that sharp indication of physical attraction, and she felt suddenly flustered and gauche.

'There might be some message or other on the answering machine,' she said foolishly.

There was – but only from her mother.

'Margaret, are you there? Oh dear, I do so hate these things! Darling, you didn't ring me. I've been expecting you to all evening. Could you come over tomorrow? For lunch, maybe? Harry will be playing golf and we could have a nice chat. Oh, love to Ros if you see her. Perhaps she could come too. It would be wonderful to be all together again – quite like old times. 'Bye for now, darling.'

'Honestly!' Maggie exploded. 'She just cannot, or will not, accept the fact that Ros is missing.'

'Probably just as well. There's no point in worrying her until we're sure there's something to worry about.'

Maggie laughed shortly. 'I can see you don't know my mother very well. She doesn't worry – unless you count fussing over Harry as worrying. She finds the real thing far too exhausting.'

She followed Mike through into the kitchen. The momentary vortex of emotions she had experienced in the car had passed now.

'So, you aren't going to ring her back?' he asked.

'Not tonight. She's probably making Harry's cocoa by now. I'll do it in the morning.' She reached across him for the kettle and suddenly there it was again – an awareness sensitising her body as acutely as a touch, though there had been no physical contact between them.

'Cocoa sounds rather nice,' he said, seemingly unaware. 'I haven't had cocoa for years. It reminds me of winter evenings in front of a blazing fire, fresh from the bath and ready for bed.'

'I take it you are talking about when you were a little boy.'

'Unfortunately, yes. My flat is all night-storage heaters. The blazing fires seem to have gone the way of the cocoa. Ros hasn't got any, I suppose?' He began opening cupboards, moving things around, and after a moment he whooped in triumph. 'Yes! What's that if it's not cocoa? I've never seen her drink the stuff though.'

'She probably uses it for cooking. You want some?'

'Why not – if there's enough milk.'

'Go and sit down then, and I'll bring it in to you.'

Ros's little sitting room was incredibly cosy – soft, squashy chintz-covered chairs, a cane table covered by a cloth, and softly draped curtains. Mike was sprawled out in one of the chairs, his feet propped up on a pouffe. He looked very much at home – and why shouldn't he? Maggie asked herself. He probably spent a good deal of time here with Ros. She set the mugs down on the table and went across to draw the curtains.

'So,' she said, deliberately drawing the conversation back to Ros's disappearance. 'What do you think our next move should be?'

'I honestly don't know.' He sipped the cocoa foaming in the earthenware mug. 'This is good!'

'Well, as I said, I'll have a good look round for spare car keys and I'll see if I can think of anyone else she might have been in contact with – check out her private papers and things. I don't like doing it but . . .' She perched on the chair furthest from Mike, putting as much distance between them as possible.

'You seem to have covered practically everything in one day and not come up with anything.'

'Well, that's not quite true. At least I've found out what she meant by "something odd" going on at Vandina.' She hesitated, almost afraid to put into words the thought that had been worrying at the back of her mind. 'You don't think, do you, Mike, that she suspected someone of being a mole and something has happened to her because of it?'

'What do you mean?'

'Well, it's big business. There could be big money at stake. If she found out someone was involved in industrial espionage they wouldn't . . . harm her, would they, to prevent her exposing them?'

He frowned. 'Sounds pretty far-fetched to me. If anyone is holding Ros I should have thought it was more likely to be a nutter.'

'Like Brendan, you mean.' She saw his disbelieving expression and hurried on: 'I'm still not happy about him, Mike. He was lying to me. He had to be. Her scarf in his flat proves that. And I've got this sick feeling in my stomach that something is very wrong. You don't think, do you, that he could have . . .'

'I am beginning to think that perhaps the police are right and we are wrong.' The cocoa was mellowing Mike; he sounded almost lazy. 'I am beginning to think Ros *has* gone off somewhere on her own account. Take this Vandina business, for instance. If she was suspicious of someone, this "mole" as you call them, she could very well have gone haring off to check out some lead. If it's all so confidential then she wouldn't want anyone to know where she had gone or why.'

'But she's been gone more than a week!'

'Not so long really.'

'And why hasn't she phoned to let you know where she is? She must know you're back by now and you will be anxious about her.'

'Perhaps I don't rate any more.'

Maggie glanced at him sharply. Had she imagined that note in his voice – a note of . . . what? Resignation? A slight edge of bitterness? She couldn't be sure, but quite suddenly she found herself remembering that Brendan had said he had seen Ros in Clifton with a man – a man who was not Mike. At the time she had thought he was simply trying to divert attention from himself – now suddenly she wondered if he had been telling the truth. Was there another man in Ros's life? Someone she knew nothing of? Had she gone off with him, perhaps? But it didn't really add up.

Mike's voice interrupted her thoughts.

'I have a feeling,' he said, 'that Ros could turn up at any time. And she will not be at all amused to find that we have reported her missing.'

Maggie sighed and shook her head. She wished she could be so sure.

When he had gone she prepared for bed, using Ros's room once again. But though her limbs ached and her eyes burned, sleep refused to come.

In spite of what Mike had said, she was still dreadfully worried about Ros. All very well for him to make light of her fears about Brendan – he didn't know the man as she did, did not know just what his insane jealousy could render him capable of. And Ros had been there, at his flat – the presence of her scarf proved it.

As for the Vandina mole business, that was yet another unsolved mystery.

But tonight it was not only her fears for Ros's safety that were preventing Maggie from relaxing. However she tried to keep from remembering it, that quirk of attraction she had felt for Mike was there too, teasing at her insistently.

It had happened, she supposed, because she had had two glasses of wine and very little to eat. But it had been so strong, so unexpected, so *exciting*! I'd almost forgotten it was possible to feel like that, Maggie thought – and thanked her lucky stars that she had managed to conceal it.

But the warmth of the memory was seductive; though she knew she was foolish to do so, she hugged it to her as she drifted towards sleep, and there was a tiny smile somewhere at the back of her mind.

She woke next morning with a blinding migraine.

They descended on her from time to time, headaches that felt as if a hot steel screw was being driven into her temple, and spreading out into a pounding skullcap of pain, flashing lights before the eyes and a nausea rising from the pit of her stomach. Sometimes they lasted for days, sometimes, if she was lucky, the worst of it was over in a matter of hours.

Maggie groaned. Oh God, she hated days like this – and especially when she had so much planned. It would have to be put off, all of it; she wouldn't be safe to drive – she could barely *think* – and even if she did manage to keep going she would probably be sick. Really, the only possible course of action was to take some of her tablets, bury her head beneath the covers and hope it would go away or at least improve enough for her to be able to keep her dinner-party date with Dinah tonight.

With a supreme effort Maggie swung her legs to the floor. As she stood up, the steel screw twisted in her temple and the pounding at the base of her skull worsened. She groped her way to the bathroom and found her pills – thank heavens she had remembered to pack them. Then she remembered that her mother was expecting her to call. Well, it couldn't be helped. She couldn't, simply couldn't, face talking to Dulcie now.

Maggie let her tablets dissolve in a tumbler of water, swallowed them with distaste, and crawled back to bed.

Chapter Eight

'Darling,' said the statuesque redhead, curling her body languorously around the man's. 'There is nothing in the whole world like making love in the afternoon. Don't you agree?'

Steve Lomax ran his hand over her breast, full and thrusting even in a reclining position, and down over her stomach, still slightly sticky from the closeness and the exertions of a few minutes ago.

'I've always liked first thing in the morning best myself.'

She laughed softly. 'I'm afraid that mornings are absolutely out as far as I am concerned. Mornings I have to wake up in bed beside my husband. If I wasn't there he would be most upset.'

'I'll bet he would, lucky bastard!' Steve said, but he knew the score. The fact that they woke up in bed together did not mean they would go on to make love together – and even if it did, he had no intention of allowing himself to be jealous. Mornings might be his preferred time but he was perfectly happy to settle for a hotel room after a delicious lunch and a couple of glasses of Courvoisier. Good food, good drink and a good woman – it was an unbeatable combination. After the hardship years on a North Sea oil rig it seemed like heaven. Besides, waking up too often beside the same woman would smack of permanence and that was not something he wanted, certainly not now, possibly not ever. Being free and single was much more his style. Especially when there were women like Jayne Peters-Browne for the taking.

He turned his head slightly on the pillow and glanced along at her, bright-red hair tousled from the rough and tumble yet still looking glamorous with her make-up more or less intact. Some women he had slept with looked terrible afterwards, flushed and crumpled, with mascara smudges beneath their eyes and all their lipstick gone – most of it on to him. Occasionally he had been moved to wonder what it was that had got him into bed with them in the first place. But not Jayne – not yet anyway. He always looked at her and wanted to make love to her again. She might have been Dinah's find as a designer; she was certainly his find as a lover! Desire moved his body again and he reached for her, pulling her on top of him and groaning with pleasure as she straddled him, taking him deep inside her with her knees drawn up on either side of his narrow hips.

'Little witch!' he murmured as she raised and lowered her body in an ever-changing rhythm.

She did not answer, simply parted those perfect red lips in a voracious smile and bent her head over his, kissing and biting at his mouth with a passion that was even more arousing than the movement of her body.

Steve closed his eyes and let the tide of delicious sensation that was part intense pleasure, part almost pain, take him over.

This was living! He wouldn't go back to the cold, backbreaking, celibate hell of the oil rig if it was the last place on earth.

Thank God – and of course, thanks to Dinah – he had absolutely no need to.

Jayne Peters-Browne looked down at the handsome face, twisted in the throes of passion, and felt alive with a sense of power and triumph. She wasn't aroused herself this time; for her, multiple orgasm had always been something to read about in *Cosmopolitan*, never a reality, but she didn't care. She had already had her fun for the day – Steve was a marvellous lover (though not quite as good as he imagined – what man was?) – but this . . . this was even better. Now, instead of being at the mercy of her own needs and desires, she was in complete control, and the knowledge of it was pure, sweet exhilaration.

For as long as she could remember, Jayne had craved power, but for years it had eluded her.

She had been born plain Jane Sweeney, the only daughter of a colliery undermanager in the Nottingham coalfields, and her father's position had placed her in a state of limbo. To the other children who lived near the Coal Board-owned house which they occupied as one of the perks of her father's job she was 'the boss's daughter', removed from them because her father was in a position to hire, fire, or generally make life miserable for their fathers, and by the fact that her house was much bigger and more impressive than theirs. But when her parents, in an effort to live up to what they thought of as their status in the community, sent her to 'private school' she did not fit in there either. Money was tight – her father was not particularly well paid, and the fees for Jane and her two brothers' schooling crippled him – so there was never anything over for the extras the other, more affluent girls, took for granted. Jane could not ride – and for most of them the Pony Club was the centre of their social universe. Her accent was all wrong. Her family had retained many of the habits of the working class from which they had risen – her father had been an ordinary collier and a deputy before studying for, and gaining, his undermanager's ticket. Worst of all, she was fat.

Unfair though it may seem, being overweight is one of the worst crimes a child can commit in the eyes of his peers. Fat children are different enough to be the butt of jokes and name-calling as bad if not worse than anything brought before the race relations or sex discrimination boards. Fat children are not often good at games. Fat children look ridiculous in the latest fashion craze – always supposing they can find it in their size.

Jane was not only plump, she was also tall for her age. Because her brothers were always hungry the family were used to 'filling' meals – dumplings and pies with suet crusts, steamed puddings dripping with jam or treacle, apple pies that were more pastry than fruit. At eleven Jane was five feet five inches tall and could match her years with her weight in stones; by the time she was thirteen and her breasts had begun to sprout she was three inches taller and had put on another stone.

To make matters worse, her mother, in an effort to save money, made most of her clothes. Given Jane's size this could have been an advantage, but since Mrs Sweeney had very little idea of what was fashionable for a young teenager in the early seventies it was a disaster. Jane looked a frump and felt a freak. She walked with a stoop to minimise her height and tried without success to hide her large hands and feet (which she frequently fell over).

Jane had a dream – that one day from the fat ugly duckling she now was a swan would emerge. She would not only be beautiful, she would be successful. And no one would ever laugh at her or ostracise her again.

Around the time of her fifteenth birthday a new art teacher came to Jane's school. She was called Miss Makim and she was quite different to any of the other members of staff and indeed to anyone Jane had ever known. Miss Makim had been a 'hippy' in the heady days of the Swinging Sixties and she had hardly changed since then. Her long hair was tied back in a bunch at the nape of her neck and she wore little or no make-up. She dressed in cheesecloth blouses, long wrap-around Indian cotton skirts and wooden-soled health sandals that clopped loudly on the wood-block school corridors. As an artist she believed in freedom of expression, as a teacher she was totally lacking in discipline, as a woman she personified all the easy-going warmth and enthusiasm of the 'make love not war' generation.

Miss Makim saw at once the enormous talent Jane possessed which others had failed to notice – because it was difficult to associate anything beautiful with Jane – and which was being allowed to wilt away for lack of nurturing. She encouraged her to explore and expand and as the talent began to blossom under her tutelage she found herself wanting to help the shy, awkward girl to blossom in other areas too.

'You must believe in yourself,' she told Jane. 'You have a great deal to give. Everyone does.'

'No one wants you when you're fat,' Jane said.

'That's nonsense. It's what's inside that counts.'

'Nobody ever seems to want to bother to find out what's inside me.'

'Perhaps because you give the impression that you yourself don't think it would be worth their effort. Other people tend to take us at our own valuation, you know. And you are very defensive about yourself. But if it's being fat that makes you self-conscious, well, you don't have to be fat.'

'I can't help it,' Jane said. 'Mum says I've got a large frame.'

'But there's no need for it to be quite so well covered,' Miss Makim said bluntly.

They were in the kitchen of her cottage; she had invited Jane over to practice her sketching, which she needed to speed up in order to make the best possible showing in the still life or life drawing in the A-level examination, which Miss Makim was determined she should take when the time came. Now, with a morning's tuition behind them, it was time for lunch.

'What do you eat?' Miss Makim asked.

Jane told her and Miss Makim listened in disbelief.

'All that? Good heavens! Why don't you have muesli or fruit for breakfast instead of fried bread and bacon? And so much starch and sugar is very bad for you.'

'What do *you* eat?' Jane asked, looking enviously at Miss Makim's willowy figure.

'Well, I'm a vegetarian, of course, so I have lots of pulses and fresh fruit and vegetables.'

'Pulses?' Jane repeated, mystified.

'Beans and things.'

'Baked beans?'

'Dried ones, mostly. There's a lot of sugar in the tinned varieties,' Miss Makim said severely. 'Look, I've got a hominy pie in the fridge. We'll have that for lunch with a nice crisp salad and you can tell me what you think of it.'

Jane quite liked it but she wasn't sure she would want to live on it all the time – or if her mother would allow her to!

'Change your eating habits and you will lose weight,' Miss Makim told her. 'Provided of course that you also absolutely give up snacking on biscuits and chocolate bars.'

Jane flushed. She knew she was guilty of comfort eating.

'If you can get down to a size fourteen you will be able to wear jeans as the others do and you'll feel much better for it,' Miss Makim told her. 'And if you could squeeze off the extra to reach a size twelve or even a ten, you would be stunning. With your height you'd be of model proportions.'

Her positive attitude fired Jane with enthusiasm. She went home determined to lose weight. But it was an uphill battle. Bad enough to feel hungry all the time, bad enough to have to be strong when she would have died for a chocolate bar or bag of crisps, ten thousand times worse when it was not only herself she had to fight but her mother as well.

'For goodness' sake eat up and forget about this slimming nonsense,' Mary Sweeney would say, slamming a plate of chips and battered fish, running with grease, on the table in front of her. 'You'll feel faint if you go out on an empty stomach.'

'But I want to lose weight!'

'Whatever for? You're fine as you are. Some of these girls look as if they haven't had a proper meal in their life.'

Jane would sigh at the hopelessness of it, pile her food on to her brothers' plates when her mother's back was turned, and go to her room to nibble the Limmits biscuits she had bought with her pocket money. Whether she would have had the necessary willpower to stick to her diet for long enough to make any difference if she had not had any extra incentive is doubtful. But she did have an incentive. She had fallen in love.

His name was Graham Toohey. His father was the new manager of one of the other collieries, he was blond and handsome, and he had 'palled up' with Jane's brother, Martin, who, at sixteen, was just the same age. The boys were always together, swimming, going to the cinema and (though their parents did not know it) to the pub. Jane was sure they met girls there and her heart ached with envy.

So far Jane's record with boys had not been impressive. At discos she was usually left hiding in a corner because nobody ever asked her to dance and she was much too self-conscious to carry on jigging all alone when the boys came and broke up the group of girls. Nobody had asked her out. Nobody had kissed her, though at Christmas she sometimes lurked under the mistletoe in the hope that someone might try. She had never received a Valentine's card, and she thought that if one with her name on it did drop on the mat it would only be someone playing a joke. She listened enviously when the other girls boasted of their conquests, but she never heard the juiciest bits because they were only related in whispers to the members of the in-crowd and Jane was not one of them. But now she was filled with fierce determination. Somehow she was going to get Graham Toohey.

To begin with she kept out of his way, determined not to spoil her chances by moving before she was ready. As the weight came off, determined not by a pair of scales, which her mother refused to have in the house, but by the way her old clothes were beginning to hang on her, Jane plucked up the courage to shop for a pair of jeans as Miss Makim had suggested. She chose a unisex shop in town and had to try them on in a cubicle with a swinging stable door – rather embarrassing since at her height far too much of her was visible over the top of the door. But she persevered, buying not only the jeans but also a cheesecloth shirt similar to the ones Miss Makim wore and which would fall loose outside the jeans to hide the remaining bulges. She then visited Boots the Chemists and purchased a dark kohl eyeliner, some pale lipstick and a pair of enormous gypsy earrings.

At home she put it all on and paraded in front of the mirror. Not bad – but still not quite right. The Kohl pencil had gone on wrong and made her look as if she hadn't slept for a week instead of achieving the sultry, smoky effect she had hoped for, and her hair looked old-fashioned.

I ought to be a redhead, Jane thought. If I were a redhead Graham would be sure to notice me.

She walked down to the corner chemist and bought a rinse labelled 'Rich Chestnut'. Then she spent the afternoon in the bathroom, waiting for the colour to take on her normally light-mouse hair and trying to get the stains from under her nails.

When she washed out the rinse the effect was startling but it suited her, emphasising the paleness of her skin and complementing her blue-green eyes. She changed her usual side parting for a centre one, and this too suited her, making her face look oval and interesting instead of moon-like. Full of excitement at her own daring she put on the new jeans and shirt and went downstairs.

Her mother was furious. She told Jane she looked like a tart, which was untrue – she looked more like a Botticelli painting, ripe and luscious – and demanded that Jane return to her normal hair colour immediately. Jane refused, lying that the colour was permanent – it was not, though it would last through six washes, according to the leaflet that had been in the box. But her father smiled in a way that almost signified approval and said: 'You look awright to me, lass.'

Jane smiled back at him and was rewarded with a wink.

Graham and Martin were out somewhere on their bicycles. Her heart pounding with the momentousness of it, Jane went into the garden and positioned herself on the lawn to wait for them. She took a magazine with her – *Cosmopolitan*, which she had bought in town and was keeping well out of her mother's way in case she should see the glaringly suggestive copy emblazoned on the cover: 'How Well Endowed Is Your Man?' 'Does Semen Make You Fat?' and 'How to Find Your G-Spot'. Jane doubted her mother would know what a G-spot was – she herself certainly had not until she had read the article – but the other titles were less ambiguous and a little shocking. Jane could not wait to read them and she quite fancied the boys seeing her with the magazine – a good 'prop' to go with her new image.

When she heard the click of the gate she wanted to run and hide. Instead, gathering all her courage, she arranged herself in model pose, chin in hand. The pose also managed to stretch the thin cheesecloth enticingly around her still-ample breasts, but Jane was unaware of this.

Graham leaned on the handlebars of his bicycle and whistled.

'Hello, Gorgeous!'

After that he always called her 'Gorgeous' and the thrill of it never palled.

'What do you mean, Gorgeous? That's my sister!' Martin said, adding rudely: 'What the hell have you done to your hair?'

Jane ignored the jibe. She got up and walked towards them. The tightness of her jeans gave her an undulating gait.

'You didn't tell me you had a sister who looked like this!' Graham said.

'It's only Jane – and she's done something peculiar to her hair.'

'It doesn't look peculiar to me,' Graham said. For a sixteen-year-old he had quite a smooth line in patter and there was a knowing, age-old sparkle in his blue eyes. 'I think it looks nice.'

'Thank you,' Jane said primly.

'Don't be so bloody soft,' Martin said crossly. He began to push his bicycle up the drive but Graham did not follow.

'What are you doing tomorrow night?' he asked Jane.

She shrugged, her heart beating very fast.

'There's a disco on in the village hall. Are you going?'

'I might be.'

'Great,' he said. 'I'll see you there.'

Jane was first excited, then terrified, then worried. What would she wear? She'd spent all her money on the jeans and shirt and she couldn't, simply *couldn't* wear one of her old home-made dresses. Next morning she got on her bicycle and pedalled over to Miss Makim's cottage.

It was now the middle of the summer holidays. Jane was afraid Miss Makim might be away, but she found her sitting in the garden and sketching the cat who was asleep under the weeping willow tree.

'Jane!' she greeted her. 'Good heavens, I'd hardly have known you.'

'I've changed my hair,' Jane said, feeling pleased.

'And not only that! My goodness, that diet seems to have worked wonders! What brings you here?'

Jane told her. 'I know it's a cheek but I wondered if you might lend me a skirt to wear with this cheesecloth blouse,' she finished.

Miss Makim smiled. 'I think I can do better than that. Come in and try some things on.'

A few minutes later the contents of Miss Makim's wardrobe were spread out on the bed and Jane had selected a looseish dress in cream cheesecloth with a handkerchief hemline.

'You look terrific,' Miss Makim said, pleased because she felt personally responsible for the transformation. 'Who is the lucky boy?'

'His name is Graham.'

'I see. Well just be careful, Jane. I should think this Graham will find you irresistible and I shouldn't want you to get yourself into a situation you are not ready for.'

'Miss Makim!' Jane said primly, but the warning struck her as funny. She was ready for any situation, after reading *Cosmopolitan* far into the night. She fancied Graham like crazy and she fancied experiencing at first hand some of the things she had read about. Like a butterfly emerging from a chrysalis Jane was more than anxious to begin on life and living, and the sensuous personality, so long submerged beneath rolls of fat but developing along with her body all the same, was ready too.

Nothing much happened that night. Graham spent most of the evening with the other boys. But he did walk her home with his arm around her waist and he did ask if she would like to go for a walk the next day.

'Oh yes!' Jane said, so excited she could scarcely breathe.

He arrived on his bicycle, which he propped up against the garage wall. Martin, put out by the direction events had taken, was very offhand with him, but Graham did not seem to mind. They walked out of the village, past the pit where her father was undermanager and into the fields between the slag heaps and the river. He put his arm around her then and began kissing her, and Jane responded eagerly. She might never have been kissed before, but she certainly liked it. And it was not at all difficult – after five minutes Jane felt as if she had been doing it all her life. But Graham, she sensed, was a little awkward. He wasn't shy, or 'backward in coming forward' as her mother would say, but there was a sort of breathless eagerness about him that made him slightly clumsy, and quite suddenly Jane felt as if he, and not she, was the novice. It was a good feeling.

When he slipped his hand inside the cheesecloth blouse she let him. She did not feel threatened, she felt powerful, and she exercised that power when he tried to undo the zip of her jeans, removing his hand firmly and placing it in the small of her back, whilst at the same time pressing herself against him in a provocative manner that seemed to come as naturally as kissing.

'Jane!' he groaned, sliding his hand back to her zip again. 'Come on, let me just touch!'

And after a while she let him.

She wouldn't go any further, though, not this time. It was much too soon, and besides, half the fun was in allowing just so much and no more, to have him begging, this handsome older boy, to play him like a fish that has taken the bait. That was the most exciting thing of all, feeling she could hold him and all his turbulent emotions in the palm of her hand.

Each time they went out she allowed him to go a little further, and when she judged she really would be asking for trouble to tease any more she suggested he should purchase a packet of Durex. It did not occur to her that this might sound calculating, any more than it occurred to her that she was not yet sixteen. She simply knew she had embarked on something she had been born to be good at.

It was a disaster, that first time, but the disaster was not her fault and she felt not diminished by it but more powerful than ever. His fumblings and his blushes and the rush with which it was eventually over made her believe more strongly than ever in the superiority of women. Never in her life had Jane felt threatened by a man and she did not feel threatened now. It was her mother, a woman, who called the tune at home; it had been the girls at school who had made her feel foolish and gauche and unwanted. Men didn't do that. With men she was Queen Bee, giving or withholding as she chose.

'Can I see you tomorrow?' Graham asked.

And playing that power game with ever increasing confidence, she replied: 'Oh, not tomorrow. I've got things to do. But there is a film on in town I want to see. Will you take me on Saturday?'

'Yes, if you like . . .' But his disappointment was obvious. Jane smiled to herself.

'We don't want to do this too often, do we? I think we should save it for really special occasions.'

And Graham had no choice but to agree.

By the end of the summer it was all over, petering out as youthful romances so often do. But it left Jane changed for ever.

In spite of constant nagging from her mother she kept her hair coloured red but she decided against losing any more weight. Boys seemed to like her the way she was, a statuesque size 14. They flocked around, attracted partly by the way she looked and partly by her reputation. The girls at school began to view her in a different light, cultivating her in the hope that they too might be sought after by the Graham Tooheys of this world.

Social success bred the sort of confidence to enable Jane to excel in other spheres too. With straight As in Art at both O and A level, she did a foundation and then a degree course in fashion design, emerging with a First. Her career took her to several well-known giants of the high street but she stayed nowhere for long. She was restless, eager to move up and move on, always looking for new challenges, new horizons to conquer.

Along the way she changed the spelling of her name from Jane to Jayne and acquired a husband, Drew Peters-Browne. She had met him at art school and had been attracted to him in the first place because his family was extremely well placed socially – aristocracy, almost – and this offered the status Jayne had always hankered after.

It was an unconventional marriage. Drew was bisexual, with a leaning more towards the homo- than the heterosexual. He had, for a time, been the keyboard player with a moderately successful rock group, and though he now wanted only to paint masterpieces he had retained the tastes he had acquired then – good whisky and fine old wines, exclusive restaurants and foreign holidays, not to mention the use of certain illegal substances. His father, though he could have well afforded to, refused to support Drew in what he considered his profligate lifestyle, and it was left to Jayne to supplement the little he made from selling his paintings.

She was quite happy to do this. Since he had reverted to his preference for men she had no sexual power over him, and holding the purse strings made up for that.

The Vandina post had cropped up when Van had been killed and Dinah needed assistance with design. It had appealed to Jayne for a number of reasons, not least that Vandina was one of the most prestigious names in the fashion world. She had applied for the job and got it, she and Drew had moved into a cottage in the area which was perfect for his work, and everything seemed set fair.

Steve was just the icing on the cake.

She had made up her mind to have him as soon as she met him – just as long ago she had made up her mind to have Graham Toohey – and she had gone after him just as determinedly. He thought he had been the instigator of the affair, of course, but Jayne did not mind him thinking that. Leave him some illusion, she thought, for the sake of his pride.

But he had turned out to be more of a challenge than any of her conquests for a very long time. For one thing he was Dinah's son. That in itself added spice. But beyond that there was a hard edge to him that somehow gave her a feeling of . . . yes, that was it, danger.

Jayne looked down at the handsome face, felt the hard muscles of his shoulders and upper arms under her hands and the strong narrow cage of his hips beneath her well-rounded ones, and smiled.

Not bad for a plain little fat girl, she thought. Not bad at all. And this is just the beginning.

Chapter Nine

By lunchtime Maggie's migraine seemed to be easing. Her eyes felt heavy, as if she had been drugged or had slept too long, but at least the terrible sharp pain, as if someone was boring into her skull with a pneumatic drill, had eased and when she dared to get up she found she was no longer shivering or feeling sick.

She padded gingerly across to fetch Ros's dressing gown, praying that this might be one of those occasions when the tablets worked quickly and the migraine lasted only a few hours instead of a couple of days. Apart from the sheer bloody misery, the desire to do nothing more than die, she always resented the time wasted; now, anxious to continue the search for Ros, she resented it even more than usual.

She went downstairs, half expecting the pain and dizziness to begin again, but moving about did not seem to make it any worse and she brewed herself a good strong cup of tea (best not to have coffee with a migraine, she had learned from experience), squashing a teabag in a mug and adding just a splash of milk.

With the tea she took two more of her tablets – her 'blockbusters', she called them – and nibbled a piece of dry toast. So far so good. Whilst she was eating it the telephone rang. The sound of the bell seemed to go right through her head and she answered it as quickly as she could.

'Margaret, is that you? Or is it that wretched machine again?'

It was her mother. Maggie's heart sank. 'It's me.'

'Where are you? I was expecting you for lunch.'

'Mummy, I never said I'd come today. I was going to ring you but I've got a migraine . . .'

'Oh really!' Dulcie's tone was reproving and Maggie found herself remembering how impatient her mother was with anything less than robust health in others. Even as children Ros and Maggie had learned to expect little sympathy; chicken pox and mumps were just another form of wilful naughtiness in Dulcie's book, contracted for the express purpose of inconveniencing her; colds and coughs were a source of extreme irritation. 'Do you have to keep hacking?' she would enquire. 'Do try to stop it – you are driving me mad!' As for Maggie's headaches, she had always maintained that they were psychosomatic. 'She doesn't understand,' Ros had said once. 'She's hardly had a day's illness in her life.' It was true – in spite of her almost fragile appearance Dulcie enjoyed the rudest of good health.

'I don't know why you get those things!' she said now with disdain. 'You should see someone and get something done about them.'

'I'm sorry.' Maggie was feeling too washed-out to argue.

'Well, just as long as you haven't disappeared too,' Dulcie said, implying that Ros's disappearance, like Maggie's migraine, was just another deliberate annoyance. 'When can I expect to see you, then?'

'I don't know,' Maggie said, her patience exhausted. 'At the moment my first concern is finding out what has happened to Ros. I'll phone you, I promise.' She put the receiver down and was immediately overcome by guilt. Why did she allow her mother to rile her? It was always the same – uncontrollable irritation followed by filial remorse. Other people didn't have this love-hate relationship with their parents – or did they? Ari certainly didn't. He adored his mother and indulged her shamelessly.

Whilst she was in the hall Maggie checked the mail box, but there was no post at all today. Then she finished her tea and made a fresh cup. The headache was definitely lifting and the relief of it made her feel more cheerful. She even thought she might be able to eat something – some tinned soup, perhaps, or baked beans? She opened the door of Ros's little larder to see what she could find and immediately saw the keys, hanging on a cup hook at eye level.

Ros's spare car keys. She'd said she'd look for them and here they were, practically presenting themselves for her attention. Maggie decided to forgo the soup and go straight into Bristol to check out Ros's car. She ran a bath and the warm water revived her further; by the time she left the cottage, albeit still moving at a slower rate than usual, the headache was not much more than a dull throb.

Driving into Bristol she found herself thinking of Mike and the spark of attraction she had felt for him; it seemed now almost like a dream sequence that had never really happened at all. And as the traffic built up for the city Maggie, who had not driven in Bristol for years, was forced to concentate hard on trying to remember which lane she should be in to get to the railway station. There were roadworks at the Bath Bridge causing congestion and confusion but she negotiated them at last, turned into the station forecourt and found a parking space. Then she set out to look for Ros's car and eventually found it, parked not far from her own.

As she had expected the car was scrupulously clean and tidy. There was a telescopic umbrella and a silk scarf on the rear seat (how Ros loved her silk scarves!), a box of tissues in the rear window and a chamois leather, a road map and a wallet containing the car's service history in various pockets. Otherwise, nothing. Maggie slid into the driver's seat and sat quietly, running her eye over the dashboard, covered now with a thin film of dust, and fighting a feeling of disappointment. Trust Ros to remove every scrap of rubbish. Her own car, she knew, would be a mine of information, however useless, on her activities of previous weeks – shopping lists and empty cigarette packets, sweet wrappers and used tissues. She yanked open the ashtray. There were no cigarette ends, of course – Ros didn't smoke – just one screwed-up stick-on ticket from a pay-and-display car park, dated two weeks earlier, and showing four hours' parking bought in the nearby city of Bath. Beyond that there was nothing.

Maggie leaned back in the seat, hands on the steering wheel.

Why did you park here, Ros? Where were you going? And why haven't you come back? Can't you tell me – wherever you are? Don't you know I'm worried about you?

Quite suddenly she stiffened. Unconsciously she had stretched out her legs into a driving position – but she had not encountered the pedals. Gooseflesh ran up her arms. She sat up, reaching out again with her legs. Her toes met brake and clutch, but that first instinctive suspicion was confirmed.

She couldn't drive the car with the seat in this position and certainly Ros, who was, if anything, an inch or two shorter than she was, couldn't have driven it either. The police had said that the fact that the car was parked here at the station meant Ros must have gone off somewhere on a train, implying she must therefore have left of her own free will. But the position of the driving seat proved one thing beyond doubt.

Whoever had driven it here and left it, it had certainly not been Ros.

When her head stopped spinning Maggie glanced at her watch. The shock of her discovery had made her head start thumping again; now all she could think of was that she wanted to talk to Mike.

The hands of her watch showed 3.24 – too late, certainly, to telephone the office of the school where he taught. They would be closed now, if she knew anything about school offices, pulling down their shutters with the last bell. Would Mike have left yet? He wouldn't be teaching now but he might be running some after-school activity or relaxing in the staff room with a cup of tea.

Almost feverish in her haste, Maggie locked Ros's car, hurried back to her own hired one and drove out into the afternoon traffic. The congestion around the Bath Bridge was worse than ever, a huge chaotic jam, and she sat tensely, edging forward nose to tail, willing a gap to open and let her through. She knew more or less where Mike's school was situated; what she didn't know was his home address. If he left school before she got there she didn't know how to contact him, and because of her dinner date with Dinah Marshall she wouldn't be seeing him this evening either.

Beyond the Bath Bridge traffic jam the road was reasonably clear. Maggie put her foot down as hard as she dared whilst searching for the road she wanted, and then the 'School' sign. She was lost; admit it, these streets all looked identical – rows of houses, all similar, a small arcade of shops, a couple of tower blocks of flats – she'd never find it, even calm and with all her wits about her, never. A couple of women were wheeling pushchairs along the pavement; Maggie pulled over and wound the window down to ask directions, her hand shaking so much she could scarcely turn the handle.

To her intense relief the women knew the school, which was, they said, just around the corner. She followed their directions and there it was – a gateway topped with a huge signboard, sprawling dirty-grey buildings and, unbelievably, a playing field where a game of cricket was in progress.

There was something almost incongruous about seeing a game of cricket being played here, in the middle of this run-down area of the city, as if a village green had somehow been uprooted and plonked down, a piece of a jigsaw that did not quite fit, and the gaggle of mini-skirted girls lounging in the sunshine to watch in no way resembled the spectators Maggie had ever seen outside a pavilion on a summer afternoon. What was good about it was that since Mike was head of PE the chances were that if a match was being played he would still be here.

Maggie parked on the perimeter road and started across the field, wondering what she would do if Mike was actually umpiring. A cricket match could go on for hours and she could hardly interrupt. But as she approached she recognised his tracksuited figure standing under the wall of the pavilion.

Engrossed in the game, he did not notice her until she reached him.

'Maggie – what are you doing here?'

'Mike – thank goodness! I have to talk to you.'

'Why, what's happened?'

She told him, the words tumbling out.

'She couldn't have been the last person to drive the car, Mike. She couldn't have reached the pedals. Whoever parked it outside the station, it wasn't Ros.'

'You're sure the seat didn't slide back when you were poking about?' His face seemed to have frozen.

'I don't think so, no. I'd have noticed, I'm sure. Mike, I think we should tell the police about this.'

'You haven't yet?'

'No. All I could think of was telling you. But it must make a difference, mustn't it? It's a piece of hard evidence. Perhaps they'll take notice now. I mean, I couldn't see anything in the car to suggest who might have been driving it, but they could get their forensic people to go over it, couldn't they? And just the fact it was dumped at the station is suspicious.'

'How do you mean – suspicious?'

'Someone wanted us to think that Ros had left it there and gone away by train. I'm frightened, Mike.'

'Calm down now.' He laid a hand on her arm. She resisted the urge to cling to it.

'I don't feel very calm. The more I find out the more certain I am something terrible has happened to her. Brendan . . .'

'You think Brendan might be behind it?'

'Well, yes, I do. He'd be capable of anything, and I know Ros was afraid of him. Brendan's tall, the seat could have been in the correct position for him to drive. Then there was her scarf at his flat. And there's something else I didn't tell you. Brendan told me he'd seen Ros a few weeks ago in Clifton with a man.'

Through the touch of his fingers she felt him stiffen slightly.

'A man.'

'That's what he said – though I'm not sure if I believe him. He could have said it to divert suspicion away from himself. I think we should go to the police again, Mike, with all these fresh bits of evidence. I think . . .'

A roar from the cricket field made them both turn. One of the batsmen had been dismissed and was stomping bad-temperedly back towards the pavilion.

'Look, Maggie, I can't really stay talking now,' Mike said. 'Leave it with me. I'll ring the police station. And if you want to, give me a buzz when you get back from Dinah Marshall's.'

'I don't actually have your number.'

'Don't you? Oh, I suppose you don't . . .' She found her diary and a pen and he wrote down the number and handed it back to her. 'I'll hear from you, Maggie. Right?'

He squeezed her hand and turned away, and she was suffused with a sudden longing to beg him to give her a little more time, as if just by his continued presence he could make the nightmare go away. She knew she was being ridiculous, that Mike was as helpless as she, and there was nothing to be gained by going over and over it – nothing but the comfort that she drew from sharing her fears. Or was there more to it than that? When she had made her disturbing discovery she had been able to think of nothing but telling Mike. She could have gone to the police herself but she hadn't – she had raced straight to him. And why? Was it more than anxiety to tell him about her discovery? Was it simply that she had wanted to see Mike?

The thought shook her to the marrow, filling her with guilt and horror. Maggie hitched her bag up on her shoulder, turned and walked back to where she had left her car.

*

Mike checked the score, held a brief conversation with his opposite number from the visiting team and went back to watching the cricket match. But his mind was no longer on it – if it had been before. Now he could think of nothing but the pieces of information Maggie had imparted.

Most damning, he supposed, was the position of the driving seat in Ros's car. From experience he knew that what Maggie had said was true; Ros always kept it pretty far forward. On the few occasions he had driven the car he'd had to move it back quite some way to accommodate his long legs. It was possible, as he had suggested, that it had somehow slid back when Maggie had been foraging about for clues, but he would have thought she would have noticed.

So, if Ros hadn't been driving when the car was parked outside the station, who had? Maggie suspected Brendan but Mike couldn't see it somehow. His solidly unimaginative and logical mind couldn't accept that the man would suddenly take it into his head to do her some harm now, when they had been separated for so long. But of course there was the fact that Maggie had seen Ros's scarf in his flat to add weight to the suggestion; if it really was the one she had sent Ros for her birthday then he must have been lying when he said he had not seen her since before Christmas.

Except that he hadn't said that, exactly. He'd said he'd seen her in Clifton with a man.

A muscle tightened in Mike's stomach. Had that been another lie, or was it the truth? As Maggie had remarked, Brendan could have been trying to throw in a red herring. But somehow he didn't think so. Though it made him both angry and sad, he was almost inclined to believe it might be the truth. There had been something about Ros in the weeks before he went away that had aroused his suspicions, a feeling that she had withdrawn from him slightly, that there were things she was leaving unsaid, perhaps secrets she was keeping. He hadn't wanted to believe it then and he didn't want to believe it now, yet he was unable to dismiss out of hand the possibility that she was seeing someone else.

The almost unexplored possibility that had nevertheless been nagging at him reared its head suddenly, striking at the most vulnerable spot in his armour – his male pride – and reopening old wounds which had nothing to do with Ros but which had been inflicted by Judy, his first wife, who had left him for another man.

Across the years the remembered pain reached out to engulf Mike. He had loved Judy with the simple, straightforward, total love of a trusting and uncomplicated man. He had believed in her, been completely faithful to her, and it had never for one moment crossed his mind that she might not respond in exactly the same way. Blind, blind, blind!

Tony Finlay had been his best friend. As schoolboys they had been inseparable and even when life took them on different courses they had kept in close touch. He would have trusted Tony, too, with his life. But that hadn't stopped the pair of them from having an affair behind his back. And one day Judy had told him, almost without preamble, that she was leaving him for Tony.

The blow to both his heart and his pride had been terrible; for a long while, hurt and bitter, Mike had thought he would never get involved with another woman. He had changed jobs, got himself a bachelor flat, made a new life. And then he had met Ros.

Ros was all kinds of things Judy was not. Where Judy had been soft and funny Ros was sharp and sophisticated, where Judy had been unambitious and apparently home-loving, Ros was the epitome of the career girl, totally wedded to her job. Her independence had fascinated Mike – there was an honesty about it that he felt had been sadly lacking in his marriage.

It was an attraction of opposites – Ros liked socialising, Mike preferred the quiet life, Ros's agile mind was scarcely ever idle, Mike could sit in silence contemplating nothing more demanding than the latest rugby result or test match score. But they were surprisingly compatible, each effortlessly complementing the personality of the other, and they fell gradually into a closer and closer relationship which Mike supposed, if he thought about it at all, must be love, though it was quite different from the way he had felt about Judy.

But although they were soon lovers and constant companions neither wanted to move the relationship on to a more formal footing. Both had failed marriages behind them, both were reluctant to commit themselves again. They enjoyed each other's company, but they also enjoyed the personal freedom that came from having their own, quite separate, homes.

Now, with a sense of shock, Mike realised that whilst rejecting commitment he had expected fidelity. Jealousy, creeping up on him unawares, gave him a brief empathy with Brendan. Had Ros cheated on him, he wondered, as Judy had cheated? Was she cheating now, with someone else? Perhaps it was just past experience that was making him overly sensitive – Ros had, after all, never given him the slightest cause to seriously believe she might be two-timing him – but the pieces of information Maggie had imparted so innocently were resurrecting old hurts and making him increasingly suspicious of Ros's motives.

Maggie had taken the position of the driving seat to mean that someone with much longer legs than Ros's had driven the car to the railway station and left it there to allay suspicion. Little pleasure as it gave him, Mike could think of a much simpler reason – that whoever it was driving Ros's car had left with her for wherever it was she had gone. Brendan had said he had seen her with a man in Clifton – this man and the person who had driven her car could be one and the same. The moment Maggie had told him about it he had seen the possible connection. That was why he had talked her out of going straight to the police with the fresh evidence. He could imagine them making the same assumption and if they were right he would end up looking a bigger fool than ever. If she had walked out on him he didn't want anyone, least of all the police, to know how much he missed her.

Mike swore under his breath and went back to concentrating on the cricket match.

Chapter Ten

Drew Peters-Browne was in his studio in what had once been a hayloft at the rear of the converted barn where he lived with Jayne, his wife. He had spent the day painting but an hour ago had decided he had done enough. He had cleaned his brushes and packed up his oils – the tools of his trade were one thing Drew was careful about – then he had put a heavy-metal tape into the sound system, fetched himself a warm beer, rolled a cannabis reefer and thrown himself down on the battered Chesterfield to smoke it.

This, he reckoned, was the best part of the day, when he could relax, the glow of satisfaction that came from knowing he had done a few hours' better-than-average work supplemented by the high that came from the music and the cannabis.

Some days it was not so good, of course. Some days when his work had gone so badly that he was depressingly certain he would never again turn out a painting that wasn't a crock of shit, the music and the drugs had the opposite effect, reminding him of glory days gone by and showing the future painted either in sombre hues or the vermilion splashes of eternal damnation. But not today. Today had been good and Drew felt good also.

He stretched himself comfortably on the Chesterfield, a lanky man in check shirt and paint-stained cords, his long hair tied back at the nape of his neck into a wispy pony-tail, and contemplated the evening ahead.

Perhaps he'd walk into the village and spend an hour in the pub. He enjoyed drinking with the locals, who called him 'arty' and treated him as a slightly eccentric celebrity. Or perhaps he'd drive into town and visit Cliff and David, friends of his at whose 'marriage ceremony' a few months ago he had been best man. They had a young man over from the States staying with them and Drew was anxious to meet him. He was hesitating over the delicious decision when suddenly he was aware he was no longer alone.

'Jayne – darling – you frightened the life out of me!' he drawled.

'If you didn't play your music so loudly you'd have heard me calling.'

'Perhaps I didn't want to hear,' he said a trifle petulantly.

'I'm sure you didn't. Nevertheless, it's time you were getting ready.'

'Ready for what?'

'For Dinah's dinner party.'

'Oh shit!'

'Don't tell me you'd forgotten!'

'I had. Completely. Do we have to go?'

'Yes, Drew, we do.'

'Oh shit,' he said again. 'They are the most boring bunch of farts ever. One of these days I shall tell them so. That should liven up their pissing stupid dinner party.'

Jayne crossed to the Chesterfield, took the can of beer from Drew's hand and stood over him threateningly.

'You can stop that, Drew, and stop it right now. You are coming to Dinah's dinner party with me and you are going to behave yourself. That boring bunch of farts, as you call them, keep you in the manner to which you are accustomed, and don't you forget it. What is more, if we play our cards right they will keep us in luxury for the rest of our lives.'

'They offend my artistic nature.'

'Haven't you always fancied a château in France or a palazzo in Italy? I will tell you here and now, you'll never make enough from your painting to buy even a hovel! Yes, darling, I know you are good, but artists are never appreciated until they are dead and that won't do either of us much good. So, be a good boy, come and have a shower and make yourself presentable and then contain your dislike of the boring old farts for a couple of hours. Right?'

Drew sighed. 'I suppose I don't have any choice.'

'No, darling, you don't.' In the doorway she turned and smiled back at him indulgently. 'Anyway, if you gave them the chance you might find out that they are not all quite as boring as you think.'

'Which one, exactly?'

Jayne's lips curved and grew full as she remembered her midday assignations. 'Never you mind, darling. And you don't, do you?'

'No, I don't mind,' he answered truthfully.

'I still don't understand, Steve, why you invited Ros's sister to dinner tonight,' Dinah Marshall said.

'I thought I'd explained,' Steve returned easily. 'She wanted to talk to you about Ros. She thinks you might know where she's gone.'

'Well I don't. I'm as much in the dark as anybody.' She hesitated, a tiny frown puckering her forehead. 'Is the sister seriously worried? She doesn't think something might have happened to her, does she?'

'What could have happened to her?'

'I don't know. But it's so unlike her to go off in this way. I must say I am a little concerned myself . . .' She was silent for a moment, then she went on: 'I don't see what is to be gained by inviting her here, though. She won't know anyone – and what if we want to talk business? We won't be able to with her here.'

'I thought putting people at their ease was one of your specialities, and you know you hate talking business at social gatherings. In any case, Jayne's husband will be here. He's an outsider.'

Dinah reached across the table to rearrange the posy of rosebuds and spray carnations that made up the centrepiece.

'Not really. Jayne is fanatical about fashion and totally involved in Vandina. She must talk to Drew about it at home.'

A wry smile twisted Steve's mouth. He was looking forward to the evening. The edge of danger that came from sitting across the table from his lover and her husband gave him a buzz of the adrenaline that he now knew was his life's blood, and tonight Ros's sister would be here too.

'You worry too much, Dinah,' he said lightly. 'Let me get you a drink. Gin and tonic?'

'Mm, I could murder one.'

She stood back, running a quick practised eye over the table settings, making sure that Joanne, who came in from the village to cook for her dinner parties, had got it right. Joanne had a degree in catering but she could at times be amazingly slaphappy about the small details that were so important.

Tonight, however, everything seemed reasonably correct. Dinah adjusted a couple of pieces of heavy silver cutlery, moved a crystal glass a few millimetres to the right and crisped the fold on a linen napkin. Then she straightened, taking the glass Steve was offering her and sipping gratefully.

He was probably right. She did worry too much, but she couldn't help it. She was a worrier by nature – that was why Van had been so good for her; he had done the worrying for her. Now she was beginning to allow Steve to do the same. She looked at him over the top of her glass and felt her heart contract with love. Oh, it was good, so good, to have a man one could rely on, and when that man was the son you thought you would never see again it made it that much better. Steve didn't totally understand the business yet, of course – how could he? It was a world totally removed from the one he had been used to. An oil rig and a fashion empire could hardly be more different. But she had every confidence in him. Already, in the short time since he had arrived, he had learned so much about the running of Vandina and she was sure he was capable of taking on a good deal more yet.

It would be so wonderful, Dinah thought, to be able to relinquish the onerous mantle of responsibility and get back to what she loved best – designing and planning; wonderful to be able to dump the paperwork and the troublesome shop stewards and the worries about tardy suppliers on to someone she trusted, not only because of his ability but because he was family, and surround herself again with sketch pads and source sheets and inspirational samples of exciting fabrics and materials. And what a luxury it would be to be able to see an idea through from start to finish instead of having to turn it over to Jayne, competent though she was. And to have time to think ideas through and create during the day instead of having to burn the midnight oil as she had done last night.

'I've asked Don to come a little early,' Dinah said now. 'I wanted to have a word with him about costings before the others arrive.'

Don Kennedy was the Vandina accountant and finance director. He had been away for the last couple of days – in fact he had flown back into Bristol only this afternoon.

'Costings!' Steve remonstrated. 'Couldn't that have waited until tomorrow?'

'I'm in London tomorrow, remember? And no, it really won't

wait. It's terribly urgent. I have to get plans underway to cover for this Reubens fiasco.'

Steve sipped the whisky he had poured himself.

'As I said just now, you worry too much. I can't see what all the fuss is about. Surely Vandina is well enough established not to be hurt by a newcomer like Reubens? You have the luxury end of the market well and truly sewn up.'

'Because we are original. Oh yes, the quality is of prime importance too but alone it's not enough. Our customers expect us to be the innovators, they like to feel they are the ones setting the trends. They expect us to lead the way, not copy others.'

'You haven't copied anyone.'

'Try telling the trade – or the public – that when Reubens have already gone public with their plans. I know it doesn't seem fair but business rarely is. That's something you'll learn, Steve. Believe me, it can be a hard lesson.'

He looked at her. There were dark shadows under her eyes – she had been up half the night, he suspected – but the outer shell, the image she presented to the world, was very much in place. Glamorous, successful Dinah – how many people suspected the insecurity that lay beneath that mask?

'So, how do you plan to sort it out?' he asked, half smiling.

'That's what I want to talk to Don about.' As if on cue the sound of a car engine and the crunch of tyres on gravel made her glance towards the window. 'Here he is now. I'll take him into the study. Look, Steve, if any of the others arrive before we've finished, can you make them welcome?'

'Of course.' He tossed back his drink, smiled at her. 'Don't worry, Dinah, I'm here. You can leave it all to me.'

'What's all this about then, Dinah? What's so urgent it can't wait for a few days?' Don Kennedy asked.

A dapper, unassuming man of unprepossessing appearance, Don had been a mainstay of the Vandina management team almost from its inception, without ever attempting to move into the driving seat. His was a face no one remembered, bland and ordinary, beneath thinning straw-coloured hair which he brushed self-consciously over his ever-spreading bald spot. But his eyes were kind, clear blue, and the rosy hue in his cheeks suggested that once upon a time he might have looked like a pink-and-white cherub.

The moment he had arrived Dinah had ushered him into the study which had once been Van's domain and which, in a way, seemed a living memorial to the man who had created and run Vandina. The original *Punch* cartoons which decorated the walls, the furnishings, tobacco brown and forest green, the huge antique swivel chair, all were of his choosing; on the leather tooled desk his heavy old inkwell and silver paperknife lay as if waiting for his return. No cigars had been smoked in the study since Van's death yet it seemed that their sweet aroma still hung in the air, and Van dominated the room in death as in life through his life-size portrait in oils which hung above the Victorian-style mantelpiece.

Don Kennedy glanced at the portrait as he always did when he entered the room in silent greeting to the man he had worked with for more than twenty years, and wondered at the way that mere oil and brush strokes could create a likeness so striking that the powerful personality seemed almost to reach out from the canvas and overwhelm in the same way the man himself had done.

Did I like him? Don Kennedy asked himself on occasions, and was honest enough to concede that liking had had very little to do with it. Admiration, yes. From the moment he had been introduced to him Don had known that here was a man who knew exactly what he wanted and would almost certainly get it, a man with determination as well as vision, a man with an IQ practically off the scale in spite of having left school at the age of fifteen with no formal qualifications. Everything about him commanded – and received – admiration. Respect? Possibly, if a little grudging. Van could be ruthless; Don had seen him in action often enough to know that he could also be unscrupulous in the pursuit of his goals – and less than faithful to his wife. But then, were these not the characteristics typical of the successful entrepreneur who needed to be unscrupulous in order to survive in the jungle of big business, just as he needed the attention of young and beautiful women to feed his ego. And Don knew that the strongest emotion he had experienced towards Van had been envy – envy for the position he had carved out for himself, envy for the personal fortune he had amassed, and most of all envy because Van had Dinah, with whom Don had been in love for as long as he had known her.

Perhaps, Don thought when he was in retrospective mood, if Van had been a less powerful personality and he himself had had a little more to offer he might have tried to win her away, but he had lacked the self-confidence even to try. Sometimes, angered by Van's infidelity towards the woman he looked on as a goddess, he had longed to tell her of his feelings for her, to try to persuade her to leave Van and go with him, but he had known it was a vain hope. Dinah had idolised Van, there had been something almost mystic about the hold he had over her, and his death seemed to have done nothing to break the spell. Don knew that although Van was dead and gone Dinah still thought of herself as his wife. To make any move towards her would be, in her eyes, an insult to Van's memory.

He looked at her now, standing beneath the commanding portrait, a slim, still beautiful woman, elegant in a little black dress which set off the shining cap of fair hair and accentuated the whiteness of her skin, and knew that all he could do was what he had always done – be there for her when she needed him.

Today her call had come when he had been back in his house for barely an hour but he had not hesitated. Something was bothering Dinah, she wanted to talk to him and so he had come gladly.

'Well?' he said evenly, adopting the half-teasing tone with which he always covered his deeper felings for her. 'What's been happening while I've been away that is so serious?'

Dinah had replenished her glass and poured him a large measure of his favourite dry sherry before inviting him to the study; he never drank spirits, they didn't agree with him. Now she sipped her gin and tonic, regarding him steadily.

'Reubens.'

'Reubens,' he repeated.

'Our latest would-be competitors.'

'Yes,' he said. 'I know who they are. What have they been up to?'

She told him.

'The range appears to be almost identical with the one I planned,' she finished. 'God knows how it happened, but it has. You know what that means. I can't possibly launch the new Vandina line the way I intended. The fashion editors would crucify me. Worse, they might ignore me altogether. Something has to be done, and quickly.'

He shook his head.

'Dinah, there's nothing I can do to help you there. I'm not an ideas man. I wish I was.'

'I know that, Don,' she said impatiently. 'Ideas are my province – and I have one. But I need to talk to you about it. I need costings urgently. And your approval to place a couple of rather large orders with the very best suppliers.'

He smiled briefly. 'When has Vandina used anyone else?'

'I know. It's the quantity this time that will make the order extra expensive.'

He turned the sherry glass between his fingers, the soft white fingers with perfectly manicured nails that belonged to a man who had never done an hour's manual work in his life.

'All right. What's the idea?'

'Luggage.' She said it breathlessly, with that little edge of excitement she always experienced when her creative juices were running. 'I want to do a range of luggage. Suitcases, large, medium and small, soft grips, flight bags, right down to easy-to-manage hand baggage. Some will be pigskin, of course – Vandina is principally leather and everyone knows it – but I also want to incorporate the other natural materials I intended to use for my new spring range – toughened hessians, for instance. That way I can work in the handbags as part of a co-ordinated whole. Customers will still be able to buy them as a one-off fashion accessory if they wish but the main emphasis will be on the idea of a total matching range of luggage with the handbag being just the last link in the chain. Oh – and I don't want to aim it solely at women. Men buy a lot of suitcases but they need hand baggage too, particularly if they are flying. There will be at least one design masculine enough for even the most macho man but a great deal more practical than the usual compromise of briefcase and grip. There will be easily accessible pockets for travel documents, a padded compartment where spectacles can be safely kept with no fear of them being damaged when the bag goes through the radar check and a specially designed toiletry wallet for toothbrushes and so on. Oh – and a shaver, of course.' She paused for breath and to sip her gin and tonic. 'Well, what do you think?'

'I think you have been very busy! When did you dream all this up?'

'Last night.'

'Just like that?'

'I have to admit I didn't get much sleep,' she said a little ruefully. 'But I wouldn't have done in any case, I was far too worried about the Reubens business. I did go to bed at the usual time but my mind was just chasing round in circles wondering what the hell to do. In the end I got up again, came down here and made myself a stiff drink. Without a doubt I can thank Glenfiddich distillery for my inspiration.' She crossed to the antique writing desk and pulled out a portfolio she had stacked behind it. 'Here are my preliminary sketches . . .' She flipped over A3 sheets of paper covered with the quick, deft drawings of the trained designer. 'This is how I see it – a distinctive shape, a distinctive and unusual blend of materials, and of course the Vandina logo. Well, say something, Don.'

Don Kennedy smoothed the hair protectively over his bald spot as he always did when he felt pressured. Dinah's enthusiasm was almost touching, her commitment to her company unquestionable. But her talent frightened him. Caution was his watchword, it had helped him keep Vandina finances on an even keel, and though he was shrewd enough to know there would be no finances to manage without Dinah's inspired vision he was still unnerved by each and every innovative step she had taken.

In the old days he had not felt he was responsible for anything but ensuring the money was there to back Dinah's hunches. Van had been there to keep an eye on things and curb her more extravagant ideas. How many times he had actually squashed a scheme of Dinah's Don had no idea – perhaps never, perhaps many times – that was something that had remained between the two of them. Now Don himself was being put into the position of arbiter and elder statesman and he didn't feel qualified to comment on the viability of anything beyond his own field of involvement.

'It's not going to come cheap,' he said. 'We haven't budgeted for a major outlay on stock in this financial year.'

'We can afford it though. We have to be able to! We're not a tin-pot little outfit, for goodness' sake. We're Vandina!'

'This is true, but we can't afford to show bad half-year figures.'

'Don, I'm doing this for the sake of our reputation. If we were to lose that then you would have to start worrying about half-year figures and full-year ones as well. This will work. I know it will!'

'Have you talked to anyone else about it?'

'You're the first. I haven't even told Steve. I wanted your OK from a finance point of view first. Now I have it I'll get things moving.'

'Dinah, I haven't given you a definite yes.'

'But you will. You will!'

'I think you should discuss it with someone who has a better feel for the market than I do.'

'I will, I promise. Now, I can't do anything about it tomorrow. I'm in London, as you know. But the following day I'll get these sketches on to the computer. I want to see dimensions and also the way the different materials will look together in rather different proportions than they were on the handbags. But I'm convinced I've got a winner here. Perhaps I should thank Reubens after all for forcing me into a rethink!'

He shook his head. It was good to see Dinah sparkling with enthusiasm but the habit of caution was too ingrained to allow him to be completely carried along by it.

'I certainly hope so, Dinah, but we'll just have to see.'

A little of the light went out of her face.

'You might be a little more enthusiastic!'

'I told you, Dinah, I'm not really in a position to judge the market.'

'But you do think it's a good idea?'

'I don't know. I wish I did but I honestly don't know. My only concern is that we shouldn't be left with a lot of expensive stock we can't sell. And I find it quite impossible to get excited about the prospect of handbags for men.'

The moment he said it he regretted it. Her finely drawn brows came together, a tiny frown creased her forehead and her mouth drooped so that for the moment it looked as if she might be going to cry. He'd seen it before, it was all part of the quicksilver change of mood from bubbling enthusiasm to dejection that was intrinsic to her character. To her employees and the union representatives, the buyers and the suppliers, Dinah might appear full of confidence; those closer to her knew the basic insecurity that plagued her. When her judgement was called into question Dinah could deflate like a punctured balloon, for she lacked the inner resource of that very belief in herself that she apparently exuded. Now, he thought, with a moment's extreme tenderness, she resembled nothing so much as a child desperately seeking approval.

He wished with all his heart he could reassure her and knew he could not. What good would it do for him to tell her yes, he definitely thought she was on to a winner, when he was totally unsure himself if it was the truth?

Silently he cursed himself for failing her. Van would have known the answer. Van would have said yea or nay and with that sure instinct for successful business he would have been right.

There was no way, Don thought miserably, that he could replace Van, either in the company or in Dinah's heart. He glanced up again at the dominating portrait as if to seek an answer. But the eyes, though burning with a long-extinguished vitality, were totally enigmatic. Van was not about to send him a message from beyond the grave.

Chapter Eleven

The car Steve had sent for Maggie – a chauffeur-driven Mercedes – had arrived promptly at seven, and Maggie was ready and waiting, smoking and pacing nervously as she wondered how the evening would turn out. She wasn't looking forward to it at all, dining with a crowd of people she did not know and who might resent her presence, and she had agonised over what she should wear, since she had no idea how formal Dinah Marshall's dinner parties were likely to be. Eventually she had settled for a long loose jacket and cigarette pants in soft autumnal shades with a cream silk camisole which she hoped would look neither over- nor underdressed. But she was still feeling far from confident and wishing fervently she had not accepted Steve's rather surprising invitation. Under normal circumstances she would never have dreamed of doing so, but these were not normal circumstances and she felt obliged to take every opportunity to learn any snippet of information that might give a clue as to Ros's disappearance, though, quite honestly, she was beginning to believe more and more that it had nothing whatever to do with Vandina and the 'odd happenings' there, and everything to do with Brendan.

As the Mercedes turned into the drive leading to Luscombe Manor, Dinah's country house, Maggie looked around with interest. It was a long drive, punctuated by a couple of cattle grids as it wound its way between green fields on both sides, past a small neat estate cottage and on to a broad gravel turnaround. The house itself was rambling – rather like a large farmhouse, Maggie thought – but the stonework had all been recently pointed and there was an air of leisured elegance about it that set it apart from a working farm.

As the driver came around to help Maggie out of the car the front door of the house opened and Steve emerged. He was casually dressed in white shirt and light-coloured slacks and Maggie was glad she had not gone more formal.

'Maggie, so glad you could come.' His tone was easy and

welcoming, the faint transatlantic twang she had noticed when she first met him adding to the air of laid-back charm. 'Do come in. The others are already here.'

He ushered her into a hallway where the stone-slab floor reminded her once again of a farmhouse, though there any similarity ended for it was furnished with a heavy old hall stand and dresser in highly polished mahogany. There were sweet peas in a vase on the dresser and a huge arrangement of dried flowers in a jug on the floor, but there was also a pair of green Wellington boots and a set of golf clubs propped up behind the door and a couple of huge striped umbrellas together with a black city gents' variety in the hall stand. They added a homely touch which put Maggie a little more at her ease. She had expected a showpiece home, but clearly Dinah and her son actually *lived* here.

Voices were coming from behind a closed door on her right but Steve ushered her past it and into a pleasant drawing room. Again Maggie was surprised at the ordinariness of it whilst at the same time wondering why she should be. Vandina was, after all, as the slogan went, 'A Touch of the Country', and this was the home of its creator. Yet she had somehow expected the trappings of wealth and privilege with which *Homes and Gardens* led its readers to believe the rich and successful surrounded themselves, rather than this chintzy room furnished in wicker and pine with squashy soft sofas and chairs piled high with welcoming cushions.

In one of the chairs a man was sprawling, glass between his hands, long legs clad in scarlet cotton trousers stretched out in front of him. Maggie's first impression was that he was quite young, then, with a slight shock, she realised that she had been mistaken. The longish hair, tied back in a drooping pony-tail, and the bright colours of his clothes had misled her. Now she saw that the face was a little raddled, long lines etched between nose and mouth, deep circles under the eyes, and cheekbones which jutted, almost blue-tinged, through the pallor of his skin.

A little embarrassed, Maggie looked quickly away towards the second person in the room – a statuesque redhead stunningly dressed in shocking pink. As Maggie entered she moved away from a corner bookcase where she had been idly examining the titles stacked there, meeting Maggie's glance with a cool half-smile.

'Maggie, meet Jayne and Drew,' Steve was saying. 'Jayne is a designer with Vandina, Drew is . . .'

'A professional layabout,' the raddled man interrupted. His voice was lazy and surprisingly well educated – definitely public school, Maggie decided, Marlborough perhaps, or Clifton College, maybe even Eton or Rugby.

'Drew is joking,' Steve said swiftly. 'He is actually a very fine artist. Drew, Jayne, meet Maggie – Ros's sister.'

Was it her imagination or did Maggie feel a slight change of atmosphere? No, ridiculous, it must be imagination. They would have known she was coming, surely? But there was something alert suddenly about Jayne, a sharpening of those green eyes, a slight but unmistakable curve to the scarlet lips that was not quite a smile.

'Ros's sister! Well!' She shifted slightly on her high heels and turned her glass between scarlet-tipped fingers with a gesture that was somehow almost sensuous.

'Maggie lives in Corfu,' Steve supplied.

'Gerald Durrell country,' Drew said lazily from the depths of his chair.

'Not quite,' Maggie said. 'I actually live near Kassiopi.'

'Near enough.'

'What will you have to drink, Maggie?' Steve asked. 'Gin and tonic? Sherry? Wine? Or something else?'

Maggie glanced at the array of bottles set out almost haphazardly on a small pine table.

'I'd love a Campari.'

'Sure. With ice and soda?'

'Please.'

'And a slice of orange?'

'Lovely.'

He knew his drinks, she thought. So many people ruined Campari by adding lemon instead of orange. She watched him make the drink, as deftly as a professional bartender, and was aware of Jayne watching her.

'So – what are you doing in England?' Drew asked. 'If I lived in Corfu I don't think I'd ever leave.'

Maggie hesitated. She had come tonight with the express intention of trying to discover something that would lead her to

Ros, but to begin on the subject now, when she had scarcely stepped inside the door, seemed inappropriate.

Steve, crossing the room with her drink, seemed to sense her hesitation and answered for her.

'Maggie came over to see Ros, of course. The trouble is Ros has taken it into her head to disappear.' He handed Maggie her drink, his eyes meeting hers almost conspiratorially, and once again Maggie sensed that momentary charge in the atmosphere without being able to identify it.

She took her drink, sipping gratefully at the slightly bitter concoction which Steve had mixed in perfect proportions.

'That is unfortunate for you,' Jayne said. Her voice was silky.

'Yes.' Again Maggie hesitated, wondering if it was still too early to talk about Ros, but she was saved again, this time by a voice from the doorway.

'Hello everyone. Sorry not to have been here to greet you.'

Maggie turned to see a slender figure with silver-blonde hair, dressed all in black, and at her shoulder a pink-faced man, no taller than the woman, with thinning hair brushed carefully across his shining pink scalp. Both were more formally dressed than any of the others, though her little black dress would have gone almost anywhere and his dark suit was probably identical to the one he wore for business.

'Dinah! We were wondering where you were!' Jayne said, kissing her rather theatrically on both cheeks.

'I had some business I wanted to discuss with Don. I didn't want to bore the rest of you with it.'

'We wouldn't have been bored. Heavens – I eat, drink and sleep the business, Drew will tell you that. What was it?'

'No, Jayne, not now . . .'

'But later perhaps,' Don Kennedy said. He was standing just behind Dinah's shoulder – like a royal consort, Maggie thought irrelevantly. 'Dinah has had a stunning new idea and she's tried it out on me. But I'm the wrong person to give an opinion. You, Jayne, would be much better qualified.'

'What sort of idea?'

'Something to retrieve the Reubens fiasco,' Dinah said, 'but I'm quite sure Maggie doesn't want to hear us discuss business. You are Maggie, aren't you? And I'm Dinah.'

She spoke graciously, but Maggie could not avoid noticing the slight stiffness in her manner.

'Yes. I'm very pleased to meet you, but I do hope I'm not intruding.'

'Not at all. Any guest Steve chooses to invite is more than welcome.' But the edge was still there and Maggie noticed she had been referred to as Steve's guest, not Ros's sister. 'May I introduce Donald Kennedy?' Dinah went on, indicating the man at her elbow. 'Don looks after the Vandina finances, but he is also one of my oldest friends.'

'I wouldn't put up with being referred to like that if I were you, Don,' Steve said.

'Oh, I don't mind. Why should I?'

'I would have thought "most valued friend" would be a more tactful way of putting it. "Oldest" makes you sound as though you are in your dotage.'

Don turned a little pinker. No sense of humour, Maggie thought. But Drew was smirking unpleasantly and Maggie experienced a wave of dislike for him. This was a man who would take a malicious delight in the discomfort of others, she was sure.

'Shall we eat, then?' Dinah suggested.

She led the way across the hall to a dining room which was furnished in much the same style as the drawing room, with cottagey rattan rather than the elegant period furniture Maggie had half expected. The curtains, still open to reveal a view across open countryside, were of a chintzy material in softly faded blues and greens, the same fabric covered a small sofa and the cushions which formed the seats of the dining chairs. The glass-topped table had been laid with bright alfresco style pottery, carafes of wine and water and a basket of Italian-style bread sticks.

'You are sitting beside me, Maggie,' Steve said, pulling out a chair for her.

'It's rather odd, isn't it?' Drew remarked lazily as he took his place on her right. 'That is where Ros usually sits. Tonight we have the pleasure of her sister's company instead.'

There was a small awkward silence. Into it Steve said easily: 'And very charming company it is too.'

Jayne was moving into the seat directly across the table from Maggie; as Steve spoke Maggie happened to glance up and catch a look that could only have been pure dislike on the other woman's face. Had that look been meant for her or was it a reflection of Jayne's feelings for Ros?

She shouldn't have come, Maggie thought uncomfortably as a pretty but rather harassed girl served them gazpacho. She should have insisted on an interview with Dinah at the office and kept the whole business of her enquiries on an impersonal level. There was no way she was going to learn anything here about Ros's disappearance. The evening was going to be nothing but an embarrassing waste of time.

Her misgivings continued as the meal progressed. But by the time pudding was served – a delicious apricot mousse covered with thick cream and tiny crisp meringues – she had begun to wonder if there was more behind her discomfort than simply being an outsider.

The others did not seem genuinely at ease with one another either. For a group of people who worked together and were supposedly friends there was an atmosphere that might almost have been described as artificial.

Drew remained aloof, reinforcing her first impression of him as an observer enjoying his own private joke at the expense of others, and Don Kennedy was quiet and seemingly preoccupied. Dinah, though she chattered brightly, seemed a trifle brittle as if there was hidden tension beneath the poise. As for Steve . . .

Since he was sitting beside her it was inevitable he should talk mainly to her, and when the conversation turned so frequently to topics of which she knew nothing, he was surely only being a good host when he made efforts to include her. But Maggie felt instinctively that there was more to it than that. She could not help noticing the sly little glances at Jayne, and she wondered if the attention he was paying her was partly for Jayne's benefit. This suspicion was strengthened by Jayne's own reaction – she had noticed and she did not like it. She was laughing too loudly but there was a hard set to her mouth and a steely sparkle in her green eyes whenever they came to rest on Maggie. Was it simply that she liked being the centre of attention, or was it more than that? With a woman like Jayne it was almost impossible to tell.

When the meal was over Dinah asked the rosy-cheeked girl to serve coffee in the drawing room, but as the others filed out she took Maggie to one side.

'You must think me very rude,' she said with a smile that made her look suddenly very young. 'I've hardly had the chance to speak to you at all, Maggie.'

Maggie flushed slightly, wondering if Dinah had read her thoughts.

'You had other guests too,' she said quickly. 'And Steve has been looking after me very well.'

'Yes.' The smile played again on Dinah's lips. 'I had noticed. But he said you wanted to talk to me about Ros. I'm not sure I can help but perhaps this might be a good moment. You are worried about her, I understand.'

'Very worried. No one has the faintest idea where she is and I wondered if she might have said something to you.'

'Nothing.'

'She didn't mention plans of any kind?'

'No. To be honest I'm amazed at her letting me down like this. I rely on Ros. Since my husband died she has been a tower of strength. The whole thing is totally out of character, especially when she knows how busy we are. I simply can't imagine why she should go off and not even let us know when we can expect her back.'

Dinah's bewilderment was obviously genuine and all Maggie's fears began to reassert themselves. During the meal, awkward though it had been, it had somehow seemed impossible to believe something dreadful had happened to Ros. Now, brought face to face once more with the fact that she really had disappeared without a word of explanation, Maggie felt the sick weight of anxiety knotting her stomach once more.

'It's not possible, I suppose, that she could have . . . gone off with someone?' she asked. 'I mean, she has a steady boyfriend, Mike Thompson, but I just wondered if there might be someone else in her life – someone she was having an affair with, perhaps – a married man, say, or . . . oh, I don't know.'

'No,' Dinah said. Her response was very quick and very definite – almost too quick and definite. 'No, I don't know of anything like that.'

'So there wasn't gossip of any kind at Vandina?' Maggie persisted.

'Not that I've ever heard. No – I'm sure not.'

'I see.' Maggie hesitated. 'There is one other thing. Ros had mentioned that there was something odd going on at work. You wouldn't have any idea what she was talking about, I suppose?'

Dinah frowned. 'Something odd? What on earth do you mean by that?'

'I don't know.' Maggie hesitated again; she had promised Liz not to mention Ros's suspicions to Dinah – but tough! All very well for those close to her to want to protect Dinah for whatever reason; the only thing that mattered to Maggie was finding out what had happened to Ros.

'I don't actually know what Ros meant by it,' Maggie said, 'but I think she may have suspected industrial espionage of some kind.'

Dinah's response was immediate. The colour drained from her face and one slender hand flew to her throat.

'Oh my God.'

'I'm sorry,' Maggie said. 'I didn't mean to give you a shock, but I thought it might be important.'

Dinah fingered a fine gold chain that circled her throat.

'It's not so much a shock exactly, more a confirmation of something I had considered myself and very much hoped was not true.'

A tingling sensation ran down Maggie's arms and concentrated itself in the tips of her fingers.

'You mean you think Ros might have been right?'

'I'm afraid I do. Something has happened within the last few days – another company has gone public with designs so similar to the ones I had planned for a spring launch that it did occur to me that there might have been a leak. I have been trying to persuade myself it was just coincidence, creative brains plugging into the same wavelength – it does happen. But if Ros suspected a mole . . . When did she say this?'

'I don't know exactly.'

'But before she went . . . wherever she has gone.'

'Obviously.'

'And well before we knew anything about Reubens copying our designs. Oh, it's too dreadful! To think that somebody inside Vandina is actually working for Reubens . . .' Her tone was rising sharply, she was verging, Maggie thought, on hysteria. But having gone so far she had to go on now, driven by the almost certain confirmation that Ros had been right.

'Look, I know this sounds melodramatic,' she said. 'But is it possible they might be dangerous?'

'Dangerous? A mole is very dangerous. He – or she – can undermine a whole company.'

'I don't mean dangerous to the company. I mean *really* dangerous – violent. Supposing Ros found out who it was – might they . . .?'

She never finished the question. Steve appeared in the doorway.

'Dinah, the coffee is getting cold . . .' He broke off, taking in their pale faces and the strained atmosphere. 'What is going on here?'

'Steve – Maggie tells me Ros suspected someone in Vandina of spying. Industrial espionage, you know?'

Steve raised an eyebrow. 'A fairly obvious conclusion, I would have thought, in view of the Reubens episode.'

'I didn't think so.'

'You wouldn't – you didn't want to.'

'Of course I didn't want to! It doesn't bear thinking about – someone we work with and trust doing something so dreadful . . .'

'Don't upset yourself, Dinah.' He put an arm around her. 'Not tonight. Not with a drawing room full of guests. We'll talk about it tomorrow.'

'But . . .'

'Tomorrow.' He glanced at Maggie. 'Do come and have your coffee.'

With an arm around Dinah he ushered them into the drawing room. The others had all stopped talking – presumably listening to what was going on.

'Dinah, are you all right?' Don was on his feet, oblivious to anyone else in his concern for her.

'Not really, Don. There's a suggestion that someone at Vandina is working for Reubens. That whoever it is leaked them the designs for the new range.'

There was a small silence, broken only by Drew's amused laugh.

'Dinah!' Steve said warningly, but Dinah ignored him.

'I'm terribly upset. I don't know what to do.'

'I've told her, there's nothing we can do tonight,' Steve said soothingly. 'We'll start investigations tomorrow. I'll conduct them myself. Don't worry, Dinah, if there is anything in this, we'll get to the bottom of it.'

'But in the meantime keep your drawings for your replacement idea under lock and key,' Don warned her.

'What is this replacement idea of yours, Dinah?' Jayne asked, her eyes sharp.

'Dinah has had an inspiration for a way to compensate for the Reubens fiasco – a range of luggage of which the bags are just a part.' In his anxiety to console her Don had obviously forgotten his earlier misgivings. 'But if Reubens really do have a spy in the camp we'd do well to keep any mention of it between ourselves for the moment. We don't want them stealing this idea as well.'

'They wouldn't dare,' Steve said decisively. 'Luggage would be much too big a venture for them.'

'How do you know?'

'I've been doing some homework. Oh, they're bold and they want to eat into our share of the market. But I doubt that at their stage of the game they have the facility to branch out that we have.'

Drew chortled again. He seemed to be finding the whole thing outrageously amusing. Jayne silenced him with a furious glance.

'How will you go about finding out who the mole is?' Don asked. 'We need to know fast or none of our future plans can be regarded as safe.'

'There are ways.' Steve was refusing to be rattled. He passed a cup of coffee to Maggie and another to Dinah as he spoke. 'The first thing is to check the credentials of everyone who has joined the company recently. Everyone who had access to the designs, that is. If that doesn't throw anything up then I shall set a trap.'

'This sounds like something straight out of a James Bond film,' Drew said lightly. 'What sort of a trap, Steve?'

'I think I shall keep the details of that to myself.'

'Which means you haven't a clue. And just for the record, dear boy, who will be checking your credentials? You are quite new on the scene yourself, aren't you?'

'This isn't a joking matter, Drew!' Don snapped, but Steve merely shrugged elegantly.

'You're quite right, Drew – as far as it goes I suppose I could be a candidate. But I'd hardly be likely to cheat my own mother's company. And in case you are in any doubt, the fashion-world contacts that can be made on an oil rig are zilch.'

'That was a preposterous thing to say, Drew,' Dinah said. She sounded close to tears. 'But then the whole thing is preposterous. Vandina employees are like a family to me. I just don't know who could do such a dreadful thing.'

'I should have thought it was obvious,' Jayne said.

They all turned to look at her, reclining in one of the squashy chairs, endless legs crossed with elegant grace in front of her. She smiled, looking from one to the other of them as if relishing the attention.

'Who?' Dinah asked sharply.

Jayne reached across to set her empty coffee cup down on the low rattan table, then stretched lazily.

'Well, Ros, of course.'

There was a moment's startled silence. Then Dinah echoed: 'Ros!'

'Ros. Wouldn't you agree she's the most likely candidate? She had the opportunity, she had the contacts, and she's missing!'

Maggie had begun to tremble with shock and fury.

'That is a terrible thing to suggest!' she blazed. 'It was Ros who suspected a mole in the first place!'

'We have only your word for that.'

'And Dinah's secretary. Ask her if you don't believe me.'

'So Liz is in on this too.' Jayne's eyes narrowed. 'But perhaps Ros was just covering herself. She knew industrial spying was bound to be a runner once Reubens went public with our designs. What better way to place herself above suspicion than to plant the idea that she had already smelled a rat?'

Dinah was becoming more and more upset.

'I can't believe that Ros . . .'

Jayne shrugged. 'What you choose to believe, Dinah, is neither here nor there. And I repeat – where is she now?'

'She's missing!' Maggie cried.

'Exactly. And *you* are here. Why? I ask myself. Have you come to take up where she left off?'

Maggie glared at the strikingly attractive face, rendered

speechless by the vitriol in the allegation, and Steve intervened swiftly.

'I think this is all getting a little bit out of hand. I suggest we drop the subject – all this wild speculation is getting us nowhere. As I said, I'll begin investigations tomorrow but until we have something definite to go on we keep this entire conversation where it belongs – between ourselves. Now, how about a game of charades?'

'How very apt!' Drew murmured. He was obviously enjoying the scene, much as an ancient Roman might have enjoyed watching gladiators fighting to the death in the arena. But the others showed little enthusiasm for the idea.

'Count me out,' Don said firmly. Dinah, still playing nervously with the chain around her neck, said nothing at all.

'I really think I would like to go home,' Maggie said. She was shaking with anger and her head had begun to throb dully again. 'Could I use the telephone to call a taxi, please?'

Dinah, standing motionless, seemed oblivious of anything that was being said, but Steve smiled with the same easy charm, totally ignoring the fact that anything untoward had happened.

'You'll do no such thing. I've given Richards the rest of the evening off. But you are my guest. I'll drive you myself.'

He ushered her into the hall, an arm lightly about her waist and the last thing Maggie was aware of as they went out through the door was Jayne, watching them with what was now undisguised hostility.

'Don't take too much notice of Jayne,' Steve said when they were installed in his low-slung Jaguar. 'She likes nothing better than causing a sensation.'

'I could see that,' Maggie retorted, 'but it was unforgivable of her all the same.'

Steve swung the car around a bend, then glanced sideways at her.

'What made you raise the subject of an industrial spy with my mother?'

'It was something I'd stumbled on. Perhaps it was wrong of me and I'm sorry if I upset her . . .'

'When you know Dinah better you'll realise she does tend to

find contact with reality distressing,' he interjected. 'She prefers to cocoon herself in her dream world where the Touch of the Country equals luxury.'

Maggie let the comment pass. She did not want to become embroiled in a discussion just now on what made Dinah's tortured genius tick.

'I'm afraid the only thing that really matters to me at the moment is finding out what has happened to Ros,' she said. 'She is my sister – and I'm very worried about her.'

'Forgive me.' He extracted a cigarette from a pack of Camels lying in the well of the Jaguar and lit it with the dashboard cigarette lighter. 'Forgive me, but why do you think something has happened to her?'

'Lots of reasons.'

'Which are?'

'Oh, I don't want to go through all of them now.'

'And what exactly do you think has happened to her? No, don't answer that. It's obvious. You think she has been murdered.'

Maggie shivered violently at the bald statement.

'Look,' he said easily. 'I know you were offended by what Jayne said, and I must confess she didn't put it very tactfully. But I have to say it seems a lot more likely than that she has been murdered.'

'Not you too!' Maggie flared.

'I know, I know,' he soothed her. 'But look at it logically. The facts do fit awfully well.'

'And I suppose like Jayne you think I am here to carry on where she left off.'

He blew smoke, wound down the window and tossed the butt out.

'Actually no, I don't think that. I think you are a very nice, very uncomplicated person and you couldn't be dishonest or deceitful if you tried.'

'Implying Ros could.'

'Implying nothing. But just ask yourself, Maggie, how well do you know your sister? Oh yes, you grew up together, of course. But you've been abroad for . . . how long? Three years? Four? A lot can happen in that time. People can change, their priorities and perspectives, almost everything about them. Maybe the Ros you used to know couldn't have done such a thing. But maybe she doesn't exist any more.'

They had reached the cottage now. Steve swung the Jag on to the turnaround.

'I'm sorry if this evening didn't turn out as you'd hoped.' He got out, coming around to open the passenger door for her. 'I know you're worried, Maggie, and I wish I could help. In fact, if I think of anything at all I'll let you know.'

He helped her out of the car, and it seemed that his fingers lingered on her arm a moment or two longer than was necessary.

'Perhaps we should keep in touch anyway.'

Something in the tone of his voice – a little too deliberately casual – and the continued pressure of his hand on her arm set warning bells jangling for Maggie.

She might have been a married woman for three years now, but she still recognised a pass when she saw one. Steve had been making a play for her all evening, in a very sophisticated, laid-back way it was true, but making a play for her none the less. Dinah had noticed it and so, she thought, had the bitchy, self-confident Jayne. Complications of this sort were the very last thing Maggie needed, and yet . . . Steve was her only means of maintaining contact with Vandina. If Ros's disappearance was connected in any way with her work then perhaps playing along with him was the best chance she had of learning the truth.

With an effort she forced herself to smile.

'That's kind of you. Maybe we should.'

'Good. I'd like the opportunity to redeem myself after dropping you into what turned out to be a less than successful evening. Can I phone you?'

'Yes,' she said.

As she unlocked the door of the cottage she heard the church clock striking eleven, the chimes carrying clearly across the valley on the still evening air.

Mike, she thought. I must let Mike know what has happened. Ring at any time, he had said, and eleven wasn't late.

She reached for the telephone, dialling the number he had given her and waiting with barely concealed impatience to hear his voice. But there was only the hollow sound of the bell ringing with relentless regularity.

She let it ring and ring, feeling a sense of urgency and desolation build up inside her and it was only when she heard the click of the automatic cut-off and the resumption of the dialling tone that she realised just how much she had wanted to speak to him.

The realisation frightened her a little, because she was uncomfortably sure that the longing was not entirely the desire to share the details of what had happened tonight. Or perhaps it was exactly that.

She was beginning to want to share with Mike a little too much.

When all her guests had left, Dinah poured herself a large tumbler of Glenfiddich, added some ice cubes, and carried it into the study.

Whenever she was worried or upset there was nowhere she wanted to be so much as here in the room that reminded her so of Van. In his lifetime he had been her support and strength; now that he was no longer with her she drew comfort from the tangible effects he had left behind. He was still here, she felt, something of the powerful essence of him had impregnated the very walls so that she felt he was close, close enough almost to reach out and touch, close enough to curl up in his arms as she had used to do. Here in the comforting stillness she could hear his voice, vibrant and strong, inspiring confidence because it reflected his own supreme belief in himself.

Had Van ever been afraid? Had he ever entertained doubts about the wisdom of his actions or his ability to overcome any obstacle that might be placed in his way? If so he had never showed them. Whatever the problem Van had known how to deal with it. He would certainly have known how to deal with this latest crisis.

Dinah sipped her whisky, hoping that the smooth ice-cold fire would calm her nerves but feeling only sickness as it hit her stomach.

She hated conflict and uncertainty, hated the feeling of betrayal that came from knowing that someone in her employ was less than loyal. It upset her to the core of her being, unsettling her precarious self-confidence, so that she shook physically, and she knew she would be awake half the night while the arguments raced around inside her head. She hadn't wanted to believe that someone she knew and trusted could do this; even when the evidence was there before her very eyes she had tried to dismiss it, as if by refusing to acknowledge it she could make it go away. But now with all the arguments ringing in her ears she could no longer deny the very real possibility that there was indeed someone at Vandina who was not who they seemed to be, someone who was working principally not for her but for her rival, Reubens.

It happened all the time in business, of course; she knew that with the part of her brain that could still think logically. But knowing it did not help. Because Vandina was an extension of herself she took the betrayal personally and was desperately hurt by it.

As a businesswoman it was her Achilles' heel, this inability to separate herself from the wheeling and dealing, the decisions that had to be made for the good of the company, the cut and thrust of the rat race. That was what Van had been so good at: he had cushioned her from it, removed all the worries and left her free to concentrate on her artistic vision – though there had been times when he had questioned even that, so that she wondered not simply whether Vandina would ever have existed without him (she knew it would not) but whether she herself was not something he had fashioned and created.

Oh Van, I miss you so dreadfully! she thought. I have to hold it all together for your sake and I don't know if I can do it.

But at least she was not quite alone. At least now she had Steve.

At the thought of him the warmth generated by the whisky began at last to creep through her veins. Thank God for Steve! He wasn't ready to take over the reins yet, he didn't know enough about the business, but already she could sense in him the same steely single-mindedness that had been Van's strength, and it both comforted her and excited her oddly to know that she had given birth to a man such as him. Soon, she thought, soon I will be able to lay my worries on his shoulders as I used to lay them on Van's.

The warmth ran and spread and she sipped her whisky again, her hands steadier now around the glass. It was almost, she thought, as if her perception of the two men was merging, Steve becoming Van, Van becoming Steve.

She glanced up at the portrait that hung over the fireplace, the commanding life-size portrait of Van in his prime.

'If only you had known him,' she said softly, then, almost as soon as the words were out she was regretting them with a rush of guilt that made her feel illogically as if she had committed sacrilege.

Van had not wanted to know Steve. It had been Van's decision that she should give him up. Through all the years, though she had grieved for her lost son, she had never questioned Van's judgement and she did not question it now. Habit was too strong.

'I'm sorry, Van – I didn't mean it. You were right. You were always right.'

His eyes looked back at her from the canvas – those deep-set eyes of such a dark blue that they were almost black seeming to hypnotise her from beyond the grave, and Dinah knew without question that all the heartache and the guilt counted for nothing. If she had her time over, she would do it all the same again.

Dinah

She was just twenty when she first met Van. She was also penniless – and pregnant.

Dinah seldom thought now of those dark days – it seemed they might almost have happened to someone else and not to her at all. But when she did think of them she found she could remember with frightening clarity the way she had felt – helpless, trapped, abandoned and alone.

Perhaps, she thought, it would not have been quite so bad if she had not led such a sheltered life and been so incredibly young for her age. It had been, after all, the start of what people blithely referred to as 'the Swinging Sixties'. But as yet they had barely begun. The taboos of the past decades were still casting their long shadow, living with a man before marriage was still regarded as 'letting oneself down' and becoming an unmarried mother was a cause for shame and disgrace.

These values had been deeply ingrained in Dinah by her mother, Ruth, herself the daughter of a Nonconformist minister. Dinah's father had died of peritonitis when she was seven – 'Divine retribution', Dinah had once heard her grandfather remark – and Dinah and her mother had left their home and moved to the rambling old manse occupied by her grandparents.

Dinah disliked the manse. It was dark and musty with wood-panelled walls, overpowering Victorian fireplaces above which countless china ornaments sat on a dark oak mantelshelf, and cabbage-rose wallpaper yellowed by age and damp. The down-stairs floors were flagstoned, apart from the parlour which had black-varnished floorboards around a faded carpet square, and upstairs was lineoleum with a scattering of rugs. There were few mirrors to reflect what little light there was – mirrors encouraged vanity, Grandfather said – and no pictures, with the notable exception of a vast pencil drawing of John Bunyan which dominated the living room. His eyes seemed to follow you wherever you went, Grandfather said, and Dinah had thought it was true. Whenever she got up to mischief she would look nervously over her shoulder and meet John Bunyan's unwinking stare.

Not unnaturally, life at the manse was dominated by religion – not the joyous hat-in-the-air religion of Dinah's best friend Mary, who was a Roman Catholic – and probably doomed to hellfire for it, according to Grandfather, who strongly disapproved of the friendship – but a stern and sober existence lived to honour a stern and sober God.

There was little laughter – Grandfather had the weary sainted look of a man carrying all the cares of the world on his shoulders, Grandma scuttled behind him like a pale timid mouse, and her mother had stopped laughing after her father had died. When Dinah laughed she felt almost as if she were committing sacrilege and she would look quickly over her shoulder to see if John Bunyan had noticed.

And that was on weekdays. On Sundays it was even worse.

Sundays meant two doses of chapel, one in the morning and one in the evening. Dinah found it dreadfully boring, sitting in the front pew dressed in her best and then being patted and patronised by the ladies of the church, out to get on good terms with the minister. She amused herself by listening to Mrs Thomas, who sang the hymns lustily in her booming mezzo-soprano and held the last notes a beat or so longer than anyone else, or counting the times old Mr Henry coughed, or even watching Grandfather's spittle sparkle in a shaft of sunlight as he spat out his sermon from the pulpit just above her.

Even worse were the hours between and after services. Practically every activity which helped to pass the time was forbidden, for the day was set aside for worship and contemplation. Reading was not allowed, unless it was the Bible or a book of Bible stories, sewing was not allowed, jigsaws were not allowed. Playing cards was certainly not allowed; Grandfather disapproved of them at any time, proclaiming them 'the works of the devil', and once when he had caught Dinah indulging in a quiet game of patience he had confiscated the pack and thrown them into the fire beneath the great Victorian mantelpiece. Dinah, tears brimming in her eyes, had watched them turn brown and curl at the edges, until the flames finally consumed them as she imagined the flames of hell would consume her if she continued to offend the Lord God by flouting His commandment to keep holy the Sabbath Day. The radio – or wireless as it was called then – was turned on only for the weather forecast and *Songs of Praise*, and afterwards Grandfather would read aloud from the leatherbound family Bible which was kept in a cupboard beside the fireplace.

Later, when she was in her teens, Dinah tried to rebel against the Sunday regime. Mary went to the coffee bar on Sunday afternoons, and one day Dinah dared to go with her, having made the excuse that she was going for a walk.

She spent the afternoon in a state of nervous excitement, too afraid of the possible consequences of her adventure to really enjoy it, drinking cups of foaming espresso coffee and feeling guilty as she listened to the pounding music of the jukebox and chatted to the leather-jacketed youths who clustered around it. This was probably the start of the path to damnation, she thought, resenting Grandfather for making her feel an outcast, yet unable to shake off the pervasive feeling of wrongdoing.

When she got home Grandfather was waiting for her, coldly furious.

'Where have you been?' he demanded.

'For a walk,' Dinah whispered, quaking.

Grandfather drew himself up to his full height. He was a big man, over six feet tall and broad-shouldered; in his best Sunday black, with his gaunt face and thick head of silver hair, he was a daunting sight.

'How dare you lie to me!' His voice, which could fill the chapel, echoed fearsomely around the flagstoned hall. 'Don't you know it is wicked to lie? I will ask you again – where have you been?'

'With Mary.'

'Mary. You mean Mary O'Sullivan?' He uttered it with the same distaste he might have said 'Lucrezia Borgia'.

She nodded, unable to look at him.

'And where have you been with Mary O'Sullivan?'

'We . . . went for a cup of coffee.'

'And where did you have this cup of coffee?'

She could not answer. Her mouth had gone dry. Grandfather took hold of her shoulder, shaking her.

'You've been to that coffee bar, haven't you? *Haven't you*?'

She was looking down. All she could see was Grandfather's shoes, shiny with polish.

'Look at me when I am speaking to you!' he ordered. 'You and that *hussy* have been to that evil place, and on the Lord's Day too. I am ashamed of you, Dinah, ashamed and disappointed. You do know, don't you, that what you have done is wicked?'

'But . . . it wasn't!' she protested weakly. 'I didn't do anything wrong.'

'There was music, I suppose? So-called *pop* music?'

'Well – yes, but . . .'

'On a Sunday! Why do they need pop music on a Sunday? It's rubbish at the best of times, inciting young people to do things they shouldn't, have thoughts they shouldn't have. But on a Sunday!' He broke off, beside himself with rage. 'The place should not be allowed to open on the Lord's Day. If I had my way I'd close it down altogether but I suppose there is a call for it from a certain type of person. But not for you, Dinah. You will never go there again. Not on a weekday, and certainly not on a Sunday. Now, wipe that lipstick off your mouth, go to your room and remain there until it is time to go to chapel. Do you understand?'

She nodded and fled, shaking, ashamed, confused. She knew deep down that she had done nothing wrong, but the habit of respect for Grandfather was too strong to break. Honour thy father and thy mother, the commandments said. Here in the manse it had been expanded to include Honour thy grandfather and grandmother. Dinah had not yet learned to argue.

But how had he known? How had he known she had not been for a walk as she had pretended? As she asked the question his voice seemed to echo in her head: 'Be sure your sins will find you out.'

Dinah's face burned with shame. It was a long time before she rebelled again.

'You've got to tell him,' Mary said. 'You've got to tell him you've got a boyfriend. You're sixteen years old and this is nineteen fifty-seven. He can't keep you locked up forever like some Victorian virgin.'

'I can't tell him! He'd kill me!'

'Then don't be surprised when Dave Hicks finishes with you. He will, Dinah, believe me. He won't go on being satisfied with meeting you behind the bicycle sheds in the lunch hour for ever. And when he ditches you it will be your own fault for not standing up to that old ogre.'

'He's not an ogre,' Dinah said, feeling honour bound to defend her grandfather. 'He's only the way he is because he thinks it's for my own good.'

'Rubbish! He just likes having you under his thumb. It gives him a kick.'

'No, he's a good man really. He must be – he's a minister.'

'Hah! A chapel bumper! He's not a real priest.'

Dinah said nothing. She hated arguing with Mary about religion. They didn't often do it – it wasn't a subject that interested either of them overmuch – but when it did arise, the divisions between them were so deep and entrenched they threatened the friendship.

Once Dinah had been rash enough to tell Mary that Grandfather had said the trouble with Catholics was that they thought going to confession was a passport to doing exactly as they pleased – they could pay lip service to repentance, say a few Hail Marys and go out and do the same again.

Mary had been furious and they had been bad friends for days. Now, because she could not bear to fall out with Mary, Dinah let the slur on her grandfather pass.

'It's no use. He won't let me go out with Dave. I know he won't,' she said, returning to the most important question.

'Then say you're going out with me. He'll never know.'

'I wouldn't bank on it,' Dinah said, remembering the episode of the coffee bar. 'It's as if he has second sight. Perhaps God really is on his side.' She shivered.

'The devil more likely,' Mary retorted. 'What about your mother? Doesn't she have any say in it?'

'Not much.'

Since returning to the fold Ruth had also returned to the childhood habit of allowing her father to dominate her. Dinah was too used to being told to 'do as your grandfather says' to have any real hope that her mother might prove to be an ally. When she was a child she had thought it was just that she was in cahoots with him, 'the grown-ups' lining up against her and inseparable in their rigid views and values. Now she was beginning to realise that, unlikely as it seemed, Ruth was just as afraid of Grandfather as she was. But it made no difference. She could not imagine Ruth ever admitting that her father might be wrong, even between themselves, let alone standing up to him on her behalf.

Dave Hicks was in Dinah's class, and she'd liked him for ages, experiencing little flutters of excitement when he looked at her, soaring on wings of happiness when he smiled. She had longed for him to like her back, but at the same time she had dreaded him asking her out because she knew she would either have to refuse or face the most dreadful rows at home. Now that it had actually happened she did not know what to do.

So far she had made excuses why she couldn't meet him in the evenings and gloried in the heady pleasure of simply seeing him in schooltime. The weather was hot and sunny, enhancing the dream-like aura that surrounded her, and each day after school he walked part of the way home with her, sometimes carrying her satchel, tennis racket or cookery basket, but never holding her hand and certainly not putting his arm around her because teachers often passed by in their cars and such boldness would not only have been frowned upon but punished.

He had kissed her – in the dark corner behind the cycle sheds – and it had been wonderful. Even the fear of being caught could not spoil the trembling excitement, the romance, the sheer intoxicating happiness that had filled her, and ever afterwards the smell of sun-warmed tarmac, the feel of rough cotton cambric beneath her fingers, even the sight of dust motes dancing in a ray of sunlight could evoke for Dinah the magic of that moment when he had held her uncertainly, his lips, clumsy and unpractised, pressing against hers. The problems had all seemed very distant then and she had wanted only to snuggle close and kiss him again and again.

But forgetting the problems in the heat of the moment didn't make them go away. All very well to say that what they had was enough for her – it wasn't enough for him. He wanted a girl he could go out with in the evenings, sometimes at least. He was becoming impatient. And with a sinking heart Dinah knew Mary was right. Unless she did something about it he was going to ditch her and find someone else, someone not restricted by thc rigid rules and regulations laid down by a dictatorial old man.

Dinah bit her lip, feeling completely trapped. She couldn't see how she could escape. Now – or ever.

When she left the school dining hall two days later Miss Derby, the much feared senior mistress, was waiting for her.

Miss Derby was hawk-faced, with iron-grey hair set in finger waves. She dressed in tweed suits and sensible shoes and lived with another woman teacher in a cottage a mile or so further along the winding road beyond the manse. It never occurred to any of her pupils that the pair might be anything more than two old maids gaining comfort from each other's company. They were frankly terrified of her. Sturdy teenage boys would choose to be caned by the headmaster any day rather than endure a tongue-lashing from Miss Derby, and being sent to 'Wait outside my room!' was a torture that made the brashest tremble and reduced the faint-hearted to a jelly of terror.

As the pupils left the dining hall and saw her standing there grim-faced they stopped talking and slipped silently by, but as Dinah attempted to do the same Miss Derby pulled her aside.

'Does Mother know you have a boyfriend?'

Dinah gazed at her, speechless with fear and surprise.

'I have passed you in my car on several occasions walking with Hicks,' Miss Derby continued. 'He doesn't live in your direction, does he?'

'No, Miss Derby.'

'So I conclude he is going out of his way to walk home with you.'

'Yes, Miss Derby.'

'I repeat – does Mother know about this?'

'No, Miss Derby.'

'I thought not. I'm sure she would agree with me that something like this could seriously interfere with your studies. You are in the fifth year – you should be concentrating on passing your examinations, not fooling about with boys.'

'But Miss Derby . . .'

'I don't intend discussing this with you, Dinah. But I think Mother should know what has been going on, don't you? I shall have a word with her.'

'Miss Derby – please . . .'

'That will be all, Dinah. Off you go now, you are causing an obstruction. Oh – by the way, it's high time you had your hair cut. It's brushing your collar in a most untidy way. And don't think you can get away with it by tying it up in one of those so-called pony-tails either. They prevent your beret from sitting properly. Come and show me next week that you have obeyed my instructions.'

She marched off, her gown – immaculate black, not chalk-stained and ragged like some of the other teachers' – swirling out behind her.

When Dinah arrived home that evening she knew at once that Miss Derby had already carried out her threat. There was no mistaking the look on Ruth's softly crumpled face, and when Dinah went to her room to change out of her uniform her mother followed, closing the door behind her.

'Dinah, I have had Miss Derby on the phone. She tells me you have been seeing a boy. Is this true?'

Dinah's heart had begun to beat very fast. 'Well . . . sort of . . .'

'You mean it is true! I told Miss Derby I was sure she must be mistaken. How could you be so deceitful and underhand?'

'There's nothing wrong in it! He only walks home with me . . .' She drew a deep breath. 'But he has asked me to go to the pictures with him.'

'Well, I hope you told him no!'

'Mum – please! He's in my year and he's very nice . . .'

'For goodness' sake, Dinah, I had hoped you'd have more sense than to bother with boys at your age. As Miss Derby said, you should be concentrating on your schoolwork. There's plenty of time for all that other nonsense when you have your exams behind you.'

'It wouldn't make any difference to my exams. We could go to the pictures on a Friday or a Saturday. I'd work really hard the rest of the week to make up for it . . .'

'You'd be distracted. You'd be thinking about him when your mind ought to be on your studies. And besides, it isn't just that. You're not old enough to be going out with boys. You don't know what he's like.'

'I told you, he's really nice!'

'He may *seem* nice,' Ruth said darkly. 'The trouble is that all men are the same; young or old they can think of only one thing. Particularly *young* men.'

'What do you mean?'

'Well.' Ruth's face became flushed, her voice flustered. It was the same way she had looked when she had had to tell Dinah about periods – nature's way of getting rid of too much blood, she had said, and Dinah, in her innocence, had wondered why such a seemingly natural, if rather unpleasant, occurrence, should cause her mother so much embarrassment. Now, of course, she knew the truth and felt a little scornful that Ruth should have lied to her. 'Well,' Ruth said now, 'they want to *do* things. Things that aren't nice, like touching you where they shouldn't. You wouldn't know about that, of course, but I am afraid it's true.'

Dinah felt the colour rise in her own cheeks. She did know about boys wanting to touch – there had been a time when it hadn't been safe for a girl to be on her own in the classroom after school because the boys would gang up and grab her, pushing their hands up under her jumper. A stop had been put to that, thank goodness, when a teacher, hearing screams, had come in and caught them at it. The boys concerned had been sent to the headmaster and the poor unfortunate girl to Miss Derby, who had accused her of inciting them. Oh yes, Dinah knew all about boys wanting to touch, but she could not imagine Dave treating her like that. What they shared was special, not dirty and horrid.

'He wouldn't,' she said. 'He's not like that.'

Ruth laughed mirthlessly. 'He *would* want to, Dinah, and you'd be putty in his hands. I don't want you going out with boys until you're older and that's all there is to it. Now promise me you'll stop this silly business and we'll say no more about it.'

'But Mum . . .'

'Keep your voice down, Dinah. I don't want your grandfather to know about this. He'd be very angry to think you were behaving this way. I shall ring Miss Derby tomorrow and ask her to let me know if she sees you talking to this boy again, so don't even think of it. Do I make myself clear?'

Dinah nodded miserably. It never even occurred to her to rebel. It was not in her nature. When her mother left her alone she lay down on her bed and cried.

*

She hardly slept that night, lying awake and wondering what she could say to Dave and if there was any way she could go on seeing him. But next day in school Dave was acting oddly. He seemed intent on avoiding her, his eyes did not meet hers once and after each lesson he turned away, laughing and joking a little too boisterously with his friends.

It took all day for the truth to sink in, but when he left straight after school without waiting for her she could deceive herself no longer. She wasn't going to have to tell Dave she couldn't see him any more. He had taken matters into his own hands.

'I told you, didn't I, that he'd get fed up with the way you were going on,' Mary said. 'I warned you, didn't I?'

In that moment Dinah almost hated Mary, who was so bold and confident and seemed to have everything that she did not.

A week later Dave was going out with Wendy Turnbull, who wore tight jumpers and giggled and primped when the boys whistled at her. Perhaps her mother had been right, Dinah thought. Perhaps that was what he *had* wanted.

It was the end of a dream.

Ever since she had been able to hold a pencil Dinah had been good at art. Her drawings were very fine, very detailed, though mostly she liked to copy other people's pictures rather than compose her own. At five she had reproduced characters from her story books, at ten she attempted the glossy pictures from the family Bible – 'Behold I Stand at the Door and Knock' and 'The Holy Family'. At fourteen she managed a detailed facsimile of the John Bunyan print and Ruth kept it on the sideboard for a week so that she could show it off to anyone who came to call.

Dinah's art teacher, Mr Robinson, had spotted her talent early on. Now he began to encourage her, though he told her it was time she gave up copying the work of others and set her own stamp on her efforts.

'You must try to be original, Dinah. These copies are all very well if you want to be a forger, but I don't think that's quite what you have in mind, is it? You must learn to draw from life. Start with the hoary old chestnuts – a bowl of fruit or a vase of flowers. It may seem a bit boring compared to what you've been doing, but it's all good practice.'

Dinah did as she was told. There was a vase of roses on the dining room table and she sat down with her pad to try and draw it. But her attention to detail meant she worked very slowly and the petals were dropping long before she had finished.

The same thing happened with a bowl of fruit. An apple had been eaten and the orange was turning dry and shrivelled-looking and still she was working away trying to get the texture of the peel right.

'It's useless!' she groaned, presenting the half-completed picture to Mr Robinson. 'I just can't do it!'

'Of course you can!' Mr Robinson encouraged her, though he did not add what was obvious to him – the reason Dinah was so dissatisfied with her work was because she had not only natural talent but also the ability to know good from bad and was setting her standards too high for her limited experience. Besides this, he knew Dinah lacked confidence in herself. That was why she so enjoyed copying the work of established artists – it absolved her of the need to bare her own soul and put her creativity on the line.

'Perhaps you should draw something that won't change shape before you finish it,' he went on, rolling up the sleeves of his baggy fisherman-knit sweater. 'What I would like you to do is to get a group of objects together that are connected in some way but which are all of different textures, and arrange them to form an interesting composition.'

'What sort of things?'

'Anything you like. Use your imagination.'

Dinah did. That night she gathered together a high-heeled shoe which her mother had once rather rashly bought but had scarcely worn, a feather boa, a leather belt with a huge shiny buckle, a pretty filmy scarf and an old trilby hat belonging to her grandfather. She borrowed a small occasional table from the sitting room and set it up in the window of her own room where the light was good. Then she sharpened her pencils, making sure she had a good range, from very soft through to hard, and began work.

Looking back, Dinah often remembered that picture and knew it had marked the beginning of her love affair with materials of all kinds. Oh the joy of etching in the little fronds of the feather, catching the fibres in the hat, shading carefully so that the buckle on the belt appeared to shine! The shoe was the most difficult to get right; she worked patiently to capture the suede straps, twisted from having been squashed under other, more sensible shoes in the bottom of the wardrobe for so long, and the high pointy heel, which shone in a different way to the metallic buckle.

When it was done she felt almost bereft, but also proud. She clipped the drawing between two pieces of card to keep it flat and took it to Mr Robinson.

He didn't lard her with praise; that wasn't his way, even though he was perhaps more aware than most of Dinah's fragile self-confidence and her desperate need of encouragement. But he let her see that he was impressed.

'You know, Dinah, we should be thinking about getting you into art college,' he told her.

Dinah's heart leaped. She was so surprised she did not know what to say. Art college – when all her friends were aiming for secretarial courses and teacher training! It didn't seem real – it was like a dream. But as the first euphoria began to wear off there was the old familiar sinking feeling lying in wait for her. She knew very well what Grandfather, and even her mother, would have to say about such a plan. It would be stamped on as firmly as coffee bars on Sundays and dates with boys had been.

'I couldn't,' she said in a small voice.

'Dinah, you could! You have real talent. Oh, you've got a lot of hard work to put in, of course, but you don't mind hard work, do you?'

'No, it's not that . . .' She hesitated, feeling disloyal. 'It's my family. They wouldn't let me go.'

'Why ever not?'

'They just wouldn't.'

'In that case perhaps I ought to have a word with them,' Mr Robinson said. He was excited by the prospect of getting her into art college; after years of teaching indifferent youngsters who looked on his classes as a 'skive' from 'real work', Dinah, with her wonderful gift, was a joy to him. He didn't want her to waste that gift, and he didn't want to lose this chance, this *one* chance, of seeing just one of his pupils go on to success. 'Will you ask your mother to come and see me, Dinah?'

'I'll ask,' Dinah said. But I don't think it will make any difference.'

As she had expected, Ruth poured scorn on the idea and Grandfather thundered warnings about the moral standards of colleges of art.

'Dens of vice!' he proclaimed. 'What put such an idea in your head? And what would fooling around there fit you for?'

'Mr Robinson says there are all kinds of things I could do. I could even teach art like he does.'

'If you want to teach there are plenty of other subjects. What about English? You've always liked that. Or religious instruction.'

'I don't want to teach religious instruction. I want to do art. Oh please, Mum, won't you just come and talk to Mr Robinson about it?'

'Dinah, there is nothing to talk about. And in any case the whole discussion is academic. I don't suppose for one moment you would get in.'

Deflated, though not in the least surprised, Dinah reported back to Mr Robinson and saw a look of mulish determination come into his eyes.

'All right, Dinah, just leave it with me,' was all he said.

A week later Miss Derby telephoned the manse.

'Mrs Marshall, I'd like to talk to you about Dinah.'

'Oh no!' Ruth wailed. 'She hasn't been fooling about with that boy again, has she?'

'No, it's nothing like that. It's Dinah's future I want to discuss. When could you come in to see me? Would tomorrow afternoon be convenient?'

'Oh . . . yes, Miss Derby, of course!' said Ruth, who was almost as much in awe of the senior mistress as her daughter was.

Dinah always considered it a minor miracle that the hated Miss Derby should have been the person who persuaded her mother to allow her to try for a place at art college. In reality, of course, it was Mr Robinson she had to thank for it. He had realised that the formidable senior mistress carried far more authority than he did, and he had gone to her with the problem. Miss Derby, who was more susceptible to his bohemian charms than she would have been willing to admit, agreed with him that it would be a feather in the school's cap to have a pupil succeed in such an unlikely ambition, and with her forceful manner Miss Derby quickly talked Ruth round.

'She thinks you should be given the chance to try for a place at one of the really good colleges,' Ruth said to Dinah, placing the emphasis on the 'good' as if that had been the deciding factor. 'She says it would be a crime to let your talents go to waste. So I have agreed – as long as you are sure it is what you really want to do.'

'Oh I am!' Dinah said, hardly able to believe her good fortune.

From the moment Ruth announced her decision the atmosphere in the manse became terrible. Grandfather remained firmly opposed to the idea – and Grandfather was not used to being thwarted. When his first protests went unheeded his fury seemed to harden so that even his silence was eloquent. He went about the manse like a huge black thundercloud shutting out the sun. He refused to talk to Ruth or Dinah; when it was necessary for him to speak to them he barked in tones that clearly displayed his displeasure. Mona, Dinah's grandmother, became more mouse-like than ever, scuttling about with a look that said she might burst into tears at any moment and doing her best to persuade Ruth to change her mind.

'Your father is very upset. You shouldn't go against his wishes like this, after all he has done for you.'

'Mother, Miss Derby says it is in Dinah's best interests.'

'Your father says these places are . . . terrible. Full of sinners. He can't bear to think of Dinah there and neither can I. He'll be ill with the worry of it, Ruth. Can't you see how grey he looks? It could bring on a stroke or a heart attack or anything and then how would you feel, knowing you and Dinah were responsible?'

But astonishingly Ruth remained firm. For once in her life she had been forced to choose between two figures of authority and for some reason best known to herself she had decided to go along with Miss Derby.

Dinah got her place on a foundation course at a college of art in the next county, 'digs' were found for her with a middle-aged widow in a terraced house just a bus-ride from the college – Ruth had insisted Dinah should stay with someone who would look after her properly – and at the beginning of term Grandfather, still glowering, still churlish, drove her there in his ancient Morris Oxford.

'I just hope,' he said, as Dinah unloaded her battered suitcase, her canvas hold-all and her brand new portfolio, 'I just hope, my girl, that you will not live to regret this.'

'Oh Grandfather, please! Be happy for me!' Dinah begged, but he turned away. In the September sunlight the long creases in his hawk-like face were deeper and more pronounced than ever; his mouth, set and hard, refused to smile.

'I hope you will have the good sense not to bring shame and disgrace on us,' was all he said.

Dinah's year as a foundation-course student passed fairly uneventfully. Away from the claustrophobic atmosphere of the manse she began to blossom in a dozen small ways. She changed her style of dressing from the prim and proper school-and-Sunday clothes and took to wearing casual jeans and sweaters, though when she went home for weekends she always dressed in a skirt long enough not to offend her grandfather. She spent what little spare cash she had on records of Elvis Presley and Billy Fury and played them on an ancient record player that she had acquired at a rummage sale. She grew her hair long and wore it loose, and once, in a fit of daring, put on a brown rinse just to see what she would look like with dark hair. She hated it and spent the next week washing and washing it, again and again, until it was gone. She also began to acquire a certain measure of independence, asking Mrs Meadows, with whom she lodged, to buy muesli for her breakfast instead of cooking the bacon-and-tomatoes or poached eggs on toast which her mother had requested as part of the deal. Occasionally she went out with some of the friends she made on the course, to coffee bars or the cinema, even, once or twice, to a dance hall, but she was certainly not engulfed by the wild lifestyle her grandfather had predicted. She was still too inhibited by her upbringing to want to indulge in the smoking, drinking and drugs that existed on the periphery of art-school life – and there was simply no time for leading the wild life anyway.

The course was a good deal more demanding than Dinah had ever imagined it could be; there was so much work to be done that she often had to stay up late at night to finish one project or another, and the circles under her eyes owed more to her efforts on some piece of coursework than to gay living.

The course was a varied one and Dinah found she enjoyed the creative tasks she was set most of all. Designing and making a receptacle to hold all her artistic bits and pieces was one she particularly enjoyed – she made hers from hessian and bits of leather and it was held up to the rest of the students as brilliantly innovative – and a nursery rhyme mobile made from wood was chosen to donate to the local children's hospital.

Towards the end of the year Dinah had to choose which course to apply for to take her over the three-year span of degree studies. She was still undecided by the time the students held their annual fancy dress ball. But the excitement – and the accolades she received as a result of the Red Indian costume she made for herself out of two or three huge chamois leathers – made up her mind for her. Better even than drawing she loved working with materials.

There was a fashion degree course on offer at the art college. Dinah applied for it and to her delight was accepted.

If the foundation course had been hard work, the fashion course was even harder. Project followed project, and because the materials were so expensive Dinah had to take a part-time job as a waitress to help pay for them. Mrs Meadows began to complain about the hours she was keeping and the electricity she burned working in her room late at night, and Dinah began to scour the college noticeboards looking for alternative accommodation.

At last she found what she had been looking for – a group of five students who rented a flat in a large house near the college wanted a sixth to help them pay the rent. Dinah went along to meet them. She was still a little shy but the students – two boys and three girls – seemed friendly in an expansive, if somewhat offhand, way and the flat was big and cheerful, though shockingly untidy, with dirty dishes and pans piled in the sink and used coffee cups and overflowing ashtrays scattered about the floor.

Dinah already knew the girl she was to share a room with – her name was Lynne Beckett and she was a second-year student. But she soon discovered that the arrangement was not quite as ideal as she had expected. Seduced by the thought of freedom she had overlooked the practical snags – no room of her own, however small, where she could leave her work and know it would be undisturbed, a bathroom where the water was more often lukewarm than hot and was almost impossible to get into in the mornings anyway, five other people using her milk and her orange juice, five other people leaving their dishes unwashed and their dirty clothes where they dropped them. Dinah was naturally tidy, she hated a mess, but no matter how often she cleared up the kitchen, next day it was as bad again, and she realised she had to choose between putting up with it or becoming a full-time skivvy.

The flat was always noisy too, music going full blast, doors banging, people laughing and talking too loudly. When she wanted an early night she was inevitably woken up by Lynne swanning in, falling over the bed or even switching the light full on.

Dinah began to long for the peace of her digs with only Mrs Meadows complaining occasionally to disturb her, but it was too late to go back. Mrs Meadows had a new lodger, a sober young man who worked in a bank, and besides, the new flat did have one rather special compensation.

His name was Neil Meredith and he was a third-year graphics student. He was tall and slimly built with brown wavy shoulder-length hair and just the hint of a beard. He also had warm brown eyes fringed with long dark lashes and a County Durham accent that fascinated her.

Neil had a girlfriend, Angie, who was in his year on the graphics course, and who looked amazingly like him. They might have been twins in their ripped jeans, T-shirts and sneakers, with their hair, almost identical in colour and length, falling over their shoulders. Angie spent a lot of time at the flat and Dinah couldn't help envying her, especially when she and Neil disappeared into his room and shut the door. But when Angie was not there Dinah fancied he paid quite a lot of attention to her. It wasn't anything she could put her finger on, just a smile that made her fold up inside or an enquiry about her work. But it was enough to make Dinah feel alive and excited, as if something very good was just around the corner.

One night when the others were all out he came into the big sitting room swinging a bottle.

'Want some?'

Dinah, who was leafing through magazines looking for material for source sheets, looked up, flushing with surprise and pleasure.

'What is it?'

'Vino. Only plonk, of course, but it all goes down the same.'

Dinah brushed her hair back behind her ears, her flush deepening.

'Thanks – but I don't drink.'

'Don't drink?' He sounded genuinely surprised.

'No. Well, at least, I never have.' She broke off, unwilling to explain about the strict taboo on alcohol with which she had been brought up and a little ashamed of the narrowness of her background and experience.

'Ah, I remember now. You're a strict Methodist, aren't you?' he said, wagging a finger at her.

'How did you know that?'

He grinned. 'I make it my business to know these things. Oh well, if you don't want to I won't force you. But you don't know what you're missing.'

Dinah bit her lip. She didn't want to appear a bore, and besides, where was the harm? Already her more relaxed lifestyle was making her question some of the rules with which she had been indoctrinated, and now she found herself remembering a conversation – argument, really – that she had once had with Mary on the subject of what her grandfather called, in his most censorious tones, 'strong drink'.

'Why is he so against it?' Mary had asked in her bouncy way. 'I don't understand, I really don't.'

'He says it's the path to damnation.'

'That's ridiculous! If it's so wicked why did Jesus turn the water into wine at the wedding feast? And you drink wine at Communion.'

'No we don't. Not wine.'

'Don't you? Really?'

'No!'

'No wonder my father says you Methodists are weird! In fact he says not drinking wine is almost blasphemous – setting yourselves as being holier than Christ.'

At the time Dinah had been shocked, but now she found herself remembering and thinking that Mary had a point.

'Well . . .' she said hesitantly. 'Perhaps I could have just a little. Just to see if I like it . . .'

'I don't want to tempt you.' He was still standing there smiling at her, holding the bottle just out of reach. For a spooky moment she wondered if this was how the devil had looked to Jesus when He was in the wilderness, offering Him the kingdom spread out beneath Him, and she seemed to hear her grandfather's resonant voice: 'Get thee behind me, Satan!' Then the moment passed and she made up her mind.

'No, there's no harm in it, is there? Only don't give me too much.'

He poured some into a cup and handed it to her. She tasted it, half expecting not to like it, and discovering that she did. Before she knew it the cup was empty. She held it out to him.

'Can I have some more?'

He laughed. 'You take the biscuit, Dinah Marshall! Yes, you can have some more if you like, as long as you don't accuse me of getting you drunk!'

She sipped more slowly, feeling her head becoming a little swimmy but liking the warm glow that might have been due to the wine and might have been because of the way Neil was looking at her, half smiling, his big brown eyes very deep and thoughtful.

They sat chatting over the rest of the bottle of wine, and when it was time for bed her project was still unfinished but she felt wonderfully, singingly happy. Perhaps after all there was a chance for her with Neil.

But next day Angie was back on the scene and Dinah had to dust down her dreams and get on with her life.

There was no telephone in the flat, only a coin-box type on the wall in the communal hall downstairs. But it did take incoming calls and when it rang it was answered by whoever happened to hear it.

One spring morning it began ringing at about seven o'clock. It rang and rang but no one answered it. Afterwards Dinah, who had been up early finishing off a design project, felt sure she *had* heard the distant shrilling, but their flat was two storeys up and she had not registered what it was or that it might be for her.

An hour later the doorbell rang. This time several of the others were up, stumbling about trying to kick-start themselves into getting ready for college. It was Henry, one of the fine-art students, who answered it and moments later he was knocking on Dinah's door.

'Dinah – are you there? You're wanted. It's the police.'

'The police!' Dinah repeated, shocked.

The constable was quite young and rather good-looking.

'Dinah Marshall?'

'Yes.'

'Could I come in?'

Dinah glanced over her shoulder. The living room was in total disarray, Lynne was sitting on the floor eating yoghurt and wearing nothing but a Mickey Mouse T-shirt and the other fine-art student was wandering about clad in a faded towel.

'Well, not really . . . What's it about?'

'I have a message for you. From home. They've been trying to telephone but couldn't get any reply.'

Dinah felt her knees go weak. 'Has something happened, then?'

'Well . . . yes. Are you sure we can't go inside?'

Dinah gripped the doorpost. 'It's Grandfather, isn't it? He's had a stroke. Grandma always said he would. Is he . . . dead?'

The policeman looked worried. 'No, it's your mother, I'm afraid.'

If Dinah's knees had gone weak before, now it was her whole body. The blood seemed to drain away and she thought she might be going to faint.

'Mum! No! You're wrong!'

'I'm afraid not. The message is that your mother has collapsed and is very ill in hospital. Your family want you to go home immediately.'

'Where is she? What hospital? What's wrong with her?'

'I'm sorry, I don't know the details,' the policeman said. 'I suggest you ring home straight away to find out.'

'Yes . . . yes . . . I will . . . thank you . . .'

She closed the door. The others were all staring, curious but not wanting to show it. She ignored them, searching in her purse for change for the phone. She didn't have any.

'Has anybody got any shillings or sixpences?'

Henry went to his room and emerged with a handful of silver. Dinah took it and ran down the stairs.

The phone at the other end rang interminably. Dinah could

imagine it echoing through the manse. At last it was answered by Mrs Miller, who came in to clean on two mornings a week.

'Is that you, Dinah? Oh dear, such goings on! They've been trying to get hold of you . . .'

'What has happened, Mrs Miller?'

'Your mother. Dear oh dear, it's terrible! She got up about half past six to go to the lav and just collapsed. Your grandmother was awake and heard her go down – bump! When she found her she was lying on the landing, half in and half out of the bathroom. I reckon she felt bad and that's why she was going to the lav. Dear, dear, what a terrible shock!'

'But what do they say is wrong with her?'

'I couldn't say. She's been took to hospital – the General, of course – rushed off by ambulance, and your gran and gramp have gone with her. They'll be doing tests, I s'pose, and we'll know more then, but . . .'

'It's all right, Mrs Miller, I'm coming home. Well – I'll go straight to the hospital. Tell Grandfather that, will you, if he rings or comes home.'

'I will, Dinah. Oh dear, I'm so sorry . . .'

'It's not your fault, Mrs Miller,' Dinah said, as if the only thing in the world that mattered was consoling the daily woman. 'And they can do marvellous things, can't they? At least she's still alive!'

But by the time Dinah reached the hospital her mother was dead. Her grandparents were still there, in a special room that was kept for relatives who had suffered bereavement. They told Dinah that Ruth had passed away ten minutes earlier and that they had been with her at the end. Mona was upset, mopping her eyes with a crumpled handkerchief, but Grandfather was almost triumphal. There was, thought Dinah, who was as yet too numb with shock to be able to begin to grieve, something almost obscene about his theatrical demeanour, face set into the same lines of traditional solemnity she had seen him wear for a hundred funerals, eyes almost gloating in his grey face.

'Your mother is gone,' he intoned. 'Gone where pain and sin cannot reach her, where she is beyond being hurt by the thoughtlessness of those she loved. How long is it since you came home to see her, Dinah? Too long. And now it is too late. You failed to come and comfort her in her lifetime, and now she is dead.'

Dinah gazed at him in horror. 'What are you talking about?'

'Your mother missed you dreadfully. The doctor tells us she died of a brain haemorrhage. But I know she died of a broken heart.'

Dinah gasped, pressing her hand to her mouth, tears brimming suddenly.

'Now, Reverend, there's no need for that,' the nurse who had showed Dinah to the relatives' room interjected. She looked shocked and angry, and she put an arm around Dinah. 'Would you like to see your mother, my darling? You come with me.'

Mona made to follow but the nurse stopped her with a wave of the hand.

'She'll be all right with me.' In the corridor she squeezed Dinah's arm. 'Don't take any notice of him, my darling. He's upset. People say all sorts of things when they are upset.'

Dinah nodded, but the tears were still blinding her and she was choked by grief and guilt. It was true, she hadn't been home as often as she should have of late. For one thing the centre of her life had shifted – her world revolved around college now. But it was not only that. There had been such a terrible fuss when she had moved into the student flat, the same sort of glowering black disapproval as when she had first elected to go to art school, accompanied by all the old recriminations, but this time Dinah had felt she really did not have to take it. All she had to do was avoid going home. The cessation of the weekend trips had been like the removal of a penance; for the first time in her life Dinah had felt the beginnings of real freedom.

But now that freedom had closed its jaws like another trap. How could she have been so selfish? She had pushed her mother on to the periphery of her life and now it was too late to make amends.

Ruth was lying in a side ward. She looked very peaceful, as if she were simply asleep, and her skin had not yet taken on the waxy pallor of death. But Dinah had never seen a dead body before and she hung back in the doorway, afraid to go in.

'Come on, my dear, she can't hurt you.' The nurse's voice was firm and kind; Dinah, who had never experienced much warmth or affection, wanted to weep at the sweetness of it. The nurse put her arm around her, drawing her gently into the room, taking her hand and laying it on Ruth's still warm one.

'You see, she's peaceful, dear, isn't she? She's lovely. She didn't suffer, you can be sure of that. Now, would you like to have a little time on your own with her? I'll leave you for a few minutes but I'm just round the corner if you should want me. Are you all right now?'

Dinah nodded. She stood beside the bed, looking at her mother. There was so much she wanted to say to her now that it was too late, and she realised that they had never really communicated at all. She had no memories at all of the early years before her father had died. Life seemed to have begun only from the time they had moved into the manse where Grandfather ruled the roost and prevented a proper mother-daughter relationship.

If only it had been different! Dinah thought. She dropped to her knees beside the bed and lifted the unresponsive hand to her wet cheek.

'I'm so sorry, Mum!' she whispered.

'What do you mean, you are returning to college today? We have only just buried your mother. It's indecent!'

The funeral, which had been held at ten thirty, was over, but those stalwarts of the chapel who were sufficiently privileged to have been invited back to the manse were still gathered in the parlour drinking tea, eating tuna and cucumber sandwiches, and speaking in hushed tones of the terrible tragedy which had overtaken their beloved minister and his family.

'I'm sorry, Grandfather, but I'm going. I've ordered a car to take me to the station.'

'Cancel it! There are people here who want to talk to you.'

'I don't want to talk to them.'

'They have come to pay their last respects to your mother. You owe it to them.'

'No,' Dinah said. 'I don't owe them anything. They're not here because of me, they're here because of you. *You* talk to them. I'm going back to college.'

'Dinah!' His face was like thunder. It was the first time he could ever remember her daring to answer back. 'I won't tolerate this behaviour!'

Dinah gazed at him with a loathing that had crept up on her unawares. Since leaving home she saw him in a different perspective; now, after spending five days under his roof she longed only to escape. There had been no loving comfort for her, no tenderness, only gloom and a heavy sense of blame. Now grief gave her a courage she had not known she possessed.

'Grandfather, I am going back to college today and you might as well make up your mind to accept it.'

For a moment she thought he would strike her, so black and angry did his expression become. Then a shudder passed through his body leaving him oddly white and rigid like a tree struck by lightning.

'May God forgive you, Dinah,' he said coldly.

It was mid-afternoon when Dinah arrived back at the flat. The bravado had gone out of her now, the grief and the stress of the last few days and the ordeal of the funeral taking their toll on her so that she felt utterly weary and drained. She let herself into the flat, not expecting anyone else to be there, dropped her hold-all on the floor behind the sofa and went into the kitchen to boil the kettle for a much-needed coffee.

'How was it, then?' The voice from the doorway made her jump. She spun round. Neil was standing there, leaning against the doorpost.

'How do you expect?'

'Awful?'

'Yes.'

'I'm really sorry, Din. I don't know what to say.'

They knew, of course, that her mother had died. She had rung to tell them and that she would be staying over until after the funeral.

'There's nothing *to* say. What are you doing home this afternoon?'

'I decided to skip lectures and do some work here.'

He had been painting, she could see – there were bright smudges of oils on his faded jeans. The kettle boiled.

'Do you want a cup of coffee?' she asked.

'No. Tell you what, I've got a better idea. Let's have a proper drink.'

'Wine? In the middle of the afternoon?'

'Not wine – vodka. And what does it matter what time of day it is? It'll do you good. Come on.'

Dinah tipped the coffee back into its jar and wiped the cups out with a tea towel. Neil was in his room. She took the cups in to him.

'Do we need these?'

'No, believe it or not we've got some glasses – courtesy of the White Hart.' He laughed, fishing for them, and the bottle, down behind the bed. 'Do you want to wash them up or do you trust me when I say I am not suffering from anything catching?'

'I believe you.' The thought that she was going to drink from Neil's unwashed glass was oddly erotic. 'I'm still not sure about vodka, though. Will I like it?'

'Try it and see.' He poured a generous measure, topped it up with orange squash and passed it to her. 'Don't drink it the way you drank the wine, though. It's spirits, remember – it will go to your head.'

She sat down on the edge of Neil's bed, sipping the drink and feeling it run rivers of warmth through her misery and tiredness. Neil was sprawled in the one and only chair.

'We didn't expect you back today,' he said. 'Not straight after the funeral.'

'There was nothing to keep me.'

'What about your grandparents?'

'Hmm.' She laughed shortly and bitterly.

'Don't you get on with them?' Neil asked.

'You could say that. My grandfather wants everything done his way, he can't stand it if anyone goes against him. He's never forgiven me for leaving home. And my grandmother – it's weird, I've lived with her since I was seven and yet I don't really feel I know her at all. She's so quiet, never offers an opinion on anything, just follows Grandfather like a shadow. It's almost as though she's not a real person at all.'

'You won't be going home very often now, then.'

'I don't feel like going home at all . . .' A tear slid down her nose and she covered her mouth with her hand, gulping hard to try and stop others following it. 'I'm sorry . . . I'm sorry . . .'

'Hey – don't cry! Dinah, don't!' He got up from the chair and sat down on the bed beside her, taking the glass out of her hand and putting it on the floor. 'Do you want a handkerchief?'

'It's all right, I've got one.' She fished up her sleeve and extracted a crumpled tissue. But still the tears refused to stop, and when Neil put his arm around her she turned her face into his shoulder, sobbing against him.

Neil held her gently, rocking her, and after a while he began to kiss her hair and then her forehead. As the paroxysm of weeping eased she became aware of the pressure of his lips. She raised her face slightly and he kissed her nose and then her cheek. She remained motionless, aware of something sharp and sweet twisting within her, and he kissed her eyes, too, gently licking up the salty wetness of her tears with his tongue.

To Dinah in that moment his nearness was more than purely physical, the nearness of a man she had been attracted to for months, it was almost spiritual. There was comfort in his touch, it meant that she was no longer alone. Dinah, who had been starved of affection all her life, responded to the warmth of those arms around her with the eagerness of a baby seeking its mother's breast. She clung to him and when his lips reached hers she kissed him back with a passion that surprised him.

He unbuttoned her crisp cotton blouse, sliding his fingers inside, and she did not protest. If anything she only clung more tightly as he stroked her breast, found the nipple and tweaked it into arousal. He pushed her gently back on the bed, sliding up to lie alongside her, and she turned to him eagerly, pressing the whole length of her body against his. Her skirt was already rucked up; still expecting a rebuff he pushed it above her hips, but the only sign of protest was of annoyance that their bodies had been separated for even a moment; she pressed herself back against him, as tight as she could, twining her bare legs around him and nestling the core of her body against his.

Neil felt a sweat begin to break out all over his body. He hadn't intended to do more than comfort Dinah; he liked her and he'd flirted with her a little, but he had not seriously considered going any further than that – he was, after all, going steady with Angie. But the way she was pressing herself against him was more than flesh and blood could stand. She really seemed to want it!

He thrust a finger deep inside her. She winced and he knew he had been right about her all along – she was a virgin. Again he pulled back. He could do without complications like this. Again she pressed against him, clinging, panting, almost sobbing.

'Please, don't leave me – don't leave me – don't stop!'

It *was* more than flesh and blood could stand. Neil forgot caution, forgot Angie, forgot everything but the demands of his own body and that of the girl beside him. It was all over quickly – too quickly – and at once the guilt was there, rushing in.

'Christ, Din, I'm sorry! I didn't mean . . .'

But she was still clinging to him, still sobbing.

'Oh, say you love me, please say you love me!'

'Dinah!' He extricated himself. 'For goodness' sake!' He looked down at her lying there on the bed with the sort of expression on her face that warned she might be going to cry again. 'Dinah – look, I said I was sorry. But you . . . you really were asking for it.'

Her eyes widened, she gave a little hiccuping sob, then sat up, straightening her clothes in terrific haste as if simply by covering herself quickly all that had happened could be undone.

'Dinah.' He reached out to put a hand on her shoulder.

She jerked away. 'Don't touch me!'

'But . . .'

'Just don't touch me. All right?'

He shrugged, turned away. 'Suit yourself.'

She slipped on her shoes and ran back to the living room for her overnight bag. In her own room she slammed the door and leaned against it, slumping, staring like someone in shock. What had she done? What in the world had possessed her? Had it been the vodka? No wonder Grandfather said drink was the road to damnation! Or had it just been that she had desperately needed someone to love and comfort her? She didn't know. She only knew that she had thrown herself at Neil like a hussy and she could not bear the thought of having to face him – or any of the others – again. Overcome with grief and shame she sank to the floor, huddling there, staring into space.

She was still there when Lynne came home an hour later.

'Oh you poor thing!' Lynne sympathised when she had persuaded Dinah to move so that she could open the door and come into the room. 'Was it awful?'

Dinah nodded mutely.

'Funerals are horrid, I know, especially if it's someone you care for. Come on, I'll make you a cup of tea. Or would you like something stronger? I think Neil's got some vodka. I'm sure in the circumstances . . .'

'No!' Dinah said hurriedly. 'Tea – please!'

She had no intention of telling Lynne that she had already had some of the vodka, and she certainly was not going to let a living soul know, if he didn't, that it had gone far beyond that.

All she wanted to do was forget. And she could only pray that he would do the same.

One June morning Dinah set out as usual for college, but when she came in sight of the utilitarian building, three storeys of soulless grey concrete which housed the school of fashion, she knew she could not bear to go in. She walked straight on across the car park, past the low prefabricated huts where the foundation-course students worked, into the lane beyond and from that into the fields that led down to a stream.

It was a beautiful morning, the sky high, clear blue and the foliage, still unspoiled by the dust of summer, fresh and green. A light breeze stirred the white flowers of the may where it made heavy bunches on the branches that overhung Dinah's path. Birds flew and swooped in the hedges and although it was still early the bees were already about, buzzing with lazy purposefulness from clover to clover. But Dinah scarcely noticed. She was too preoccupied, locked in the private world that had imprisoned her ever since the awful truth that she might be pregnant had begun to dawn.

Strange how it had crept up on her, the constant nausea that she had initially put down to grief, the realisation that in spite of a constant niggling pain in the pit of her stomach her period was not going to come. At first she had thought grief might be to blame for that too – everyone knew that emotional turmoil could upset the balance of the cycle and the more you worried about it the more you put if off. But all the time she had somehow known that was not the reason. When she was three weeks overdue she had had a little bleed that had lasted half a day, accompanied by the most severe stomach cramps she had ever experienced, but she had welcomed them, thinking that here was the proof – everything was all right. But when the bleeding suddenly stopped she began to worry again. Why did she have this dull heavy ache? Why did she feel so sick all the time? Why were her breasts changing? The nipples hadn't been dark like that and covered with little white bubbles – had they?

Day by day the feeling of dread grew more intense, even creeping into her dreams so that she woke trembling, her face wet with tears.

Dinah told no one of her fears – keeping her secret seemed the single most important thing. Neil had hardly spoken to her since that afternoon and she was hurt but not surprised. She knew he was embarrassed by what had happened and she blamed herself entirely. She did not want him to realise she was pregnant as a result of that brief encounter; her pride would not allow it. But something had to be done. She could not pretend for ever that nothing was happening to her. At the moment she did not show – her body was as slim as ever apart from a slight thickening of the waist – but she would not be able to hide it for ever.

That lovely June morning Dinah walked by the river trying to clear her head and make plans of some kind. If she stayed at college much longer not only would Neil realise she was pregnant but so would all the others. Dinah was suffused with a hot and debilitating flood of horror at the prospect and she found herself beginning to tremble. She would have to take a year out at the very least and go right away, she decided. But when the baby was born – what then? Adoption was the obvious answer, but that thought was horrific too, making her stomach contract as if to keep the baby safe inside her, and Dinah was suddenly quite sure she could never bring herself to part with it.

If I went right away from anyone I know, maybe I could bring the baby up myself, she thought. She would have to get a job to support them both, of course, and it was unlikely to be the sort of career she had hoped for. But it was the only option that offered hope rather than despair, a positive step. For a moment Dinah felt almost cheerful, as if she were setting out on a great adventure, then, as suddenly, she was terror-struck at the enormity of what she was proposing to do.

But for all her confusion there was one solution she did not consider for even a moment, and that was going home. She would not give her grandfather the satisfaction of knowing he had been proved right. Whatever she did to sort out this mess, Dinah was determined she would do it alone.

Christian Van Kendrick Junior, or Van, as he liked to be known, was not feeling best pleased. It was not part of his brief to have to interview applicants for the more menial jobs in his father's boot-making factory – at least, he did not consider it was. His father, however, Christian Senior, seemed to think differently.

'I have to go out,' he had said. 'I have to go and see the bank manager. You can do the interviews for me. There are only three of them and they are all after the one operative's vacancy. You know what we are looking for – someone steady and reliable, a hard worker who won't go sick for a week every time he has too much to drink at the working men's club on a Saturday night. A man with a young family is probably best. He will need the money regularly as well as doing a bit extra to make up on the piece work.'

'Why not let Jim Pratten see them?' Van suggested.

Jim Pratten was the charge hand. He had been with the company for years – ever since Christian Van Kendrick had come to England from Holland just before the last war and set up his little factory manufacturing industrial safety boots. In Van's opinion, Jim was the obvious person to conduct the interviews – he was the one, after all, who would have to work with whoever was taken on, and if he couldn't spot a good operative after twenty-five years he had no business being in the position he was.

But the old man would have none of it.

'I'm asking you to do it, Christian. It is all good practice for you – for when I retire and you take over. Now, the first interview is at three o'clock, and here are the letters of application . . .'

Van's mouth tightened angrily. He knew it was useless to argue – in the end his father would have his way. He was the most stubborn man imaginable; sometimes Van thought of the legend of the Dutch boy who had saved his town from the flood water by sticking his finger in the hole in the dyke, and mused that his father could very well have been that boy – he would have stood there too, hour after hour, with his finger jammed in the hole, if he had made up his mind to it. Perhaps stubbornness was a national characteristic of the Dutch.

Van picked up the sheaf of papers fastened together with a metal clip, which his father pushed across the desk towards him, and slammed out of the office.

As he crossed the machine room Jim Pratten looked up and acknowledged him with a mock salute that reminded Van uncomfortably of a tug of the forelock. He nodded curtly – no point trying to talk over the noise of the machines, and in any case he had nothing to say. He went into his own office, put on the light – a single bare bulb in a plain white plastic shade directly over the desk – and closed the blinds on the window that looked out on to the factory floor.

His father's office was a mirror image of this one, though with no curtain or blind at his window, but Van could not stand the feeling of being in a goldfish bowl and so he had installed the Venetian blind. Pulled to the right angle it enabled him to look out and watch the operatives at work without them being able to see him.

Van sighed, acknowledging the truth that he had avoided for so long but which was now constantly on his mind. He hated the factory, hated the soul-destroying mundaneness of it, the feeling that Kendricks was a little family concern that would never – could never – grow beyond its humble origins. Most of all he hated the feeling that it had somehow trapped him with tentacles as unyielding as his father's stubbornness and would never let him escape.

There was no doubt in Van's mind that Christian Senior intended the factory to be his son's destiny. Even before he could walk he had been taken there in his pushchair and as he grew older his father would take him on a tour of the cutting room and the stitching lines, holding him by the hand to make sure he did not hurt himself on any of the machinery and explaining what was going on. In those days he had loved the noisy whirr and the smell of leather, loved to hear the stories of how his father had come to England from Amsterdam, fallen in love with his mother, married her and bought the small run-down factory premises whose previous occupant had gone bankrupt during the depression.

'They laughed at a Dutchman making boots,' Christian would say. 'They thought we wore only wooden clogs. But I showed them. Oh yes, I showed them.'

The young Van had listened to the stories and never tired. It was only later that his enthusiasm had begun to wane. It was not easy, he thought, to remain fascinated for very long with safety footwear, and the thick-soled heavy-duty boots which were Kendricks' stock in trade were unbelievably ugly. But they sold well – and that was what constituted the trap. Cheap, serviceable, unexciting boots were mandatory wear for thousands of working men, and Kendricks had captured a slice of the market with their reputation for value for money. The factory was not making a fortune but it was ticking over nicely; though the Van Kendricks were by no means rich, they were, by any standards, comfortably off.

Van was now thirty years old and he knew he had a great deal to thank the family business for – his comfortable childhood, his education, the standard of living to which he had become accustomed – but it didn't make him like it, or the part he had to play in it – any better. His father might be content within his limited horizons; Van was more ambitious. He found Christian's pride in his life's work faintly irritating, and the expectation that he would simply carry it on, maintaining it on the same lines without expanding or diversifying, was a millstone around his neck.

It was not the long hours that his father expected him to put in that he minded – Van was not afraid of hard work. But if he was to devote his life to the business as he knew his father intended him to, then he wanted to play for higher stakes.

Many times in the last few years Van had tried to persuade Christian to allow him to develop the business, but the old man had reacted with characteristic stubbornness.

'It's a good family business,' he would say. 'We don't want it to get too big. Better to be able to run it ourselves. I know everyone who works for me. I've watched their children grow up.' The Christmas party for the children of his employees, when Christian himself dressed up as Santa Claus to hand out an orange, an apple and a small present from the huge ten-foot Christmas tree, and the annual outing to Weymouth, when Kendricks hired, and filled, two charabancs, had featured in the works calendar for as long as Van could remember.

'But we need to expand,' Van argued. 'Times are changing and we should be changing with them. Big is beautiful these days. There won't be any more room, soon, for the little man. If we don't modernise and streamline our operation we shall be squeezed out.'

'I won't have a lot of newfangled working practices. Quality is our trademark.'

'Quality need not be sacrificed.'

'I have run this factory my way for nearly thirty years. It is doing very well the way it is, thank you.'

'Well, we really should have another line,' Van said, changing tack. 'If the demand for safety footwear was to disappear we'd be finished.'

'Tch! Working men will always need boots.'

'Not to the same extent.' Van could feel himself losing patience. 'It's no use behaving like a dinosaur. Can't you see times are changing? Men don't have to walk miles to work any more – they don't even have to travel there on firms' coaches. They drive their own cars. And when they get there machines are doing most of the heavy work. Give us another twenty years and people will be more interested in what they wear for leisure than for work. We have to be ready for that.'

'Kendricks is known for its safety footwear. In this part of the world Kendricks *is* safety footwear.'

And he had remained unmoved, no matter how persuasive the arguments Van put forward.

On occasions, totally frustrated by his father's entrenched stand, Van had considered leaving and setting up on his own, but he had no capital with which to do it, and without his father's support, no collateral for a loan. Besides this he had no idea what product he could launch without the starting point of safety footwear, which was the only business he knew. In spite of an incipient ruthless streak Van could not bring himself to do this. It would break his father's heart if he set up in competition, and in any case it would be a bad move commercially – as Van had already observed, the market for heavy-duty boots was a contracting one; with both him and his father fighting for a share of it the likely outcome would be that they would both go under.

No, there was nothing for it, Van decided, but to stick it out and continue to try to change his father's mind. Failing that, he could only look forward to the day when his father retired and control of Kendricks came to him. Then he would be in a position to translate his ideas into action. The old man would probably still try to run the show from the sidelines but Van was determined that when he was in charge he would do as he liked. Just as long as it was not too late – just as long as Kendricks was still solvent and providing a strong enough base to provide him with the launching pad he needed.

For a man of Van's temperament the waiting was far from easy. The old man was nearly sixty now but he showed no signs of being ready for retirement. He still rose with the dawn and walked the two and a half miles to the factory as he had done for the last thirty years, rain or shine; he still maintained the same paternalistic outlook, fondly watching through the window of his little office as the workers turned out his beloved boots, and frequently touring the factory floor to check quality at first hand or to enquire about the health of the wife and family of one of the hands. And he still issued instructions which amounted to orders to Van, although he had graced him with the honorary title of Factory Manager.

Van sighed, reached for his box of slim panatellas and lit one. Then he pulled the letters of application toward him and leafed through them. Two men and one woman – or, more accurately, one girl, a student. Not a very satisfactory applicant – if he had been running the business he probably wouldn't even have bothered calling her for interview, but it was his father's policy to see everyone who wrote in for a job. 'They took the trouble to apply, the least I can do is give them an interview,' he would say. As if, Van thought, that was supposed to make them feel better when he turned them down!

Van glanced at his watch. The first of the applicants was due to arrive in half an hour. That would give him just time to get some of his correspondence out of the way. He rang through for the secretary he shared with his father.

'Could you come in for dictation please, Jean?'

Then he pushed the little pile of job applications to the back corner of his desk to make way for more pressing matters.

Dinah arrived for her interview ten minutes early. Punctuality had always been a habit with her, for it had been drilled into her since childhood.

She sat in the narrow passage outside the receptionist's office, hands in their black cotton wrist-length gloves clasped in her lap, looking the picture of composure, but feeling utterly sick inside.

Through the window which gave on to the office she could see the receptionist clattering away on her typewriter, never glancing up for even a moment, and though the door, flaking dark-brown paint, was closed, she could hear the constant whirr of the machines, a depressingly monotonous sound. She did not like what she had seen of the factory so far; it was repressive and old-fashioned, a far cry from the future she had imagined for herself, but what choice did she have? She needed a job and this one, if she could get it, would have certain advantages. The pay, though not brilliant, would at least keep her while she waited for the baby to arrive, and sitting at a machine would be better than standing in a shop or waiting at table in a café where she would be on her feet all day. And at least she could sew. She had always been good at needlework and she could not imagine that stitching boots would be so different from making a dress.

The door leading to the factory opened and a slightly built man dressed in a sports coat of cheap tweed material and poorly cut slacks came out. Dinah glanced at him expectantly but he walked straight past her and out through the door. Another applicant for the job? Dinah wondered, and felt her heart sink. Perhaps Kendricks were looking for a man.

The minutes ticked by. Dinah looked at the receptionist, still typing furiously in the little office, but the girl seemed to have forgotten that she was there. Then the door opened again and another man came out, a thickset man with dark springy hair and eyes of such a dark blue they were almost black. He was in shirtsleeves but the shirt was immaculate white, worn with a grey and blue striped tie and dark-grey trousers that were obviously part of an expensive, well-tailored suit. Gold cufflinks gleamed at his wrists. He exuded confidence and power.

Dinah stood up, smoothing the wrinkles out of the pencil-slim black skirt which was beginning to be a little too tight around the waistband.

'Miss Marshall?' The man's voice suited him, low and crisp with just the hint of a West Country burr.

Dinah nodded. The navy-blue eyes ran over her appraisingly.

Dinah felt he could see right inside her and know things that were as yet her secret and hers alone. She felt her cheeks begin to grow hot.

'I am Van Kendrick.' His eyes came to rest on her face, his mouth, with its full, rather sensuous lower lip, curved into a cool smile. 'Sorry to have kept you waiting. Perhaps you would like to come through.'

'I don't quite understand why you want to work for us, Miss Marshall,' Van Kendrick said. 'Boot operative seems an unlikely choice of job for someone with your qualifications.'

Dinah swallowed at the lump of nervousness in her throat. She had anticipated being asked something like this and she was ready for it.

'I can't afford to stay on at college. I lost my mother recently.'

'I see.' He looked at her, saw again the vulnerability behind the composure which had constituted the first impression he had had of her, and understood – or thought he understood. She was hurting inside and the hurt was born of grief and a safe world torn apart. She was very young, he thought, and also very attractive. Van was a bachelor still but he had known plenty of girls. They flocked to him, drawn by his striking good looks, his money and his personality – that blend of charisma and a ruthlessness which, though not yet fully developed, was there in embryo just the same. But none of them, no matter how pretty or how accommodating, had affected him the way she was affecting him. He looked at her and found himself wanting to please her, wanting to see the way that delicate-boned face would light up when she smiled. But even as the thought crossed his mind he dismissed it, recognising it as nothing but foolish sentimentality which had no place in business.

'I'm not convinced this would be the right job for you,' he said. 'It's hard work and it can be monotonous. To be frank I should think you'd be bored stiff in no time at all and I can't afford to have to keep recruiting and training new staff.'

Her face fell; she sat forward in her chair scrunching the little black gloves to a ball between her hands.

'I wouldn't let you down. I really do need the job.'

He eyed her steadily. 'I'm sure there must be others, better suited to your qualifications. What exactly were you studying?'

'Fashion design. And I'm terribly interested in shoes.'

The first small flame of excitement darted inside him. He tried to ignore it.

'I'd hardly describe the footwear we make as shoes – not in the sense you mean, anyway. We're light years away from the fashion industry.'

'But they're leather, aren't they? I love working with natural materials. I did a project on shoes and matching accessories. Oh, I know what you mean about your boots. I can see they are not very interesting . . .' She broke off, biting her lip as she realised what she had said, then rushed on: 'But the point is, I'd be learning the technical side. Then perhaps sometime in the future . . .' Again she broke off, embarrassed, he guessed, at having more or less admitted that she had no intention of staying at Kendricks long enough to collect her gold watch.

He smiled, the excitement flaring inside him again as a plan began to take shape.

He had been looking for a way to branch out the moment the old man relaxed his hold a little. Perhaps, sitting right here in front of him was the very person who could help him achieve that ambition.

He thought of the two applicants he had interviewed already this afternoon – solid, unimaginative men with young families to support, exactly the kind of worker his father had in mind. Either of them would have fitted the bill, either would prove, in all probability, to be hard-working and reliable. Then he looked again at the girl, at the lovely face, eager, young and alive, and thought he could glimpse the exciting creative mind which lay behind it. His father would have chosen one of the men, he knew, but his father wasn't doing the interviewing. The choice was his – and how he was going to enjoy making it!

'Very well,' he said. 'The job is yours, Miss Marshall, if you want it. When could you start?'

Instantly he was rewarded by the lovely smile that he had known would be there, just waiting to be turned on.

'I could start on Monday,' she said. 'And thank you, Mr Kendrick. Thank you very much!'

*

One day when Dinah had been working at the factory for just over a week Van sent for her.

Instantly her heart began to beat a little too fast for comfort and she felt sick with apprehension. He wasn't satisfied with her work. He was going to get rid of her. And what would she do then?

She closed down her machine and crossed the factory floor to his office, tapping at the door and waiting for him to call for her to go in.

Van was sorting through some papers in a box file on one of the big dusty slatted shelves.

'You wanted to see me, Mr Kendrick?' she said hesitantly.

'Dinah. Yes.' He turned his dark-blue gaze on her and she felt her colour deepen. 'How are you getting on?'

'Fine.'

'You're not finding the work too much for you?'

'No, it's . . . fine.'

It was a lie. She didn't like the work at all; it was boring, just as he had said it would be, and the tough leather needed for boots was difficult to manage and hard on her hands.

'Good. Dinah, I want to talk to you. Won't you sit down?'

Nervously she eased herself into the same chair she had sat in for her interview, but instead of sitting opposite her he came around the desk and perched on its corner, arms folded, legs stretched out in front of him.

'I remember you telling me that as a design student you were particularly interested in shoes.'

'Yes.' That had been a lie too. She *had* done a project on shoes, but only because the assignment had forced her to. But she had thought it sounded good and might tip the balance in persuading him to give her the job.

'I was wondering if you'd be interested in putting your talents to work for me. I have long wanted to produce something a little more exciting than safety footwear but I'm not entirely sure of the best way to go about it. I was hoping you might have some ideas you could contribute.'

Dinah was so surprised her mind went a total blank.

'What sort of ideas?'

'Well, obviously we haven't the right set-up here for fashion footwear. Our machinery is geared to heavy-duty stuff and our operatives wouldn't have the right skills. No, what we need is something that uses the talents and equipment Kendricks can provide but which would cater for a different section of the market – leisure wear, perhaps. I don't really know. That's where I was hoping you might come in.'

'Well . . . I . . .'

'Look,' he said, 'don't think I expect you to come up with a brilliant idea like a conjuror pulling a rabbit out of a hat. But give it some thought. Perhaps we could talk about it again. Over a drink, perhaps. Or dinner.'

He saw her startled look and smiled. He knew that to most of his employees 'dinner' meant the midday meal; perhaps Dinah thought that was what he was suggesting. 'Evening dinner,' he said indulgently.

Bright wings of colour tinged her cheeks.

'Oh, I know what you mean. But my landlady cooks for me when I get home.'

'Surely she wouldn't mind if you gave her a break for once?' he said easily.

Dinah hesitated. She thought that in all likelihood Mrs Brooks, with whom she was lodging, *would* mind. She was that sort of person, ready to take offence at anything, imagining slights where none were intended, reading implied criticism into any comment that was not unmistakably praise. And her cooking certainly left something to be desired – tasteless stews, lumpy gravy, greasy fry-ups. Dinah, who quite often felt nauseous in any case, had found herself yearning for the good nourishing food Mrs Meadows had provided, or even the frugal but wholesome fare she had been brought up on at home in the Manse, and the prospect of a restaurant or even a bar meal – especially one she would not have to pay for – was a tempting one.

But it was not fear of Mrs Brooks's displeasure that was making her hesitate so much as fear of herself and the emotions Van awakened in her every time he looked at her with those navy- blue eyes or simply passed by her machine. She did not even have to see him to know he was there – the strength of his personality was as palpable as if he had reached out and touched her, and a weakness would spread through the very core of her where she imagined she would feel the first fluttering movements of her baby. It was madness, she knew. No one had ever affected her in quite this way before – not Dave Hicks and certainly not Neil. Even though at the time she had thought herself in love with them it had simply been the normal attraction of a girl for a boy who might, if she was lucky, feel the same way about her.

But this . . . this was more akin to the idolisation of a movie star or a pop singer, glamorous but distant and unattainable. There was no chance Van would notice her, even under the best of circumstances. He was so much older than she was, and though she had discovered he was not married she thought that someone as mature and attractive as he was must certainly have a girlfriend or even a fiancée. He also came from a totally different world – he was sophisticated, well-off, 'the boss' with a lifestyle to match. Even if things were not . . . as they were . . . he would never look twice at her; since she was almost three months pregnant it made the dream even more impossible.

That was probably the reason he was having this effect on her, she thought; pregnancy was making her overemotional and silly. But knowing it did not alter the way she felt about him, never quite reached that perverse little core deep inside her that would not let go of the irrational certainty that this was the man she had been meant for, the man she would one day love – and go on loving for the rest of her life.

Yet strangely that day when he asked her out to dinner she believed him when he said it was because he wanted to talk business, and though she was thrilled by the invitation she was half afraid to accept in case she was unable to hide the way she felt about him.

Van being Van, however, he did not give her the chance to accept or refuse. He simply carried on as if there was no question about it.

'I would prefer to discuss my plans away from the office,' he said. 'I don't want anyone to know what I have in mind just yet. Which brings me to my other point – I'd appreciate it if you didn't tell anyone about this. There are times in business when it is best to be a little discreet.'

She nodded. 'I won't say anything. I don't talk much to the others anyway.'

'No.' He had noticed how isolated she seemed. 'So – shall we say tomorrow evening?'

'Oh, I don't know if I'll have thought of anything by then . . .'

'Don't worry. We can talk about the ideas you *might* have. Shall I pick you up? About seven thirty?'

'I'll meet you somewhere,' she said hastily. She did not want Mrs Brooks to see her going off in a big and impressive car, and she was embarrassed for Van to see the grimy little terraced house that was, for the time being, her home. 'I'll be in the square, by the war memorial.'

He smiled. 'All right.'

He was still smiling when she left his office.

Dinah scarcely slept that night. In itself this was not unusual – she had had plenty of sleepless nights since the awesome discovery that she was pregnant. But this was different. Instead of tossing and turning, miserably wrestling with her own problems, she lay wide awake, her mind busy with the exciting challenge Van had set her. By morning she had one or two ideas, and at work in the factory she continued to turn them over in her mind while her hands were busy guiding the stiff leather through the machine.

She saw Van once or twice but he scarcely acknowledged her, treating her to the same cursory nod he gave the other employees, and she found herself wondering if he had had second thoughts and might leave her waiting for him in vain. But when she reached the war memorial on the dot of seven thirty he was already there, his blue Jag parked with the engine running.

'There's a little bistro I know,' he said when she was seated in the passenger seat beside him. 'I thought we'd go there.'

Dinah nodded, relieved he was not taking her anywhere too grand. She had agonised over what to wear; she had never had many clothes and some of them no longer fitted her properly. Eventually she had settled for a simple blue dress, high-waisted and only semi-fitted, with a boat neckline that showed off the smooth slope of her shoulders, and broderie anglaise trimming on the bodice. Van was dressed formally in a dark suit and silk shirt with a quietly patterned tie, and Dinah wondered anxiously if he had changed his mind about his choice of venue when he had seen what she was wearing.

These fears were allayed, however, when they reached the bistro – a tiny place, mid-terrace, that might almost have been mistaken for a fairly unassuming house – for Van gave his name, saying he had made a reservation, and they were shown to a table at the rear of the restaurant overlooking a small but picturesque garden.

The smell of garlic wafted out to greet them. It had the effect of making Dinah instantly hungry and she nibbled on a bread stick as they waited for their first course to arrive – mushrooms in a wonderful creamy sauce and flavoured with garlic.

'You'd like some wine, of course,' Van said perusing the wine list.

Remembering the effect alcohol could have on her Dinah shook her head. 'Could I have water?'

'Of course.' He ordered a bottle of Chablis and also water, but when the wine waiter brought the bottle, nestling in a silver ice bucket, and he had tested and approved it, he looked at her questioningly.

'Why don't you have just one glass? It's very good.'

Dinah hesitated. She did not want to appear totally gauche.

'Well, all right. Just one, perhaps.'

But after a few sips she left the wine untouched. For one thing she really was afraid it might go to her head, for another she did not really care for the taste of the wine. To her untutored palate the fine dry wine compared unfavourably with the Sauternes she had drunk with Neil.

'Well,' Van said, 'have you had time to think over what we were talking about?'

He was mopping up the last of his mushroom sauce with a hunk of bread; Dinah, rather shocked by what she knew her grandfather would consider dreadfully bad manners, could not bring herself to do the same.

'Yes, actually I have,' she said. 'I've had a couple of ideas but I don't know what you'll think of them.'

'Try me.'

'You said perhaps you could expand into the leisure market, and the closest thing to the lines you do at present would be walking boots. For hiking, you know, or maybe even climbing. I'm not sure how they would differ, that's something I'd have to find out. For walking, for instance, comfort would be paramount. But they'd be big and chunky and serviceable, just like the ones you make at present.'

'Uh-huh. Go on.'

'Then there are riding boots. Riding seems to be getting really popular, especially with little girls. Where I come from it was only farmers or people with pots of money who rode, but since I've been here I've noticed strings of ponies walking out around the lanes and several boards advertising riding schools. I think . . .'

'Where did you come from?' he interrupted.

'Gloucestershire. And last time I was home I noticed it was the same there. Stables giving lessons, children on . . .'

'Whereabouts in Gloucestershire?'

Her eyes narrowed; he saw that the shutters had come down. She did not want to talk about her home background for some reason, but her reluctance only made him more curious.

'Where in Gloucestershire?' he pressed her.

'A place called Staverley. But I thought we were talking about my ideas, not me.'

A slight smile twisted his mouth. So for all the eager compliance, in spite of that air of shyness and uncertainty, she could bite.

'Of course. Go on.'

'Well, obviously riding boots are a rather different proposition. They need to be made out of large pieces of leather so it could be expensive – you wouldn't be able to cut out avoiding the flaws as you do at present. And again it may well need to be softer, better cured.'

He nodded, impressed with the amount of thought she had put in and how much she already knew about boot-making. He was not too happy with this riding boot idea, though, and he said so.

'The trouble as I see it is that they would be horrendously expensive. You're quite right about needing larger perfect sides of leather and they don't come cheap. People might baulk at paying the price. A lot of the children I see out with the riding school wear Wellington boots – and good luck to them. They are multi-purpose – and they're cheaper to replace when their feet grow.'

Her face fell and he felt almost guilty.

'I'd have to get some market research done before embarking on something like that,' he went on. 'Though there might be a way around it. Some of the synthetics are very good these days. I'll give it some thought. Any other ideas?'

'Just one. I was thinking about the strips of leather – offcuts do you call them? – that are left over. I hate to see them wasted and I thought of a way of using them.'

'Yes? How?'

'Sandals.'

He shook his head. 'We don't do fashion, or children's shoes. That really is going away from the Kendrick set-up.'

'Sandals for men.'

'The pieces wouldn't be big enough for that.'

She laid down her knife and fork. Her eyes were shining again with excitement.

'I'm not thinking of conventional sandals. I'm thinking of sort of thongs. Biblical-style sandals for young men. The way they dress is getting more casual, they don't want to look like their fathers. They want to wear jeans and casual shirts, beads even, and they need some kind of footwear to go with that look. What's more, biblical-style sandals could almost be unisex. Girls could wear them too. If you were using up offcuts you could turn them out really cheaply, and if they didn't sell you wouldn't have lost very much. But I think they might be a hit.'

Van felt suddenly as if all the hairs on the back of his neck were standing on end. She had something, this half-trained, unsophisticated girl. He'd sensed it the first time he'd seen her when she had walked into his office; now he was certain of it. Exactly what it was she had he couldn't explain, but perhaps it was the ability to look ahead, not back, to forecast trends and set fashions. In the safe, unexciting world of industrial footwear he had seldom had the opportunity to know, much less work with, anyone who possessed that rare gift, but he thought he was looking at it now. She could be wrong, of course, and so could he, but somehow he didn't think so.

The waiter was at his elbow, refilling his glass. Van raised it and though she had scarcely drunk anything so far, she did the same. But even as he smiled indulgently at her and drank the toast his natural caution and his predilection for being in a position to pull the strings was taking over.

Don't let her know how excited you are. Keep her dependent on the need for your approval.

As long as Dinah thought he was the only one who recognised

and appreciated her talent she would be in his power. Lose that and he might lose her. At that moment, for a great many reasons, that was something Van was very anxious should not happen.

Dinah was happy, happier perhaps than she had ever been in her life.

The bleak little room at her digs which had so depressed her when she moved in seemed almost homely now; with her own knick-knacks decorating the heavy old dressing table and a huge teddy bear that Van had bought her sitting on her pillow it was a place where she could be alone with her dreams.

Mrs Brooks's sour nature did not bother her any more, and the monotony of her job had ceased to matter. As for the future, Dinah refused to allow herself to think beyond the next time she would be with Van, and with a little practice this habit began to be as easy as it was comfortable. Physically she was feeling much better; the debilitating nausea which had scarcely left her during the first months had gone now and Dinah managed to create a dream world for herself into which the reality of her condition scarcely intruded at all.

Van was her whole world now. She was obsessed with him, he filled every corner of every thought from the time she woke in the morning until the moment she fell asleep at night, and even then he invaded her dreams. She loved the way he looked, loved the uncompromising lines of his face and those incredible dark-blue eyes, loved the resonance of his voice with that slight soft burr, loved the squareness of his shoulders, the solidity of his build. But at the same time she knew that the reason she loved them was because they were the outward manifestations of his personality, they reflected the power and the determination, the steely inner strength, the hard edge that she had only glimpsed at first but which was becoming more and more pronounced.

And of course it was not only Van himself she loved – though in all conscience that should have been enough. She also loved what he was doing for her, opening up a world she had scarcely known existed, both in a real and in a more cerebral sense.

He had taken her out several more times since that first evening, sometimes for a drink, more usually for a meal, but wherever he took her it was in a different league to the places she had frequented as a penniless student, restaurants where the prices on the menu were always in double figures and the size of the bill, when she caught sight of it once when he was signing his American Express chitty, made her gasp. Always there was wine, and although she still drank very little, afraid of the effect it might have on her, she was beginning to get used to the dry taste of it and to like the way it felt on her tongue. She enjoyed the learning process, enjoyed feeling like a child let loose in a glorious adult world, enjoyed being fussed over and pandered to by waiters who took her coat and pulled out her chair for her and spread a napkin on her knees, and if they looked a little askance at her cheap chain-store dresses she never noticed it.

But perhaps they did not look askance – they did not dare. They were too much in awe of Van, who commanded respect even in those places where he was not known. Any derogatory thoughts they might have had regarding his companion they kept very much to themselves.

Always when he took her out the pattern was the same. First, at the beginning of the meal, would come the business discussion, when they would talk over Dinah's ideas, then, later, the conversation would become less formal. Sometimes Van would try to get her to talk about herself, probing gently into her background. But Dinah did not want to talk about herself. She did not even want to think about herself – or at least not the real Dinah. She wanted to continue to live in this dream world, playing a part like an actress, taking on a whole new persona, until she not only believed in but almost became a different person with no problems, no complications, no murky past or uncertain future. Her answers were evasive and when he pressed her she found herself inventing little lies that added to the romantic unreality in which she had begun to live.

When he questioned her about her home she described the house where she had lived as a small child, never mentioning or even thinking about the manse. When he asked her about relatives she said she had none and then, as an afterthought, invented a family of cousins in New Zealand because the idea appealed to her. Mostly, however, she managed to steer the conversation away from herself, gently turning the questioning on to Van.

This was surprisingly easy; Van always enjoyed talking about himself and in Dinah he found an attentive and admiring audience. He related the story of how his father had started the business, he told her of the stranglehold in which the old man still held it, and of his own efforts to modernise the whole operation.

'He won't have a thing changed if he can help it,' he told Dinah. 'I was even named after him. He wanted to know there would still be a Christian Van Kendrick at the head of the company when he is dead and gone.'

'I think that's rather nice,' Dinah said.

'Nice? Being known in the family as "Little Christian"? I used to hate it. I felt I had no identity of my own.'

Dinah was amazed. She found it almost impossible to imagine the small, balding man she knew as Mr Van Kendrick Senior dominating anyone, much less the dynamic Van.

'How did you come to change your name?' she asked.

'Oh, when I was at school boys were referred to by their surnames and my friends soon shortened it to "Van". My parents still call me Christian, though. Even "Little Christian" on occasions.'

Dinah laughed. She had, thought Van, the most infectious laugh he had ever heard, a little giggle that sounded as if champagne bubbles had gone up her nose.

'And when do you think they'll stop calling you that?'

'Perhaps when I finally get control of the business. Perhaps never.'

When the meal was over and the evening at an end Van would drive her home. She had given up caring about him seeing the mean little house where she had her digs – what was the point when all he had to do was look up her address in the staff file? As for Mrs Brooks, Dinah no longer worried whether or not she saw the impressive car and what interpretation she put on it if she did. Mrs Brooks was a part of the real-life world which Dinah had chosen, for the moment, to ignore.

Sometimes when he drew up to the kerb outside her digs Dinah would find herself wondering if he might kiss her goodnight and wishing that he would. Sitting there, tingling with awareness, she could almost feel her flesh drawing towards him, imagine the way it would feel if he were to put his arm around her, pull her towards him. The very air seemed charged with the imminence of it and yet inside she felt very still, poised and waiting. But Van made no move towards her, no matter how she willed it so. In fact he rarely even switched off the engine, but finished whatever conversation they were having with it running, then leaned over and opened the door for her. Whenever he did this she thought for one blinding moment he was indeed going to kiss her, then, as she realised he was not, she would experience not only disappointment but also embarrassment in case he should have been able to read her mind and know what she had been thinking.

'Thank you,' she would say hastily, sliding out of the car and avoiding all contact with his arm. 'Thank you for a lovely evening.'

'My pleasure,' he would say, and then the engine note would change from a near-silent idle into the throaty yet totally under-control roar that somehow reminded her of Van himself, and he would be gone.

Dinah would stand for a few moments on the pavement before searching for her key, looking into the darkness that had swallowed him and relishing the wonderful rosy glow that suffused her.

She must not, of course, expect a single thing from this relationship. But she wished with all her heart that it could go on for ever.

Van was waiting, for what he was not entirely sure. A sign, perhaps, or simply an instinct that would tell him the moment was right.

He could not understand his own reluctance to move on, to take the next step and the next in their inevitable, unchangeable sequence, until his relationship with Dinah became a full-blown affair. It was not something he had ever experienced before. When he wanted a woman – and he had wanted plenty – he had always made his move swiftly and decisively. He had seldom been rejected and when he had it had never bothered him unduly; he had shrugged his shoulders, considered the loss to be more the lady's than his own, and moved on to fresh pastures. But this time it was different. This time he did not want to take the risk. To push her too far, too fast, might be to lose her. That, more than anything, was what he was afraid of.

But why? Was it her talent, which could help him to expand the business on the lines he wanted, and which excited him so, that was too precious to chance? At first he had been sure that was it. He had, in fact, been quite certain it was that talent that made her attractive to him. He had forgotten, or almost forgotten, that he had felt drawn towards her even before he had known she was more, much more, than just a student drop-out. Yet it was those very same qualities which fascinated him now – the innocence, the vulnerability, all overshadowed by something else, some edge of depth and mystery which he could not fathom.

It was when he broke the habit of a lifetime and opened the Venetian blinds at the window between his office and the factory floor so that he could sit at his desk and watch her work that Van acknowledged to himself that his interest in her was much more profound than simply her artistic talent. It gave him pleasure to see her sitting at her machine, golden head bent so that the delicate lines at the nape of her neck were exposed. He found himself wanting to touch her neck, to run his fingers over the arched sinews down to the curve of her shoulder and breast, and when she smiled, that lovely illuminating smile that took her rather serious features and made them beautiful, it called to something in the depths of his being, twisting his heart and awakening responses he had forgotten it was possible to experience.

When he took her out he enjoyed not only her enthusiasm for the ideas to which she had obviously given so much thought but also her delight in the whole experience. He sensed she was totally unused to the way of life to which he was introducing her and took pleasure in broadening her horizons and watching her wonderment.

It would be the same, he thought, when he eventually made love to her. She would be lacking in experience, might even be a virgin, but he would enjoy teaching her. The very idea of it was more erotic by far than the liaisons with the sexually accomplished women he was used to. With his enormous appetite for such things he rarely failed to enjoy their expertise, but the memory of them did not fire him as the thought of making love with Dinah fired him. That was a fantasy which had the power to put him into a state of arousal whenever he allowed himself to indulge it.

So far he had not made one single move towards her and he

marvelled at his own self-control. He still went out with other women – he had two in tow at the moment, a beauty queen he had met when he had been one of the judges in a recent Miss Modern Venus competition, and the wife of one of the partners in his firm of solicitors. Both were sexually voracious, if inclined to be a little demanding emotionally, and neither of them was able to do anything to make him want Dinah less.

It was, he thought, the very fact that he had placed her out of bounds sexually that made her seem so very desirable. Take her, and the magic might wear off. Yet still he could not bring himself to make the move, though for the life of him he could not put his finger on exactly what it was that made him hold back. When they were alone together he quite often had the feeling that she wanted him to touch her; the desire hung in the air between them so tangibly that the denial of it seemed almost to create an awkwardness of its own. But there was also a part of her that seemed to need space and distance. In spite of her apparent ingenuousness he felt oddly certain that he did not know her, that she was holding back from him some very important part of herself.

He caught it sometimes in her eyes; he would be talking to her across the table in some restaurant, watching and enjoying the light in her face, and then perhaps he would ask her some question about herself and suddenly the shutters would come down. For a moment he would glimpse not simply wariness but fear, sharp and clear, as if she was seeing something he could not and recoiling from it. Then almost as quickly it would be gone and she would be smiling, not that wonderful sweet smile that came from the depths of her soul but a quick, nervous smile that he sensed was part of the defence mechanism. She would answer him then, but oddly there was always a feeling of unreality about her reply, as if she was an actress playing a part, not a woman opening up to him with details of her life.

What was she hiding? he wondered. What was it that made her draw back from telling him the truth about herself? And what was it that projected a defensive wall that repelled any advance he might try to make in spite of the fact that she also seemed eager to welcome it.

Dinah was an enigma, but one he was determined to solve one

day. It was just a matter of waiting for the right time and the right place. Then, he was sure, his patience would be amply rewarded.

At the same time as he was falling in love with Dinah, Van was also turning the schemes she had suggested for the factory over in his mind and by the end of August he was ready to put at least two of them to his father.

The riding boots, he decided, would have to wait – there was market research to be done and the possibility of alternative materials to be looked into – but he had discussed her suggestion of walking boots with his product engineer and between them they had come up with a prototype that seemed to take in all the features necessary for comfort and durability. Marketing, which he had felt might cause a problem, had been solved by Dinah herself. Why try to sell through a middleman, she had said. Why not advertise a mail-order service in the columns of the popular press? She had done a little drawing of the boot, captioned it 'Lightfoot through the country', and he had a feeling that if the boots were realistically priced it just might pull in some orders.

As for the sandals, they were easier. Because they were basically unstructured there would be no need for special lasts to be made – the old boot lasts gave the dimensions of the foot and all that was required was to add thongs and straps to a leather sole. But Van thought that if he could actually show his father a prototype pair he might have more chance of persuading the old man to venture into this new market than if he merely took him the drawings. The ideal opportunity to do some experimenting would present itself when Kendricks closed down, as it did every year, for its fortnight's summer break, the last week in July and the first in August.

'Are you going away for the holiday?' Van asked Dinah towards the middle of July.

At once he saw the wariness in her eyes. Then she shook her head.

'No. I've no plans.'

'Neither have I.' It was not strictly true. He had booked himself and his car on to a ferry to France, where he had intended to tour as and when the fancy took him. But a holiday – any holiday – always struck him as a shocking waste of time. He was usually bored after the first few days and only frustrated at not being able to work. And this year in particular he had no desire to be anywhere that was not within reach of either Dinah or his work.

'Look, I'll tell you what I'm thinking. The factory will be closed for two weeks and my parents will be in Italy. They go there every year. It would be the perfect opportunity to try to make both the sandals and the walking boots. I'd like to see how they turn out when there's no one looking over my shoulder.'

The light came back into her eyes.

'*My* sandals? The ones I designed?'

He smiled at her childlike delight.

'Yes. Of course. Would you be prepared to give up your holiday to do it? Then when the old man comes home I can show him the finished article and try to talk him into producing some more. In fact I intend to do more than try to persuade him, I am going to insist. This factory is my future, and it's time I had some real say in running it. Well – are you willing?'

'Of course!'

He could not resist one more little probe.

'There's no one who will be expecting you to go home?'

'No one. I did think I might spend a couple of days with Mary, but there's nothing definite arranged.'

Van was instantly alert. It was the first time Dinah had ever mentioned anyone from her past.

'Mary?'

'Mary O'Sullivan. An old school friend of mine. Well, she's Mary Colbourne now, married, with a little boy, but I still think of her as Mary O'Sullivan.'

Was it excitement that her designs were going to take shape that had made her less cautious? Van tried to press home the advantage.

'You were at school with her in Gloucestershire?'

'Yes. She was my best friend. We've always kept in touch.'

'And though she's no older than you she's married, with a child?'

'She's a Roman Catholic,' Dinah said as if that explained everything, but he had seen the hint of the shadows returning and wondered why.

Had Mary perhaps stolen Dinah's boyfriend and married him?

Surely she wouldn't want to keep in touch if that were the case. But there was something, something in Dinah's past that she wanted to keep hidden, and in some way it had to do with marriage and babies. If she were not so young and obviously inexperienced he might almost have thought she had been married herself. But the naivety belied that and it did fit with her story of having been at art school, which he was fairly certain was true.

'So, what do you want me to do?' Dinah asked, and the moment passed.

'Just be here during the holiday. We'll crack this thing together.'

'Oh yes!' she said. 'Oh Van, I shall enjoy that!'

They both enjoyed it. It was the most tremendous fun, stealing into the factory where all the machines stood silent and dust motes danced in the shafts of sunlight that streaked through the unshuttered windows.

Van had collected her at nine thirty on the first Monday of the holiday. His father had left for Italy the previous day and Van parked his Jag in the space reserved with his father's name. Though there was no one but Dinah to see it it gave him a good feeling, as if he were already head of the firm instead of just the heir to the throne. He unlocked the factory with his huge bunch of keys and they went in. Everything had been turned off for the holiday – even the water supply. Van went around flicking switches and loosening taps and Dinah filled the kettle to make them coffee, which they took with them on to the factory floor. They were much too eager to get to work to want to waste time.

For three whole days they worked solidly. The first samples were useless – the sandals were not merely casual but untidy, the boots would have crippled a walker within the first half-mile. They went back to the drawing board, modifying and refining, and tried again. Better, much better. The sandals looked stylish, if totally unconventional, and Dinah reiterated her suggestion that they might sell to women as well as men. Van, who had made the boots in his size, put them on and went for a walk first around the factory floor then around the car park, and pronounced them 'almost there'.

'You know what I think?' he said to Dinah.

She shook her head, still neatening one of the straps on the sample sandal.

'I think we should give these boots a proper trial in the field. Scotland, the Lake District – you name it. It is the holidays after all.'

He saw the quick wings of colour rise in her cheeks and thought they spelled disapproval for the idea. Then she said in a small, downcast voice: 'You mean you're going to go away after all?' and he realised she had misunderstood him and the reason for her flush was dismay.

'Not just me,' he said. 'You too. Where would you like to go?'

He saw it then, that same smile of pure happiness that had transformed her face when he had first given her the job. Happiness, surprise, and an element of disbelief.

'Me?'

'Yes, you. Why not? You've earned it.'

The smile faltered suddenly. 'But I can't afford to go on holiday.'

'Did anyone ask you to pay? Go on – where would you like to go?'

'Exmoor,' she said. 'The Doone Valley. I'd like to see the church where Lorna was shot.'

He laughed. 'It's just a story!'

'Maybe. I'd still like to see it.'

At that moment he would have taken her anywhere in the world that she wanted to go.

'All right,' he said. 'Exmoor it is. How soon can you be ready?'

'Any time.'

'In that case,' he said, anxious not to give her time to change her mind. 'We'll go tonight.'

He telephoned through on the office phone to book rooms in a hotel in Minehead – the Gateway to Exmoor – then drove her home, giving her an hour to pack, and picked her up again.

'I don't think Mrs Brooks approves at all,' Dinah said, giggling, as he put her battered suitcase into the boot beside his own smart monogrammed leather one. 'She thinks I'm a scarlet woman!'

And so you will be, if I get the chance! Van thought with a touch of wry humour. Aloud he said: 'Take no notice. She's just a narrow-minded old biddy.'

Dinah giggled again. 'Yes,' she said happily, 'she is.'

She was, he thought, more relaxed than at any time since he had known her. It was as if the totally changed circumstances of the last few days had lifted the barriers that little bit more and pushed whatever it was that haunted her into the past where it belonged. His spirits rose. Perhaps away from familiar surroundings the time would be right to unravel the enigma that was Dinah and manoeuvre their relationship into a more intimate phase.

The hotel was on North Hill where the wild and beautiful expanse of Exmoor creeps right down to the outer perimeter of the town and the wide blue bay spreads out beneath. It was late by the time they arrived; they had dinner in the hotel restaurant, all pristine white napery, heavy old silver and sparkling crystal, and watched the sun go down in a blaze of red until it disappeared into the sea. Van made no move that night. Better to let her relax completely, sink into the wonderfully unreal state that comes with holidaying in a romantic setting.

The next day they breakfasted in the same huge dining room and Dinah ate ravenously – stewed fruit, bacon, tomatoes and scrambled eggs, toast and marmalade and coffee. Van, used to seeing her pick at her meals when he took her out to dine, was amazed at her appetite. He had noticed recently that she seemed to have put on some weight – scarcely surprising if she tucked so much away each morning!

Breakfast over, they drove out on to Exmoor. Dinah gazed enraptured at the ever-changing scenery – the deep wooded valleys with streams running through, the wide and wild expanses of moorland, green and purple and gold where the heather and gorse grew in great spreading patches amid the scrubby grass. Van felt a softening inside as he looked at her, experiencing again the same desire to please her that he had felt the first time she had walked into his office.

At last they stopped and Van laced himself into the boots he had made.

'Moment of truth!'

Dinah laughed. 'They'll be fine – I know they will!'

'I hope so – since it's *my* feet that will be covered in blisters if they're not!'

There were no blisters, but the boots did rub his ankle bone.

He eased the boots off, sitting on a boulder, and examined the raw spot.

'Is it my feet or the boots?'

Dinah had dropped on to the scrub beside him, bending over the offending boot, prodding at the high collar that encased the ankle.

'It's got to be the boots. It doesn't matter how peculiar your feet are . . .'

'Thank you!'

'. . . they have got to be comfortable. For you – or anyone. Perhaps if we added a little padding from there . . . to there . . .'

'When do we add it?'

'As soon as we get back to the factory.'

'And what about me? How do I get back to the car now?'

Dinah smiled mischievously. 'Well, you could go barefoot! Or maybe I could make some padding now. Just to try. Here, let me . . .'

She pushed the boot on to his foot. He winced.

'Ouch!'

'Wait a minute.' She searched in her bag for a clean handkerchief and placed it under the collar of the boot. As her fingers grazed his skin he winced again, not from pain now but from the sharp arousing pleasure of her touch. She glanced up anxiously, thinking she had hurt him, and her clear, troubled eyes sent a bolt of desire through the core of him. He reached out and touched her hair, running his fingers through its silky softness, curling around the base of her skull. She sat motionless, looking up at him, her hand still resting on his foot. He bent forward, never taking his eyes off hers, and pulled her gently towards him. He had never wanted a woman more than he wanted her, but he knew instinctively that he must not rush her even now.

A tremor ran through her as his face came closer to hers, but it was gentle, like the wind whispering through the bracken. In that moment the past with all its pain, and the lurking uncertainties of the immediate future ceased to exist. There was only Van. The touch of his hand on her hair was her cradle and her grave, the whole of her life was there in the circle of his arms. He was the only one who had ever mattered, could ever matter, she would walk through the fires of hell to be with him, sacrifice anything just to have him look at her this way, hold her, love her. Dinah felt her soul rise within her, taking wing to meet him. And as it did so a tiny detached part of her was whispering that there would never be another moment quite as perfect as this one, when they would be quite alone, quite separate not only from the rest of the world but also from their own fears and ambitions, anxieties and dreams, cut off in a universe of their own making and surrounded by galaxies of stars.

His lips touched hers and suddenly it was not only her soul but her body that was yearning, the hard sensual mouth crushing hers with a terrible tenderness. She let go of his foot and somehow was in the gap between his knees, her hands gripping the powerful blades of his shoulders, back arched, head bend back beneath his kiss so that her throat curved like a swan's. His arms were around her now, circling her waist, as she pressed forward against him. After long minutes, very gently he held her away, looking at her.

'Do you know how long I've been wanting to do that?'

She shook her head. Her lips were swollen, her eyes luminous.

'I think I only invented this holiday so that I could get you alone. Did you know that?'

Again she shook her head. She had no words.

He kissed her again, delighting in the way her lips responded, speaking the volumes her voice refused to utter. Then he stood up.

'Shall we go back to the hotel?'

She knew what he meant and for an instant it was as if he had douched her with ice-cold water. This habit of living each moment for itself and never looking ahead had really got a hold on her; lost in the euphoric aura of romance she had simply refused to acknowledge the natural progression of events. Now a great wave of panic washed over her, not because she did not want Van to make love to her – she did, oh, she did! – but because she was suddenly terrified that he would be bound to realise her condition. Her body was still remarkably contained, it was true, her stomach muscles were strong and she was carrying the baby high so the bulge was almost all in her midriff and waistline. But her breasts were full and swollen, the nipples dark and spotted with white nodules. If he saw them he would surely know . . .

'Dinah?'

Love flooded her and she knew that if she let this moment slip away it might never come again.

'Yes,' she said. 'Let's go back.'

He pulled her to her feet, kissed her again. In the quiet that surrounded them, Dinah could hear bumble bees and crickets, all the tiny sounds of nature. For the rest of her life they would be synonymous for her with perfect, unsullied happiness.

'Thank God I can get these bloody boots off now!' Van said when they reached the car. He sat in the driving seat, kicking them away and slipping his feet into his own comfortable brogues. 'No one in their right mind would pay good money for them as they are, I assure you.'

Dinah was too happy to do anything but laugh.

'Don't you realise that's my design you are maligning?'

'We'll get it right. I'll get Jim Pratten to work on it.'

'But I . . .'

'Don't worry about it. You stick with the ideas – leave the master craftsmen to sort out the details.'

There was something slightly patronising in the way he said it. Dinah experienced a slight pang of deflation, which was instantly forgotten as he reached over to squeeze her hand.

The hotel was quiet, a few guests taking afternoon tea and pastries in the lounge. Van collected their room keys from the reception desk. Dinah was waiting for him on the stairs. He slipped an arm around her waist.

'Your room or mine?'

The dark imp of reality tapped her shoulder once more. She pushed it away.

'Yours.'

She wanted it to be his room. She wanted to see his things around her, holding her safely in his world. Her own room was full of cheap clothes and her tatty suitcase, looking totally out of place on the impressive luggage rack. Her room was evidence of her past, portent for her future. Her room was too close to reality.

He unlocked the door, drawing her inside, and she felt no fear, only a sense of rightness. Though it was less than two hours since he had first kissed her, the courtship had already in a sense been gone through in the long evenings when they had talked endlessly and nothing more.

She looked around. The late-afternoon sunshine was slanting in through the partially drawn curtains, lighting a room that was curiously impersonal. The maids had obviously been in, the room had been cleaned and the bed made, but it was clear that in any case Van was meticulously tidy. His clothes were all hanging out of sight in the wardrobe, not draped around as her own were, on the dressing table there was only his hairbrush and a pair of gold cuff-links to add a personal touch to the hotel's information folder and the courtesy tray with kettle and neatly stacked cups and saucers.

Van pushed the door closed, dropped the room key on to the dressing table beside the hairbrush and took her in his arms. At once desire flooded her, blotting out thought. He kissed her, then began unbuttoning her blouse, and the fear returned, urgent now.

'Couldn't we pull the curtains . . . please?' she whispered.

He looked at her with love and indulgence in his eyes. She was such a child, so shy. He would teach her to enjoy lovemaking, to glory in the sight of his body and his enjoyment of hers, to watch the act and so appreciate it with every one of her senses. But it would take time. For now he would humour her and do it her way.

He crossed to the window and drew the curtains. They were thick, lined with heavy material, and they shut out almost all of the light. He went back to where she stood, arms wrapped protectively around her body. A moment's doubt assailed him.

'Dinah . . . you are sure?'

She nodded. He could hear her breath, soft and uneven. As he reached for her, slipping his hands inside her blouse and unfastening the strap of her bra, she moved closer to him so that her body was entirely hidden from him, and again he wondered. Even now she was holding back, keeping within herself that very private place he could not reach. But he wanted her too much now to worry about it. She was shy, that was all, inexperienced and perhaps slightly ashamed of it.

'Darling, relax!' he said, the endearment slipping easily off his tongue though he could never remember having used it to a woman before. 'I won't hurt you. Just let it happen.'

Her skirt was simple pink gingham trimmed with white broderie anglaise, full and gathered. When he unbuttoned the waistband it fell to the ground. Beneath it she was wearing a petticoat made of layers of stiffened net in rainbow colours; easy, too, to slip that down. It lay at her ankles in a sighing heap and he slid his hand behind her knees, lifting her out of it bodily and carrying her to the bed.

In the dim light he could see the curves of her body, a little more rounded than he had expected, as she lay on top of the covers. He undressed himself swiftly then knelt beside her, stroking and kissing her until he felt her beginning to respond again. Yet even in response she was curiously passive. Van was used to women who knew how to make love with the skills of a courtesan, who expressed their desire with positive actions, who were prepared even to take the initiative. Dinah did none of these things. Though he could sense the quivering need that was electrifying her body she lay almost completely still, waiting for him to call the shots, and he realised he liked it, that for him it was more arousing to be totally dominant than to be made love to, however skilfully.

He lay down on his side next to her, turning her so that they lay face to face. He kissed her again, holding her pressed close so that he probed her gently, and she gave a soft, low cry and arched against him. For a few moments more he moved rhythmically until he sensed both from the movements of her body and the rising urgency of her breath that she was in the upward spiral of excitement which leads to climax. Then and only then did he enter her.

Lying pressed into the pillows, Dinah felt she had moved into another dimension. The excruciating sweetness, the mounting desire, the brief moment of pain, the utter delight of having him fill her, move in her, possess her.

'Please . . . oh please!' she whispered, but she did not know what it was she was begging for because already she had everything she could desire and it was wonderful . . . wonderful! Then: 'Don't stop! Don't ever stop!' and she knew it was because she wanted this glory to go on forever, the sensation of body and mind and spirit all swirling upwards to the stars.

'Come with me,' Van murmured, sliding his hands beneath her and raising her so that the tilt of her body brought them still closer together. And suddenly the sweetness was reaching screaming pitch, so sharp she could scarcely bear it and she knew this was the moment to hold on to, *this, this*.

Afterwards, subsiding into the warm rosy valley of

contentment, she twined her arms around Van's broad back, holding him within her as long as she could. Only when he slipped from her did she allow that it really was over.

'Oh Van, I love you,' she whispered.

He squeezed her gently but said nothing, rolling on to his side and taking her with him. She was becoming drowsy now; though it was still only late afternoon she felt her eyelids closing.

Beside her Van too relaxed in the afterglow, and a few moments later, still locked in one another's arms, they slept.

Something was wrong. Van knew it but could not for the life of him put his finger on what it was.

He had sensed it almost immediately after that first ecstatic lovemaking. When they had woken Dinah had clung to him as if she could not bear to be parted from him for even an instant. At his suggestion she had run a bath, but whilst she was taking it she had locked the door, and when she emerged she looked slightly drawn, although the warmth of the water had raised a rosy flush in her cheeks.

'Come here,' he said to her, and although she did as he asked he sensed that she had gone away from him again. Frustration made him irritable; he could not understand her withdrawal, the stiffness in every line of her body as he held her. Yet when he said a little coolly: 'Perhaps we had better get dressed for dinner,' she clung to him, her tight closed eyes and puckered mouth suggesting she might be close to tears.

At dinner it was the same; she ate little and seemed preoccupied. She did not want a pudding; he went to the sweet trolley to choose from the impressive array of desserts and as he returned to their table he noticed that her face, in repose, was indescribably sad.

It was as if that shadow that lurked at her shoulder was back, he thought, only darker and more insistently threatening than before. He filled her glass, thinking it might help to relax her, but she drank little, only sipping at the good French wine he had selected.

Afterwards they went for a walk, down the hill to the sea front, and the burden went with them. Van's impatience grew. Was this how virgins behaved when they had just succumbed for the first time – wallowing in doubt, resenting the loss of their virginity? It was so long since he had made love to anyone but the most experienced of women and he could not recall ever having encountered such a reaction before, but he thought it must be that. He would have to be patient with her and teach her that there was no need for it to be this way, he decided.

He made no attempt to make love to her again that night, but next morning as she faced him across the breakfast table she reminded him a little of a piece of diamond-cut crystal, so sharply brittle was she. The cloud, he knew, was still there beneath the shining exterior. It had not gone away, it was simply hidden.

He drove her to Porlock. They sat by the weir, watching the fishing smacks in the bay, then they went on, up the steep toll road, back on to the moors, seeking out the villages where thatched cottages nestled together behind their gardens, bright with the old-fashioned flowers of summer – hollyhocks and delphiniums, phlox and snapdragons. They had lunch in a country pub and afterwards he headed for the spot she had said she most wanted to see – the Doone Valley.

They parked on the road, looking down towards the church where Lorna had died, and glancing at Dinah he saw that her eyes were full of tears. In that moment irritation gave way to tenderness. He put his arm around her, turning her to face him.

'What is it, darling? What is the matter?'

She shook her head. 'Nothing.'

'There must be something. You don't cry for no reason – nobody does.'

'Oh – it's being here, I suppose.'

'But you wanted to come.'

'I know, but it's so sad! Love can be, can't it?'

'Perhaps. But it's nothing to cry about.'

She sat silently staring down the valley.

'It's not Lorna Doone and John Ridd you're crying about at all, is it?' he said. 'You have been behaving strangely all day. Is it because of what happened last night? Because if it is, that's nothing to cry about either. You wanted it to happen, didn't you?'

'Oh yes!' There was no mistaking the fervour of her tone.

'And so did I. We've both wanted it for a very long time. So what is it? You're not worried that I might have made you pregnant, are you? Because if you are – forget it. I can promise you I didn't.'

He heard her gulp, deep in her throat. Then she said dully: 'No, it's not that.'

'What then?'

Tears were welling in her eyes and he felt a sudden bolt of jealousy.

'Is there somebody else? Somebody you can't forget?'

'No. No! Oh, please do stop going on at me! There's nothing wrong. I'm fine. I'm probably just tired – I didn't sleep much last night.'

And she would say no more.

They returned to the car and drove on, and gradually he sensed her mood lifting, returning to the forced elation of the morning as if she had made a conscious decision to put whatever it was that was troubling her behind her.

That night they made love again, this time in her room, and though she once again insisted that the lights should be out her response had that same feverish quality he had noticed in her all day. When it was over they lay side by side, his hand resting on that slightly rounded stomach and he was surprised when she took it and moved it higher, so it lay instead on her ribcage.

'Do you want me to go?' he asked, though it was the last thing he wanted.

She curled herself around him.

'No, please stay!'

It was some time during the dark reaches of the night that it came to him that he wanted to marry her. He had woken to feel her there beside him, heard her regular breathing and reached for the warm softness of her. She moved slightly, murmuring something he could not make out, and with the suddenness of an electric shock he realised he never wanted to leave her.

The thought startled him. Never before had it occurred to him to want to make one of his many relationships permanent. He enjoyed his freedom too much, enjoyed playing the field, taking his pleasures with no strings attached. He had seen himself as one of life's natural bachelors, wedded only to the ambition that would one day bring him all the prizes he desired. A wife had had no place in his plans. But then he had never before known a woman like Dinah, never before been in love.

The realisation that this had all changed frightened him a little. But even as he tried to tell himself that the madness would pass and he would get over it he knew he did not want to. Loving her made him vulnerable and Van did not like being vulnerable. Marry her, make her his, and he would be in control again, both of himself and of her.

But the desire was not only selfish. He wanted to give to her too, to make her happy, to teach her to trust and to banish forever whatever it was that clouded her horizon. He wanted her there to share the fruits of his success, wanted them to do things together, not just the lovemaking but also the adventures and the striving, even the sheer hard work, as they had shared the making and the trial of the new walking boots and the sandals that he thought of as the 'Bible boots'.

The wonder of discovery filled him and he thought how odd it was that someone as ingenuous and childlike as Dinah should have reached his heart where more sophisticated women had failed. And yet at the same time it was not strange at all but absolutely right, for her very naivety filled a gap in him, making him feel strong and powerful whilst at the same time that unreachable core of her fascinated him and posed a challenge.

They had one day left, one day before they had to return to reality, to the factory and everyday life. He could no longer bear the thought of her sitting at her machine with the other workers, knew it would tear him apart to look through his office window and see her there, one of the least important of his father's employees, when he wanted her beside him. As for his other lady friends – it amused him to think how outraged they would be to know that they had been usurped by this little girl.

But how proud he would be! She was beautiful already – when she was dressed, with his money, in designer clothes, she would be stunning. And he would teach her everything she needed to know to fit into his world.

Tomorrow he would ask her to marry him, he decided. And in spite of all that had gone before, in spite of the doubts she inspired in him, it never occurred to him for one moment that she might refuse.

*

He took her to Tarr Steps, in the heart of Exmoor, and on the way back he detoured again to the Doone Valley.

Van was not a romantic but knowing how she felt about the place it seemed only right to him that it should be here that he asked her the question that had not left his mind since those sleepless hours last night.

'Lorna never made it to the altar in the church,' he said, sitting on the ridge and holding her hand. 'Would you like to do it for her?'

She glanced up, puzzled, and he knew she had not understood.

'Would you like to be married there?'

She laughed, a soft little intake of breath.

'Would I . . .? I don't know. What a funny question!'

'It isn't meant to be funny. I don't even know if the church is used for services any more, let alone for weddings. But if it is, would you like to be married there . . . to me?'

She still looked puzzled, as if she half understood but was afraid she might be mistaken.

'For goodness' sake!' he exploded. 'I'm asking you to marry me, Dinah!'

'Oh!' It was there again in her eyes before she quickly turned her head away, that shadow that had no substance, and for a moment he felt sick inside, as if she had hit him. He had made love to her, and the ghosts were still there. He had asked her to marry him, and the ghosts were still there. What could he do to drive them away? Though he was churning inside with unfamiliar emotions his voice was hard, almost expressionless.

'I take it, then, that your answer is no?'

She turned back. He was reminded of a gazelle poised for flight.

'Oh Van, there's nothing in the world I would like better than to marry you. Only . . .'

'Only what?'

She hesitated, eyes distant. Then she lowered her lashes, shook her head.

'Nothing.'

Would she never tell him? He wanted to catch her, shake it out of her, but he knew he could not do that. One day, in her own good time, she would tell him. Until then he would have to be patient.

'Will you marry me, then?'

She buried her face in his chest. 'Oh Van, I love you so much!'

It was, he thought, not quite the answer he had expected, but he knew that for the moment it was the best he could hope for.

They drove home next day. Dinah was very quiet but also very loving, her hand resting on his thigh as he drove, her head against his shoulder.

They did not talk about marriage again. He would give her time to get used to the idea, he told himself, and besides, he could use a little time to get used to it himself! Reaction to the hasty decision had begun to set in; he didn't regret it, no, certainly not that, but he did want time to adjust to the enormity of what he had done.

They ate *en route* at a country pub, and he loved the fact that they were treated as a couple. Back in Over Stowey he drove her to the little terraced house where she had her digs and stopped outside.

'Thank you,' she said, oddly formal.

'Thank *you*,' he replied, 'for the happiest few days of my life.'

'At work . . . will we . . .?'

'Tell anyone? We will tell them just as soon as you are ready.'

'And the boots? Do you think they will be all right?'

He frowned. The boots were, at that moment, the furthest thing from his mind.

'I'm sure they will be. The basic design is good and the experts can work on the technical details.'

'Mm.' She nodded. She looked, he thought, satisfied.

'Do you want me to come in with you – carry your case?'

'Oh no, better not. Mrs Brooks is a funny soul.'

'Mrs Brooks is going to have to get used to me – for a little while, anyway.'

'Yes,' she said reflectively. 'Yes, I suppose so. But not tonight.'

He placed her case on the doorstep, then took her by the shoulders to kiss her lightly.

'Goodnight, darling.'

'Goodnight.' It was almost a sob, and then suddenly she threw her arms around him, burying her face in his chest. Embarrassed, he tensed. He was too old and too sophisticated for such a public display of passion. But before he could even attempt to extricate himself she released him again, picked up her case and turned away. Her key was in the door and she did not look round at him. But somehow he had the impression that she might be cryng.

'Dinah . . .' he began to say.

'Goodnight, Van,' she said again, and he wondered why for one ridiculous moment he thought she had said not 'goodnight' but 'goodbye'. Then the door had closed behind her and there was nothing left for him to do but return to the car and drive home.

Next day Dinah did not turn up for work. Van had arrived early – he always did, but today he had even more reason than usual for wanting to get to the factory; he was anxious to put the modifications for the walking boots in hand, and he wanted to see Dinah. But her place was empty and her clock card in its wallet remained unmarked.

Van was puzzled but also almost unnaturally worried. All very well to tell himself that the likeliest reason was that she was not well and taking a day off – he was sickeningly certain it was more than that. All very well to rationalise that since Mrs Brooks had no telephone, if Dinah was poorly she would not feel like walking to the kiosk at the end of the street to call in sick, yet still all his instincts clamoured alarm. All thoughts of tackling his father about the production of the boots were forgotten. At eleven o'clock Van told his secretary he was going out, took his car and drove to Wellington Street.

The weather had taken a turn for the worse. This morning it was drizzling and beneath the overcast sky the terrace of grey stone houses that gave directly on to the street without even the smallest of gardens looked depressing and unwelcoming. A couple of worn-out-looking women laden with shopping in plastic bags turned to stare curiously as the Jag drew up outside Mrs Brooks's house. A Jag here was not a common sight.

Van rang the bell. For a long while there was no reply, then he heard slippers shuffling across the lino. When the door was opened it was obvious that Mrs Brooks was in the middle of the weekly wash. Her hair hung limply across her thin face, the sleeves of a shrunken cardigan were pushed up to her raw-boned elbows and she was wiping puffy red hands on the skirt of her wraparound overall.

'Yes?' she snapped.

'I'm sorry to disturb you, Mrs Brooks. I've come to see Dinah.'

The woman sniffed, wiping her face with the back of her hand. 'Huh! You'll have a job to do that.'

'Isn't she well?'

'She's gone.'

'Gone?' Somehow he had known it already and yet it was still a shock. 'Gone where?'

The woman shrugged. 'How should I know? All I can tell you is that she packed up and left, first thing this morning. It's a good thing I take my rent in advance, I must say.'

'You mean . . . she's not coming back?'

'That's what I said, isn't it?' She peered at Van suspiciously. 'Do you know anything about it? Who are you, anyway?'

'I'm her employer,' Van said. 'Did she leave a forwarding address?'

'No. I asked her what I should do if there was any post for her and she said there wouldn't be. Well, if there is I shall just put it back in the box marked "Gone Away". I'm sure I can't be bothered if she can't.'

'Could I see her room?' Van asked.

The woman looked taken aback. 'What for?'

'In case she left anything.'

'She didn't.'

'I'd like to check for myself all the same.' Van spoke with authority and Mrs Brooks reluctantly gave in.

'I've stripped the bed, mind you,' she said, leading the way up the stairs. 'I'm washing the sheets and pillowcases right now.'

As Mrs Brooks had said, every one of Dinah's personal possessions had gone. Without them, and with the bed stripped, exposing bare, stained mattress, it had a bleak impersonal feel that made it impossible to imagine that it had been Dinah's home for almost as long as he had known her. Van checked the drawers, each lined with yellowing newspaper, and opened the wardrobe, empty but for a jangling collection of wire hangers.

'You see?' Mrs Brooks was watching from the doorway, an expression midway between satisfaction and pained outrage on her thin, worn face. She was torn between annoyance at her lodger's sudden departure and pleasure at seeing him thwarted, he decided, and realised with a sense of hopeless frustration that there was no point pressing her any further.

'Miss Marshall doesn't owe you anything, I take it?'

'I told you, I take a month's rent in advance. Mind you, I should have been given notice. I might have trouble letting again,' she added hastily.

Van's lips tightened with dislike.

'You might indeed,' was all he said.

Van sat behind the wheel of his Jaguar, staring into space. He was unaware of the mean street now, oblivious to passers-by staring curiously. He was still in shock, his mind reeling with unanswered questions. Where had Dinah gone – and why? Yet at the same time there were facets he could see with startling clarity – Dinah with tears in her eyes, Dinah clinging to him, Dinah walking away from him without a backward glance: 'Goodbye, Van.' He was certain now that that was what she had said – not 'goodnight', but 'goodbye'. Part of him had known it even then but he had refused to accept it. But why? *Why?* Because they had made love? Because he had asked her to marry him? If she didn't want to she had only to say so. Or did she think working with him afterwards would be impossible? That could be it. She had not wanted to hurt him by outright refusal and had taken fright at the thought of having to face him again. She had not after all said she would marry him. The omission had jarred on him then and it jarred on him now. But she had said she loved him and he believed her. So why should she pack her bags and go without a word to him or anyone? It did not make sense, but instinctively he knew it had to do with that part of her that he had never been able to reach and the shadow that came between them.

What was it she was hiding? Some secret sorrow? Something she was ashamed of – her background, perhaps? Whatever it was he couldn't imagine it could be anything so very terrible. Knowing Dinah and her ingenuousness she had probably exaggerated whatever it was, built it up in her mind until it assumed unacceptable proportions. He would find her, worm the secret – whatever it was – out of her and assure her that nothing was more important than their being together.

Van started the car, driving automatically in the direction of the factory. Already he felt the loss of her like a physical pain, an emptiness growing and spreading to touch every part of him. But shocked and hurt though he was, he had no doubt but that he would find her again and make right whatever it was that was wrong between them. He needed her, on both a physical and an emotional level, and also as the catalyst for his dreams for the future. Dinah, with her elusive talent, was the other, missing half of his ambition. Together they would move Kendricks into a whole new dimension. That was the way he had planned it – that was how it would be. Her disappearance now was merely a hiccup.

Van, with his dynamism and determination, would refuse to allow it to be otherwise.

Mary Colbourne, née O'Sullivan, put her baby son Patrick down for his afternoon nap and went back into the house. In the cluttered but homely kitchen Dinah had just finished drying the lunch dishes, now she stood, still twisting the damp tea towel between her hands, staring listlessly out of the window into the small sunny back yard where the tall scarlet and pink geraniums in their terracotta pots made splashes of brilliant colour against the grey, and the coach-built pram, protected by a cat-net, had been parked in what little shade was provided by the side of the house.

Mary looked at her friend sadly and shook her head. Dinah was under a great deal of strain – and it showed. Her face was pale and drawn, her eyes puffy, and beneath the cheap cotton shift, patterned with flowers the same shades as the geraniums, the bulge of her spreading waistline was clearly discernible.

'Dinah, we have to talk,' Mary said. 'We have to decide what you are going to do.'

It was almost a week since Dinah had arrived on her doorstep, and one look at her had told Mary that something was dreadfully wrong. Dinah had confirmed it – she had left her job and her digs and had nowhere to go. Could Mary take her in for the time being until she sorted herself out?

Mary had agreed. She had a spare room and Dinah was welcome to that as long as she needed it, she said. She was certain that Bob, her husband, would not mind – he knew how lonely she got since being confined to the house with the baby while he worked long hours and all the overtime he could get in his trade as a plasterer to make enough money to pay the mortgage. But she was puzzled. The last she had heard from Dinah was when she had thrown in her college course and gone to work in a boot factory – a very odd thing for such a talented student. Now it seemed that that too had gone by the board. And Dinah was clearly distressed – and, thought Mary, suspiciously plump. It did not take her long to get Dinah to admit she was pregnant – with her spreading waistline there was little point in denying it. But any details of her predicament were a closed book.

'I don't want to talk about it,' Dinah would say, and Mary had let things ride, not wanting to upset her more by pressing her further. But a week had gone by and Mary did not feel she could wait any longer. Bob was beginning to ask questions – and in any case Dinah, for her own good, had to be made to face up to the fact that she was pregnant.

'Din, we have to talk,' Mary repeated, but Dinah continued to stare out of the window. It was the pram with little Patrick in it that she had focused on, Mary realised. She sighed.

'I'm going to put the kettle on and make us a cup of tea,' she said firmly. 'Then, whether you like it or not, we are going to talk.'

'Oh Mary, I don't want to! Not in the way you mean. Let's talk about the old days . . .'

'Dinah, in case it had escaped your notice, you are expecting a baby. Ignoring the fact won't make it go away. Have you seen a doctor?'

Dinah shook her head.

'Well you *must* see a doctor. You could be endangering your health and the baby's too.'

Dinah was staring unseeingly into the middle distance.

'Do you think it's too late for me to have an abortion?'

'Dinah!' Mary was shocked. 'You mustn't even think of such a thing! It's illegal, immoral and probably dangerous. And any fool can see it's far too late for that now. How far gone are you?'

'Five months.'

'Far too late.'

'I wish I'd thought of it earlier.'

'Dinah Marshall, will you stop talking about abortion! It's a wicked thing even to think of taking human life. That's what you would be doing. Killing a baby, your baby – a baby just like little Patrick.'

'All right, all right, don't go on about it! It's too late, like you said. I've just got to go on and have it.'

'Dinah.' Mary took the tea towel from her hands and steered her to a chair, sitting her down. 'I'm your friend. We've always been friends, haven't we? Won't you tell me about it?'

Dinah shrugged. 'There's nothing to tell. I got drunk and let things happen. That's all there is to it.'

'What about the father? Does he know you are pregnant?'

'No, and I don't want him to know.'

'What about your grandparents?'

Dinah laughed hollowly. 'I certainly don't want *them* to know! You can just imagine what they would say, can't you? Anyway, I never want to see Grandfather again as long as I live.'

'Which won't be very long, the way you're going,' Mary said flatly. 'You must have at least *thought* about the future.'

'Not really. I left college before anyone guessed and I got a job to tide me over while I worked out what I was going to do. But then . . .'

'Yes?'

'I suppose I just stopped thinking about it.'

'Why? Why, Dinah?'

There was a long silence. Then Dinah said: 'Because I met someone else.'

'Who?'

'His name is Van. Van Kendrick. He owns the factory where I worked – or at least, his father does. He's really special. I love him, Mary. I tried to forget what was happening to me, pretended it was all a bad dream. It was such a relief to put it all to the back of my mind and pretend I was just ordinary, like everyone else, and that maybe . . . we could . . .' Her eyes began to fill with tears.

Mary put the cups down on the kitchen table and sat down opposite Dinah.

'But he didn't notice you, I suppose.'

Dinah looked up. 'Oh yes, he did. He really liked me. That was just it. It was wonderful. He asked me to work on some designs with him, for new things for the factory to make. It was easy to forget about the baby then. I was so busy. We made these walking boots, just him and me, when the factory was closed for the holiday. And then we went away together.'

'Holy Mother of God!' Mary exploded. 'You don't mean you let him, too!'

'Yes.'

'Dinah Marshall, you have been kicking over the traces and no mistake! And to think I thought you were the prim and proper one!'

'Oh Mary – don't *you* start on me!'

Mary sighed. 'All right. Tell me. Now he's had his wicked way with you he doesn't want to know any more.'

Dinah's eyes widened. She looked almost startled.

'Oh no, you're wrong. He asked me to marry him.'

'What!'

'He asked me to marry him.'

Mary waved her hands in an expressive gesture.

'So what went wrong? Why are you here?'

'Well, I could hardly marry him, could I? Not the way I am. And I couldn't tell him either.'

'Why not?'

'I couldn't bear to. He thinks . . . thought . . . I was a virgin. I couldn't tell him I was pregnant.'

'He made love to you. He must know!'

'I made sure the lights were out. I don't want him to know, Mary. It would spoil everything.'

'It seems to me everything is spoiled now!'

'Not everything. Not what we had together. At least this way he'll remember me the way he thought I was. If he knew . . . oh Mary, don't you see? He'd hate me, and I couldn't bear that.'

'He'd be shocked, I suppose, but if he loves you . . .'

'No. I couldn't inflict it on him. Not someone else's child.'

'I suppose you know what you are doing. You seem to have made up your mind.'

'Yes,' Dinah said, 'I have. I knew, as soon as he asked me to marry him, that I couldn't let it go on any longer. I either had to tell him or get away. And I couldn't tell him.'

'So you ran away. What point is there in that?'

'I don't know. I don't know!'

'Dinah, let me write to him. Let me tell him.'

'No!'

'If he loves you . . . if you love him . . .'

'No! If you write to him, Mary, I'll never forgive you!'

'All right,' Mary said wearily. 'But we have to make plans of some sort, Dinah. You can't stay here indefinitely.'

'But you said . . .'

'I know what I said, but I was thinking about a holiday, not you moving in for good. You've got to see a doctor, you've got to see a social worker, you've got to make arrangements for what you'll do when the baby is born. Are you going to keep it?'

'I suppose so . . .'

'There are places, I think, where you could stay for a while when the baby is very young. Mother and baby homes. Dinah! Are you listening to me?'

But Dinah had gone far away again.

Mary sighed. She was very fond of Dinah and wanted to help her. But this was all more than she had bargained for.

'I'll get in touch with social services for you, but then you have got to help yourself,' she said firmly.

But secretly she was wondering if she could find out exactly where Dinah had been working, and if perhaps she would go against Dinah's wishes and get in touch with this Van Kendrick.

After all, something had to be done.

Two days later Mary was washing nappies when there was a knock at the front door. Bob was at work – as usual – and Dinah had gone down to the shopping arcade to buy vegetables and bread. At least having her here meant another pair of hands to help with the chores; Mary, in spite of her contentedly domestic nature, was constantly amazed at how much work a baby made, and wondered, as she struggled with the round of feeding, bathing, and washing nappies and Babygros, for which there never seemed to be enough hours in the day, how on earth Dinah would manage all alone.

Now she sighed at the interruption, wiped her hands on a kitchen towel and headed for the door. If it was Jehovah's Witnesses she'd soon send them away with a flea in their ear, she thought crossly.

But the man standing on the doorstep did not look like a

Jehovah's Witness. He was tall and good-looking, impeccably dressed. Mary looked at him questioningly.

'Yes?'

'Mary Colbourne?'

She nodded, puzzled.

'Good. I do have the right house then. I wonder if you can help me? I'm looking for Dinah Marshall. You are a friend of hers, I understand. Would you have any idea where I might find her? My name is Van Kendrick, by the way.'

Mary was amazed – on reflection she had taken Dinah's story with a pinch of salt. The idea that her employer, well-to-do man of the world, had asked her to marry him seemed altogether too far-fetched, and Mary was well acquainted with Dinah's capacity for dreaming and the way she used her fertile imagination to help her through when reality became too much for her. It wasn't that she lied exactly, either to herself or to anyone else, but she did have a way of embellishing the truth, twisting it to make it more acceptable, that stemmed partly from her almost pathological desire to please. It was Mary's opinion that Dinah's grandparents had a lot to answer for, but with her own two feet firmly on the ground she could not understand how retreating into a dream world could ever really help when it was obvious that sooner or later one would have to emerge to find reality waiting, all the more daunting for having been ignored.

Perhaps, Mary had thought, the employer had made a pass at Dinah, perhaps he had picked her brains for ideas for his merchandise – or perhaps Dinah had imagined the whole thing. Either way she felt sure in her own mind that the proposal of marriage must be simply wishful thinking on Dinah's part, and the fact that Dinah had refused to allow her to contact him seemed to bear that out. Certainly the last thing she had expected was to have him turn up on the doorstep, looking for Dinah. She wiped the palms of her hands, still damp from the washtub, on her apron, looking at him with the shrewd blue gaze that was part of her Irish heritage.

'Mr Kendrick. Yes, Dinah has mentioned you.'

She saw a muscle move in his cheek.

'You do know where she is, then?'

'Yes, I do.' She tipped her head, birdlike, to one side. 'Why do you want her?'

A look of astonishment crossed the handsome features, followed almost immediately by one of annoyance.

'What sort of a question is that?'

Mary stood her ground.

'Quite a straightforward one, I'd have said. Look, Mr Kendrick, Dinah is a very old friend of mine. I care about her. She's going through a very difficult time at present and I don't want her worried or upset.'

'The name is *Van* Kendrick,' he said slightly pompously. 'Christian Van Kendrick. I assure you, the last thing I want is to cause Dinah any distress. Quite the contrary. So if you could just tell me where I could find her . . .'

Mary looked hard at him. She wasn't sure she cared for him. Yes, he was good-looking. Yes, he had an aura of magnetism and power. Yes, he had pots of money, judging by the sleek Jaguar drawn up at the gate. But he was also arrogant, with a sense of his own importance, and she fancied he was not only used to getting his own way but could make things very unpleasant if he was thwarted. But what could she do? She had no intention of lying to him, and besides, whatever she might say, Dinah needed all the help she could get.

'You'd better come in, Mr Van Kendrick,' she said. He followed her into the tiny parlour. 'Sit down.'

'Thank you, but I'll stand.'

'Very well.' Mary positioned herself in the doorway, folding her arms and attempting to look straight at him. It was not entirely easy; with her short Irish legs and his impressive physique he was almost a foot taller than her. But she held his gaze anyway, her round face set into the fierce lines that could make Bob, her husband, quail when they were directed at him.

'Are you the father of her baby?' she asked.

She saw his face change. If she had been harbouring any suspicions that perhaps he already knew about Dinah's condition they were dispelled in that moment. She saw his shock, saw his guard drop briefly so that there was vulnerability where a moment ago there had been arrogance, and realised he most certainly had not known.

'Are you telling me Dinah has a baby?'

'Not yet. But she's expecting one. In early December, I should think, though she hasn't had her dates confirmed – she hasn't even seen a doctor. She has spent the last five months trying to pretend it wasn't happening, as far as I can gather. But she *has* to see one – and soon. And she has to make plans for the future. Burying her head in the sand won't make it go away.' She paused, then continued: 'I wanted to get in touch with you. Dinah forbade it. She didn't want you to know. How do you come to be here, by the way?'

'Dinah left without a word to anyone as to where she was going. I've been trying to trace her by piecing together what little I know about her. I knew the part of the world she came from, her home town, and I knew your name. She's talked about you. I thought you were my best bet.' His face hardened. 'Who is the father of her baby?'

'A student, I think – someone she knew at art school.'

'She told me she left art school because her mother had died.'

'Oh, that's perfectly true.' Mary found herself flying to her friend's defence. 'Her mother did die.'

'But obviously it was not the only reason. The young man abandoned her, I imagine.'

'She never told him. It was a very casual affair, I think.'

'Dinah seems unwilling to tell anyone anything. Where is she now?'

'She's gone to the shops.'

'You mean she is staying here with you?'

'For the time being, yes. If you'd like to wait she'll be back soon.'

For a moment he hesitated, then gave an impatient shake of the head.

'No – no, I won't wait. And perhaps it would be better if you didn't tell her I'd been here.'

He was moving towards the door. Mary experienced a flash of protective anger. The swine! Now that he knew the trouble Dinah was in he couldn't get out fast enough. Dinah had been right in thinking the truth would drive him away.

'Don't worry,' she said coldly. 'I won't be the one to tell her. I don't want to see her hurt any more than she already is. Because, God bless her, she has no more sense than to be in love with you. I said she should have told you the truth – I told her that if you loved her too you'd stand by her, whether it was your baby or not. I see now she knew you better than I did. Oh, don't worry, I won't break her heart by telling her she was right all along about you, Mr *Van* Kendrick.'

She ushered him out, praying that the distinctive Jaguar would be gone before Dinah came back and saw it. Then, burning with outrage and dislike, she returned to the kitchen and vented her anger on the tub of nappies.

Van was stunned. He got into his car and drove – too fast, and with little regard for other traffic. When he had been hooted at several times he pulled into a lay-by and switched off the engine, folding his arms across the steering wheel and laying his head against them.

So, he had found Dinah – and he had also discovered her secret. He knew now what the shadow behind her eyes meant – and he wished to hell he did not.

In ignorance Dinah had been to him all the things he had wanted her to be: pure, sweet, innocent, childlike. Now he knew she was none of these things. She was carrying another man's child and had been all the time he had known her. She had lied to him, she had deceived him, and he felt as if his world had, quite literally, turned turtle.

Van took out a cigar and lit it with the dashboard lighter, but the smoke tasted acrid on his tongue.

Of all things he had not expected this. As he had chased around the country trying to follow up the scanty pieces of information that might lead him to Dinah it had never for one moment occurred to him that the reason she had run away might be because she was pregnant. And yet of course it made perfect sense. He couldn't believe he could have been so naive as not to have thought of it before, let alone that he could have been so unobservant that he had made love to her and not realised. Well now he knew, and the knowledge was a sickness deep inside him. The pain of knowing that his madonna was sullied, the even worse pain of knowing that someone else had not only been there before him but had given her the one thing he never could – a baby.

Van had been nineteen years old when he had contracted mumps. His friends had thought it a huge joke – they had gathered to mock his swollen face and neck, calling him 'Hammy Hamster', and he had joined in the merriment. But not for long. The doctor had warned him of the possibility of serious side-effects, and later tests had proved that his fears were well founded. Van had become sterile. It was virtually impossible for him ever to become a father.

At nineteen the news had not affected Van very deeply. Once he knew his virility would not be impaired he had shrugged his shoulders and looked on the bright side – what a stud he could become if he did not have to worry about leaving a string of illegitimate progeny in his wake! But as he matured he had found that there was a certain hollowness in knowing he would never father a child. Not for him the chance to pass on a family business as his own father hoped to do. What he achieved must be done in his lifetime and what he did he must do for himself, not for his descendants.

Because he was strong and single-minded Van adopted this philosophy and made it his own. He had no time or energy to waste on bitterness or regret for something which could not be changed. But there remained within him a small sensitive spot which reacted with illogical violence to any reminder of his own inability to fulfil man's intended role in the scheme of things and procreate. It made him angry, anger not directed at himself or the illness that had robbed him of his fertility, but an anger that was all the more frustrating and destructive because it lacked a focus. It seethed and boiled in his blood, knotted in his stomach, crawled just beneath his skin. He could not father a child. But Dinah – his Dinah – had found someone who could. She had slept with this unknown man who possessed what he, Van, lacked, and all the time they had been together his seed had been growing inside her.

Van stubbed out his cigar. He wanted to be sick. His senses were numbed a little by shock, but he knew that when it began to wear off there would be layer upon layer of pain. Yet at the same time, in spite of his horror and revulsion, he knew he still wanted Dinah, even more, if that were possible, than he had before. He loved her, needed her with a desperation he had never expected to experience. He needed her as a man, with his heart and with his body. And he also needed her as the inspiration for everything he hoped to achieve professionally. The combination was compelling; he knew there was no point in fighting against it, no point weighing odds or considering anything but the demands of fate. She was his destiny, whether he liked it or not, and he was hers. They had been meant for each other, flaws and all – useless to do anything but try to make the best of it.

Van wound down the windows of the Jag and took a few deep breaths of fresh air. It was scented with the sweetness of summer, with cow parsley and hot, dry grass. He knew, as he smelled that particular combination, that it would ever after remind him of this moment.

Leaving the window down he started the engine. Then he turned the car back the way he had come.

Dinah was upstairs, in the little front bedroom that Mary was allowing her to use.

She had been feeling dreadfully tired and drained the last few days, and she had taken to going to her room and lying down for half an hour, supposedly to read. But she couldn't concentrate on reading, she couldn't concentrate on anything. The words blurred in front of her eyes and her thoughts churned until she thought she was going mad.

What was she going to do? Mary was quite right, she had to make plans and it wasn't fair to expect Mary to make them for her – she had her own life to get on with. Perhaps, Dinah thought, she had been wrong to impose on Mary at all, but she hadn't known what else to do. She had had to get away from Van and there had been nowhere else to go, no one to turn to. And somehow she hadn't been able to face striking out alone again as she had done when she left college. Then she had been worried, but positive. Now she felt frightened and panicky and very, very lost.

And this awful tiredness didn't help.

Did everyone feel like this? Dinah wondered. If so, how did women who had other children to cope with manage? But perhaps it was just her, perhaps there was something wrong. She still hadn't seen a doctor to tell her otherwise. A tiny nugget of hope flared at the back of her mind. Perhaps she was going to lose the baby. That would solve everything. She would be free and everything would go back to being as it had been before.

Except of course that it wouldn't. Nothing could ever be the same again.

Tears filled Dinah's eyes. If only she had met Van before any of this happened! That was ridiculous, of course. If she hadn't become pregnant she would never have met him at all – she would still be at college. And it was no use wasting energy thinking like that. She had to pull herself together, face the doctor and the social workers, decide where to have the baby, where she was going to live afterwards and how she was going to support them both. But she simply did not know where to begin and lacked the will to try.

Dinah got up from the bed and crossed to the window, sitting on the floor with her elbows resting on the sill, staring out at the hot, dusty August afternoon. Her stomach felt heavy and uncomfortable; strange when she thought how well she had managed to conceal it until now – since she had been at Mary's it seemed to have increased in size overnight, but perhaps it was just that she was not making the effort any more.

She heard a car turn into the street and looked towards it listlessly. A Jag – like Van's. The pain in her heart was sharp and insistent, just above the place where she sometimes felt the flutter that she knew was the baby.

The car came to a stop outside the house. Dinah's breath caught in her throat, the first stirring of realisation affecting her physically long before her mind had registered the truth. The door was opening, a man was getting out. Van! Dear God it wasn't just a car *like* Van's – it was Van! She leapt to her feet in a flurry. He mustn't see her like this – she couldn't bear it! This horrible cotton shift dress straining over her bulge, her hair – oh God, just look at her hair, what a mess! In fact, did she want to see him at all? Should she hide, lock the door, pretend she was asleep, anything, anything, until he went away again?

The panic rushed up at her, she felt it mounting in her in a hot flood tide, but her hands were icy cold, her legs shaking, weak and useless.

Dinah thought: I've got to sit down! But suddenly the bed looked a dreadfully long way away. She took a step towards it. The room swam around her. Another step, but it was like walking in water. Her legs buckled beneath her and she sank, quite gracefully, to the floor.

*

She could hear Mary's voice calling to her – 'Dinah! Dinah!' – but it sounded a very long way off. Then there was another voice, *his* voice, and she somehow knew that the hand holding hers belonged to him. Her eyelids fluttered, the mists cleared a little. She opened her eyes fully and he was there, the face she loved close to hers. Oh Van, Van . . .

Mary was holding a glass to her lips. Brandy. The smell of it made Dinah feel a little sick.

'No . . .' She pushed the glass away.

'Have some water,' Van said.

It was lukewarm, from the carafe beside her bed which she kept there because she often woke in the night and needed a drink and which she had forgotten to empty this morning. But it moistened her lips and revived her a little, though she still leaned back heavily against his arm.

'What are you doing here?' she asked muzzily.

He wiped a trickle of water from her chin with his finger.

'I've come to take you home,' he said.

They were married by special licence three weeks later in a registry office ceremony, because it created less fuss and in any case Dinah could not face a place of worship. Her grandfather, who was her legal guardian since she was not yet twenty-one, refused his permission, so they had to apply to the courts to reverse his decision and then he refused to attend the ceremony. Only Van's parents and Mary, Bob and little Patrick were there to see them make their vows. Dinah looked utterly beautiful in a twenties-style dress of cream silk that skimmed her thickening figure, and though she was still pale her skin had the incandescence of happiness.

Van's parents were less happy. They liked Dinah well enough, but a pregnant twenty-year-old machinist was hardly the bride they would have chosen for their son. Christian Senior had had a few choice words with Van about the whole affair, particularly since he assumed they were going to have to live in the family home, for the time being at least. As a result Van found a suitable house to rent within easy reach of the factory whilst negotiations went on for a permanent home. On the day, however, they put their very real doubts to one side and managed to smile for the wedding group photographs. In fact, Van's mother, looking at Dinah's shining face, wondered if perhaps she had been wrong to worry. The girl was beautiful and sweet and Van looked like a man who had everything he could wish for. Kissing her new daughter-in-law on the cheek, she prayed that he would continue to feel that way.

Dinah was eight months pregnant when Van knew for certain that he could never accept another man's baby as his own.

When he had returned to Mary's house that day in August nothing had mattered to him but having Dinah back with him, and when he had seen her lying on the floor of the cramped little bedroom he had known that whatever the circumstances he wanted only to marry her, take her home and look after her. The child she was expecting seemed unreal, not even a consideration, and in the excitement of arranging the wedding and finding somewhere for them to live he had scarcely given it a second thought. But as she became more obviously pregnant his revulsion began to return, just a slight twinge at first, then growing day by day until it became an obsession.

Had Van been an introspective man he might have realised that he had not given himself time to adjust to the situation as it was in reality before making his decision to marry Dinah with all it entailed. But Van was not introspective any more than he was cautious. He acted swiftly and sometimes rashly and he had little time for the faint of heart or the fence-sitter. Van the entrepreneur, the man of action, was curiously lacking in imagination; he acted on instinct, sometimes blundering blindly after what he wanted with no thought for the consequences. This impetuous side of his nature often brought spectacular success, but equally it occasionally brought disaster. As the time for Dinah's baby to be born drew closer Van knew without a doubt that this was one of the latter occasions. The sight of her swollen body was anathema to him. He did not think he would have liked it very much even if it had been his baby she was carrying; as it was it was much worse, a constant reminder that there had been someone else.

Dinah had tried to tell him once about the way it had been but he had retorted, rather harshly, that he did not want to know. It was true, he did not, but it ate away at him just the same. He became irritated by her bulk, by her seeming inability to be comfortable in a chair, in the car, in bed, and by her constant tiredness. He no longer wanted to take her in his arms and feel that monstrously swollen belly pressed against him. He could not bear to see her naked. He thought of how she had insisted on making love in the dark on that sweet stolen holiday and how he had planned to show her how to enjoy seeing as well as touching – what irony! Now it was he who wanted to make very sure that her body was under wraps. Once he had come into the bedroom and caught her in the act of putting on her nightdress, and the sight of her swollen breasts and distended stomach had seemed to him grotesque contrasted with her still slim and shapely legs.

'For goodness' sake, Dinah!' he had snapped. 'Do you have to?'

He had seen the hurt flare in her eyes but it had not moved him. He was too concerned with his own feelings. That night he slept in his dressing room. From that day on Dinah had been careful to dress and undress without a moment's nakedness, in his presence at least. But even her modesty was irritating to him.

He began working longer and longer hours, but there was little satisfaction at work either. His father was taking an entrenched attitude over the footwear he and Dinah had designed – he had agreed to produce a few pairs of the walking boots, but positively refused even to consider the sandals.

'They are right outside our line,' he said. 'It's not the way I want to go.'

Had he been feeling less truculent Van might have considered that getting the walking boots into production was at least fifty per cent success for his scheme and been satisfied to leave it at that for the time being. As it was he saw only that his father was again frustrating him.

'We have to diversify and the sandals are an excellent way of doing that. They won't even cost much to make since they use up oddments.'

'They will also use up the time of men who are better employed doing what they know. And what about the soles? They can't be cut from scraps. I don't want to do it, Christian.'

'Father, we need a second string if we are ever to grow.'

'Grow? Who wants to grow? This is a good business we have here, just the right size.'

'Tin-pot.'

'I beg your pardon? If that is how you feel about it, Christian, I suggest you go away and start your own business. I won't be told how to run mine by anyone, least of all my own son, who has benefited from it all his life.'

Van sighed. 'I'm sorry.'

'I should think so too! You have hurt me, Christian. One day perhaps your son will do the same and then you will know how I feel. It is not nice, being criticised and told what to do by one's own son.'

Van winced. 'I shall never have a son,' he wanted to say. 'It is not my child Dinah is carrying.' He did not; the question had never been raised at home and he knew that his parents assumed that the doctors had been wrong when they had said he was infertile. They thought, quite naturally, that the baby was his, and he had been too proud to correct the mistaken assumption. But his father's comment reminded him cruelly that the child was not his and that he did not want it. He could not bear the thought of having to see it every day of his life, could not bear to share his home – and his Dinah – with this unwanted intruder. He would be an appalling father, he knew, directing all his resentment at the cuckoo in the nest. He did not want to have to care for some other man's child and he was certainly not going to hand his life's work on to him. He hated the baby now and he would hate it even more when it was there, demanding love and attention and money. Perhaps in the end he would even hate Dinah for foisting it on to him. The fact that he had married her knowing about the baby made no difference. He could not – would not – take the charade any further than he had to.

Van thought about it and he came to a decision. When Van came to a decision it was, as far as he was concerned, a *fait accompli*.

'I can't do it!' Dinah said. She was white with shock and horror. 'Van – you can't be serious! I can't give my baby up for adoption!'

'And I can't keep it,' Van said flatly. 'I've tried to accept it and I can't. I'm sorry, but there it is. At least I'm being honest. Better to face up to it now than to ruin all our lives.'

'It wouldn't ruin mine – it's my baby!'

'But not mine. And it would certainly ruin our marriage.'

'Van, I couldn't! I couldn't!'

'Dinah.' Van adopted a reasoning tone. 'You must know how I feel. I should think it's been plain enough these last weeks and it is going to get worse. What sort of a life would your child have, knowing that his father hated him? Now if he was adopted he would have two loving parents who really wanted him. Surely you can see the sense of that?'

'I can see that you've gone mad! I won't talk about this any more!'

'Dinah . . .'

'Be quiet! Be quiet!' Tears were streaming down her face. Love for her stirred him, then he glanced down at the bulge of her stomach and hardened his heart.

'All right, Dinah, if that's the way you want it. But please realise I am in deadly earnest about this. I will not have this child. I will not bring him up as my own. If you insist on keeping him you can consider our marriage over.'

She took a step back as if he had hit her, hands flying to her mouth.

'Van . . .'

'I mean it. The choice is yours. Me – or the baby. You can't have both.'

'I thought you loved me!'

'I do love you.' His voice softened. 'I love you very much. We can have a wonderful life together, you and I. We are right together, two halves of a whole – and not only in marriage but in business too. We proved that, working on the new designs together. You have the talent and the vision, I have the business acumen and the wherewithal. We could start something new together, branch out and build a company of our own that would be exactly the way we wanted it. And we'd have each other. Wouldn't that be better than you fending for the baby all alone? What sort of a life would that be for you or the baby?'

'I don't believe I'm hearing this . . .'

His voice hardened again. 'You are hearing it, my dear. I'm sorry, but my mind is made up.'

Dinah began to feel sick. She was starting to learn that when Van said his mind was made up no amount of argument or pleading would change it. Once, she thought, she might have been able to sway him, but not now, not with her body so swollen and ugly he couldn't even bear to look at her. And even then, she thought, it might not have worked. Van was totally intransigent, he saw things in black and white, never the shades of grey between. If he had turned so decisively against the baby she did not think that anything on earth would change his mind.

And in a way she understood. She had known right from the start, hadn't she, that there was no way he would accept the situation. That was why she had run away. But Van had come after her and for a little while she had dared to believe she had been wrong. But she had not been wrong. She had been right first time. Van wanted her but not the baby. And that was precisely what he intended to get, no more, no less.

She wiped her face with a shaking hand. 'It's all very well, but what would you tell people? Everyone knows I'm pregnant – your family, friends, employees at the factory, everyone! And they all think the baby is yours. How could you possibly tell them you had had your baby adopted?'

'I've thought of that.' He turned, ostensibly to open a window, but somehow she knew it was to avoid having to face her. 'I'll book you into a private nursing home where I can buy absolute confidentiality. They will arrange the adoption for us – and a very suitable one I know it will be. And we will simply tell all those people you mention that the baby did not survive.'

She gasped then and simultaneously the child kicked within her.

'It happens, doesn't it?' he went on. 'Babies are stillborn, or survive only a matter of days. No one would question you too closely. They would be too afraid of upsetting you. It would work, Dinah. It has to work. Then we can simply get on with our lives.'

It was a nightmare; she felt she was being strangled by the tentacles of some gigantic sea monster and eaten alive. To have thought she was safe – and then to be given this terrible ultimatum!

Yet had she thought she was safe? In the beginning, maybe, but lately . . . no. She had sensed Van's revulsion and known the cause of it. And the knowledge had been a torment. It was too much to ask – too much to ask of any man, and particularly one like Van. Beneath that totally confident exterior lay an Achilles' heel, some insecurity she did not understand. And though his rejection hurt her, yet still it was Van's feelings that were most important to her, more than the baby's, more than her own, more than anything in the world. She worshipped him, she adored him. He was her life: her past, her present and her future. She could not even contemplate losing him now – it was unthinkable. If to keep him she had to give up her baby she would do so. The choice, however painful, was already made.

Strangely, she did not blame him. Van was what he was – if he were not she would probably not love him. And at least, as he had said, he was honest about his feelings. Better that than to see him growing to hate the child that was being passed off as his own, better that than seeing their own relationship deteriorate beneath the pressures and the strains. No, she did not blame Van – typically, she blamed only herself. The imperfection was hers, her own irresponsibility was the root cause of the whole mess. She could not expect Van to pick up the pieces.

Except that he was going to. Not that he was going to put them back together exactly as she might have hoped, but at least he would make some sort of order out of chaos. If she let him play things his way all the burden would be lifted from her shoulders. Van would look after her. In the midst of her pain Dinah knew there was nothing that mattered to her more.

He was a beautiful baby. She saw him only once but she would never forget him. He had big blue eyes that seemed to gaze at her for a moment before closing contentedly, a button nose and soft rosebud mouth, and a mass of dark hair covering his slightly pointed head. She looked at him in wonder, lifting one tiny hand with its little pearly-pink nails and stroking it gently with her thumb. Then she held him close against her breast, breathing in the baby smell of him, loving the warm softness and suffused with a rush of tenderness that made her want to weep at the wonder of it.

She wished then that she could keep him, wished with all her heart that things could have been different. But it was too late now. All the arrangements were made – there could be no going back.

When they took him away she did not protest. She felt calm in a curiously fatalistic way, though her eyes were so full of tears she could scarcely see him properly. She had been told that a couple were already waiting for Stephen, as she had called him. They were delighted with him. But beyond that she knew nothing. Confidentiality was absolute. He had gone, she knew not where, only that he was loved and wanted very much. The knowledge was a sweet, poignant pain, a comfort and a life sentence.

When she was strong enough Van took her home and she had to endure the sympathy of those who thought that her baby had been stillborn. At times she had to struggle with herself not to cry out: 'He isn't dead at all – he isn't! He is alive and well!' But at other times it was easy, for she *was* grieving and Van's family and friends respected her silences and her tears and did not press her to talk when she wanted to be silent.

For a long while she thought the pain would never go away. She ached for her baby, an empty, searing sense of loss that throbbed in her breasts, full and tender in spite of the injections to stop the milk coming in, and pulled in the muscles of her retracting stomach. She stretched out her arms to the empty air as if to hold him, then wrapped them around herself, sobbing in an ecstacy of grief. At night she lay dry-eyed, staring into the darkness, longing for him, wanting to see him just once more. She tried to find the words to ask Van wasn't there please some way the decision could be reversed – couldn't he *please* get her baby back and accept him as his own? But the words remained unspoken. It was too late. She couldn't get him back. And even if she could it wouldn't work.

Gradually, the pain began to lessen and the terrible fits of depression came less often – though over the years they would never go away entirely.

There were other things to fill her life now. Van had found them a new home, a farmhouse which he was having renovated, and Dinah immersed herself in planning decor and choosing furniture. Their funds were far from unlimited – Van's salary was quite modest – but Dinah still had far more cash to play with than she had ever had before and she allowed her imagination full rein as she chose chintzes and wicker, soft natural shaded fabrics and warm unvarnished pine. Only when she came to decide upon the decor for the smallest bedroom did the blackness creep up on her again; this room would have been the nursery. She sat in the middle of the bare board floor, with the boughs of the old apple tree tapping softly against the window, and wept for the baby who would never grow up here, never know this house or her love.

When the decoration of the house was complete and they moved in, she was like a lost soul for a time. But not for long. Christian Senior was still proving stubborn about manufacturing the sandals and Van was becoming restless.

'Bugger the old man – its time to branch out on our own!' he said to Dinah.

'Branch out – how?'

'If he won't sanction expansion at his damned factory, we'll do it ourselves – here.'

'*Where* here?' Dinah asked. A little pulse of excitement had begun deep inside her. There was something electrifying about Van in this positive, dynamic mood that stirred her own latent longing to express the ideas that were simmering away in the depths of her creative mind.

'The old barn could be made into a workshop. The roof is sound; if I had lighting installed, some workbenches and a machine or two, we could make a start – on a small scale at least.'

'With the sandals, you mean?'

'Yes, and anything else you can manage to dream up. Accessories of some kind, perhaps. But not shoes. We don't want to tread too much on the old man's toes.'

Dinah giggled. 'If he's wearing Kendricks' safety boots he'd never notice.'

Van frowned. A sense of humour did not number among his qualities.

'I know he's refused to do anything that smacks of fashion but there's no point upsetting him. See what you can come up with.'

'I'll think about it,' she said, feeling the excitement stir again, making her feel she was standing on the brink of a new and exhilarating adventure, and promising herself that the moment she was alone she would indulge in the almost forgotten luxury of giving free rein to her creative talent.

'Good girl. Come here.'

Van held out his hand to her and she went to him, laying her head against his chest. It was so nice that things were right between them again.

Van seemed to have wiped Stephen from his mind; he never referred to him or his existence. Once or twice Dinah had mentioned him and seen Van's face change, darkening, clamming up.

'It's over now,' he said. 'Best just forget it.'

Dinah knew she could not forget so easily but the sense of loss made her all the more desperate for Van's love and approval.

The revulsion he had felt when she was pregnant seemed to have gone now; they made love often and he was teaching her to enjoy every aspect of physical contact. But though she was a willing pupil his previous rejection of her had gone deep and she could not shake free of the fear that one day he might reject her again. Had it been the fact that the baby was not his that had made him turn away from her in disgust – or had it been the altered shape of her body? Suppose he should feel the same when the time came for them to start a family? She couldn't bear to go through it all over again – and certainly Van had not mentioned trying for a baby of their own. Dinah prayed that she would not become pregnant again by accident, and so far her prayers had been answered.

But her insecurity went even deeper. It was a darkness inside her that she could not explain, unless it was that she had lost Van once and so she might lose him again. Close as they were, and deeply in love, there was a part of him she could not reach and knew she would never possess.

When Van asked her to suggest some more ideas for what he thought of as his pet project it seemed to Dinah not only an exciting challenge but also a wonderful opportunity to impress him with her skills and show him that she was not just a foolish girl who had managed to get herself 'into trouble'. The ideas she had had for the footwear factory had been all very well, but they had been limited to the criteria of fitting in with existing production methods and tailored to appeal to Christian Senior. The walking boots were already doing very well in the markets to which they had been introduced, but they were still boots for all that, and hardly inspiring, and the riding boots had never got off the ground at all. As for the 'Bible sandals', though she was quite pleased with the concept, it was not what she would have chosen to design.

Now Van had suggested accessories and the word opened up a

whole new world to her. Accessories was certainly something she could be enthusiastic about – a wide range to give full scope to her skills.

There were still limits to be observed, of course. She couldn't come up with anything too complicated or complex – they simply did not have the facilities to produce anything beyond the most simple, for there would be room for perhaps only one cutting table and one or two machines at most – but Dinah did not mind that. She had always preferred the classically simple, her taste was for something she had never before been able to indulge – quality, with a hint of the original. Now, carefully bearing in mind that to begin with at least she and Van would have to make up anything she designed themselves, Dinah began her search for ideas.

Since Van's background was in leather, that was an obvious starting point; to it she added her own love of the natural. Searching through countless glossy magazines, scribbling and sketching the ideas for bags and belts that came to her then and at the oddest moments – in the bath, cooking dinner, even, sometimes, in bed – she was at last able to forget her baby, at first for minutes, then hours, then eventually days at a time. At first she was shy and reluctant to show her sketches to Van, and she remembered with a twinge of poignancy how ready she had been when she had first known him to share her inspirations. Now she felt curiously protective, both of them and of herself, as if she was afraid they might suffer the same rejection as Stephen. Perhaps, she thought, it was simply that it was much more important now that Van should like her ideas, because on them the future was to be based; in her heart, though, she acknowledged it was more. Last time around she hadn't known how ruthless Van could be. Now she had first-hand experience of it and she had been left with the bruises.

Van's reaction when she showed him the first set of sketches seemed to bear out her fears. He was at best noncommittal, at worst dismissive.

'They are run-of-the-mill. Not original enough.'

'They are original!'

'Not so as you'd notice. There are belts just like that on market stalls all over the place.'

'I've never seen any!'

'Try going to Portugal, or one of the Greek islands. They're good quality, some of them, too.'

Dinah tried not to be hurt. She went away and tried again, letting her imagination run riot. But this time Van's reaction was even less encouraging.

'Oh my God, Dinah, what have we got here?'

'You said to be original,' she said defensively.

'Yes, but these are completely over the top. Where the hell would you find a market for these – apart from Carnaby Street, perhaps? Can you imagine anyone actually carrying that bag? And we've got to make the stuff, remember. Plaited leather is all very well, but . . . What we want is something simple but exclusive to us. A sort of trademark, to stamp our identity in the minds of the public right from the beginning. Do you understand?'

Dinah nodded. She understood. It was just that she was beginning to lose faith in her ability to do what he wanted. For days the new ideas she needed refused to come, she walked around in a daze, she wept, she pummelled her head with her fists. She thought she was going mad, or having a nervous breakdown, or both. When she could bear the four walls of the house around her no longer she went out for a walk, hoping that the fresh air would blow the cobwebs away but finding to her frustration that the cotton-wool cloud enveloping her had gone along too.

It's no good – I just can't do it! she thought. Oh please, please, let me have just one little inspiration, one really good idea, just to show Van I *can* do it!

Afterwards Dinah always remembered that moment in absolute detail, for it seemed to be the beginning of everything. One moment a sense of helplessness was choking her, the next she looked down and saw a grass snake, its movement a perfect graceful curve through the scrubby grass. It was there so briefly and then gone, but in her mind's eye she could see it still – the markings on its skin, the fluid way it moved. Dinah caught her lip between her teeth; the idea was not just taking shape but exploding in her brain so fast she didn't know if she could catch it.

For the first time for weeks she had gone out without pencil and paper. She hurried home, thoughts racing. When Van came in from the factory at six that evening he found the back door –

and all the other doors in the house – wide open, with the exception of the smallest bedroom, which Dinah had taken to using as a den.

'Dinah, are you all right?' he called anxiously.

Dinah was sitting in the middle of the floor surrounded by pages from her sketch pad. She looked up and smiled, that wonderful come-alive smile that could make his heart turn over.

'I think I've got it,' she said, and he knew from her tone that this time she probably had. But he exercised caution all the same.

'Tell me.'

'Come and see!' She pulled him down on to the floor beside her. 'You see this little grass snake? He's our trademark. See how beautiful he is? He curves into the buckle for a belt and his tail flicks to make a join at the back. Or he can decorate a bag, or even make a clasp. I know you don't want to do shoes, but if you did you could put him around the back of the heel – like this – and if ever, ever, we could get our own fabric printed I'd work him into the design for a silk scarf. Now – what do you think? Don't you think I'm brilliant?'

He had to smile then too. The idea *was* brilliant, exactly what he had been looking for. But he didn't want her to get too carried away.

'Well done,' he said, with more restraint than he was feeling. 'Yes, I think that is one we can use.'

Van decided they would trade under an amalgam of their two names – Vandina. Their logo was the grass snake and their slogan was 'A Touch of the Country'. Van had dreamed that up and Dinah had greeted it with all the enthusiasm he had denied her.

They made the belts in the barn which Van had converted into a makeshift workroom, and to begin with they employed a staff of one.

Fred Lockyear had been with Kendricks from the time he was demobbed from the army in 1945 until he retired, six months previously, at the age of sixty-five. He was a solid and reliable, if unimaginative, craftsman, and he was only too pleased to oblige when Van visited him and suggested he might come out of retirement to work a few hours a week for the new enterprise.

'To tell you the truth I'm bored stiff stuck at home,' he told Van.

'The missus complains I'm under her feet all the time – and I could do with earning a few bob to help make my pension go a bit further.'

When it came to cutting and stitching Fred's hand was as steady as it had ever been, and Dinah took over for the artistic snake emblems which Fred referred to as 'the twiddly bits'.

Van handled the marketing himself. There was no way they could mass produce the belts, and in any case Van did not want to. Their very exclusivity was their selling point – the fact that each was handmade and slightly different. Van went direct to the big London stores, Harrods and Harvey Nichols and Swan and Edgar, and came home with his order book full. Fred and Dinah worked flat out to fill the orders – and within a week the stores were back requesting repeat orders and a sight of any new lines Vandina might produce.

Scenting success, Van sent Dinah to her little studio to refine some more of her ideas ready for production, and Fred brought in his daughter, Mandy – who had also worked for Kendricks before leaving to get married and start a family and who was now glad of the chance of a few hours' work a week – and a cousin, similarly placed, who had been a glove machinist.

'I feel I'm being overrun by Lockyears!' Dinah confided to Van, but she did not mind. They were all good workers, and besides, the cousin's previous work experience had given Dinah another idea – why not gloves? With the help of the cousin, a plump, jolly woman named Marian, she designed a glove with the trademark snake worked in stitching at the wrist.

Glove-making required a different machine. Van went to see the bank manager and arranged for a loan to cover the capital expenditure, and the gloves went into production. Once again, they were a huge success, and since some of the work on them could be done at home, by hand, Marian suggested that some of her former colleagues could be employed as outworkers. In between designing and stitching her 'twiddly bits' Dinah found herself parcelling half-made gloves for the outworkers to collect, checking their handiwork and keeping records.

Now there were simply not enough hours in the day – she was up with the dawn and scarcely ever in bed before the small hours. She did not mind the hard work – being fully occupied meant she had no time for fretting over Stephen – but there were times when she felt she was being dragged away from what she did best: planning and designing. Vandina was, she thought, a little like Frankenstein's monster – it seemed to have acquired a life of its own, taking her over body and soul.

Christian Senior was becoming awkward too. Like everyone else he believed that the baby had been stillborn and at first he had viewed his son's enterprise with a certain amused indulgence, thinking it a harmless amateur operation to give Dinah something to occupy herself and keep her mind off her tragic loss. But as Vandina grew and prospered, with Van still handling the marketing and accounting himself, he began to feel less kindly towards it.

'You are spending too much time fart-assing about,' he told Van bluntly. 'You're hardly ever in your office these days. All you seem to think about is Dinah's damn-fool fripperies.'

'Dinah's fripperies, as you call them, are doing very well indeed.'

The old man snorted. 'A flash in the pan. You'd better stop to think which side your bread is buttered.'

'That is exactly what I am thinking of. I'm looking to the future, and I don't believe it lies in industrial footwear.'

'Industrial footwear pays your salary.'

'For how much longer? I've been telling you for years – working conditions are changing. But you won't listen to me. You're too damned blinkered. You refused to sanction any changes at the factory, so I've taken it into my own hands.'

'At the expense of what I pay you to do!' Christian was becoming angry. Reluctant though he was to admit it, he was experiencing the first niggling doubts that Van might be right; the orders for industrial footwear *were* falling, not disastrously – yet – but certainly the pads were no longer as full as they had once been and it was a long while since the machines had worked at full stretch. The trend worried Christian, but it was not in his nature to admit he might have been wrong, even when the evidence was staring him in the face. Instead he reacted as he always did when doubts assailed him – by digging himself into a yet more entrenched position.

'As far as I am concerned you have two choices,' he growled. 'Either give my company your undivided attention or else get out.'

Van was shocked. He had not expected it to come to this. But he could be as stubborn as his father – and as convinced that he was in the right.

'Very well,' he said calmly. 'If that's what you want.'

'Dammit, Christian, it's *not* what I want! You know that. I built this firm up from nothing – when I retire I want you to take over.'

'Then let me do things my way.'

'Van Kendricks make working boots. It's what we are known for.'

'Correction – it's what *you* are known for. I am going to be known for high-quality fashion, made to Dinah's designs.'

The old man's patience finally snapped.

'Then damn well get on and do it.'

'I will,' Van said coolly.

'But don't come running to me when the bank calls in your loans and you can't keep a roof over your head. I won't bail you out and you might as well know it. And don't think you can manage your wild schemes on my time. You're fired!'

'Very well,' Van said. 'But just remember you are the one who made the decision, not me.'

He went straight to his office and cleared his desk. The quarrel had left a bad taste in his mouth, but at the same time he felt exhilarated with a wonderful sense of freedom. For too long he had been crown-prince-in-waiting. For too long he had had to work in his father's shadow and he had known, deep down, that that would never change. The old man would not retire and leave him to run things his way. Even if he came to the factory less and handed over control nominally it would still be his hand on the reins. Van felt a huge surge of freedom, and with it excitement. From here on in he would be his own man.

It was not, of course, quite as easy or trouble-free as it sounded.

A production company with just a handful of employees operating out of a converted barn as an innovative sideline was one thing – transforming it into a profitable business that would keep him and Dinah in the manner to which they were accustomed was quite another. It had to grow, and grow quickly, if it was to survive, increasing output and turnover many times over. But it had to grow in the right way. Not for Vandina a descent into mass marketing. Exclusivity was its life's blood.

Over long days and longer nights Van evolved a two-pronged strategy.

On the one hand he set about looking for premises that would accommodate a much larger operation; on the other he explored the avenues for market expansion.

The question of premises was solved more quickly and easily than he had dared hope – a local firm who had made electrical components had recently gone into liquidation and Van was able to secure the lease on the factory space and warehousing for what he considered a reasonable outlay. It would have to be gutted and re-equipped, of course, and in order to raise the necessary finance Van had to be able to produce plans and forecasts for vastly increased turnover and profitability.

In some ways it was a classic chicken-and-egg situation but Van revelled in the challenge of it. He left Dinah to make the necessary marketing approaches to the most exclusive British suburban stores and took off on a whistle-stop tour of the shopping capitals of the world, a Gladstone bag containing samples in one hand, an order book in the other.

Three weeks later he was back. Buyers in all the major stores had enthused over 'A Touch of the Country'. He had gained important orders in New York; Bostonians, wooed by the exclusivity, were enchanted. A boutique chain with outlets in the most glamorous shopping malls throughout the Far East had placed a sizeable order – guests at the luxurious Peninsula in Hong Kong, visitors to Penang, Singapore and the Philippines would be able to buy Vandina belts, gloves and wallets. Van had also approached the glossy magazines about advertising – better one horrendously expensive advert in American *Vogue* than a dozen in the cheaper, more down-market publications. And it had already paid dividends – the advert had sparked interest in the editorial department and there was talk of a feature on the new, very English, very exclusive Vandina.

It was time now to work around the clock. Finance had to be raised, the new factory properly equipped, staff recruited, orders for vastly increased supplies of raw materials placed. Van seemed to thrive on the pressure of it alll – he was a powerhouse of energy who could survive quite comfortably on four hours' sleep a night – but Dinah was less resilient. Lack of sleep made her edgy; combined with the stress of worrying about whether they could do it at all, let alone successfully, she sometimes felt her nerves were close to breaking point. She was losing weight, too – burning so much nervous energy and never stopping to eat proper meals were taking their toll. But she did not want to worry Van, so she soldiered on.

There were ups and there were downs, there were times when it seemed the whole operation was fated to collapse about their ears, but somehow they survived, building, building all the while. Thanks to vision, sheer hard work and not a little luck Vandina not so much crept as exploded on to the fashion scene. The rich and stylish were proud to claim they had been the first to discover it; an item bearing the little trademark snake became an accessory which proclaimed not only the wherewithal to shop in the world's top stores but also the mark of the trendsetter.

Towards the end of the first year, just as it seemed that success was within their grasp, Dinah's health finally gave out. The strains on her both mentally and physically proved too much and she suffered a nervous breakdown. The doctors prescribed Librium and a complete break; Van packed her off for an extended holiday in the south of France, but he made sure she took her sketch pad with her.

It was her salvation – and also marked the beginning of a new phase for Vandina. Sitting in a shady spot on the balcony of her apartment, with a warm breeze fanning the pages of her pad, Dinah dreamed up new ideas that would widen Vandina's range – bags and purses, little leather photograph frames around which the grass snake curled enticingly, and even, at last, some designs for the complementary silk scarves which would of course have to be made by a specialist under licence.

By the time she returned she was almost completely recovered, though still not weaned off the Librium. In her absence Van had redoubled his efforts – the workforce now numbered thirty full-time employees in addition to the outworkers, a sales manager, an accountant and a quality controller. But Van refused to relinquish overall control. He still took all major decisions, listening to the promptings of his own instincts rather than advice from others, he still insisted on personally overseeing every aspect. He had the power now that he had always wanted and he used it as despotically as his father had done. Vandina was, quite simply, his life. He did not intend to let anyone else take the smallest part of it from him and he did not intend to share the credit for its creation – not even with Dinah, whose inspiration it had been.

They had been married for almost five years and Vandina was an established success story when Dinah's maternal instinct began to reassert itself. Christmas was approaching; the shops were full of toys and excited children clamouring to see Father Christmas, and the atmosphere of frenetic family gaity had reawakened the sharp, poignant longing she still felt for little Stephen, making her wonder where he was and wish she could buy presents for him and see his face light up when he unwrapped them.

It was of course an impossible dream, she knew that. But alongside it another dream was nudging her more insistently with every day that passed – the desire to be pregnant again, this time with Van's baby. No amount of hard work and success in the business could take away the desperate need to hold her child in her arms, and this time, she thought with hope, it would be different. Another baby would not replace Stephen in her heart – no other child could ever do that – but at least she would know the joy of seeing him grow up, at least there would be something to fill the great yawning hole in her heart.

There was another reason, too, why Dinah wanted a child. Lately Van had been coming home later and later so that Dinah was often alone, and she wondered how even a workaholic such as he was could find business matters to occupy him night after night. She had not criticised or questioned – Van hated both. But she thought that perhaps if he had a son or daughter to come home to he might raise his head and see something outside the four walls of Vandina.

One December evening when Van arrived home at a reasonable hour she broached the subject. They had eaten dinner and were relaxing in front of the big inglenook fireplace where a log fire was blazing and occasionally spitting sparks on to the rough stone surround. Dinah was curled up in one chintz-covered chair; she rested her chin on her hand and looked across at Van, sprawled in the other, a glass of brandy on the small drinks table at his elbow, smoking a cigar.

'Van, I've been thinking. We're pretty secure now financially, aren't we?'

He looked across at her curiously. 'I don't think we're on the verge of bankruptcy, no.'

'It's a bit better than that, surely?'

'Business is good, yes, though it has to be to pay off the loans. But why the sudden interest in our financial affairs? Have you been overspending on the Christmas cheer?'

She shook her head, a rosy blush rising in her cheeks.

'Nothing like that. It's just that I was wondering . . . do you think perhaps we could start thinking about a baby?'

She saw his face change, eyes narrowing, the long lines that had begun to appear between nose and mouth deepening. Her heart sank.

'Don't look like that, Van, please! Wouldn't you like a son, or even a daughter perhaps? I know I would. I want us to be a real family. I know we never seem to talk about it but I . . .'

'No,' Van said. His tone was hard and uncompromising.

'What do you mean – no?' Dinah asked, shocked. 'We want a family sometime, don't we? So why not now?'

He ground out his cigar into the chunk of rock fashioned into an ashtray.

'I don't have any particular desire for a family, now or ever. Children are nothing but an encumbrance.'

'You've never said that before!'

'I've never liked children. Spoiled brats, most of them, sucking you dry and giving nothing in return.'

'Surely you don't *look* for anything. The joy comes from just having them . . .'

'Not for me. We don't need children. We have each other and the business. Why rock the boat? Do you want another drink?'

He drained his glass and got up to refill it, effectively closing the conversation. She gazed at him, numb with misery.

'But I want children!' she said, her voice rising. 'I can't help it, but I do!'

He turned, looking at her, wondering if he should tell her the truth – that choice was not on the agenda. But he knew he could not. His infertility was his secret, he did not want to share it with anyone, and especially not with Dinah who was all too obviously fertile to a fault. And in any case he had spoken the truth. He did not want a child. Not any more. He had lived for so long with the knowledge that he could never be a father that he had not only accepted it but also rationalised it. He was not missing anything, it was his good fortune to have one less thing to worry about.

'Doesn't what I want count at all?' Dinah asked.

The latent sense of inadequacy manifested itself in anger.

'I should have thought you have everything even you could want,' he said cruelly. 'You have a nice home, money to spend as you wish – and God knows, you are not afraid to spend it. You have the opportunity to exploit your bent for design and be recognised for it – that alone is something many young designers with more talent than you have would give a great deal for. I have made you a household name, Dinah, and you ask whether what *you* want comes into it! There is a word for that sort of attitude. The word is ingratitude.'

'That's unfair!' she retorted, the colour rising in her cheeks. 'You make it sound as though I had nothing to do with our success at all!'

'The original idea was yours, I grant you, but you'd not have been able to do anything with it if it hadn't been for me. I've employed craftsmen to translate your ideas into viable merchandise, I've put up the money, I've marketed you. Without me, Dinah, you'd be nothing. I'm not sure you would even have had the ideas without me to goad you, and what ideas you did have would have remained on the drawing board. Make no mistake, I have made you what you are and you would do well to remember it.'

She turned away, tears of humiliation stinging her eyes. She wished she could argue, but she could not. She did not want to fight with him. All she wanted – all she had ever wanted – was his approval and his love. Van was her world. If he did not want a baby then she would not try to force the issue.

She ran to him like a child, clinging to him, needing to grow again through his forgiveness. It was almost as if she *were* a child again, the repressed little girl, threatened by the all-seeing eyes of John Bunyan and his new incarnation, her grandfather. Whenever things went wrong Dinah felt, however irrationally, that she was somehow to blame.

'I'm sorry, Van. I'm sorry!'

Van held her and after a while she felt the stiffness begin to ease out of his body.

'It's all right,' he said. 'Calm down, Dinah.'

'I love you, Van. And you're right, we don't need anything but each other, do we?'

'No,' he said.

But he was not telling the truth.

Van had taken his first mistress while Dinah was in the south of France recovering from her nervous breakdown.

The affair had been brief; Van took what he needed and when he had had enough he dismissed the woman – a temporary secretary at Vandina – from her job and from his life. But the affair had reawakened his taste for variety in his sexual life; the novelty of being married to Dinah had worn off and Van was realising that monogamy was not for him.

Over the years there were to be many women, mostly one-night stands but a few longer-lasting relationships which Van was as adept at ending as he was at everything he did; when he tired, the lady in question was despatched as efficiently and relentlessly as a used cigar butt. One or two were to prove awkward but Van always found the most appropriate pay-off. Surprisingly, he managed to keep Dinah in ignorance of his deviations, or perhaps she simply did not want to know. For her, ignorance was bliss, and whatever the reason Van's exploits never became an issue between them.

As the years passed Vandina became more and more successful, a mini-empire producing lines that were sought after by the rich and discerning the world over, whilst Kendricks, the boot firm, contracted steadily until at last there was nothing left for it but closure.

'Perhaps you had something after all,' Christian Senior said to Van the week before he died. It was the closest he ever came to admitting that his son had been right and he had been wrong.

Van acquired his private pilot's licence – for business reasons, he said, but when he bought himself a Cessna he flew it often for pleasure.

Dinah took things a little more quietly. Her work was still her joy; to it she added a passion for opera and ballet. She learned to ski and took winter holidays in Gstaad and St Moritz, and in the summer she usually spent a month in the Ardèche, where she had recuperated from her nervous breakdown.

That was well behind her now, the last prescriptions for Librium never filled.

As for her desire for a family, she never mentioned it again, any more than she mentioned Stephen, though thoughts of him haunted her still.

Van was her life, he was all she had ever really wanted. No one, Dinah thought, could expect to have everything. As Van had pointed out to her that long-ago December evening, she had been luckier than most – luckier, certainly, than she had ever had any right to expect.

And then Van was killed, and for a time that secure world had fallen apart. But once again fortune had been on her side. Totally unexpectedly, Stephen had returned to her, and his coming had gone some way to fill the awful yawning gap.

In a strange way she felt that Van was with her still. When she was worried or upset she would go to his study and sense his presence, strong and powerful as ever.

In life, in death, Van would always be with her.

Only now there was Steve too.

Chapter Twelve

On the evening Maggie was at Dinah's dinner party, Mike went to visit Brendan.

He was deeply disturbed by what Maggie had told him; the position of the driving seat in Ros's car was almost indisputable evidence that someone other than Ros had been driving it when it was parked at the station, and it had become inextricably entwined in his mind with Brendan's assertion that he had seen her in a Clifton bar with a man. It was possible, of course, that Brendan was lying. Maggie suspected him of being connected with Ros's disappearance, Mike knew, and if he had indeed finally snapped and harmed her in some way then it would follow that he would be anxious to throw in as many red herrings as he could to put Ros's relatives – and the police – off the scent. But either way, Mike thought it was time he spoke to Brendan himself.

When he had finally wrapped up his school team's cricket match he drove home and fixed himself a scratch meal – a tin of corned beef, some tired-looking salad and a jacket potato baked in the microwave, washed down with a can of lager. While he was eating he switched on the TV, catching the end of the local news coverage, but there was nothing to hold his interest – the threat of job losses at a local manufacturing firm, primary school children dressed up in the costumes of the last century to commemorate some centenary or other, an old woman who might have worn one of the original mobcaps and pinafores as a child grinning toothlessly – and dazedly – as she was given a bouquet of flowers to celebrate reaching the grand old age of one hundred and five. The pictures blurred before Mike's eyes. He was just about to switch off when the recap of the headlines began. A body had been found in woodlands. Mike stiffened, nerves taut and jangling suddenly, like the trip wires of a dozen alarm bells.

Ros. The thought hit him simultaneously with the newsreader's words. Then, seconds later, he heard the newsreader qualify the statement – the body was that of a man who had not yet been formally identified but whom police thought was probably a tramp who had been sleeping rough. Mike experienced an enormous rush of relief, but the shadow of dread, raised so suddenly by those first blank words, remained. 'A body has been found in woodlands.' Mike put down his knife and fork and pushed his plate away. He was no longer hungry. He took the remains of his supper to the kitchen and dumped them in the pedal bin. Then he went upstairs, showered and changed.

Brendan, you bastard, I'm coming to see you. I have a few questions to ask you and you had better come up with the right answers.

Mike had never before been to Brendan's flat but he found it easily enough from Ros's descriptions and rang the bell beside the name card in its plastic box. It was a while before the intercom buzzed into life, and Mike was just beginning to think Brendan must be out when the man himself answered with a curt: 'Who is it?'

'Mike Thompson. I want to talk to you, Newman.'

'Mike Bloody Thompson. Well I sure as hell don't want to talk to you.'

'It's about Ros.'

'I don't care what it's about. I'm going out and I'm late already.'

'It won't take more than a few minutes.'

But Brendan had gone. Mike put his finger on the bell again, keeping it there. After a minute the intercom crackled again and Brendan's voice bellowed: 'Fuck off, Thompson, and leave me alone.'

'Not until I've spoken to you.'

'I don't talk to scum.'

'We'll see about that,' Mike said.

His temper, slow to rise, was up now. He'd stay here all night if he had to. But if Brendan was going out it was unlikely that would be necessary. Mike went back to his Citroen, parked in the communal yard at the back of the flats, got in and waited. After about ten minutes the door opened and Brendan came out.

Mike recognised him at once, though Brendan had put on quite a lot of weight since his broadcasting days. Tonight he was looking less raddled than when Maggie had called on him. His jet-black hair was gelled into a fashionable style and he was wearing a white jacket over a black shirt. Reactolite glasses covered his permanently red-rimmed eyes. Mike got out of his car and walked over to him.

'Brendan my friend. I said I'd wait.'

'And I said I didn't have anything to say to you.' He made for his car – a BMW which had once been a symbol of his success but which now looked as if it had seen better days; one wing had been buckled and the indentation was gathering rust. Mike followed him.

'I'm trying to find out what has happened to Ros. You know she's missing?'

Brendan laughed unpleasantly. 'Left you, has she? Just like she left me? Yes, I had heard.'

Mike controlled the temptation to rise to the bait.

'Don't you want to find out what has happened to her? She was your wife, after all.'

'Perhaps someone should have reminded her of that.' Brendan was searching amongst his keys for the one that would unlock his car. Mike wondered how he could detain him, short of physical violence.

'I'm worried about her, Newman, if you're not.'

'For fuck's sake, isn't it obvious? She's gone off with another man.'

Again Mike suppressed the instinct to retaliate sharply.

'What makes you think that?'

'It's obvious, isn't it? When a woman goes off there's always a man. Particularly if the woman happens to be our own sweet Rosalie. She never could keep her knickers on. Haven't you found that out yet? But then perhaps you don't know her as well as I do. And aren't you the lucky one?'

Mike controlled the urge to hit the Irishman.

'You told Maggie you saw Ros with a man in Clifton,' he said between gritted teeth.

'Maggie?'

'Ros's sister.'

'Oh, that Maggie.'

'Who was it?'

'How the hell should I know?'

'Well, what did he look like?'

'I don't remember. Just a regular guy. Well endowed, but then he would be, wouldn't he? Ros wouldn't bother with one who wasn't.'

'And you only saw him the once?'

'Yes – and I'd never seen him before. Satisfied?'

'No, I'm not. Was he dark? Fair? Ginger?'

'Look, Thompson, can't you get it into your thick head – *I don't remember*. He was white, right? About thirty, smartly dressed, good-looking. That's all.'

'OK,' Mike said. 'You don't remember. Well I suggest, Newman, that you start trying to remember. Because if we don't find Ros things don't look good for you.'

'What the hell have I got to do with it?'

'Because if Ros hasn't gone off with someone, if something a good deal more serious has happened to her, then you are Prime Suspect Number One. You've threatened her often enough – she was scared to death of you, Maggie will testify to that. And you are lying when you say that's the only time you have seen her recently.'

'What are you getting at?'

'Maggie sent Ros a scarf for her birthday which, as we both know, is in May. She found it in your flat. So don't try to tell me the only time you have seen her was in a bar in Clifton.'

There was a moment's silence. Brendan had stopped searching for his key.

'It's the bloody truth,' he said at last, but Mike noticed that a haze of sweat had broken out on his forehead.

'So how did you come to have her scarf in your possession?'

Brendan pulled out a handkerchief, a huge square of royal blue to mop his forehead, and managed to knock his glasses askew. He looked, Mike thought, thoroughly rattled.

'She left it behind in the bar that night,' he blustered.

'How very convenient.'

'It was on the back of her chair after she left. I took it home to return to her sometime.'

'But you haven't.'

'Because I haven't seen her. Christ, what is this?'

Mike's hand shot out, pinning Brendan against the car. Brendan was a big man, but Mike, fit from all the sport he played, was stronger.

'I'll tell you, Newman. If Ros doesn't turn up soon, safe and well, I shall go to the police about the scarf – so you had better get your story straight. And you'd better start trying to remember who it was you saw her with too. Do I make myself clear?'

'Get off my back, Thompson!' But the sweat was trickling now in rivers down Brendan's pasty face. Mike had the distinct impression he was afraid – and not just of the threat of physical violence. The note of panic in his voice was more profound than that. He was keeping something back, Mike was certain, but he was at a loss to know how he could find out what it was.

A car turned into the communal parking area. Mike relaxed his grip on Brendan and the other man shook himself free, straightening his jacket and glowering at Mike.

'Do that again and I'll have you charged with assault.'

'If anything has happened to Ros you'll find yourself charged with something a lot more serious than that.'

Brendan unlocked the door of his car and got in.

'Forget her, Thompson, she's just not fucking worth it.' He started the engine, slammed into gear and pulled away. Mike stared after him, impotent in his anger, and wondering whether he dared break into Brendan's flat to see if he could find any more evidence that Ros might have been there. The tenants who had come home whilst he was talking to Brendan had left the main communal door ajar, perhaps they intended going out again. He crossed and pushed it open, then with a quick look round to see if anyone was about, climbed the stairs. But Brendan's own front door was securely locked. There was no way in.

Mike cursed. Perhaps his best bet was to go to the police again. Would they obtain a search warrant? Somehow he doubted it. At the moment they just did not seem interested in the case. If anyone was going to find out what had happened to Ros it was going to have to be him – and Maggie.

He stood for a moment deep in thought. Perhaps if he were to get a photograph of her and show it around someone would remember having seen her – the station staff at Temple Meads, for instance, the booking office clerk or the ticket collector. Ros was the sort of woman men did notice.

The thought jarred on Mike. Men noticed Ros, and if Brendan was to be believed, Ros noticed men. In this, at least, Mike thought her ex-husband was telling the truth and the suspicion did nothing to make him feel better. Perhaps it was the Judy syndrome all over again and Ros had simply walked out on him for another man he knew nothing about. With an effort he pushed the thought aside. It would be all too easy to guard his pride and do nothing. But if something *had* happened to Ros inaction would be no help to her at all.

Mike drove home, found a good photograph of Ros, and visited the railway station. But he drew a complete blank. No one remembered having seen a girl looking like Ros. There were other staff, of course, not on duty at the moment. If Mike would like to leave the picture . . .

Mike was unwilling to do that. He would get copies made and come back again, he said. Then he toured the bars and restaurants in Clifton, asking the same question. He had a little more success here, several waitresses and barmen thought they recognised Ros, but none could come up with any concrete sighting and no one could remember who they might have seen her with. At last, sick at heart and demoralised, Mike treated himself to a drink at The Channings. It was late when he got home again. He noticed he had forgotten to put his answering machine on, so he had no idea if anyone had tried to call him. Well – tough.

Mike drank a glass of milk and headed for bed.

When she woke next day Maggie's first thought, apart from the ever-present worries about Ros and the constant nagging anxieties about her own marriage, was that she could hardly put off contacting her mother any longer. As a maternal parent Dulcie might have many shortcomings but for all that she was still her mother, and the longer Maggie put it off the worse it would be for her, she knew. Dulcie would have stoked up such a sense of grievance that she would be quite impossible and the visit would be even more uncomfortable than it might otherwise have been.

Besides, Maggie thought, it was always possible she did know something without realising she knew it. Ros might have said something to her to which she had attached no importance – Dulcie's powers of deduction were limited and her concentration span practically zero.

Maggie telephoned suggesting she should drive over for lunch, and though her mother's faintly pained tones did not bode well for the visit, she agreed.

'I'll see you later then, Margaret. If something doesn't happen to sidetrack you in the meantime, that is.'

'I'll be there, Mother,' Maggie said patiently. 'I do usually do what I say I am going to.'

'Do you, dear? Then you must have changed a good deal. At least, it may be that you are reliable where your friends are concerned, but with your family it's always been another matter.'

'I'll be there in a couple of hours,' Maggie said grimly.

She made herself some breakfast, showered and dressed. The weather had taken a turn for the worse again; it was chilly and damp with a strong breeze blowing the bedraggled-looking roses in Ros's small front garden. Maggie got into her car and headed for Wiltshire, hoping she could find the way. Navigation had never been her strong point but her mother would never accept the excuse of getting lost as a reason for being late.

Dulcie always referred to the home she shared with the Colonel as a 'cottage', but compared to Ros's genuine article the description was a misnomer. In fact the Ashbys occupied a pretty country house, set in extensive gardens on which Dulcie lavished most of her time and interest. The fact that the lion's share of the hard work was done by a gardener was lost on her; she always referred to 'my roses' and 'my sweet peas' as if she personally nourished and tended each one, when in fact Maggie could not remember ever seeing her actually wield a hoe or pull a weed. Instead she loved to float about with a wooden trug on her arm, planning, criticising and admiring.

'I'm so glad I put the rhododendrons *there*,' she would say; or, 'My phlox are an absolute picture this year – I'll divide them next autumn and make an extra bed.'

To this the Colonel would merely grunt. In his opinion a garden was something which should be left entirely to the hired help so that all Dulcie's attention could be focused on his own well-being.

Today, because of the inclement weather, Dulcie was not in the garden when Maggie pulled into the driveway. Maggie went round to the back door, which was flanked by a conservatory, rang the bell and pushed the door open.

'Mother, it's me!'

Dulcie floated into the conservatory. In her pale trousers and tailored shirt she looked, Maggie thought, ridiculously young. Only the carefully coiffured hair and the network of fine lines around her nose and mouth betrayed the fact that she would never see sixty again. She kissed Maggie, then held her away, frowning slightly.

'Darling, what have you been doing to yourself? You've lost weight. Haven't you been eating properly?'

Maggie suppressed a sigh. Every time she saw her mother she said the same thing.

'I've been this size for the past ten years, Mother.'

'Hmm, I don't know about that. But then of course I so rarely see you.'

'You are looking well, Mother,' Maggie said, changing the subject.

'Am I? I suppose I know how to make the best of myself. Even though I am a perfect martyr to arthritis, and my back goes out at the least excuse.'

Maggie knew about the back trouble – it had always seemed to occur whenever there was an occasion her mother wanted to avoid – but the arthritis was a new one.

'I didn't know you had arthritis.'

'Oh dear, yes! In my hands.'

Dulcie extended them for inspection. Maggie could see no evidence of arthritis – her mother's fragile wrists and slim, tapering fingers with perfectly manicured nails looked to her much as they always had done.

'Sometimes I can hardly bear to hold a knife and fork,' Dulcie murmured plaintively. 'But I try not to complain. Harry fusses over me so if I do. Now, we don't want to talk about my little ailments, do we? Come into the drawing room, dear. I have the coffee pot on.'

The drawing room was small but genteel and, as always, perfectly ordered, cushions plumped, glossy coffee-table books on gardening set out rather pretentiously. Harry was sitting near the window, a cup of coffee on a low table at his elbow, reading the *Daily Telegraph*. He folded it carefully as Maggie and Dulcie entered, managing to make the gesture appear somewhat ungracious, and stacked the paper neatly into a rack strategically placed near his chair.

'Margaret! Your mother was expecting to see you yesterday, you know.'

'I never said I'd come yesterday,' Maggie protested. 'And anyway, I had a migraine.'

'Oh dear, do you get those too?' Dulcie enquired. 'I used to suffer from them dreadfully – I expect you remember. I have been known to lie in a darkened room for anything up to a whole week, but I don't seem to get them quite as badly nowadays. By the time you are my age, Margaret, you probably won't get them at all. And they are obviously not as serious as mine used to be.'

'No, I don't expect they are, Mother,' Maggie said.

Dulcie poured coffee into bone-china cups ('I hate pottery – so clumsy!' she always said) and passed one to Maggie, who perched rather uncomfortably on the edge of a brocade-covered chair.

'So, how is Ari?' Dulcie asked with perfect conversational politeness yet somehow managing at the same time to convey her disapproval.

'He's well. Working hard as usual.' Maggie had not the slightest intention of discussing her marital problems with her mother who would, she knew, delight in them whilst pretending concern.

'And his family?'

'Yes.'

'They don't know how lucky they are,' Dulcie sighed. 'It must be wonderful to be so closely knit.'

'Oh Mother, you know you'd hate to have me and Ros under your feet all the time.'

'Darling, what a thing to say! I should adore to be allowed to share in your lives. I realise where you are concerned that is simply not possible, but Rosalie . . . She lives so close by and yet I scarcely ever see her.'

Maggie's heart came into her mouth and she found herself wondering suddenly whether any of them would ever see Ros again.

'Mother, I am very worried about Ros,' she said.

Harry snorted impatiently and Dulcie sighed.

'So you keep saying. I'm afraid I fail to see what all the fuss is about. Rosalie does her own thing. She always has.'

'Not to this extent. Even Mike doesn't know where she is.'

Dulcie sniffed eloquently. 'The PE teacher, you mean. I expect

Rosalie has found someone more suitable. I never did think he was her style. Even Brendan, unfortunately as he turned out, had more about him. He was a radio personality after all. But a *PE teacher* at that dreadful school . . .'

'Has she ever mentioned anyone else to you?' Maggie asked.

'Good heavens, no!' Dulcie sipped her coffee elegantly. 'There was that Vandina man, of course. She used to talk about him rather often. But that was some time ago now.'

'What Vandina man?'

'The main one – Van something. He sounded foreign. But I think he's dead now. Rather a pity – he would have made a good match for Ros.'

'If you mean Van Kendrick, he was already married.'

'Was he? Oh well, that doesn't seem to stop young people nowadays.'

'He was her boss,' Maggie said. 'Nothing more.'

'If you say so, dear. Personally I think there was more to it than that.'

'Mother, you know how fanatical Ros is about her work,' Maggie said, irritated. 'Van Kendrick's name would have been bound to crop up in conversation.'

Dulcie shrugged. 'Well, since he's dead I suppose it's all academic anyway. And you are right about Ros being fanatical where work is concerned. I really don't know where her drive comes from!'

Not from you, that's for sure, Maggie thought crossly.

'Has Ros seen Brendan recently, do you know?' she asked, changing tack.

'Not that I know of. I was saying the other day, we never hear Brendan on the wireless these days. Do you know why that is?'

'I think he lost his job, Mother.'

'Lazy toad,' the Colonel interjected.

'I beg your pardon, dear?'

'His name came up at the Rotary lunch a couple of weeks ago. Old Forsythe said he'd applied to them for a job. Naturally he didn't get it. With a reputation like his they wouldn't touch him with a bargepole.'

Alan Forsythe, a fellow Rotarian, was a leading light in the local commercial radio station.

'You didn't tell me that!' Dulcie said, piqued.

'Didn't want to upset you, old girl. Thought it better not to, in view of the things that were being said about him.'

'What sort of things?'

'Oh, gone completely off the rails. Forsythe thought he'd gone a bit batty, due to drink probably. Said he was quite irrational and seemed to be going blank-o. Had trouble remembering his own name, according to Forsythe.'

'Oh surely not!'

'Well, you know what I mean. Seen it in the army when a fellow drinks too much – he loses himself. Alcohol destroys the brain cells. It'll be his liver next, mark my words. He'll be dead of cirrhosis before he's forty.'

'Oh dear, I do hope not! Perhaps Rosalie is better off without him.'

'Believe you me, she is.'

'He did behave very badly towards Rosalie,' Dulcie conceded. For a moment she was lost in thought, her butterfly brain working overtime as she put together, for the first time, unpleasant and conveniently forgotten happenings from the past with the more ominous aspects of the present situation. 'You don't think he has harmed Rosalie in some way, do you?' she asked anxiously.

'I don't know, Mother,' Maggie said. 'But I think he could be capable of it.'

'Oh my goodness! Do you suppose we should go to the police?'

'We already have – remember?'

'Oh yes, of course – they came here. But do they know about Brendan? Perhaps *you* should phone them, Harry, tell them what sort of man he is. If you were to mention Alan Forsythe's name, tell them what he knows about him, they would surely take notice.'

'All Forsythe said was that he is useless these days as a broadcaster. There's no law against that, unfortunately,' the Colonel replied testily. 'Don't upset yourself, my dear. What are you thinking of, Margaret, frightening your mother in this way.'

'But if Rosalie . . .'

'Harry's right, Mother,' Maggie said. 'There's nothing new you can tell the police. They seem convinced Ros has gone off of her own accord – just as you were. There's no point getting yourself into a state. There could be any number of explanations for her disappearance.'

Dulcie thought again for a few moments, then brightened.

'You're right. Let's put it out of our minds and talk about something different. Goodness knows, we see you so seldom, we don't want to spoil it by being morbid!'

Her short concentration span exhausted and her ability to shut out anything which might trouble her reasserting itself, Dulcie steered the conversation towards the mundane and the frivolous and, most of all, to herself. When Maggie left, midway through the afternoon, Ros had not been mentioned again.

Driving back to Bristol Maggie tried to convince herself that her mother was right to refuse to be worried. In all probability there was a perfectly rational explanation for Ros's disappearance which she and Mike had refused to acknowledge because it did not suit them to. Dreadful as it was to imagine that something horrific had happened to her, at least it left the image of the Ros they loved intact. But if she had run off with someone else or if she was, as Jayne had suggested, the Vandina mole, taking the salary of one employer whilst actually working for another, and betraying the trust placed in her, then she immediately became a different person, someone Maggie did not know at all. Dulcie, however, looked at it in quite a different light. She could, it seemed, happily accept Ros for whatever she was in the most simplistic way.

Back at the cottage Maggie parked the car, wondering what to do next. The feeling of helplessness and utter frustration was beginning to get to her. She had seen all the people who might be able to help and had come up with nothing. And Ros was still missing.

There was an official-looking envelope addressed to Ros in the mail basket; Maggie took it into the kitchen, tearing it open as she went. She had no qualms now about opening Ros's mail – if she turned up safe and well and was angry about the invasion of her privacy so be it. In the meantime Maggie was anxious to learn everything she could about her sister's life in the search for a clue. On this occasion, however, when she realised that the envelope contained a bank statement she did wonder momentarily whether she was going too far by prying into Ros's finances. But she cast her eye down the statement all the same, noting Ros's healthy bank balance, the input of her substantial salary and a number of large standing orders – her mortgage repayment, insurance premiums and a budget account transfer. Then, somewhere at the back of her mind, alarm bells began to jangle and she ran her eye once again down the column of outgoings.

The statement was a bi-monthly one and in the early weeks regular withdrawals had been made using a cashpoint card. But towards the latter part of the statement there were no such withdrawals. Maggie traced the date of the last one – two days before Ros had disappeared. After that – nothing. The only recent outgoings were a few standing orders and a couple of cheques which obviously pre-dated her disappearance.

Maggie felt sick with sudden dread. Surely if Ros had gone away she would have needed cash by now? The final withdrawal was not a particularly large one – the same fifty pounds that Ros apparently took out for spending money every week. And there were no recent cheques or Switch transactions either, nothing to indicate that she had paid hotel or restaurant bills, nothing to cover a train fare from Bristol to anywhere.

It was possible, of course, that if she was with someone then it was he who was picking up the bills. But Ros was nothing if not independent – she liked to pay her own way. Then again, perhaps she was using Access or Visa, but there was no large payment in the statement which might indicate a credit card bill. And in any case surely she would need *cash*, to make small everyday purchases if nothing else.

Maggie's feeling of foreboding deepened. She glanced at her watch. Mike should be home from school by now – unless he had another cricket match. She went back into the hall, but before she could pick up the telephone it began ringing. Telepathy, she thought. Mike is ringing me. She snatched it up.

'Hello?'

'Maggie? It's Steve Lomax.'

For a moment, her mind elsewhere, she couldn't think who Steve Lomax was. Then she remembered.

'Steve. Hello.' It was difficult to keep the disappointment out of her voice.

'I was wondering if perhaps I could take you out for a drink this evening.'

'This evening?' She was thinking quickly. She had hoped to see Mike this evening, but Steve was a definite link with Ros, a contact with Vandina. If Brendan had nothing to do with Ros's disappearance then something connected with Vandina offered the only other real possibilty.

'Perhaps you already have other arrangements,' he was saying smoothly.

'No . . . no, I haven't any plans for tonight.'

'Then can I persuade you to spend it with me?'

'All right. Why not?'

'Good! Shall I pick you up? Say about eight?'

'Fine. I'll look forward to it.'

She put the phone down, then picked it up again and dialled Mike's number. But it was only his answering machine.

'I need to speak to you,' she said. 'I shall be going out at about eight. Perhaps if you get in before then you could call me.'

She replaced the receiver, and only then did she realise she was trembling.

'So – what was all that about, darling?'

Steve Lomax replaced the telephone receiver and swung his blue leather swivel chair around to see Jayne Peters-Browne standing in the doorway of his office.

Her pose was studiedly sultry – and striking – one hand raised against the door jamb so that the creamy silk of her blouse strained over her full breasts, one hip thrust provocatively forward, but instead of the usual rush of desire he felt only irritation.

As a lover Jayne was matchless; he did not think he had ever known a woman with more to offer. He liked her voraciousness; the fact that she was totally uninhibited was a sensual turn-on. Making love to her was like making love to an active volcano, stimulating, satisfying and somehow darkly dangerous. But the fact that he took her to bed did not give her the right to invade the other areas of his life. It didn't mean she had any claims on him – and it certainly did not mean she could walk into his office uninvited and quiz him on private telephone calls she might overhear.

'Did you want something?' he asked coolly.

For a moment she looked slightly nonplussed. Then her

expression hardened, green eyes sharp, full lips taking on a downward droop.

'Yes, as a matter of fact I did. I wanted to ask you about the plans Dinah has to reverse the Reubens débâcle.'

He leaned back in his chair, eyeing her narrowly. 'Why?'

Again he caught her uncomfortable reaction to his curt reply and suppressed a smile; Jayne was becoming transparent, he thought. She was displaying the first signs of the vulnerability that comes with emotional involvement. But again she recovered herself so quickly that he almost wondered if her momentary discomfiture had existed only in his imagination.

'You're awfully grouchy this morning, darling. What's the matter?'

'There is a door to my office, in case you hadn't noticed. I'd appreciate it if you'd knock on it like any other employee.'

This time her response was a quick blaze of anger.

'But I am not any employee!'

'During business hours you most certainly are.'

'I disagree. Leaving our personal relationship out of it – though to be honest I don't see why I should – I would remind you that I am the senior designer with this company. I didn't realise I had to make an appointment to see you.'

'There's no need to be facetious, Jayne. All I'm asking is that you don't come barging in when I am on the telephone. I think I have a right to my privacy.'

Her eyes blazed. He was fairly certain she had heard enough to know he had been making a date with another woman, and for a moment he thought she was going to confront him with it. But if this was so, she obviously thought better of it.

'All right, *Mr* Lomax,' she said pointedly. 'Would you like me to go out and come in again so that we can begin our conversation on a more sensible basis?'

He swivelled his chair back to face his desk. Desire for her was beginning to stir again. She really was very attractive when she was angry. But he had no intention of letting her see it. 'Treat 'em mean, keep 'em keen' the old saying went. Steve was a great believer in it.

'There won't be any need for that – as long as it doesn't happen again. Come in, sit down. Now, what was it you were asking me?'

'I was asking about Dinah's plans. I can't do my job properly if I don't know what she has in mind.'

'I'm afraid I can't enlighten you. You'll have to talk to Dinah about that.'

'Dinah is in London today. I need to know immediately what she has in mind. If we intend to put a whole new line into production in the spring there is no time to be wasted.'

'I don't think one day will make much difference,' Steve said easily. 'And in any case I don't believe it will concern you. As far as I can gather – and I have to say at this point that I am almost as much in the dark as you are since it was sprung on me, too, last night – as far as I can gather Dinah is dealing with the design and development of her idea herself.'

'But Don Kennedy explicitly said he wanted me in on it!'

'That's not quite what he said. He suggested your opinion would be of value. But it's not for Don to interfere in the design side. He's the money man, pure and simple. Dinah has the last word on the way things are done.'

'That's ridiculous!' Jayne fumed. 'I was hired as chief designer. I have a right!'

Steve felt his desire stir again. He had a brief erotic fantasy in which he threw her, spreadeagled, across his desk and made love to her among the files and correspondence. But he exercised an iron control which hid from her any inkling of what he was feeling.

'Perhaps I should remind you, Jayne, that whatever the terms of your contract, my mother *is* Vandina. The original idea was hers, the early designs were hers and hers alone. She built this company from nothing and if she wants to take complete control of her new project then neither you nor anyone else is going to stop her. What is more, you certainly do not have the right to interfere.'

'I understood she no longer had the time to design and that was why she needed me. She can't do everything, and she has the company to run . . .'

'I have been able to take some of that load off her shoulders and I shall be taking more and more, leaving Dinah free to do what she is best at – design projects.'

'Do I detect a heavy-handed hint here?' Jayne demanded. 'Is my position being undermined?'

He shrugged. 'That's not for me to say. But if you don't like the way things are, well – you know what to do, don't you?'

'I don't believe I'm hearing this!'

He smiled; he was enjoying himself.

'Oh, I wouldn't worry about it. You'd be unlikely to be without a job for long. You're good at what you do, I admit it. Other companies would be queuing up for your services. And Reubens would be top of the list, I am sure.'

He saw the furious colour rise in her cheeks and almost laughed aloud. He'd gone too far, probably; if Jayne did take him at his word and leave he knew Dinah would not be best pleased. But he was fairly certain Jayne would not leave. There was too much to keep her at Vandina.

'Right,' he said, changing his tone now that he had demonstrated his mastery. 'I'll tell Dinah you'd like to be copied in on the new plans, though I'm quite sure she intended to discuss them with you anyway. She'll be back in the office tomorrow and the designs will come with her. Dinah refuses to be parted from her brainchildren for even a moment, I'm sure you know that.'

Jayne did not answer. He could see she was still fuming.

'And about us . . . give me an hour to do some work, then come back – if you like,' he said. 'The boardroom is empty and there's a key in the door. I don't think we've ever made love there, have we?'

She had been on the point of leaving. In the doorway she swung round.

'Steve – fuck off!' she said.

But she returned an hour later anyway, just as he had known she would. He took her to the boardroom, locked the door behind them and adjusted the Venetian blinds to make it impossible to see in from outside. Then he made love to her, not once, but twice, on the dark-blue carpeted floor, and the spat that had taken place earlier only added spice to the encounter.

'The perfect end to a busy day,' he said after the first time.

Jayne was sitting up, buttoning her silky blouse.

'Busy doing what?'

'Checking files. Trying to discover the identity of the Vandina mole.'

'And did you find anything?'

'Not yet. But I will . . . I will.'

'I still think Ros is the prime suspect.'

'Do you? Oh, I'm not so sure.'

And then, with his typically insatiable appetite, he reached for her again.

Chapter Thirteen

Maggie was in the shower when the telephone rang, and at first she did not hear it over the rushing of the water. When she turned the flow off and realised it was ringing she dived for a towel and rushed dripping downstairs, afraid that whoever was on the other end might give up and ring off before she could answer it.

'Hello?'

'Maggie? It's Mike. I found your message when I got home.'

'Mike.' She felt weak with relief. 'Thank goodness! I was beginning to think you'd disappeared too! I tried to get you last night as well but you were out.'

'Yes.' But he did not say where he had been and she did not ask.

'How did your dinner party go?'

'All right, I suppose. I didn't find out anything, if that's what you mean. But it seems there *has* been a mole at Vandina and last night the finger was pointing at Ros.'

'What the hell do you mean?'

'My reaction exactly – at least, at first. And then I got to wondering if it might be possible. There's been a big security leak – a rival company has come out with a spring range that seems to have been pinched from Vandina. This other company went public with the designs just this week and of course it does look awfully bad for Ros. The way they see it she disappeared at a very opportune moment.'

'Maggie, you can't be suggesting that Ros . . .?'

'I didn't suggest it – they did – but I did wonder if we ought to at least consider it as a possibility. But now something else has happened – something very worrying – and I've changed my mind again.' She went on to tell him about the bank statement. 'Surely she'd have needed money by now wherever she is,' she said.

'I'd have thought so, yes,' Mike said grimly.

'I'm so frightened! I've got this awful feeling something dreadful has happened to her.' She was hoping, praying, that he would argue and tell her she was being foolish, but he did not.

'I'm going to get on to the police about this,' he said. He sounded as worried as she was. 'When I've spoken to them I'll be right over.'

'Oh Mike, no, I'm sorry, but I'm going out.' She wished heartily now that she was not; all she wanted was to see Mike but it was too late to change her plans now.

'Tomorrow then? It's Saturday, and for once I don't have a cricket match or anything. No one seems to want to play our boys – they're too bloody rough! But I do have an activities day on Sunday, so I'll be tied up then.'

'All right, but I'm going to have to go now. Steve will be here to pick me up and I'm nowhere near ready. In fact I was in the shower when you rang.'

There was a tiny silence, then Mike said: 'Oh, *Steve*, is it?'

'Steve Lomax. Ros's boss's son.'

'Oh yes,' he said, and his tone was hard. 'I know who Steve is. Well, watch yourself, Maggie.'

'I will.' But as she put the phone down she was wondering just why he had sounded so angry and what it was he knew about Steve Lomax and disliked.

By the end of the evening Maggie had decided that whatever his reasons Mike was right – she did not like Steve very much either.

He was charming, yes, perhaps a little too charming, as if the syrup had been dolloped on with a spoon and spread about to create the right effect. He was courteous and attentive – the perfect gentleman. He was intelligent and good company. But Maggie thought he was also conceited and there was an edge of something else she did not quite understand, a hint of something darkly dangerous. In one respect it added to his attraction, and she thought that to many women Steve would probably prove irresistible.

That edge had come, she imagined, from the life he had lived. He had been a diver at one time, he had told her, working on an oil rig in the North Sea. From what little she knew of such things she guessed it was dangerous work, a maverick existence, certainly very different from the life of luxury he lived now. Maggie had looked at him across the table at the country pub where he had taken her and noticed the exquisitely made shirt, which she was sure was Turnbull and Asser, open at the neck with apparent carelessness to reveal a heavy gold chain, the stylish but immaculate haircut, the Rayban sunglasses tucked into his top pocket, and thought that this was a man who might once have been a rough diamond but had now been cut and polished to a degree which she found positively off-putting. To her mind he was trying too hard to be both suave and macho and for her, at any rate, it did not work. She much preferred the genuine maleness of someone like Mike, who probably threw on the first thing that came to hand and looked in the mirror only once a day, to comb his hair and shave.

'No news of Ros, I suppose?' Steve asked, offering Maggie a Camel.

She shook her head to both the question and the cigarette, lighting one of her own export Silk Cut instead.

'No. Nor at Vandina?'

'No. I'm sorry if Jayne upset you last night with what she said about Ros. She likes to be dramatic.'

'She did upset me a little,' she admitted. 'But I know my sister better than to take notice of such wild accusations.'

'Someone at Vandina *is* passing information about future plans to the opposition. It's not something to be taken lightly.'

'Whoever it is it is certainly not Ros,' Maggie said firmly. 'In fact I'm beginning to wonder if Ros might have discovered the identity of the mole and that's why she has disappeared.'

His eyes narrowed behind the haze of cigarette smoke.

'What are you saying?'

'It's a serious business, isn't it, espionage of any sort? This isn't spying on the international scale, I know, but where companies like Vandina are concerned there must be a great deal of money involved. I know it sounds melodramatic, but is it possible that if Ros discovered who it was who was playing these very expensive games and threatened them with exposure something might . . . happen to her?'

His lip curled up a fraction; he looked incredulous and almost amused.

'Like what?'

'I don't know. But something serious.'

He laughed outright. 'You've been watching too many spy films.'

Maggie tapped ash from her cigarette, rolling it nervously around the rim of the ashtray.

'Maybe I'm wrong about the industrial espionage connection. But I do honestly think that something dreadful has happened to Ros. I don't want to think it, believe me, but the signs are not good.'

'What signs, exactly?'

She told him, finishing with the latest piece of evidence, the bank statement. Catalogued all together it made a bleak and damning picture.

'Yes,' he said when she had finished. 'I begin to see why you are so worried. Look, if there is anything I can do . . .'

His hand slid across the table to cover hers; slightly embarrassed she removed it.

'There is one other thing. Her ex-husband, Brendan, claims to have seen her with a man in Clifton, and it wasn't Mike, her boyfriend. You wouldn't have any idea who it might have been, I suppose?'

He shook his head. 'If you mean do I know anyone else who might figure in Ros's life, the answer is I have no idea – though she was quite a girl. Did this Brendan tell you what the man looked like?'

'Not really. White, aged about thirty. That's all he could say.'

'Hmm. That description would fit a good proportion of the entire male population.'

Maggie sighed. 'I know. It's hopeless.'

'Another drink?'

'Yes, all right.'

She watched him go to the bar, saw the way the barmaid responded to his suntanned, blond good looks and the way he was chatting her up, and wished more than ever that she had not come. She had learnt nothing new and Steve made her uncomfortable in a way she could not quite put a name to. Perhaps it was that after three years of marriage she had got out of the habit of being alone with an unattached man and she did not know how to handle it any more. Maggie made up her mind to escape as soon as she could.

When he returned with the drinks the conversation turned away from Ros, and Steve entertained her with anecdotes of life on an oil rig. He was amusing but a little boastful, the hero of every tale, and Maggie sensed he had moved his chair a little closer to hers.

'I think perhaps I ought to be going home,' she said.

'Really? It's only just after ten.'

'I know, but I am expecting a phone call. From my husband,' she added. It was a lie, but she thought suddenly: Perhaps I should ring Ari. She had been hoping he would ring her – at least it would show he was thinking of her – but he had not.

'You're married then?' Steve sounded surprised.

'Yes. Hadn't you noticed my ring?'

'I had, but I didn't know it meant anything. A lot of people are married, as far as it goes.'

'I am most definitely married,' she said. 'I came over to see if I could find out what has become of Ros, but my husband couldn't get away. He has his business to think of.'

'I see.' But his manner had changed marginally and when he left her he did not suggest another meeting.

Again Maggie thought of ringing Ari but it was now a quarter to eleven. Taking the time difference into account it would be almost one in Corfu. If he was at home he might very well be in bed and asleep. If he was not . . . Maggie decided she did not want to know if he was at home.

She made herself a cup of Ros's cocoa and sat for a while drinking it. Then she went to bed.

Sometime in the night Maggie woke. The wind had got up; a branch was banging intermittently against the window, but she did not think that that was what had woken her. It was her mind, chasing furiously around after something she could not quite catch.

She turned on to her back and lay trying to figure out what it was that was bothering her. Then quite suddenly she knew . . . and wished she did not.

In the darkness she seemed to hear Steve's voice, with its slight transatlantic drawl: '. . . If you mean do I know anyone else who might figure in Ros's life, the answer is I have no idea – though she was quite a girl . . .'

Was quite a girl, not *is*. Did that mean that Steve thought Ros was dead?

The wind slapped the branch against the window again and moved through the shrubs in the garden so that it sounded for all the world as if there was someone out there, creeping about. Maggie shivered and pulled the duvet well up under her chin. She did not think she had ever felt more alone in her life.

Mike arrived soon after ten. Maggie had been up since dawn, restless with the kind of frustrated energy that destroys when it has no directional outlet. She was pale from anxiety and lack of sleep with dark smudges accentuating the tiredness of her eyes.

Mike took one look at her and said firmly: 'We are going out.'

'Where? Have you got some kind of lead?'

'Nothing to do with Ros. We are going out to give you a break.'

'But we can't just do nothing. Not with Ros still missing.'

'There is nothing we can do. Not a thing. I went to the police last night and told them about Ros's bank statement and I have the impression they may take a little more interest now. They are the ones to do it, Maggie. We have exhausted every avenue we can. And exhausted is the word. If you don't take a break and relax a little you are going to crack up. Who would that help? Certainly not Ros.'

'We could take her photograph around . . . show it to a few more people.'

'It won't do any good. She's not a missing teenager who might be discovered sleeping rough somewhere. We would need blanket coverage to get us anywhere at all . . . Hey! That's a thought! I wonder if we could interest the newspapers in this? If they ran the story of her disappearance together with her photograph then maybe there would be some response! Especially if the nationals picked up on it!'

'Do you think they would?'

'I don't know, but I should think there's a story there – especially with you having come over from Corfu especially to try and find her. The only snag is . . .'

'What?'

'If she *has* simply gone off with someone else we shall look prize fools – especially me. And I should think she would be furious with us.'

'If she's done that she would only have herself to blame for not keeping us in the picture. And I don't mind looking a fool. I'd far rather that than find out I was right to be worried, wouldn't you? Oh Mike, let's do it, please! Let's do it now!'

With the prospect of action her tiredness was dropping away.

'It's Saturday,' Mike reminded her. 'The papers are probably on a skeleton staff.'

'There must be somebody working there! What would go in Monday's edition if there wasn't?'

'True. Do you want to phone then?' He still sounded doubtful. It was a major step for him, Maggie realised. Once they went public with the story of Ros's disappearance the full spotlight of publicity would be turned on him. It was all very well for her, she didn't live here, wouldn't have colleagues, friends and acquaintances all speculating about her personal life. She wouldn't have to go to work and face the barrage of questions, the innuendoes. Going public would turn Mike's very ordinary private world into a circus – and if indeed Ros had ditched him and gone off with someone else then it would cause him the most appalling embarrassment. But Maggie was beginning to be sickeningly sure Ros had not gone off with someone else – not of her own free will, anyway.

'Don't let's phone,' she said. 'They may try to fob us off. Let's go to the office. At least we would be doing something positive. It's this not being able to do anything that's driving me mad.'

He sighed. 'All right, Maggie, I'll take you,' he said.

The *Western Daily Press*, together with its sister paper the *Bristol Evening Post*, occupied an impressive office block on Temple Way in the centre of Bristol. Saturday-morning traffic roared in a ceaseless stream beneath the underpass and around the roundabout on which it stood.

As Mike had suggested, the offices were half empty for the weekend, but a reporter attached to the news desk came down to see them, a young woman in her mid to late twenties who introduced herself as Sheena Ross. She listened to what they had to say, her biro flicking busily over the pages of a reporter-style notebook in a series of unintelligible squiggles that might have passed for shorthand, and studied the photographs of Ros that they had brought with them.

It was, she told them, a story that needed to be properly investigated and presented. She would talk to her editor about how it should be handled and be in touch with them – probably on Monday. But for the first time Maggie felt someone was actually listening and believing.

'If the paper take it up then perhaps at last the police will feel obliged to take us seriously,' she said to Mike as they left.

'I think they might already be doing that.' He took her arm, steering her back towards the short-stay car park. 'At least yesterday I didn't feel I was being dismissed as a complete crank.'

She nodded, but it didn't really make her feel any better. It didn't mean Ros was safe; if anything it made her fears more real.

'What would you like to do, then?' Mike asked.

'Nothing. I don't know how you can even suggest running around enjoying ourselves under the circumstances.'

'I am not suggesting a wild party. I just think it's very necessary for both of us to try and relax a little if we don't want to crack up altogether. If it was a nice day I'd suggest a picnic at Ashton Court, but as it's not we'll go down to the Watershed, unless you have a better idea.'

'You know I haven't!' she snapped.

He ignored her bad-tempered response, driving through the centre of the city to the picturesque development on the floating harbour, where an attractive row of shops and restaurants and the exhibition buildings where the wine fair was held each year fronted the water. Dozens of small craft were tied up at their moorings and a river boat was plying for trade.

'A trip up the river – just the thing to calm frayed nerves,' Mike said.

'For you maybe. Not for me.'

'For anyone.'

In spite of herself Maggie had to admit it was relaxing. In better weather and under different circumstances she thought she would have enjoyed it very much. Whenever the conversation threatened to turn to Ros, Mike steered it away again, talking about his job, the restoration project in progress on Brunel's great iron ship, the *Great Britain*, which they passed – anything to keep away from the great dark shadow which haunted them. When they stepped back on to the quayside they had coffee and pastries at a waterfront café and trawled the shops. At a craft stall Maggie bought an amethyst brooch which took her fancy, though she was immediately overtaken by a feeling of guilt that she could do something so frivolous whilst Ros was still missing.

'What would you like to do about eating this evening?' Mike asked. The afternoon was wearing on, the crowds beginning to thin out. 'Shall we look for a pub doing bar food on the way home?'

'No. Let's eat in.'

'A takeaway, you mean?'

'No, I'll cook something.' Inexplicably Maggie suddenly felt she wanted to be busy. 'And let's not have it at the cottage. Everything there reminds me Ros is missing. Could we do it at your place?'

'If you like. But it's in a bit of a mess . . .'

'I promise not to even notice.'

Mike took her into Broadmead and drove a couple of circuits around the town centre while she went into Marks and Spencer and bought food and a bottle of wine.

'What's on the menu?' he asked when he picked her up again.

'Wait and see.' Almost without realising it Maggie was beginning to enjoy herself.

Mike occupied the basement flat of a tall old house facing on to one of the less salubrious stretches of the river. It was surprisingly large and light and, considering what he had said, not nearly as untidy as Maggie had expected. His unwashed breakfast things and an empty cornflake packet adorned the draining board, newspapers and a sports schedule he had been working on were spread over the thirties-style golden oak dining table, and a tracksuit and trainers lay where he had dropped them in the tiny bathroom, but compared to Brendan's chaotic living conditions it was a palace.

'I have a woman who comes in twice a week to clean up,' he said by way of explanation. 'She keeps things under control. Left to my own devices I should soon sink in a sea of muddle.'

'I don't believe you,' Maggie said. 'Now, just show me where everything is and leave it to me.'

'If you're sure . . .'

'Quite sure.'

'Would you like a drink to be going on with?'

'What have you got?'

'Not a lot. Lager, the dregs of a bottle of whisky . . . You could start on the wine if you like but it won't be cold yet. Wait a minute – I think there might be some red left in a wine box – I had it for a party and I never drink the stuff myself.'

'That'll be fine.'

Mike retrieved the box from a shelf and managed to squeeze out a glassful for Maggie, then he helped himself to a can of lager from a six-pack in the refrigerator.

'I'll leave you to it, then.'

He went into the living room; a few minutes later when Maggie put her head round the door to ask him where to find aluminium foil she saw that he had thrown himself full length on to the shabby overstuffed sofa – also thirties-style – and was watching motor racing on television.

'Sky,' he said a little guiltily. 'I indulged myself. Sport is the only thing I watch television for – this way I can get a constant diet of it.'

She smiled and went back to the kitchen, thinking how much she liked him. There was a solidity about him that was incredibly comforting, far removed as it was from any flamboyance or conceit, and at the same time he was easy to be with, a man so confident in his own masculinity that he had no need to resort to aggression or overt domination to massage his self-image, and she could not imagine him indulging in womanising either.

Lucky, lucky Ros!

When the meal was ready Mike bestirred himself from the sofa, sweeping all his papers into a pile and dumping them on an already overflowing magazine rack. Then he set two places with huge oval basket-weave mats and stainless-steel cutlery with startling red handles, and opened the bottle of Chablis.

'Am I allowed to be told now what we're having – or do I have to wait and see – and guess?' he asked.

Remembering Ros's exotic concoctions, Maggie laughed.

'I don't think you'll have any difficulty recognising what I've got for you!' she teased.

The food was simple but delicious – salmon steaks with tiny new potatoes and a selection of baby vegetables, followed by summer pudding running with rich red fruits and dairy ice cream.

'This is one of the things I really miss,' Maggie said, wiping blackcurrant juice from the corners of her mouth with her fingers. Mike did not seem to have any napkins.

'Summer pudding?'

'Marks and Spencers food. Nobody does cooked chicken with skin that tastes like theirs. And their sandwiches! Out of this world!'

'You'll have to persuade them to open a branch in Corfu.'

Maggie laughed. Almost without realising it she had relaxed, the tensions draining away with every sip of wine. Mike had been right – today had been exactly what she'd needed, an oasis of normality in which to recharge exhausted batteries.

'I can't see them doing that somehow. But it would save me a fortune in postage – or Ros, anyway. She buys underwear and tights and things for me and sends them out. At least she did . . .' She bit her lip as the mention of Ros brought it all flooding back.

'Tell me about Corfu,' Mike said hastily, pouring coffee from a cafetiere. 'I've never been there.'

She followed his lead, determinedly turning the conversation away from Ros, though the hollow ache of anxiety was back inside her.

'I thought everyone had been to Corfu. In the summer the island seems to be overrun by the English – and, of course, Germans and Italians too.'

'Living there is a very different thing to being on holiday, though. You must have found it very strange at first.'

'I guess I still do in some ways – attitudes mainly. I enjoyed getting used to the food and the sunshine and the boutari and siesta. But I don't like the fact that Ari won't let me get a job and I find the closeness of the family claustrophobic. They tend to live in one another's pockets far more than we do.'

'But you get on well with them?'

'Well enough, I suppose. Though to be honest, they weren't exactly over the moon that Ari wanted to marry a foreigner, and of course I had no prika – dowry. A good daughter-in-law should bring a few olive groves with her at least. Having nothing was rather a black mark against me. Just the first of many, I'm afraid.'

He raised an eyebrow and she went on, slightly embarrassed: 'No, I'm afraid I'm something of a disappointment to them. But what really gets me is the fact that although family solidarity is considered so important it's only his family that count. Ros is *my* family but there was the most ridiculous fuss when I wanted to come to England. Ari couldn't – or wouldn't – understand that I simply had to come over and try to find out what had happened to her. He was really quite unreasonable about it.'

Mike spooned sugar into his coffee. 'I don't know that I blame him for that. If you were my wife I don't think I'd be too keen on you running all over the world without me.'

There was something in the way he said it that brought the quick colour to her cheeks – and not just because of the implied criticism. But before she could reply the telephone began to shrill. Mike got up and went into the hall to answer it, and she sat toying with her cup of coffee, telling herself she was mad to read anything at all into his words; that she was overwrought, emotional, imagining things . . .

She heard Mike come back into the room and did not look round, afraid he might somehow be able to read her thoughts.

'Well,' he said, returning to his place, 'that was odd.'

'Who was it?'

'Nobody. Just a lot of crackles and whines. Then the line went dead.'

'Wrong number perhaps.'

'Perhaps. But it sounded distant, almost, the way international lines sound when they're not working properly. You didn't give your husband this number did you?'

'Of course not.'

'Oh well, if it was something important I guess whoever it was will ring again. Shall we clear this up and sit back?'

They carried the dirty dishes to the kitchen and Maggie drew a bowl of water and washed up while Mike dried and put away. But he was still thoughtful and for the moment the ease of communication between them had gone.

'You're very quiet,' Maggie said, emptying the water away and wiping down the sink with a slightly tatty dishcloth.

'Just thinking.'

'What about?'

'Oh . . . wondering if it might have been Ros on the phone. Perhaps I have blown this whole thing up. Perhaps she's just gone off with someone else and she was trying to ring and tell me so. After all, Brendan did say he had seen her with another man.'

'You can't believe what Brendan says. He's a pathological liar and he is also insanely jealous. When he and Ros were married he was forever accusing her of having affairs with everyone she met.'

'Perhaps she gave him cause.' He was leaning against the cooker, arms folded, body language studiedly casual. But his eyes were narrowed, his expression suddenly hard.

'Not Ros!' Maggie flew to her sister's defence. 'She wouldn't!'

'She did.' There was something vaguely shocking about the flatness of his tone, a certainty that brooked no denial.

'Ros . . . had affairs? How do you know?'

'Oh, let's just say I know. One was her boss at Vandina – the big white chief Van Kendrick himself.'

'They had an affair?' Maggie asked, but already she was remembering how her mother had hinted at something of the kind.

'They certainly did. Hot and holy while it lasted.'

'Did Dinah know?'

'Van was a womaniser by all accounts. If Dinah did know she turned a blind eye to it. Anyway, that was all over a long time ago. Van was killed in a plane crash, or died of a heart attack at the controls and then crashed – they never knew which for certain. The plane burst into flames and Van was too badly burned for the autopsy to have any real meaning. But the fact remains, have an affair they did.'

'I see. And you think . . .'

'I don't know what I think any more.' Mike moved suddenly, throwing the tea towel down on a work surface. 'Let's go and sit down.'

'I ought to be going . . .' But she didn't want to. She had enjoyed today and she did not want it to end. Even this unwelcome conversation was better than no conversation at all, alone in Ros's cottage with her thoughts, with the branch slapping against the window and the wind sounding for all the world like someone creeping around in the garden.

'You don't need to go yet, do you?' Mike said.

'No, I guess not.' It had been easy to be persuaded.

They went back into the living room. Mike put the coffee pot on again and Maggie noticed an ancient record deck tucked away under the heavy oak sideboard.

'Can we have some music on?'

'Yes, if you like. I should have suggested it before but I didn't think. I tend to go for peace and quiet.'

'What have you got?' Maggie asked, investigating the untidy pile of LPs and a few tapes.

'Not a lot. I'm not the world's greatest music freak.' He joined her, squatting on the floor. 'The 1812 Overture and Ravel's *Bolero* – not exactly late-night coffee-drinking music.'

'What about this – Chris de Burgh?'

'That's Ros's.' Again there was something very final in his voice, and Maggie picked up the vibes. Ros's tape held too many memories of Ros. 'Lady in Red' might even describe her – Ros wore a lot of red. In his present mood Mike did not want reminding.

'Here we are – this will do.' It was Simon and Garfunkel. She passed it to him and he put it on. The strains of 'Bridge Over Troubled Water' filled the room.

'I'm by your side . . . When darkness comes . . .'

Maggie experienced a sudden wave of bittersweetness. She bent over the tapes to tidy them but succeeded only in knocking the pile across the floor.

'Oh no, I'm sorry . . .'

'Don't worry about it.' He dropped back to his knees and together they retrieved the tapes, restacking them. 'I really should organise them better . . . Oh my God, the Bay City Rollers – shades of my youth! Red tartan tam o'shanters – remember? No, I don't suppose you do. You'd be too young.'

'I used to see them on children's TV on Saturday mornings . . .'

They were laughing, relaxed again. Then suddenly their eyes met, laughter dying away. Mike reached for her, a hasty, instinctive movement, yet somehow it seemed to Maggie to happen in slow motion. One moment they were looking at one another, the next his mouth was on hers and she was kissing him back with a hunger she had not known was in her, drowning in a rush of desire which had crept up on her unnoticed and which seemed to obliterate all thought, all feeling, beyond her sudden aching need for him. His arms felt good about her, the smell of his skin was sweetly sensuous, the taste of his lips aroused responses in her, the compelling power of which she had forgotten. It was so long, so long since she had wanted someone so much that it hurt. The world around her seemed to stand still whilst all the electric energy of the universe was locked within her, so explosively concentrated that she felt she would burst wide open from the wonderful singing, pulsating pressure of it. She remained motionless in the circle of his arms and felt as if her very soul was being drawn into her lips, then, slowly, the rest of her began to be drawn to him as if his body was magnetising hers, the core of him drawing her own core with a power so intense the reverberations of it echoed through every vein and not only her arms and legs pricked and tingled but her fingers and toes also. She moved then, just a tiny wriggle that brought her hips against his, and felt the sweet sharp tug of an invisible cord in the depths of her as her most sensitive nerves registered the contact. Her breath caught in her throat, she wriggled closer still, relishing the moment but wanting more, still more.

Was it possible to experience so much delight and still climb higher? To be in someone's arms, two layers of clothes between, and experience such exquisite awareness? Her conscious mind was neither asking nor answering, yet instinctively she knew that it was, though in those few moments she had already reached a peak of sensual joy usually achieved only at the moment of climax. She pressed against him, lost in a world where nothing existed beyond the two of them and the rightness, the inevitability, of their closeness. Then, almost without warning, the perfection shattered. Mike's arms were no longer about her, his lips no longer on hers. She felt him go from her, opened her eyes and saw him moving away.

The sense of loss was unbearable, the absence of touch a physical pain. She wanted to cry out from it. Instead she crumpled to a sitting position, feeling strangely vulnerable as well as cheated.

'I'm sorry.' Mike's voice was rough. 'I shouldn't have done that.'

'I wanted you to.' She said it softly, humbly. The admission only seemed to increase her vulnerability to the emotions that were tearing her apart and to the sense of hurt.

'Then you shouldn't.' He sounded angry. 'You're a married woman, for God's sake. I know that and so do you. You have a husband waiting for you in Corfu. No wonder he didn't want you chasing off on your own. You're all as bad as one another.'

The unfairness of it stung; suddenly she was close to tears.

'You don't understand . . .'

'I understand very well. I understand enough to know I'm not going to do what some bastard did to me. Come on, I'll take you home.'

She did not move, only wrapped her arms around herself. She was trembling, the tears welling in her eyes.

'Mike, don't, please! Ari . . . well, it isn't quite the way you think.'

'In what way?'

'In every way. Oh, I know it would be wrong but . . .' She broke off, shame at her own emotions and at how close she had come to betraying Ari overcoming her. It wasn't just the physical betrayal that had been so imminent; she had also been on the point of baring her soul, breaking the confidences that are between a man and wife. She was not sure which was worse; both were damning.

'You're right,' she said in a small voice. 'I expect I'm overtired and overemotional and I've probably had too much to drink. I'm sorry.'

'Dammit, Maggie, stop apologising!' He still sounded angry but in a different way, as if he was no longer angry at her but at himself. 'I was the one to blame. Let's have another cup of coffee and forget it happened.'

But they both knew they would not forget. For the moment the warmth and closeness had gone, the wave of desire which had almost swamped them broken, but the swirling eddies were still there, washing around them. Maggie looked at him and still felt the pull towards him, a pull that was more than the need for comfort and companionship which had at first disguised it, the indefinable attraction that sparks sometimes between one man and one woman. She wanted him, she knew that now. Her body had demonstrated what her senses had refused to acknowledge. She wanted him more than she had ever wanted anyone in her life. No sense of shame, no telling herself it was wrong could stop that.

She remained sitting on the floor, hugging herself with her arms and shivering slightly whilst he went into the kitchen to make more coffee. He brought it back and set it down on the carpet beside her, taking his over to the sofa. Paul Simon was singing 'Scarborough Fair' now and the wistfulness of the tune seemed to echo Maggie's aching emptiness.

'What did you mean when you said things between you and Ari weren't quite the way I thought?' Mike asked. He said it conversationally, but the underlying tension told her he had probably been turning it over in his mind whilst he had been making the coffee.

She bit her lip. 'Just that, really. But I shouldn't have said it at all. It was very disloyal of me.'

'Disloyal?'

'To Ari. It's not right to discuss my relationship with him. It's something between the two of us.'

'I see. Do I take it that means you are not happy?'

'Mike . . .' Again she struggled with her conscience; this time the desire to explain won. 'Not really,' she said. 'We do have our problems.'

'Because of the culture divide, you mean?'

'Partly. But it's not only that. There are . . . other things.'

'Such as?'

'Just . . . things. I don't want to talk about them.'

'Another woman, you mean?'

She looked up sharply. 'How did you know?'

He shrugged. 'It's not so difficult to guess. From my own sorry experience I tend to expect women to be the ones who are faithless, but I'm not so naive that I don't know men are just as bad – perhaps worse.' He poured a coffee and put it down on the low table beside her. 'I'm sorry for what I said just now. I don't believe you are a woman who plays fast and loose. In fact I'm damned sure you're not. It was myself I was angry with for taking advantage of you.'

She looked up at him, felt the longing twist within her again.

'You weren't taking advantage of me, Mike – honestly. Perhaps it's wrong of me but I think I have been wanting something of the sort to happen all day – maybe before that even.' She paused, a little tremble coming into her voice. 'And I certainly want it to happen again.'

'So – tell me about Ari.' His voice was rough.

She told him and this time she left nothing out. She told him how she had met Ari and fallen in love, how she had gone to Corfu to marry him against all advice, full of hope and determination to make it work. She told him how hard she had tried to be the sort of wife Ari and his family expected, accepting the differences in lifestyle because she loved him and because this was what she had taken on. She talked of her failure to become pregnant and how Ari blamed her entirely for it, refusing to seek help because of his fierce Corfiote pride. She told him how everything had begun to fall apart, about her desperate loneliness, the feeling she had somehow been consigned to a backwater where life was passing her by. And when there was nothing left to tell but her certainty that Ari was having an affair with Melina she told that too, starting with the late-night drinking sessions with the boys about which, though they were common practice amongst Greek men, she had begun to be suspicious, on to the other pointers, such as the perfume which clung to his jacket, right through to his refusal to deny that he was having an affair with his secretary.

'The awful thing is, he would probably be better off with her,' she said, acknowledging the truth of it fully for the first time. 'You were right about the culture gap being the root of the trouble. With Melina that wouldn't be a problem. I think Ari regrets marrying me. And Melina would probably give him a child too. Corfiote women seem to be unusually fertile.' She said it without bitterness but the sadness was there all the same.

'I see,' he said. 'You weren't exaggerating, were you, when you said you weren't happy?'

She sipped at the coffee which had gone cold as she talked.

'Now tell me about you. It's not fair these confidences should be so one-sided.'

'Me? There's nothing to tell.'

'I'm sure there must be.'

'All right.'

He told her about Judy, who had destroyed his confidence – and his life – by walking out on him, and reiterated that he was afraid that Ros might have done the same.

'Man's pride is his Achilles' heel,' he said, self-mocking.

'You mean it would be your pride that would suffer most if Ros *has* gone off with someone else?'

'I'm beginning to think so, yes.'

As they had talked an intimacy had developed between them,

an intimacy on a far deeper level than the explosive physical attraction which had overtaken them earlier.

'More coffee?' Mike asked after a while.

'Better not. I'll never sleep. I don't suppose you happen to have a Perrier?'

'Sorry. I don't move in the Perrier-drinking circles, I'm afraid.'

She smiled. That was so obviously true – and she was glad. Much of Mike's attraction lay in his very ordinariness. Steve would probably have Perrier by the caseload. But he could not hold a candle to Mike.

She got to her feet. 'I really must make tracks.'

'Do you want to go?' His tone was loaded; she knew what he meant. Earlier, when the physical attraction had flared between them he had put a stop to it because he had thought that she was happily married. Now he knew the truth about Ari, and he was prepared to begin again and take the encounter to its logical conclusion.

But somehow talking about it had had the opposite effect on Maggie. The moment for giving way to physical passion had come and gone. Though she could still look at Mike and want him, she had reminded herself too forcefully of her obligations. When Mike had taken her in his arms and kissed her there had been no time for reasoning, only reacting. Now her mind was in control of her body once more and it was telling her that she was married to Ari and Mike belonged to Ros.

'Yes,' she said. 'For tonight I think I do.'

'All right.' He got her coat and helped her into it. As his hands touched her shoulders she almost weakened, so strong was the longing for him, but she held herself in check. Maybe . . . maybe when this was all over it would be different. Maybe if she could tell Ros to her face that she was falling in love with her boyfriend, maybe if she left Ari, maybe if she could sort everything out there would be another time when Mike would ask her to stay and she would not refuse. But not tonight. And maybe not ever . . .

They went down to the car. It was a fine night now; the stars were shining. Mike unlocked the door and she slid into the passenger seat. As they drove out of town the sound of sirens wailing carried faintly on the night air and Maggie thought she caught a glimpse of a blue flashing light somewhere across the city. But she was too lost in her own thoughts to give it more than a second's fleeting notice.

Chapter Fourteen

Sheena Ross, the reporter from the local daily newspaper, had called on Brendan around three o'clock that afternoon.

She was young and keen with an eye to getting on to one of the nationals when she had served her apprenticeship in the provinces and after she had spoken to Maggie and Mike she had got herself a coffee and lit a cigarette, sitting in the big deserted office and thinking about what they had told her. Sheena had a good nose for a story and she scented one now. This could be her big break – and it was her good fortune that it had come in on a Saturday when she was covering the news desk virtually single-handed. Also to her advantage was the fact that the telephones were unusually silent – no fires, no emergencies of any kind, nothing for the moment to distract her.

Sheena studied her notes, transcribing some of them back into longhand in case memory failed her and her rather haphazard shorthand let her down. A missing woman might be nothing or it might be very big indeed. At its most dramatic it might turn into a murder. Sheena had worked on a couple, following the human-interest line, but neither had offered very much in the way of meat. This one, if it developed, would be different. It was steeped in just the sort of detail that would make reporting it a joy and reading about it a three-course meal for the avid reader – a victim who had a high-powered job in the world of fashion, and the highly successful local fashion house Vandina at that, a boyfriend who would be well known locally because of the number of children who had been through his hands, and a sister who lived in Corfu. Add to all that the fact that Ros Newman had once been married to local broadcaster Brendan Newman and the story had enough spice to make headline news for days. Sheena stubbed out her cigarette, already savouring the possible triumph of a front-page byline and headed for the newspaper's archives to see what she could learn about Brendan Newman.

The telephone rang a few times whilst she was wading through the file of cuttings and each time she swore at the interruption. None of the incoming news was of much interest or importance – the secretary of a local drama group was anxious to get some coverage for a forthcoming production, someone rang in to say a longtime director of a football club somewhere out in the sticks had died. Sheena dealt with them efficiently but impatiently, taking the briefest of notes and transcribing them into short reports on the word processor, anxious only to get back to the story that was fascinating her.

She snatched a sandwich lunch, eating it with her head still buried in the files she had unearthed, and after taking a few more mundane calls fetched her bag, her coat and her car keys. She left the office, locking the door behind her, and headed out in search of Brendan Newman, who was, after all, the focus of human interest in the story.

'Whatever Happened to Brendan Newman?' she thought, paraphrasing 'Whatever Happened to Baby Jane?' as she drove through the heavy Saturday-afternoon traffic. That was one thing the files had not told her. But Sheena meant to find out.

As usual Brendan was hung over. He had surfaced at about midday, swallowed his usual palliative of Alka-Seltzer followed by a couple of cups of strong black coffee and a cigarette. His mouth tasted foul and the cigarette made his head thump dully but he smoked it anyway. He was half watching the sports coverage on TV when the doorbell rang. He stubbed his cigarette out in the already overflowing ashtray and went to answer it.

'Yes?'

'This is PC Nicholls, Redland Police Station.'

Brendan swore. What had he been up to the previous night? As usual most of the evening's activity was no more than a blur in his fuddled brain.

'What do you want?'

'It's about your wife.'

'My wife? Ros, you mean?'

'That's what I said, sir.'

'She's not my wife. We're divorced.'

'Just the same, I'd like to talk to you, sir.'

Brendan hesitated. He did not want to talk about Ros to

anyone, especially not the police. He was sick to death of people asking him about Ros. He wanted to forget her and the pain she had caused him. Besides this the very mention of her name stirred up a well of discomfort deep within him, a discomfort that was almost fear. But telling the police to piss off wouldn't do any good. If anything it would simply make things worse. Brendan pushed the release button to unlock the communal entrance, slid the chain off his own front door and opened it.

He recognised the policeman as he came up the stairs as the same one who had called before.

'What the fuck is it this time?' he asked rudely.

'It's about the disappearance of your wife – your ex-wife. Have you seen or heard anything of her since we last talked?'

'No.'

'No phone calls, no letters – nothing?'

'I just said that, didn't I? But there's nothing unusual in that. Ros and I don't have anything to do with one another now.'

'And there's nowhere you can think of she might be? Anyone she might be with?'

'Look, we've been through all this before. Why don't you ask her boyfriend or her sister?'

'We have asked them, sir. Nobody has heard anything from her and she has not made contact with any of her friends. In fact we are beginning to take her disappearance very seriously.'

'What the hell do you mean?'

'I mean, sir, that it's looking rather suspicious and we are concerned for Mrs Newman's safety.'

Brendan had begun to sweat. 'Her *safety*? What are you implying?'

'I think you know very well what I'm implying.' The policeman's face was expressionless and somehow it only added weight to his words. 'We are beginning to wonder if Mrs Newman is still alive.'

The sweat was trickling down Brendan's forehead now. He wiped it away with the palm of his hand.

'Of course she's still alive! She's a young woman, for Christ's sake!'

'That doesn't necessarily mean a thing, does it, sir?' The policeman stepped closer. 'Would you mind if I took a look around?'

Brendan barred his way.

'Yes, dammit, I would mind! What is this?'

'Just to establish she's not living here. It won't take long.'

'Of course she's not living here!'

'Then you won't mind if I check for myself.'

'Oh, all right – if you must. But make it quick.' He stepped aside, going into the kitchen to get his cigarettes. He could hear the policeman moving about the flat, opening and closing doors. He lit a cigarette and his hand was shaking.

After a few minutes the policeman appeared in the doorway.

'Satisfied?' Brendan asked.

'Well, she's not here, certainly. That will be all for the moment, sir. If you do hear anything from Mrs Newman you will get in touch, won't you?' In the doorway he paused, looking back. 'You weren't thinking of going anywhere, were you?'

'What is it to you?'

'If you were I think we might like to know about that too. Good day, sir.'

When he had gone Brendan kicked the door shut and threw all the locks. Then, in spite of his aching head and protesting stomach, he poured himself a large whisky and tossed it back, neat.

He didn't like this – he did not like it at all. All very well to bluster and act as if he felt confident in front of other people; inside he felt like a shivering jelly.

So – the police were beginning to treat Ros's disappearance as suspicious. Inevitable, really – it had to have happened sooner or later. But it was still an unpleasant shock to have that po-faced police officer standing in his kitchen and saying – what was it? – 'We are beginning to wonder if Mrs Newman is still alive', and saying it with a look that seemed to suggest he thought Brendan might have something to do with it.

Oh Ros, Ros, Brendan murmured, and simply speaking her name made his heart contract painfully. What was it about one particular woman that could do this to a man? He'd always been able to pull the birds. When he was a radio personality they'd come flocking, and even now he could still pick up a dolly when he wanted one – turn on the charm, flash the wallet, talk about the glory days and they succumbed, flattered to think they had been singled out by a celebrity, even if in reality his star had set over the distant horizon. He loved them and left them, careful never to get involved, smiled over the letters they wrote him – 'If you really meant it when you said I was special, Brendan, I will be the happiest girl alive', or even: 'Please phone me at the above number – my husband is away for another week' – and promptly forgot them.

But not Ros. Ros was different, though he could not for the life of him have said why. There was something about the tilt of her head, the way she walked, her smile, that had got under his skin. From the first moment he had met her he had been besotted and nothing that had happened since had ever changed that. He had come to resent her, hate her even for the success that she had achieved whilst his own career was faltering. He had been angry, hurt and jealous all in turn and sometimes all together. He had hated her for her sharp tongue and for her air of superiority, and had hated himself for what he felt to be his inadequacy where she was concerned. And when all his emotions had become too much for him and the drink was in him he had been violent towards her because it was the only release he knew. But none of this had altered the way he felt about her. Nothing could change that. Nothing ever would.

Brendan had fetched the whisky bottle and topped up his glass. Drink was his best friend. It helped him to forget and that was what he wanted – wasn't it? Except that these days even when his brain was too muzzy to make sense of his thoughts the pain and the sense of sick foreboding were still there inside him, even if he couldn't remember what had caused them. And sometimes he thought he ought to remember. He really ought to remember everything . . .

When the doorbell rang around three o'clock his first thought was that it was the police again, and he toyed with the idea of ignoring it. But it rang again, insistently, and if only to stop the noise, which echoed painfully through his aching head, he answered it angrily.

'Who is it?'

'*Western Daily Press*. Could I have a word with you, Mr Newman?'

'If it's about my wife, no, you couldn't. I have nothing to say about her.'

There was a slight pause, then the disembodied voice said: 'No, it's not about your wife. I wanted to interview you. About your career.'

Brendan experienced relief – and egotistical pleasure. The fog in his brain lifted a little. Automatically he glanced at his reflection in the hall mirror – crumpled slacks, the shirt he had worn last night thrown on again because it had been to hand. Not the image he wanted to project to his public.

'It's not a good moment. Could you come back later?'

'I'd rather it was now, Mr Newman. I do have deadlines to meet.'

Deadlines. Christ, he couldn't let her get away! She might change her mind and decide not to come back at all.

'All right. Give me a minute.'

He went into the bedroom, emptied his drawer to find a respectable casual shirt and slacks, and combed his hair. There was no time to shave. Lucky for him designer stubble was fashionable.

He went back to the buzzer. 'All right, I'm opening the door now.'

When she came up the stairs he saw that she was young and not unattractive. His practised eye took in a sharp elfin face slightly lost in a shoulder-length curly perm; a loose linen jacket and a skirt short enough to reveal good legs. Brendan was glad he had taken the time to change. He smiled at her, his hangover forgotten as his easy professional manner took over and the well-known charm began to ooze.

'You found me then – all the way to the top of the stairs. Most of my visitors give up at the first landing. I'm Brendan Newman.'

'Sheena Ross. It's good of you to see me, Mr Newman, and I'm sorry if it's inconvenient.'

'Not at all,' he said, forgetting the inconsistency. 'Can I get you a coffee?'

'Thanks, that would be nice.' She was looking around with a keen professional eye. 'It's a nice place you have here. A wonderful view.'

'Not so bad, is it?' He hunted for mugs. Miraculously there were two, washed up, on the draining board. 'Sugar? Milk?'

'No, black, just as it comes.'

'Do you want to talk here or shall we go in the other room?'

'Here will be fine.' She put her bag down on the kitchen table, extracted a notepad and pencil and also a pocket-sized cassette recorder.

'What is it all about anyway?' Brendan asked, setting a mug of coffee down in front of her.

'I want to do a series on local personalities. Profiles, really.' She said it smoothly; the delay while he had changed had given her plenty of time to plan her line of attack.

'And what made you choose me?'

'You are a big name in local radio. You're also, if I may say so, interesting as a person.' She paused, giving him a conspiratorial look. 'So many celebrities are frankly a bit boring when you get down to brass tacks.'

Brendan laughed, his ego flattered.

'You're right there – and don't I know it!'

'So – you wouldn't mind if I asked you a few questions?'

Brendan sat down opposite her. 'Fire away.'

'How did you come to get into radio? Were you a journalist?'

'Me? No, I wouldn't have the patience. I was a musician – I played the sax. The radio station wanted to do a series on jazz. I knew the producer. He asked if I'd like to present it.'

'And you were an instant success.'

'More or less. I'd kissed the Blarney Stone, talking came easily to me. And people seemed to like me. The series was extended to a regular spot and then before I knew it I had my own show.'

'That's what I thought. All this is pretty well documented in our archives, Mr Newman.'

'Call me Brendan.'

'Brendan. I just needed to check with you that I had the facts straight. Now, if you don't mind I'd like to ask you a few more personal questions. You say you kissed the Blarney Stone. What else is it about you that you think appealed to your listeners?'

Brendan considered. 'I suppose I say what I think. Even if it is a bit outrageous. I like to tear down a few icons. People enjoy being shocked, don't they? They say: "I like listening to Brendan Newman – you never know what the hell he's going to come out with next."'

She laughed, her pencil flicking busily.

'Do you see yourself as sexually attractive – a sex symbol?'

'Me?' Brendan sat back, assuming an expression of false modesty. 'Sure, what is there about me that's attractive?'

'A great deal, I'd say – and obviously I'm not the only one who thinks so. Don't you consider yourself even a little bit good-looking?'

'I never think about looks. Beauty is only skin-deep, my old mother used to say.'

'Not everyone is as introspective. You must have had women telling you they found you attractive.'

'Well, I suppose so. I could tell you a story or two . . .' Brendan branched easily into some of his well-worn anecdotes. He was enjoying himself, his former ill humour forgotten as he relived the better moments of his glory days. So relaxed was he, he scarcely noticed when Sheena began to steer the conversation towards the real purpose of her visit.

'It must have been difficult for your wife, having all these other women chasing after you.'

'Ros, you mean? Sure, she took it in her stride.'

'She didn't mind, then?'

'She reckoned it was confirmation of her own good taste. Which of course it was.' He caught her eye and winked.

'It wasn't the reason, then, why your marriage broke up?'

'No, it wasn't.' Momentarily the pain was back, encroaching on his feeling of well-being. 'We don't have to talk about Ros, do we?'

'I think our readers might be interested. After all, she was lucky enough to be your wife. An enviable position, many of them would think.'

'Unfortunately *she* didn't.'

'Didn't what?'

'Appreciate me,' he said with what he hoped was endearing honesty. 'That is why I'd rather not talk about her.'

'But surely it shows a whole different side of your personality. And besides . . . I believe she is missing. How do you feel about that?'

The warning bells began to ring in Brendan's head.

'I've told you – I don't want to talk about Ros.'

'You obviously care for her. Aren't you concerned about what might have happened to her?'

'Who says I care for her?'

'Oh come on, Mr Newman. You were married to her. You can't shut someone out of your life so easily. Especially if something terrible has happened to her.'

'Like what?'

'Supposing,' Sheena said evenly, 'she has been murdered?'

She was watching him closely; she saw his expression change, saw the panic come into his eyes, saw those first beads of sweat that seemed to form whenever Ros's disappearance was mentioned break out on his forehead. For an instant it was all there in his face, then he turned away, reaching for a cigarette.

'Who says she's been murdered?'

'Her sister seems to think so. And so does her boyfriend.'

'Mike Bloody Thompson! Have you been talking to him?'

'Well, yes, to be honest . . .'

'Honest! You must be joking! That's why you're here, isn't it?'

'Not entirely. I . . .'

'Oh yes it bloody is! You don't want to do a feature on me at all, do you? Who the hell would? You wanted to talk about Ros – bloody Ros! I suppose you think I killed her, do you?'

'Mr Newman . . . Brendan . . .'

'She was a whore, a bloody whore!' Brendan shouted. He was on his feet now, totally out of control. 'Do know what I'm talking about? Yes, of course you do. Well, that was Ros, for all her fancy ways. I tell you, she got what was coming to her. And now get out of here, before you end up the same way she did!'

'All right, Brendan, there's no need to be like this!' Sheena was attempting to be conciliatory but every vestige of colour had drained from her face. She was scrabbling her notebook and pencils into her bag and as she did so Brendan grabbed the cassette recorder.

'I'll take that. Now – get out!' He flung open the door.

Trying to retain at least an outward appearance of calm, Sheena held out her hand. 'My property, please!'

'You'll be lucky! Get out of here before I . . .'

She went. She had faced ugly situations before but none uglier than this.

'You'll be hearing from our legal department,' she called back up the stairs when she was safely out of his reach. 'Don't think you can get away with this!'

'Bitch!' he yelled after her. 'Stupid interfering bitch! Why couldn't you keep your nose out of it?'

He heard the main door slam and the sound of a car being driven, very fast, out of the communal car park. He went back into the flat and hurled her cassette recorder at the wall. She'd never use that tape, damn her, and if she wrote anything about him, one fucking word, he'd sue the paper for libel . . .

Brendan refilled his glass with neat whisky and drank it as though it were water. His head was aching again, his stomach felt sour. As the excesses of his temper receded the blackness began again, the all-pervading sick dread.

So it wasn't only the police who thought Ros was dead, the papers were on to it too. And what a field day they would have with it! Ros Newman, ex-wife of the broadcaster Brendan Newman – the *failed* broadcaster Brendan Newman. It would all be there, all the elements of a big news story. They would spare him nothing. Already he could see the headlines, the photographs, the whole bloody shooting match.

Brendan refilled his glass yet again but the whisky did nothing to make him feel better now. It only deepened his depression, filling him with disgust and self-loathing.

He was a failure, a worse than useless git. Wasn't that what they had called him at the radio station when they sacked him? Now all the world would know about the mess he had made of his life – and they would brand him a murderer too. Brendan was not sure which was worse, but he did not think he could stand any of it any more.

He carried his glass into the living room, opened a fresh bottle of whisky and sank down on to the low sofa, head in hands, thinking about his life. He'd had it all – money, a career, a beautiful wife – and he'd let it all slip through his fingers. The gods had given him so much, and what had he done? Wasted it, thrown it all away. His career was over and Ros was dead. And now the vultures were moving in.

If only he could *remember*, Brendan thought. If only he could remember exactly what had happened that last time he had seen Ros. But he couldn't remember. His fuddled brain cells wouldn't let him. There was a murky cloud obscuring it. Perhaps it was because he didn't want to remember. But perhaps soon he would be forced to, forced to face things he would rather forget.

Afternoon slipped into evening, the light began to fade from the day. Night was coming to the city. Suddenly Brendan did not want to face the night alone. Not tonight – not ever again.

He got up, his toe encountering the bottle and kicking it over. Whisky spilled out on to the carpet. Brendan did not even notice. He got his jacket and went out, not bothering to lock the door behind him. The sounds of the city carried softly, distantly, on the night air. He walked like a man in a dream, only it was not a dream he was experiencing but a nightmare, a nightmare closing in, a nightmare that would not go away.

The suspension bridge loomed up before him, Brunel's masterpiece of engineering, spanning the gorge where the tidal Avon flows out to the sea. The bridge was illuminated, making a great curving arc of brightness against the dark sky. Brendan went slowly across the walkway beside the traffic-carrying road until he was almost to the other side where Leigh Woods sweep down to meet the river. Then he walked back again towards the Clifton end and leaned over the parapet.

To his right the floodlights were reflected in the water; immediately below him there was only inky blackness. The tide must be out, leaving only a narrow stream of water along the mud. It didn't matter. He did not need the water to drown in. The fall, from this height, should be enough.

Slowly, deliberately, Brendan climbed up on to the parapet. He felt quite calm now, filled only with a sense of purpose. It was going to be easy, so easy. One move, one slip, perhaps a moment's fear as the air rushed past him, and it would all be over. No more failure, no more pain, no more guilt. The newspapers could write what they liked about him, it would no longer matter – to him at any rate. He stood, poised, gazing into the blackness below.

A shout shattered his trance. He looked in the direction of the sound and saw a figure running towards him, calling something to him. Brendan could not make out the words but he knew he could not wait around to find out. No one was going to stop him now, no one was going to thwart him this time. He had made up his mind and for once he was not going to fail in his intention.

Brendan braced himself.

'I'm sorry, Ros,' he said.

Then he jumped.

Chapter Fifteen

Mike heard the news as he grabbed a quick bowl of cornflakes before leaving for his school trip.

A man had fallen from the suspension bridge the previous evening. Police had recovered a body. The man had not yet been named.

Mike went on with his cornflakes, scarcely even registering what he had heard. It wasn't that unusual. People jumped from the suspension bridge with monotonous regularity. Sometimes they travelled quite long distances to do it. Mike shook his head, an indication to himself of his total incomprehension of what could drive any man to take his own life, particularly that way. He had fallen once when rock climbing; he could still remember the sickening feeling inside him as the air rushed past and the jarring thud as he hit the ground, knocking all the breath out of his body. That had been a short fall compared with the one from the suspension bridge at low tide but he wouldn't care to repeat it. Not that they all died, of course, the people who jumped. Sometimes their fall was broken by scrub on the river banks or by the bridge itself, sometimes they lay horribly injured on the mud flats for hours before anyone realised they were there, sometimes they drowned.

If I was going to kill myself I'd get in my car and drive like hell at some very large immovable object, Mike thought. But he could not, in all honesty, imagine ever getting to such a state himself and he found it almost impossible to identify with anyone who had.

Poor stupid fool, Mike thought. Money problems, woman trouble, whatever, none of it was worth taking your own life over. Things had a way of sorting themselves out. Insoluble as any problem seemed in the present, five years hence and it was hard to remember what all the fuss was about.

He switched off the radio and went to pack his rucksack with crisps, Mars bars, a squashed-looking meat pie that he rather fancied might be past its sell-by date and a Thermos of coffee.

A day in the company of a coachload of twelve-year-olds stretched before him uninvitingly. All part of the job, he knew, but today he resented it.

What he really wanted to do was spend the day with Maggie.

Maggie did not put the radio on that morning and consequently she did not hear about the man who had fallen from the suspension bridge. She slept late, was horrified to see the time when she did wake, and was about to leap out of bed when she remembered – there was nothing to get up for. Mike was away on a trip, she had nothing whatever planned and in all honesty there was not a thing she could do towards finding out what had happened to Ros.

In any case, Ros seemed to have been relegated almost to the back of her mind. Ever since Mike had telephoned to say she was missing, Maggie had thought of little else and anxiety for her sister had obsessed her. Now, suddenly, it was as if that obsession had burnt itself out, exhausted by overkill, and instead her thoughts were almost exclusively of Mike whilst her body remembered with disturbing clarity just how she had felt last night when he had kissed her.

The sense of guilt was still there, of course, reminding her that neither she nor Mike was free, but it didn't stop the feelings of excitement and anticipation that tingled and teased somewhere in the depths of her, couldn't prevent her from longing to see Mike again or blot out the image of his face that was there, tantalisingly, in front of her closed eyes. Maggie had forgotten in the months and years of desperately trying to make her marriage work what it felt like to fall in love. Now every nerve ending, every fibre of her being conspired together to make her remember. And in spite of knowing it was impossible, as well as wrong, she was ridiculously, soaringly happy.

She lay quietly, savouring the happiness and trying not to think about the reality, that with Ros and Ari standing between them it would be impossible for things to turn out the way she knew her heart wanted them to. Ari seemed a million miles away, the long shadow of Ros had no power to touch her this morning. If Mike was here, if she was going to have to face him in a few hours, the choices would have to be made and she knew she would decide just as she had done last night to step away from the rubicon rather than cross it. But Mike was not here. For the moment, at any rate, she could allow herself the luxury of pretending, of allowing her dreams full rein.

She closed her eyes, remembering the feel of his mouth on hers and the responses of her body, wrapped her arms around herself and pretended they were Mike's. Soon, whether she had any plans for the day or not, she would have to get up and let go of the delicious illusion. Perhaps she would telephone Ari, or at least try to telephone him – being Sunday he would almost certainly be at home in Kassiopi. No woman, not even Melina, would be able to change the habits of a lifetime; not even the prospect of a day of illicit and steamy love would be compensation for his mother's disapproval. But she was not ready to do it yet. Let the dream last just a little longer . . .

Relaxed at last after the stress and strain of the previous week, Maggie began to drift once more into a light doze. When she did she dreamed of Mike. He was standing on a path that ran through a dense woodland. He was holding out his arms to her and smiling.

'I'm coming, my darling,' she said. But the branches of the trees were slapping at her and her feet seemed to be bogged down in quicksand. Try as she might she could not reach him.

'Isn't it wonderful to have a really fine day at last? We'll eat al-fresco at lunchtime – in fact I think we might go the whole hog and have a barbeque,' Dinah said. 'What do you think, Don?'

Don Kennedy smiled indulgently. Personally he did not like eating outdoors at all. He preferred a proper meal, taken at a leisurely pace at a table inside, with fine wine in the best crystal and no sudden gust of breeze to make his cigar burn unevenly, but he did not want to put a damper on Dinah's enthusiasm, which was at times almost childlike and which he always found utterly charming.

'I'm sure either would be very pleasant,' he said easily. 'Do whatever you like, Dinah – as long as you don't expect me to cook the barbeque, if that's what you're having. My efforts are always less than edible and no one really wants burnt sausages or undercooked chicken, do they?'

'It won't be sausages or chicken. It'll be steak. And Steve has the knack of making them taste wonderful,' Dinah said happily.

'That's settled then. I'll ask Mrs Brunt to prepare them and some interesting salads. I really do think we should make the most of a fine day while we have the chance.'

She went in search of the housekeeper, moving with that quick grace which never failed to please him. She was like a gazelle, he thought, a slim fair-haired gazelle, pretty to look at but much too easily hurt. If only he could protect her from the harsh realities of life! He would never hurt her as Van had done, never do anything to cause her pain. And he would kill, with his bare hands, anyone who did. But he was not in a position to look after her as he would have liked. She was fond of him, he knew, and since Van's death she had come to depend on him more and more. But that was the extent of it. She had never encouraged him to come any closer and he was afraid to force the issue in case he overstepped some invisible boundary and destroyed the relationship that existed between them. It might not be as much or as close as he would have liked but it was very precious to him. Better to have Dinah as a loving friend than not at all.

Tyres crunched on gravel outside the window. Don looked out to see Steve's car pulling in and grimaced. He had been hoping for a little longer alone with Dinah before Steve returned – he had gone out to buy the Sunday papers, Dinah had said, but he had been gone some time and since he was obviously doing something more than simply popping into the nearest newsagent's Don had thought – hoped – that he would be a good while longer.

Don always found Steve's presence a little annoying. Dinah gave him her full attention to the exclusion of everyone else and Don felt her slipping even further away from him. Don was not sure that he liked Steve very much but he was honest enough to suspect that feeling might be rooted in jealousy. If Steve had not turned up so soon after Van's death Don might have been able to consolidate his position as Dinah's supportive confidant. But even feeling as he did, Don knew it would have been churlish in the extreme to deny her the happiness that had come from finding her son again, and in any case such wishful thinking would be a pointless exercise. Steve was here, back in Dinah's life on every level – business as well as personal. No amount of wishing would make him disappear again.

His reflections on Steve's role in Dinah's recovery from

mourning Van were vindicated when, a moment later, Dinah came hurrying in, her face rosy with pleasure, clutching a cellophane-wrapped bouquet.

'Look, Don, aren't they lovely? Steve got them for me at the garage down the road. Wasn't that sweet of him?'

'Very,' Don said, thinking that Steve certainly knew how to give Dinah pleasure. The house was always full of flowers, most of them delivered ready-arranged by the most exclusive florist in a fifteen-mile radius, and it would not occur to most people, himself included, to buy a bunch of flowers costing less than five pounds along with the petrol. But Steve had, and Dinah, without a doubt, appreciated it.

'Are we going to have five minutes alone?' he asked now. 'I want to talk to you about these plans you have to redeem the Reubens fiasco.'

'Oh – yes . . . Well, let me just put these in water. I'll arrange them later and they should have a good drink first anyway. It's so dreadfully hot and dirty outside these garage shops – I feel Steve almost rescued them!' She laughed. 'Give me two seconds, Don, and I'll be back.'

She flitted out again and Don heard her talking to Steve in the kitchen as she drew a jug of water, her voice animated with the special happiness that always bubbled through in his presence. He hoped fervently that Steve wouldn't butt in on the short time he would have alone with Dinah – he knew Jayne and Drew were expected for lunch. But to his relief when Dinah returned she was alone.

'Right – what were you going to say to me, Don?'

'I've looked at the costings for your ideas. It's going to be very expensive. It will have to go before a full meeting of the board, of course, but I have to tell you I am a little concerned. With this level of financial commitment we can't afford to get it wrong. I feel the marketing department should investigate thoroughly before we commit ourselves.'

'There's no time for that, Don. We need to move quickly to get the range into production.'

'I'm concerned the outlay will show badly on our half-yearly figures, that's the trouble. Full order books may not be enough to convince the bank manager that you are not taking one hell of a risk. And besides, are you sure we have the capacity to expand so drastically at a moment's notice? Production Management should be in on this one before a decision is taken. Have you consulted with them?'

'Not yet, but I know they will do whatever is necessary.'

'You must talk to them, Dinah, sooner rather than later.'

'I'll talk to them tomorrow, I promise. But I want to keep the element of surprise. The fewer people who know until the last possible moment the better. I don't want Reubens or anyone else for that matter getting wind of this. If there's a spy in the camp and we don't know who it is the closer to our chests we can play it, the better.'

As she spoke the word 'spy' her face clouded, evidence of her distress – and distaste.

'You still don't know who it is?' he asked.

'No, but Steve is working on it. I'm sure he'll come up with a name soon.'

'Steve thinks he already has.'

Engrossed in their conversation, neither had noticed Steve in the doorway. He came into the room, casually elegant as always, dressed for relaxation this morning in a blue denim shirt and expensively cut jeans. A pair of Raybans jutted from the pocket of his shirt and though the recent weather had been less than summery he looked bronzed and fit, his hair streaked blond as if he had just spent a fortnight soaking up the sun on a continental beach.

'You've found out who has been passing information on our range?' Don asked.

'I think so, yes.'

'Well – who is it?'

'I'd rather not say at the moment. I have a few more enquiries to do first.'

'Couldn't you at least let us in on what you've learnt so far?'

'I'd rather not.' Steve glanced at Dinah. 'You're not going to like it. If I'm right it's very bad news indeed. That's why I want to be certain of the facts before I start throwing accusations about.'

Dinah had turned very pale. 'You mean . . .?' Her voice was faint.

'Please – don't press me at the moment.'

'But Steve, we need to know,' Don said. 'We have to get a discussion going on Dinah's new designs and we need to have some idea who we can, or can't trust.'

A car approached up the gravel drive. They all looked towards the window, the tension of the moment splintering. Jayne and Drew were arriving for drinks before lunch. Steve moved to the door where he stood for a moment, hand resting casually on the jamb. His china-blue eyes were narrowed in his tanned face, his expression one that might almost have been triumph. For the first time, he had them almost exactly where he wanted them. Dinah, of course, had reached out to him eagerly but even she had been cautious where the business was concerned. And Don Kennedy . . . Don resented him, Steve sensed, and had done his best to slow his progress to the heart of the company. Now he felt the beginnings of power. It was a heady sensation.

'I don't think you need have any worries on that score, Don,' he said evenly. 'If I am right, Dinah's plans are quite safe.'

'How can you know that?'

'Let's just say I know, and leave it at that for now.'

He left the room, heading for the front door to greet Jayne and Drew.

Dinah turned to Don. She was trembling.

'What does he mean, Don? Who does he think . . .?'

'I don't know. We'll have to wait until he chooses to tell us.'

'You don't think . . . *Ros* . . .?' Her voice was shocked and low. 'I know it was suggested before but I simply couldn't believe it of her. But how can he be certain the new designs won't fall into the hands of our competitors if the spy is still working for us? Ros is the only one not around any more.'

'It's no use speculating.' Don touched her arm. 'We'll just have to trust Steve, I'm afraid.'

But even as he said it, it galled him.

'You're right, I suppose.' Already Dinah was reverting to character, trying to push to the back of her mind the things she did not want to think about. Outside the window Steve was greeting Jayne and Drew, kissing Jayne and taking her arm, bending to say something to her. 'You don't think, do you . . .?' she said suddenly.

'What?'

'That Steve and Jayne are . . .' She hesitated, a small frown puckering her brow. 'Sometimes they seem very . . . intimate.'

Don shrugged, his mind still on the spy business.

'Of course not. She's a married woman.'

'Being married doesn't stop people . . .'

'I know that, Dinah,' Don said with just a hint of impatience. 'But I feel sure a young man as eligible as Steve has no need whatever to dally with someone who already has a husband. Besides, he wouldn't want to . . .' He broke off, catching himself just in time.

'Wouldn't want to what?'

Don went to pick up his coffee to cover his sudden embarrassment. Steve wouldn't want to queer his pitch at Vandina, he had been going to say. He wouldn't want to do anything to mar his golden image in case Dinah disapproved and his chances were spoiled. Thank goodness he had stopped himself from making such a tactless remark, however true he suspected it might be.

'If anything I thought he was interested in Ros,' he said.

Dinah brightened momentarily. 'Do you know I thought the same thing! But now *Ros* . . . Oh Don, I don't know, sometimes I feel so helpless – as if I'm in a hall of mirrors where nothing is quite what it seems! Is that very stupid of me?'

'No, Dinah, it's called life.'

'Why does it all have to be so upsetting? Honestly, I just don't know who I can trust any more.'

He looked at her standing there, so apparently sophisticated and yet so vulnerable, and felt his heart contract.

'You can trust me, Dinah, I promise you.'

A sudden smile lit her face and she laid her hand on his arm.

'Oh yes, Don,' she said. 'I know I can trust you.'

When she had finally got up and eaten a leisurely breakfast Maggie decided she could no longer put off trying to ring Ari. The international lines were busy but eventually she managed to get through – only to have the telephone answered by her mother-in-law.

'Ari? No, he's not here. He's gone out in the boat. Later, perhaps . . .'

'You will tell him I rang?'

'I will tell him.' But her mother-in-law sounded less than welcoming and Maggie found herself wondering. Who had Ari taken out in the boat? Might it be Melina? In spite of her own wandering emotions the suspicion still had the power to hurt.

After another coffee Maggie decided to spend what was left of the morning cleaning the cottage. In Ros's absence a fine layer of dust had settled over everything and so far Maggie had not had time to do more than keep the bed made and wipe crumbs and coffee stains from the working surfaces in the kitchen. Now, with the hours stretching ahead, frustratingly empty, Maggie thought the best possible therapy for her confused mood might be to set to and return the place to its usual gleaming perfection.

She dressed in jeans and a casual shirt, assembled the vacuum cleaner, duster and a can of spray polish and began to work. An hour later the ground floor of the cottage was clean and sparkling and Maggie carried her tools upstairs to begin on the bedrooms.

The task was not, however, as therapeutic as she had hoped it would be. It was disturbing to be tidying up the things that Ros had left lying around, reminding Maggie all too sharply that her sister was missing and making her feel uncomfortable, as if she was committing some act of sacrilege. Would Ros ever again arrange things the way she wanted them? Maggie was sickeningly afraid she would not and she redoubled her efforts as if by getting rid of every speck of dust, every cluster of fluff, she could tip the odds in Ros's favour.

The cleaning done, Maggie decided to cut some flowers to fill the empty vases. She took the kitchen scissors into the garden where Ros's roses were in full wonderful bloom, but though at a distance the bushes were laden, close to Maggie found it difficult to decide which to cut. To take the scissors to any of them seemed a crime almost akin to murder. As she was hesitating over the decision the telephone began to ring and she abandoned the idea of cutting any at all and hurried back into the house.

Perhaps it was Ari, she thought hopefully, back from his sea trip and returning her call. But there were no telltale crackles on the line and the voice at the other end, though masculine, was most definitely not Ari's.

'Ros Newman?'

'No, this is her sister, Maggie Veritos.'

'Would I be able to speak to Ros Newman?' The voice sounded as if it belonged to a Londoner, Maggie thought.

'I'm sorry. She's away. Can I help at all?'

'I shouldn't think so. I really wanted to speak to Ros – or rather, she wanted to speak to me. My name is Des Taylor. Would you tell her I called? And that I shall be here for another week?'

Maggie hesitated, wondering if she should tell Des Taylor that Ros was not merely out but missing, and decided against it. She couldn't go into all that now.

'Does she know where to contact you?' she asked.

'Yes, but she may not have a phone number. Would you like to take it down?' Maggie reached for a pencil and copied it down – as she had thought, a Greater London code.

'What did she want to speak to you about?' Maggie asked, unwilling to let this new contact go, however unpromising the conversation so far. But Des Taylor was not inclined to be forthcoming.

'I think that's between me and Ros,' he said.

Maggie felt the hairs on the back of her neck begin to prickle.

'Please . . .' she began urgently. But Des Taylor had gone.

Maggie stood for a moment, deep in thought. Of course it was possible that this telephone call had nothing whatever to do with Ros's disappearance. But then again, perhaps it did . . .

Well, at least she had a telephone number. When she had talked to Mike they could decide whether to contact Mr Taylor, whoever he was.

At Luscombe Manor the alfresco lunch was over but the party had remained outside, taking advantage of the pleasant weather. Dinah and Don were sharing the swing seat, chatting over glasses of iced coffee, while Steve, Jayne and Drew reclined on sunbeds, lazily turning the pages of the Sunday supplements before abandoning them altogether to lie with the sun warm and bright on their upturned faces. After a while Steve, who soon tired of inactivity, got up.

'I'm going for a swim.'

Instantly Jayne, too, sat up. 'I think I'll come with you.' She glanced at her husband. 'Drew?'

Drew shifted position languidly, turning on to his stomach.

'You go ahead. Water doesn't agree with me.'

Jayne smiled. It was exactly the response she had expected.

'No one could accuse you of being overenergetic, could they?' she said lightly.

'Or of cramping your style,' he replied without even opening his eyes.

Jayne smiled again. Their relationship really was rather satisfactory. In fact most of her life had turned out rather satisfactorily.

'Have a nice rest.'

Steve was standing on the path waiting for her. She caught up with him, lazily linking her arm through his the moment they were screened from Dinah's view by the riot of shrubs and bushes.

He glanced at her, a look midway between amusement and irritation, and casually but deliberately disengaged his arm. Jayne flushed but said nothing. She was beginning to realise that however passionate the intimate moments they shared, she could not take anything for granted where Steve was concerned. Well, so be it. She didn't like the fact that she could control neither him nor their relationship but it was part of the attraction he had for her all the same. If it had been easy there would be no challenge – and Jayne liked a challenge. Besides which . . .

I don't believe I have ever wanted anyone as much as I want him, she thought, feeling the easy powerful grace of him next to her although they were now a foot apart. And in the end I'll get him, oh yes I will!

'I want to talk to you, Jayne,' Steve said.

'Oh? What about?'

'Later,' he said. 'I'm going to have my swim first.'

Dinah's large open-air swimming pool was flanked by a pool house, an octagonal stone-faced building that not only accommodated the plant but also changing rooms, showers and a solarium. Jayne kept a costume there – since coming to work for Vandina she was a frequent-enough visitor to make it worthwhile. Now, in the pink-tiled ladies' room, she slipped out of the strapless white dress she had worn for lunch and reached for her costume, which had been left on a peg to dry the last time she had used it. As she did so her reflection leaped at her from one of the full-length mirrors – her body pale but voluptuous, breasts full but firm, hips curving invitingly from hourglass waist to slightly heavy thighs.

Jayne turned slightly to produce a sideways view of her figure, eyes narrowing critically as she assessed the rounded stomach and fleshy droop of her buttocks. Was she putting on weight? She fancied she might be. Time to watch her diet and perhaps do some firming exercises. The last thing she wanted was for the plumpness that had marred her teen years to take over again. Men liked a little flesh, no matter what the beauty pundits said, but it was possible to have too much of a good thing.

She wriggled into her costume, bright red with a design of yellow flowers and emerald leaves, and surveyed herself again. Better, much better. The swimsuit was built with all the figure-controlling wizardry of a corset but it was done so cleverly that no one would ever guess. The invisibly structured bra lifted and divided her breasts, the elastic fabric smoothed away any hint of an unwelcome bulge and held those offending buttocks firmly in place. Jayne twisted her hair into a knot on top of her head with a matching scrunchy and reached for a yellow towelling wrap. Then, pushing her feet into wedge-heeled gold mules, she went out to the pool.

Steve was already swimming, cutting a perfect crawl through the turquoise water. She stood watching him for a moment, admiring the athletic grace of the stroke and the way the muscles and sinews in his back and shoulders rippled with understated power. Was there any activity that could match really stylish swimming for sheer sexiness? she wondered, and felt the familiar weakness deep inside that always accompanied the anticipation of pleasure to come.

She dropped the towelling robe on to the huge grey slabs which edged the pool and stood for a moment, hand on hip, fingers lightly touching the outward spot beneath which the yearning had stirred, but Steve ignored her, executing a perfect tumble-turn and swimming another length of the pool, and she lowered herself into a sitting position, legs trailing in the water which, though heated to a comfortable eighty degrees, felt cold to her sun-warmed skin. Still he ignored her and she slipped down into the water, gasping as it engulfed her and swimming in a large circle with a wide, gentle breaststroke. There was no way she could match him for swimming prowess, she knew, and she would not even try, and she knew better than to interrupt his serious exercise with any attempt to initiate a water game.

Eventually, when he had completed the number of lengths he had set himself, he swam towards her, head up now rather than flat between his rhythmically curving arms.

'All right,' he said. His breathing was just slightly fast, the breathing of a man who has stretched, but not overstretched himself. 'We'll talk now.'

A tiny pulse had begun to beat in Jayne's throat.

'You are making this sound very mysterious,' she said.

'Am I?' He hauled himself out of the water so that the muscles in his upper arms bunched and the sinews – and the droplets of water – glistened on his broad back.

'I'm not ready to get out yet,' she said, attempting to retain some control over the situation but managing only to sound petulant.

'Suit yourself. I can wait.'

She swam another circle, aware that her breaststroke was less than championship standard; but he was not watching her anyway. He had flung himself down on one of the plastic pool beds, spreadeagled for the sun to dry him. Jayne swam slowly to the small ladder at the side of the pool, climbed out and went towards him.

'I'm here now.'

'Sit down.' He reached out lazily and positioned another pool bed alongside his own. She reached for the robe, drying her face with it before shrugging it on and sitting down. She was shivering a little, though whether from being wet or some other reason she could not be sure.

He was still lying prone, eyes closed, face turned slightly away from her. But when he spoke the deceptively relaxed pose did nothing to lessen the impact of his words.

'I *know*, Jayne.'

She felt the shock like a line of fine wire drawn tight between each and every one of her nerve endings.

'You know what?' she asked, her voice forcedly light.

'About you, of course, darling.'

'Steve, what are you talking about?' But she already knew.

He rolled his head over then so that he was looking at her. He was smiling slightly but his eyes were cold.

'Don't play the innocent. I know what you've been doing.'

'Steve . . .'

'You are the mole at Vandina, aren't you? You might have been hired as Dinah's chief designer but that's a cover. In fact, my love, you are an industrial spy.'

She was shivering violently now. She held herself very taut so that he would not see it.

'What makes you think that?'

'I've been doing some digging. And I didn't have to dig very deep. I started by drawing up a shortlist of suspects and I soon found it was a good deal shorter than I'd imagined it would be. First, the mole had to be in a position to be able to get hold of information about future plans. That cut out most of the workforce. Then it was likely to be someone who had joined the company recently. Likely, I say – it wasn't impossible that a long-standing employee should turn traitor, but most of Dinah's closest associates have been with her for a very long time indeed and they have demonstrated their loyalty over and over again. One thing no one can doubt is Dinah's ability to engender loyalty. Most of her employees worship the ground she walks on. Then again, the likelihood is that the mole would have other contacts in the fashion industry. You fitted the bill on all counts, Jayne.'

'Really?' Jayne said coldly. 'And do you really think I would risk my plum job with an established company like Vandina for an upstart outfit like Reubens?'

Steve sat up, splaying his legs across the plastic pool chair. The sun gleamed dully on his bronzed skin but she felt no rush of desire now, only cold fear.

'That was what puzzled me, I must admit. So I began digging. And what did I discover? Really, I don't think there's any need for me to spell it out. I think you already know what I'm going to say.'

'Do I? Try me.'

'All right, if you insist. I discovered that one of the people who put up a great deal of money to finance Reubens has a name not dissimilar to your own. Lance Peters-Browne. Now there's a coincidence, wouldn't you say? A very big coincidence. Peters-Browne is not, after all, a very common name, is it?'

She did not answer. Her teeth were chattering.

'Drew's father,' Steve said. 'He is behind Reubens, isn't he?

That's why you were quite prepared to risk your position at Vandina. You stood to gain a good deal more than simply a prestigious job if Reubens was successful. The financial rewards, both now and in the future, would be enormous. You probably saw yourself in a position similar to Dinah's own. It must have been very tempting. A rosy future indeed.'

Jayne drew the towelling robe very tightly around herself. There was no point denying it. Steve knew too much.

'So,' she said. 'When are you going to tell Dinah about me?'

A little smile curled Steve's lips. He swung himself around so that he was facing her.

'I don't know. I haven't made up my mind yet.'

'For goodness' sake! Surely you might as well do it and get it over with!' She stood up, made to move away. He caught her hand, stopping her.

'I'm not sure about that. For one thing I don't actually relish the thought of upsetting her. Dinah is very fond of you – she's already distressed to think someone might be betraying her; it will be even worse when she knows it is you. I'd like to choose my time. After all, I don't think there will be any more leaks now, do you?'

She glared down at him. 'How can you be sure of that?'

'Because, Jayne, you really would be a fool to queer your pitch. After all, Reubens hasn't made it big yet and perhaps now it never will. I'd say that without you tipping them off about our plans they will be all at sea. And in a straight fight we can see them off with no trouble – strangle them at birth. Vandina has an unassailable position and a reputation second to none. If you are stupid, Jayne, you could very easily finish up with nothing. But I don't think you are stupid – far from it.'

'It's nice to know you think that of me, at least.'

'Oh, I do. I have a very high opinion of you – in many ways.' His eyes moved over her and in spite of the stress of the situation she felt the familiar stirring of desire. Recognising the weakness she fought it, gathering together all the scattered remnants of her composure and looking coolly at his hand in a silent command to him to remove it from her own.

'Well, if you have quite finished, I suggest we join the others.'

'I haven't finished. Not quite. As I said, I do have a high opinion of you, darling. You are a quite incredible woman. We could be very good together, you and I, if you would only work with me instead of against me.'

'Meaning?'

'As I said just now, I think I can safely say there won't be any more leaks of our plans – at least not unintentional leaks. But there might be circumstances where a leak might work to our advantage. Do you know what a double agent is?'

'Of course.'

'Well you might consider using your talents in that direction. If Reubens believe you are still working for them it could be very useful. If your information flow dries up altogether they might become suspicious. So I suggest you still feed them titbits – useless, of course – and when the time comes you can pass on something not only useless but designed to throw them on to totally the wrong track. Carefully planned, it could help to speed up their demise.'

'You mean you want me to help you ruin Drew's father?'

'I think Drew's father has enough substance not to be ruined so easily. But anyway let's not look at the negative side. Let's be positive. You and me, running Vandina together. Doesn't that appeal to you?'

'But . . . Dinah . . .'

'Dinah won't be in charge for ever. She's not as young as she once was, in spite of appearances. In any case, you can leave Dinah to me.'

She smiled. Her fear was evaporating, being replaced by a sense of excitement. How was it Steve could do this to her? Loving him was like walking an emotional tightrope. He could build her up, knock her down, destroy all her defences and then just as suddenly instigate this heady anticipation for what lay ahead. But it was all part of the irresistible attraction he held for her.

'You are the devil incarnate,' she said. 'I'm going to get dressed.'

She went into the pool house, not looking back though she could feel his eyes following her. In the changing room she stripped off her still-wet costume and ran the shower. She was about to step into it when she heard him in the room behind her and her heart began to pound. She had known he would come but she gave no indication that she was aware of his presence.

She stepped into the shower, turning her face up to the cascade of warm water, stretching her arms backwards so that her breasts lifted too. He came up behind her, taking her breasts in his hands and pressing his body against hers. She went weak again but she stood quite still, enjoying the contact and the sensations that it aroused. Steve – power and danger. Steve – whom she could hate and desire at one and the same time.

He turned her to him, their bodies, slippery from the water, sliding and clinging. She arched against him and he entered her, taking her while the water cascaded over them. When it was over she cried out but he turned away from her with an abruptness that was hurtful, and she understood. This time he had taken her not only from desire but to set the seal on his mastery of her.

'Get dressed, then,' he said. 'It's time we were getting back to the others.'

He was standing there, naked yet not in the least vulnerable. He looked strong and confident, a man who knew exactly what he wanted and that he would achieve it. She experienced a flash of anger.

'Don't think I'll always do exactly as you say.'

He smiled. It was not a nice smile. 'Oh, I think you will.'

'Perhaps this time it suits me. But we all have our Achilles' heel, Steve. I'm not alone in that.'

She did not know why she had said it, she was simply hitting out blindly in an attempt to redress the balance somewhat, but instantly she saw a moment's unguarded wariness in his eyes. Almost at once it was gone again, his expression hardening to hide whatever it was she had seen revealed, but Jayne knew with a flash of excitement that there was something; unwittingly she had touched a raw nerve.

'Are you trying to be clever?' he demanded roughly.

Jayne reached out to grasp the tiny advantage with both hands. To fight Steve was the only way to retain his respect – and her own.

'No, I'm not trying to be clever – just stating facts. We all have something to hide, don't we? Only some of us hide it better than others. And some things are more important than others.'

Again she spoke purely from instinct, again she saw the wariness flash in his eyes.

You are hiding something! she thought triumphantly. There is something you don't want anyone to know – and you think I know what it is!

His hand shot out to imprison her shoulder, his fingers biting hard into her bare flesh. She shivered from a sharp knife-thrust of exhilarating fear.

'Don't meddle in what you don't understand! Just do as I say – right?'

Her lip curled. She no longer felt totally the underdog.

'Very well. Just as long as we are partners, Steve.'

He said nothing, just shot her a look.

'Get dressed,' he said after a moment, then he turned and walked out of the pink-tiled changing room.

Jayne towelled herself dry, ran a comb through her hair and slipped on the white dress. Steve's finger marks still stood out, red weals on her shoulder, but there was no other evidence of their violent coupling.

She lingered for a few moments, playing the conversation over in her mind as she adjusted her make-up. So – he'd found her out. It was almost a relief. But she had also learned that he had something to hide. Remembering the partnership he had more or less offered her, she smiled again. Oh yes, it could be far better than anything Reubens could offer, position and power in an established company – and Steve too. It could all work out very well, particularly if she could discover what it was that he did not want anyone to know. Except that it hardly mattered that she was still ignorant of whatever it was. He *thought* she knew. That should be enough.

By the time Jayne emerged from the changing room there was no sign of Steve. She made her way back through the gardens to join the others.

They were all still there just as she had left them, Dinah and Don on the swing seat, Drew dozing, face down, on the sunbed. And Steve was with them, standing at Dinah's elbow, towering over her as he talked to her.

It was almost symbolic, Jayne thought. Steve had Dinah in the palm of his hand. Through him she, too, would gain a measure of control.

Chapter Sixteen

Mike arrived home shortly after six. He fixed himself a meal by reheating some bolognese sauce from the freezer and cooking a pan of fresh pasta, and carried it into the living room, switching on the television and positioning his chair so that he could watch while he ate.

The national news came on at six thirty-five but Mike paid scant attention to it. He was, to his dismay, thinking about Maggie again, and he wondered what the hell was the matter with him. He had been thinking about her on and off all day, disturbing thoughts that he cursed himself for having but seemed powerless to prevent. Somehow she had got under his skin and she was there with him every waking moment whether he was actually thinking about her or not.

When had it begun? he asked himself in a rare bout of self-examination, but he couldn't come up with an answer. It had happened so insidiously. At first she had simply been Ros's sister but somewhere along the line the balance had changed.

For some time now he had entertained doubts about his relationship with Ros, he realised. At first they had been camouflaged somewhat by the suspicion that he could not totally trust her, and though he had backed away from a serious commitment, fooling himself that he was simply afraid she might let him down as his wife had done, he had begun to wonder if perhaps there was more to it than that. If he had been completely in love with Ros wouldn't the trust have followed automatically? And wouldn't he have been prepared to risk being hurt if he had wanted her enough? More likely the caution had been born of an instinct which had told him that Ros was not the right woman for him, and fear of his pride being dented again had made him determined to hold on to her.

But since he had found her gone he hadn't really missed her as a man should miss the woman he loved. He was concerned, yes, but Ros had become less and less important – the priority had shifted so that finding out what had become of her had stopped being an end in itself and become, in part, an excuse for seeing Maggie.

He hadn't realised the way he had begun to feel about her, hadn't admitted it to himself, until last night. And then, all at once, it had hit him and he had realised with a sense of shock just how much he wanted her.

Mike shovelled spaghetti into his mouth as if assuaging his hunger for food could also assuage that other hunger that was eating away at him – hunger for Maggie – even though he knew very well it could not. Maggie had a husband in Corfu and a fierce sense of loyalty to him, even if the marriage was less than happy. She had made that quite clear. When this was all over she would go home to Corfu and her husband and her less-than-perfect marriage and he would just have to accept it. Except of course that it was not that easy.

The main news ended and the national weather forecast came on. A depression was heading in towards the south-west. The south-west and me both, Mike thought grimly.

The familiar face of one of the local presenters appeared on the screen reading the local headlines. Mike was still only half listening, then, suddenly, the newscaster's words seemed to burst through his state of inattention.

The man who had fallen to his death from the suspension bridge the previous night had been named as local broadcaster and musician Brendan Newman.

Mike froze, a forkful of spaghetti halfway to his mouth. For a moment he thought he must have misheard but no, a photograph of Brendan was being flashed on to the screen. Mike stared at it stupidly, still hardly able to comprehend what he was hearing. The photograph disappeared, the newscaster moved on to the next topic and still he stared, the words replaying themselves in his ears.

Brendan – dead. Brendan – the man who had fallen from the suspension bridge. No, not fallen – jumped. No one fell from the bridge by accident – at least he'd never heard of anyone who had, unless it was an industrial accident. If Brendan had gone over the side it must have been deliberate. But why the hell should he do something like that? Unless . . .

Ros, Mike thought. Brendan *did* have something to do with

Ros's disappearance, and he knew we were on to him, so he has taken the coward's way out and killed himself. He put down his fork, still coiled with spaghetti. He was not hungry any more.

Did Maggie know about this, he wondered? Had she, like him, just heard it on the news? Perhaps – and then again, perhaps not. He went to the phone, picked it up, put it down again. If she knew, she would almost certainly ring him; if she did not he did not want to tell her this way. She was going to be dreadfully upset, better that he should be there with her when he broke the news.

Mike carried the remains of his supper into the kitchen, scraped it into the bin and piled the plate and saucepans into the sink. Then he fetched his jacket and car keys and went out, slamming the door shut behind him.

Maggie had not heard the news. When there was nothing left in the cottage to occupy her she had gone for a long reflective walk and when she had returned she had turned the radio on, filling the emptiness with music and inconsequential chat whilst she made herself a sandwich and ate it.

When she heard the knock at the door she was surprised – and a little disturbed. She could not think who could be calling on her – unless it was the police with some news, which, under these circumstances, was almost bound to be unwelcome. Tense with dread she answered the door to find Mike standing there.

Her first reaction was one of relief. Then she saw his grim expression, telling her without words that something was seriously wrong, and fear returned all of a rush. 'Mike! What is it? What has happened?'

'Let's go inside.' He led her into the kitchen. 'Sit down Maggie.'

She remained standing. 'Why?'

He could tell from her reaction that she did not know.

'Please, Maggie, sit down. There's something I have to tell you that is going to come as a shock.'

She blanched. 'Ros?'

'No, not Ros.' He pulled out one of the kitchen chairs and eased her into it. 'It's Brendan.'

'Brendan? What about him?'

'There's no easy way to say this. Something rather terrible has happened to him.'

'What?'

'He's dead.'

'Brendan!'

'Yes, I heard it on the local news. He fell from the suspension bridge last night.'

'Oh my God!' Her eyes, blank with shock, met his. 'You don't think . . .?'

'That he committed suicide? Well – that is the obvious conclusion.'

'Shit!' She was silent for a moment. 'Brendan! I can't believe it. I know he's, well, an unpredictable character, but *suicide*! I never would have thought . . . Do you suppose he was drunk?'

'I suppose it's a possibility.'

'He must have been drunk. He'd never do such a thing otherwise. I don't think he'd have the guts.' She shivered. 'Oh God, it's too awful to even think about! You are sure?'

'I heard this morning there had been a fatality at the bridge last night but he hadn't been identified. But just now, on the six thirty bulletin, the man was named as Brendan. There's no doubt, Maggie.'

'Oh, poor Brendan!'

Mike looked at her with concern. The full implications had obviously not hit her yet.

'I'll get you a drink.'

'There's tea in the pot . . .'

'You could do with something stronger than tea, and so could I.'

He went into the sitting room and returned with a bottle of whisky and two glasses. Maggie remained seated at the table, chewing on her fingernail, as he poured generous measures and dropped cubes of ice from the refrigerator into them.

'Here – drink this.'

She gulped at the whisky, coughed as it burned her throat.

'Mike, do you think it's possible that Brendan . . . might have done something terrible to Ros and couldn't live with the knowledge any longer?' she asked after a moment.

So it *had* occurred to her.

'The thought did cross my mind,' he said uncomfortably.

'Oh God.' Her voice rose slightly. 'If he did . . . we might never find out what happened to her.'

He covered her hand with his, trying to comfort her.

'We don't know it was that. There may be no connection.'

'Perhaps not. But I don't like it, Mike. You don't know how violent he could be. I've seen for myself. And I've also seen his remorse. He did love her, you see, very much. But he couldn't control himself – in any way at all, really. That was the trouble.'

Mike swallowed his own whisky and refilled the glasses. Comfort from a bottle – Brendan's downfall. The irony of it was disconcerting.

'What happens next?' Maggie asked.

'In what way?'

'What do we do now?'

'God knows – I don't. To be honest I think we have done all we can. We'll have to leave it to the police. Maybe now Brendan has done this they'll take the whole thing more seriously.'

'They must, mustn't they? I mean, every day Ros is missing it becomes more . . . well, ominous. Perhaps they'll search Brendan's flat and find . . . something.' She shivered, a small shudder at first, then more convulsively. The darkness was closing in, the shadows taking on substance.

'You're cold,' he said, touching her arm. 'Get a jumper or something.'

She got up, obedient as a child, and went upstairs to fetch a cardigan.

'It's not really cold,' she said when she returned. 'It just feels cold because everything gets more and more like a nightmare I can't wake up from.'

He looked at her, loving her, wanting to comfort and protect her, remembering all too clearly how she had felt in his arms and the eager response of her lips. How would she react if he went to her and held her now? Perhaps that first time she had been caught unawares; certainly later she had made it clear that she simply wanted to be taken home. Make another move now and it was quite possible she would reject it. More than possible – likely – and the result would be the sort of nasty embarrassing situation that would put an end to the ease of their relationship.

He got up.

'I'll tell you what I think, Maggie. I think I should take you out.'

'Where?'

'I don't know – anywhere. For a drive, a drink. It's a nice evening and we could both do with a breath of fresh air. Come on.'

'All right. Give me a minute to put on some lipstick.'

'You look fine just as you are.'

'No I don't. I'm a mess. And if we're going to stop at a pub . . .'

He held up his hands in mock surrender. 'All right – if you must.'

She disappeared up the stairs and he prowled around the kitchen, waiting. Ros's kitchen. Ros's possessions. Yet already there was something of Maggie superimposed. It was a trifle disconcerting.

A few moments later she was back. She had changed into tan slacks and a cream cotton sweater, combed her hair and applied a little make-up. He felt his stomach contract at the sight of her and warned himself: Don't be stupid. Don't say or do something you will regret.

'Ready then?'

'Ready.'

She went round closing the windows and locking the back door, taking, he thought, a little more time than was absolutely necessary to ensure they were all secure. This business was beginning to put her nerves on edge, he realised. As he opened the door of his car for her to get in he caught a whiff of her perfume – scarcely perfume, really, more a light flowery fragrance that stirred his senses again.

'Let's go.' His voice had a faintly rough edge.

He drove out on to the main road and turned in the direction of the Chew Valley lakes. Inevitably there were still a few cars drawn up along the roadside that skirted the vast expanse of still water and parked in the designated lots beneath the trees, couples strolling or sitting to enjoy the pleasant evening, a family playing cricket whilst their two dogs acted as unofficial but enthusiastic fielders. Mike parked and they got out and walked to the very edge of the lake, sitting on a low stone wall. The sun was going down now, a ball of fire sinking towards the water which reflected its rosy glow; ducks moved lazily, wildfowl skimmed the surface, dived and rose again. The peace was almost soporific and Mike could sense that Maggie was at last beginning to relax. They sat for a long while, not talking, watching the sun dip lower until it disappeared in a bank of low cloud and a chilly wind began to whisper in over the water. He got up.

'Drink?'

'Why not?'

'Poor Brendan,' she said when they were back in the car. 'He must have been very unhappy to do something so dreadful.'

She seemed to have forgotten her earlier suspicion that it might have been guilt that had driven Brendan to suicide, and Mike chose not to remind her.

They found a country pub and went inside. Again the atmosphere was relaxed, peaceful, far removed from the gloom of gathering horrors that had pervaded the cottage. Maggie got out her purse.

'I'll get these. What will you have?'

'Lemonade and lime. I had my fair share of whisky earlier on – I don't want to go over the limit.'

She smiled. 'Since I'm not driving I don't care. I'm going to have a glass of wine.'

She bought the drinks and they carried them over to a corner table.

'What sort of a day did you have?' she asked, sipping her wine, and Mike realised that she was making a conscious effort to avoid returning to the unpleasant subjects that were stil uppermost in both their minds.

'As you'd expect . . .' He regaled her with a few anecdotes and again sensed the shadows receding as she laughed at his stories and the wine relaxed her still further.

They were still there when the landlord called last orders, and Mike saw Maggie's expression cloud. The evening and the brief respite it had brought had come to an end. Now it was back to reality.

Darkness had fallen, soft and complete apart from a sprinkling of stars, and the headlamps of the car cut a swathe through the blackness as they drove back to the cottage.

'Will you come in for a nightcap?' Maggie asked as they drew up outside.

Mike hesitated. To be alone with her in the cottage would be to invite temptation. In spite of his earlier determination to keep things cool he was not at all sure he would be able to resist it.

'I don't think so,' he said. 'Some of us have to get up for work in the morning.'

'Of course.' She said it lightly but he sensed her disappointment. 'Mike – I just remembered something. It may be nothing, of course, but a man phoned for Ros today.'

Instantly he was alert. 'A man? For Ros?'

'Yes. I forgot all about it. I suppose this business with Brendan drove it right out of my head. He said his name was Des Taylor and that he was returning Ros's call. No – wait a minute, he couldn't have said that, because he gave me a number where she could reach him. If she'd telephoned him she would have known it, wouldn't she?'

'Did he say what it was about?'

'No. He was only on for a couple of minutes. It was a London number.'

'And you took it down?'

'Yes.'

'Right.' Mike's voice was hard. 'In that case I'll give Mr Des Taylor a bell and find out what it's all about.'

He was getting out of the car, angry for no reason he could explain except that the fact that strange men were ringing Ros had touched a raw nerve. Maggie caught at his arm.

'Not now, Mike.'

'There's no time like the present.'

'Oh please! Not tonight! I really can't take any more . . .' Her voice was almost tearful and his anger died, replaced by tenderness. She'd had enough for one day; the Brendan business, coming on top of everything else, had really shaken her. He wouldn't do anything to upset her further. The call to Des Taylor would have to wait until tomorrow.

He put his arm around her, feeling her shoulders rigid with tension and quivering slightly from overstretched nerves.

'It's all right, sweetheart. Don't worry. Do you want me to see you to the door?'

She nodded, then, without warning, buried her head in his shoulder.

'Maggie?' he said.

'I don't want to be on my own, Mike.' Her voice was muffled.

'Oh Maggie . . .'

'I know I'm being stupid, but I just don't want to be in that cottage on my own . . . not tonight.'

Oh Christ, he thought, how much can flesh and blood stand?

'You are not being stupid, Maggie,' he said gently. 'I know how you feel. But I can't stay with you. You must know that.'

She raised her head. Her eyes were full of a longing so deep he felt he could drown in it, and her lips, slightly parted as if to make a fresh plea, looked more kissable than ever.

The last of Mike's resolve ebbed away. The hell with it! he thought – and kissed her.

It was some time before they left the car and went into the cottage, and by the time they did they both knew what was going to happen. But it was so inevitable now, and so good, that Maggie found both the shadows and the guilt slipping away until they no longer mattered. Ari and Corfu were a world away, the tensions and shocks of the day were relegated to the periphery of awareness, vaguely unreal, totally unimportant. She was living now only through her senses and each one of those was heightened to a pitch that was sweetly, burstingly unbearable.

She clung to him as he unlocked the door with her key and put the lights on, not wanting to let go of him for so much as a single second.

Mike. His name was a soaring aria in her heart, synonymous with the glow and the sharp singing desire. I love him, she thought, and she wanted to shout it from the rooftops, only his mouth was covering hers again, so instead she repeated the words with every fibre of her being, sliding her arms around his neck, twining her body to his and feeling the instant response.

His lips left her mouth, running a line of kisses down her chin and neck and her skin seemed to tingle with sharp awareness wherever they touched. With a swift movement he lifted her as easily as a child, carrying her into the sitting room, setting her down on the chintzy sofa and kneeling beside her. Then they were kissing again with all the fervour of two people who had wanted nothing else almost from the moment they had met.

For a little while, lost in the joy of allowing themselves at last to indulge that desire, it was enough. But not for long. Soon his hands were on her breasts, sliding up beneath her loose cotton sweater, and she moved only to allow him to begin to undress her.

Oh, the touch of his hands on her sensitised body! Oh, the feel of his back beneath her fingers, broad, smooth, muscular. Her head swam. She was not thinking now, only feeling, and every one of her senses was full of him.

Afterwards, when she remembered the glory of that first time, savouring every detail, every delight, Maggie was surprised to find that she had only a hazy recollection of how she had come to be lying on the hearthrug, totally nude. She supposed he must have lifted her there, or perhaps she had moved of her own volition, still in the circle of his arms, so that it was no more than a fluid progression, but she could not be sure. What she did remember with arousing, sensual clarity, was the urgency and the wonderful sense of calm; the look of his body as he lowered himself to the rug beside her – the hard lean body of a man who plays a great deal of sport, tanned from the open air; and the feel of skin against skin as they reached hungrily for one another, burrowing closer, closer, until they were one. That she would never forget; that she would remember for ever. His weight upon her, making her feel both trapped and submissive, and at the same time gloriously free, the first moments of utter stillness when they lay, afraid to move in case it ended before they had savoured the joy of completeness, and then the fevered activity of lovemaking that would not, could not, wait a moment longer for fulfilment.

In spite of that mutual postponement it was over too soon. If she were to die now, at this moment, it would scarcely matter, Maggie thought, because she held the whole world within her arms and her body. For long wonderful seconds she floated, high above the summit of the tallest mountain, then gently descended to a plateau where once again thought was coherent, if contented, a lovely languorous state of complete satisfaction and happiness.

Reality was encroaching, yet still it did not matter. Ari, Ros, Brendan were there once more, yet they were shadow figures. Only Mike was real, still holding her in his arms. She trailed a finger from his shoulder to his chest, twining it into the mat of dark hair, and pressed her lips to his skin, touching, tasting, replete with love.

'Maggie,' he said softly, and she found her own voice.

'You won't go, will you, Mike? You won't leave me?'
And his voice was rough but also totally comforting.
'I won't go, Maggie. I won't leave you. Not tonight – not ever.'

Chapter Seventeen

They slept that night in the narrow bed in the spare room. It was less than comfortable, for Mike was a big man, but sleeping together in Ros's bed was one thing they could not bring themselves to do. The cramped conditions and the unfamiliarity of being in one another's arms made for a restless night but neither of them minded. They made love twice more, once in the small hours when they woke to find themselves already almost at the point of union, warm, sleepy, yet already aroused, and once in the first rosy light of dawn with the birds chorusing in the trees outside the window and the early sun streaming in through a gap in the curtains.

Afterwards, as they showered and shared breakfast, the glow of newly discovered love was still with them, suffusing everything, even the ever-present problems, in a soft haze.

'I wish I didn't have to go to school,' Mike said, drinking freshly-brewed coffee from Ros's big French-style earthenware cups.

'I wish you didn't have to.'

'I'll get away from school as early as I can and see you at home this evening.' They had already decided that she should move in with him – one night in the narrow bed had been romantic, too many would be exhausting. 'Will you be all right?'

'I'll be fine. I'll make my way over when I've cleared up here.'

But when he had gone, driving off along the lane, she experienced a moment's utter loneliness and for a moment the shadow of the nightmare was there again, hanging over her like the sword of Damocles. When the engine of his car had died away into the distance the quiet of the morning was unbroken, with not even the usual sounds of the countryside to disturb it – no birds singing now, no cows coughing or mooing, just the occasional sharp rustle of movement in the hedges to prove she was not the only living thing in this strangely silent world.

She went back into the cottage. The clutter of used breakfast things on the table was comforting – the sight of two cups and saucers, two plates made her feel as if Mike was still there with her. She washed up, then went upstairs to attend to the bedroom. It seemed to her that the aura of love was still in the small sunny room, the sheets still warm from where their bodies had lain entwined, the dent made by Mike's head still evident in the pillow. Warmth flooded her, a soft weakness in the pit of her stomach, and she sat for a moment on the edge of the bed, remembering and enjoying.

How could she feel like this – so totally blissful – when she had been so sure that if she gave way to her emotions she would feel nothing but guilt? How could she be so utterly happy knowing she had betrayed both Ari and Ros? But she did. They were still oddly unreal; only Mike loomed large, filling the horizons of her world, and she thought: Don't question it now. There will be time enough later for guilt and recriminations. Enjoy it while it lasts, store up every single blissful moment against whatever the future may hold.

She stripped the bed, took the sheets and pillowcases downstairs and bundled them into the washing machine. She turned on the radio, singing along with the music as she worked, but when the news headlines came on on the half-hour she turned it off. She didn't want to hear Brendan's death mentioned – and they were sure to mention it. She didn't want the shadow of reality to encroach on her fragile happiness.

While the washing machine was working she packed the things she would need to take to Mike's into her suitcase – practically everything she had brought with her since she had travelled light – clothes, toiletries, her nightdress, though somehow she could not imagine she would need a nightdress, if last night had been anything to go by. Another warm glow suffused her body at the thought. Already she could hardly wait to be in his arms again.

She had almost finished when the telephone rang. She ran down the stairs eagerly, part of her hoping it might be Mike, though common sense told her he would be teaching by now.

'Hello?'

'Margaret? It's me, your mother.'

Her heart sank. 'Oh hello, Mother.'

'Margaret, have you seen the papers?'

'Oh.' Back to reality with a jolt. 'You mean . . .?'

'Brendan. Margaret, it is too awful! I mean, I never did like the man, but this . . .' Her voice tailed away. 'It's all over the front page of the *Western Daily Press*. And Rosalie is mentioned too.'

'What does it say?'

'That she is missing. That no one knows where she is. And you are quoted as saying you are very worried about her. They even seem to know you are over here from Corfu. How did they know that?'

'It's a long story. We thought, Mike and I . . .'

'Yes, Michael is named too. Rosalie's current boyfriend, they call him. Really it is most embarrassing! I only hope not too many of our friends read it. Most of them take the *Telegraph*, of course, but just the same . . .'

As always Maggie felt her irritation beginning to mount at what she considered her mother's shallowness. Ros was missing, Brendan was dead, and Dulcie was worrying about what her friends would think!

'Harry says the whole thing is disgraceful,' Dulcie continued. 'He feels the implication is that Brendan might be connected in some way with Ros's disappearance. It's ridiculous, of course, not to say libellous . . .'

'I don't think one can libel the dead, Mother,' Maggie said, her tone sharper than she intended. 'And if the publicity can do something to help find Ros, then I think it's worth a little embarrassment.'

Dulcie bridled. 'There really is no need to take that tone with me, Margaret. And I still think it is ridiculous to suggest that anything dreadful has happened to Rosalie. I wish you would put such an idea out of your head.'

'Mother . . .'

A ring at the doorbell. Maggie jumped at the chance to end the conversation.

'There's somebody at the door. I am going to have to go. I'll phone you back.'

'Very well. I shall be out this afternoon, though. It's my day for the Townswomen's Guild.'

'I'll catch up with you sometime.' She replaced the receiver and went to the door.

'I wondered if I could have a chat with you, Mrs Veritos.' It was Sheena Ross, the reporter from the *Western Daily Press*.

'Oh yes. Come in. Would you like a coffee?'

'Love one. Look, I'm sorry to just descend on you but I think we need to talk.'

'Of course.' Maggie made the coffee and Sheena sat down at the kitchen table, open pad in front of her.

'You've heard about Brendan Newman, of course.'

'Yes. And I understand you've run a front page on the story today.'

'Have you seen it?'

'No, but my mother has. She was just telephoning me about it. She's not happy.'

'Sorry about that. I thought you wanted publicity. And in any case, Brendan Newman is still news, though he's not the public figure he was. How do you feel about his death?'

'Shocked.'

'Understandably. What do you think made him do such a thing? Always assuming it was suicide, of course.'

Maggie was aware of alarm bells beginning to ring. On Saturday the publicity had seemed like a good idea; now she was not sure exactly what sort of demons she was unleashing.

'I honestly don't know.'

'You don't think it might have been guilt?'

'I told you – I don't know. To be honest I can't tell you any more than I told you on Saturday.'

'Then perhaps you could fill in some background details about your sister,' Sheena said, shifting tack. 'What sort of a person is she? And her job – she works for Vandina, I understand.'

'Yes.'

'Tell me about it.'

Perhaps some of her mother's discomfort with the situation had rubbed off on her, Maggie thought, for she now felt curiously reticent. How could it possibly help find Ros to have all kinds of personal details plastered over the press? But since she had been the instigator she did not see how she could back off now. She answered the reporter's questions giving as little away as possible.

'What about the boyfriend?' Sheena asked.

'Mike?'

'Yes. They have a good relationship?'

'Oh . . . yes . . .' Maggie flushed slightly. 'As far as I know . . .'

The reporter's sharp instinct picked up the slight hesitation.

'There wasn't any trouble between the boyfriend and the ex-husband? Jealousy – that sort of thing?'

'Brendan was always jealous. There was nothing new in that. But he and Ros were divorced. She had every right to new relationships.' She glanced at her watch. 'To be honest, I don't see where this is getting us. Have you got everything you want?'

'For the moment.' The reporter closed her notebook with a snap. 'I'm on my way to the police station now. If I need anything more I'll be in touch. And likewise, no doubt you'll let me know any developments?'

'Yes.' Maggie wondered if she should tell the reporter she would be contactable only at Mike's and decided against it. She didn't want to encourage speculation on that front. Just the smallest hint could be very damaging. Dealing with the press was all very well but it was a little like having a tiger by the tail. You never knew what they would make of something, how far you could trust their discretion and even whether or not what they printed would be accurate.

The washing machine had finished its cycle and as the day was warm with a fresh breeze Maggie decided to hang out the sheets and get them at least partially dry before leaving. There was no hurry, after all. Mike would be at school until four o'clock. Maggie put the sheets on the line then pottered about the cottage, her mind butterflying over the momentous and varied events of the last days.

Just before midday the telephone rang. Mother again, Maggie thought, going to answer it. But it was not her mother – it was Mike.

'You're still there, then?'

'Yes. I've been clearing up and I've had the *Western Daily Press* reporter here. Brendan's death seems to have made the story big news.'

'I've seen the headlines. You're all right though?'

'Yes.'

'Just thought I'd ring and make sure. Oh, and there's something else I thought of. With all this blowing up I wondered if it might be a good idea to go over to Vandina and collect Ros's personal things.'

Maggie experienced a twinge of discomfort. 'What do you mean?'

'Ros dealt with a lot of her personal affairs from the office. She used to say she might as well make use of her secretary and the office franking machine. She looked on it as one of the perks of her job. It occurred to me that since she's not there any more it might be wise to take possession of anything . . . personal. Now the newspapers are interested you can never be quite sure what they will do.'

'Vandina wouldn't hand anything over to them without Ros's say-so, surely?'

'I wouldn't think so, but reporters can be very persistent – and tricky. I just feel we should have the whip hand over what they do, or don't, get hold of. Could you go over and see to it, do you think?'

'Well – yes, I suppose so. If you really think . . .'

'I do.'

'All right. I'll go now. I've got nothing else to do.'

'Good girl. I'll see you about four.'

'Yes, see you.' She replaced the receiver, warmed through and through simply by hearing his voice, though her initial reaction was to wonder just what he was going on about – she could not imagine Ros would have left anything really confidential at Vandina. If she had, of course, she could see his point. It wouldn't be very nice if the papers got hold of details of Ros's private life. But she was not too keen on the prospect of simply turning up at Vandina and demanding Ros's belongings. For one thing it might be very inconvenient for them, for another she was not enraptured at the thought that she might very well run into Steve. It could all be very embarrassing, she thought. Far better to ring and warn them she was coming.

She picked up the phone again and dialled the Vandina number, wondering who she should ask for. Dinah, perhaps, in view of the fact that she had been her guest the other evening? Or was that taking advantage of the invitation? Best, perhaps, to speak to Dinah's secretary.

A few moments – and a burst of *Eine Kleine Nachtmusik* – later, Maggie found herself connected to Liz Christopher, explaining that she would like to collect any of Ros's personal possessions that might be in the office and asking when would be a convenient time for her to call for them.

The secretary sounded surprised, and a little upset.

'Oh dear, does this mean you think Ros won't be coming back?'

'No, it doesn't mean that,' Maggie said swiftly. 'It's just that since we don't know where she is I think it would be a good idea to have her things here, at home.'

'I see,' Liz said, though she clearly did not. 'Give me an hour or so and I'll get them up together for you, Mrs Veritos.'

'Thanks,' Maggie said. She had been hoping to go more or less straight away as she was anxious, now, to get to Mike's flat. But she could hardly quibble over an hour. Maggie glanced at the clock, decided it was close enough to lunchtime, and went into the kitchen to make a sandwich. After lacking appetite for days she was suddenly ravenously hungry. Was this what love could do? If so she had better be very careful or she would be putting on weight. But for the moment, she simply did not care.

Liz Christopher replaced the receiver and glanced up at Jayne Peters-Browne who was perched on the corner of her desk.

'That was Ros's sister, Maggie. She wants to collect Ros's personal things. Now why in the world should she want to do that?'

Jayne swung one leg idly. 'She doesn't trust us, I suppose.'

'I've said I'll get the stuff ready for her, but do you think I ought? I mean, I know she's her sister but Ros might not want her personal things handed over to her. And anyway, I don't like the thought of doing it. I know I shall feel I'm prying.'

Jayne laughed. 'What a hindrance scruples are! If it makes you queasy leave it to me. I'll do it.'

'But you're so busy . . .'

'Not that busy,' Jayne said, a slightly bitter note creeping into her voice. 'Dinah is still playing her cards close to her chest about her new spring range. I should be in on it, helping her with the design. It's mortifying not to be allowed to do the job I was employed for.'

'Oh, I'm sure she'll copy you in on the plans soon,' Liz soothed. 'But in any case, it's just not your pigeon to havc to sort out office affairs. I wouldn't expect you to . . .'

'Rubbish!' Jayne said forcefully. 'I've offered to sort Ros's things out and I will.' She did not add that her offer of help was far from being altruistic – she was actually relishing the thought of having *carte blanche* to rummage through Ros's personal belongings. 'I'll go and do it now. Have you got a key to open her filing cabinet?'

'It's open. We've had to have access to the things she was working on in her absence.'

Jayne slid off the corner of the desk, smoothing her skirt down over her thighs, and went into Ros's office. With the windows shut, the chair set precisely behind the desk and Ros's pens and pencils lined up neatly on the blotter it had something of the abandoned air of the *Marie Celeste*.

Some files which had been needed were piled neatly on the desk but Jayne ignored them, opening drawers and flicking through the papers inside to look for anything that might be considered personal.

After a few minutes' searching Jayne was feeling vaguely disappointed. Correspondence with an electrician Ros was contracting to do some work on the cottage and an oriental rug importer from whom she clearly intended to make a purchase hardly constituted the sort of titillating discovery she had been hoping for. In another drawer was a glossy magazine and a couple of wallets of photographs – Jayne flicked through them eagerly but they were all innocuous, mostly of Mike and Ros herself, obviously taken on a day out to a garden somewhere when the rhododendrons had been in bloom – Stourton, perhaps, or Heaven's Gate. There were two letters from a friend in Scarborough relating domestic anecdotes and a postcard from someone on holiday in the Dordogne. Hardly epoch-making, any of it. Jayne put it all together in a large manila envelope and, without much hope, opened the smallest drawer in Ros's desk and drew out a pink cardboard wallet.

A wad of correspondence had been stuffed loosely inside; Jayne extracted it and noticed that the top letter – addressed to Ros at her home address – was headed with the name and logo of an Aberdeen-based corporation, Excel Oil. Instantly her attention was alerted – wasn't that the company Steve had worked for before coming to Vandina? She flipped quickly through the papers; copies of letters which Ros had obviously typed herself on her small portable machine rather than getting Liz or one of the typists to do them for her, and a sheaf of notes, handwritten, that read almost like a diary. Jayne felt her skin begin to prickle and she read the whole file again more slowly, thoroughly digesting the contents.

By the time she had finished Jayne could hardly contain her excitement. When she had offered to sort through Ros's personal things she had done it from motives of nosiness, nothing more. Yet now she held in her hands information that could very well be synonymous with a barrel of dynamite.

Jayne sat back in Ros's chair, a smile curving her generous mouth as she reflected on the strange tricks fate could play. Only yesterday Steve had threatened her because he had learned her secret, only yesterday her position had seemed untenable, her future insecure and out of her control. But also yesterday she had gleaned the first inkling that he, too, might have something to hide. And now, like a gift from the gods, she had discovered what it was. Nothing concrete, of course, just a second-hand rendering of Ros's suspicions. But somehow Jayne had no doubt at all that they were well founded.

'Well, well, Steve!' she said aloud, though very softly and very triumphantly.

Steve was in his office trying to check progress schedules against projected delivery dates, but concentration was not coming easily. In general he was able to be single-minded about whatever he was doing – useful in almost any situation, vital to his very survival when he had been working as a diver – but today he found himself wandering off at a tangent so frequently that any continuity in his work was not so much difficult as impossible. And the tangent was Jayne Peters-Browne.

When he had unearthed the fact that she was the mole at Vandina, conducting industrial espionage on behalf of Reubens, Steve had been not so much angry as amused. The fact that she was being both duplicitous and daring only enhanced the attraction she held for him and he had enjoyed the feeling of power over her that the knowledge had given him. His affair with Jayne had always been a game; now a new element had been introduced and the result was oddly refreshing.

From the point of view of the company the fact that Jayne had been less than faithful bothered him not at all. He had no emotional ties to Vandina; he did not feel, as Dinah did, that his favourite child had been violated. He had wanted to discover the culprit and put a stop to the espionage only because if Vandina's profits and image suffered as a result he would suffer with them. The healthier the company, the bigger the profits, and the better off he personally would be, both financially and status-wise. He could draw a bigger salary, claim more expenses, have a better car at the company's expense, and ultimately he would come into an inheritance all the more worth having. A mole might have threatened all these things if the leaks had proved increasingly damaging.

But once he had realised that Jayne was the person he was after, the threat to his lifestyle had receded to the point of being nonexistent. Had he discovered any one of the company's other employees doing the same thing he would have dismissed them instantly. But not Jayne. He could handle her. He *had* handled her – and he had enjoyed doing so. The leaks would stop now, he was certain. Whatever Jayne's connections with Reubens, the deal he had offered her was worth more.

Only one thing had bothered him – the comment she had made that he had something to hide. But on reflection he was fairly sure that that had been no more than a shot in the dark, a way of trying to defend herself by the prescribed method – attack. He could not really believe that Jayne, or anyone else for that matter, could possibly know the truth about him. He had covered his tracks too thoroughly and thought through every eventuality, every juncture where things might go wrong. No, she had just been whistling in the wind, he was sure – but it had been unnerving, all the same, that moment when he had thought that somehow she had stumbled upon his secret.

The door to his office opened and Steve looked up, expecting it to be Dinah, who was the only person who had the right to enter without first obtaining his permission. But it was not Dinah.

'Jayne!' The fact that he had just been thinking about her so that she had practically eavesdropped on his thoughts made his tone even sharper than it would otherwise have been. 'I thought I made it clear the other day that I expect you to knock before barging into my office.'

Jayne only smiled and came right on in, closing the door behind her and leaning against it.

'Don't be like that, darling! I just popped in to make arrangements for our lunchtime rendezvous.'

He eyed her coldly. 'We don't have a lunchtime rendezvous – not today, at any rate. I plan to spend my lunch break with my mother.'

'Ah, your *mother*!' Her voice was silky soft, yet overlaid with hidden meaning. 'I'm sure she would understand if you told her that something quite unavoidable had come up. She really is very understanding where you are concerned, isn't she?'

He ignored the innuendo. 'I have no intention of telling her any such thing. Why should I?'

'Because I am asking you to, darling.'

He almost laughed – almost, but not quite. There was something vaguely disquieting about her totally confident manner.

'I'm sorry, Jayne, but you don't call the shots around here.'

'Oh darling, I think I do – now.' She smiled again, coming across to lay a hand that was strangely possessive on his shoulder.

Steve felt a slight sweat breaking out on the palms of his hands.

'What the hell are you talking about?'

'As I said to you yesterday, we all have something to hide, don't we? I'm an industrial spy, and you are . . . Well, we both know what you are, don't we? But it would be such a pity if Dinah were to find out. She wouldn't like it at all if she knew how you had deceived her. So you see, darling, I don't think you can afford *not* to do what I want. After all, you have a great deal more to lose than I do.'

A great icy wave washed over Steve. It wasn't bluff – she knew. How the hell she had found out he could not imagine, but he no longer had any doubts that she really did know the truth. As always in moments of crisis he became immensely calm, his brain working overtime, every sense and instinct as sharply alert as an animal at bay and fighting for its life.

'Are you trying to blackmail me, Jayne?' he asked, playing for time.

She laughed, a chuckle low in her throat.

'Don't let's call it blackmail! No, we are a mutual protection society, aren't we? You keep my secret, I'll keep yours. Only I really think we should talk about it over a bottle of champagne and . . .' Her fingers trailed up to his neck, running tantalisingly through the hair that grew down over the collar of his shirt, '. . . *other* things . . .'

'Champagne!' he said, ignoring those teasing fingers that only a few short hours ago would have driven him wild with lust. 'Well that sounds like an offer I can't refuse.'

'I knew you'd see it my way, darling. Shall I organise it – usual place?'

'No,' he said smoothly. 'I've got a better idea. Didn't Drew say yesterday that he was going to London today? That means there is no one at your house – and one place we have never made love is your bed. Wouldn't that be fun? Don't worry about the champagne – I have some on ice and it should still be cold by the time we get there.'

She hesitated. It wasn't quite what she had had in mind, but then again there was something deliciously titillating about the idea.

'Will we go together?'

'Better not. Take the rest of the morning off, Jayne, go home and . . . get things ready. I'll join you when I've finished off here – and squared it with Dinah.'

'All right.' Her lips curved. 'I'm so glad you see it my way. But then I knew you would.' She moved to the door, slinky as a well-fed cat. 'See you later, lover.'

'Yes.' He managed a smile back but as the door closed after her it fell away like a mask. He got up and paced to the window, working and formulating the plan that had occurred to him, instinctively almost, the moment he had realised she not only knew but intended to use her knowledge against him. It would be easy – so long as he covered his tracks properly. Already he had swung things his way and lulled Jayne into a false sense of security. She really thought, the silly bitch, that he would allow her to maintain a hold over him. It only went to prove she really did not know him at all.

After a few moments he buzzed through to Dinah's office.

'Dinah, look, I'm sorry, but something has just come up and I'm going to be a bit late for lunch. I'll see you there, right?'

'All right. Look, we'll leave it altogether if it's not convenient. I don't mind, honestly.'

'No – I'll be there,' Steve said. 'In fact you can go on and order for me if you like. I'll have sirloin steak and all the trimmings.'

'If you're sure . . .'

'Yes, sure.'

He replaced the receiver and fetched the bottle of champagne from his office refrigerator, wrapping it in a big brown envelope so that it would not be too glaringly obvious to anyone he passed on the way out. Then he went to the small cloakroom that was *en suite* with his office, combed his hair, washed his hands, and went through the pockets of the jackets that hung there looking for something. When he found it he drew it out, looking at it thoughtfully. A fine silk scarf – perfect. He twisted it experimentally around his hands, then pushed it into his pocket. It was going to be risky, of course, something of this kind always was, but he didn't see that he had any choice, and in any case, risks were something Steve had never shied away from. He lived dangerously and so far the rewards had been high. For years now Steve had had a motto, a maxim to live by: 'I take no prisoners.' Never, it seemed to him, had it been more apt.

'I take no prisoners.' He never had and this time he certainly would not. The stakes were far too high.

Dinah walked down the corridor to Don Kennedy's office. He looked up from his desk as she entered, smiling the pleasure he never failed to experience when seeing her unexpectedly, even after all these years.

'Good news, Dinah, I think I've sorted out the finance for your new venture.'

'Wonderful! I knew you'd do it. You always do. But that's not why I'm here, believe it or not. I've come to ask if you'd like to have lunch with Steve and me – well, with me, at any rate. Steve was supposed to be taking me out but he's going to be late and I don't fancy being there on my own. Will you escort me?'

A slight pink flush coloured Don's baby-smooth cheeks. Dear God, he thought, she can make me feel like a teenager again whenever she looks at me with those beautiful eyes of hers. Aloud he said: 'I'll be honoured, Dinah. You know you don't need to ask.'

She smiled at him. 'I know, Don. And it is wonderful to feel that in this wickedly uncertain world there is someone like you I can rely on. Will you drive me?'

'Give me ten minutes, Dinah, and I'll be with you.'

As Dinah emerged from Don's office she saw Steve disappearing down the stairs, off to whatever urgent business had claimed him, obviously. She raised a hand expectantly to wave to him but he did not turn around and he did not see her.

Jayne was in the bedroom when she heard Steve's car draw up outside. She glanced out of the window, watching him park well out of sight of the road, then walk around to the back door, and a satisfied smile curved her lips. She hadn't expected him for another ten minutes or so – he must have virtually dropped everything and come straight over. Whether his haste was because he couldn't wait to be with her, drinking champagne and making love, or whether it was because he was anxious to find out exactly how much she knew she could not be sure, but she hardly cared any more. The advantage in the power-struggle games they always played had swung around to her and she could not imagine losing it again. What she knew was too big, too important. The fact that he was here now proved that – if she had had any doubt about it.

Jayne paused for a moment in front of the mirror, retying the sash of her black satin négligé and settling it more smoothly around her shoulders. Beneath it she was wearing a black basque; the whaleboning pushed up her ample breasts to give a tantalising cleavage at the open neck of the négligé. Steve had once said he liked her in black and she wanted to look good for him. Power through knowledge of him was all very well, but she did not want to lose that other power she exerted with such proficiency – the power of sex. Satisfied with her attire, she touched her lips with a scarlet lipstick – black could so easily drain the colour from her creamy-complexioned face – and went downstairs to let him in.

'I see you got the champagne,' she said, glancing at the bottle which he had taken out of its wrapping in the car.

'And I see you are ready and waiting for me.'

She smiled at him, a secret, knowing smile, then fetched two flutes.

'I think we should drink a toast to our new arrangement, don't you?'

'And I think we should drink it in bed.'

'Eager, aren't we?' she teased.

'Why not? Life is too short to waste precious time, especially when you are looking so very delectable.'

'All right. We'll do it your way – this time.'

She led the way up the curving open-plan staircase to her bedroom, a gloriously extravagant room decorated all in white – frilled white lace on the four-poster bed, white painted walls, ankle-deep white carpet. She went to the bed, turning back the beau-duvet and plumping up the pillows before arranging herself in a seductive pose.

Steve took off his jacket and laid it carefully across a chair beside the bed, then opened the bottle of champagne, poured some into each of the two flutes and handed one to Jayne.

'Here's to us, darling.' She raised the flute, smiling at him across the rim.

'Here's to success in all our enterprises.' But he barely tasted his, putting his glass down on the dressing table whilst he undressed swiftly and joined her on the bed.

'Steve! I don't know what I've done to deserve this!' she murmured as he took the glass from her hand and began kissing her.

'Don't you, darling?' He was easing the négligé from her shoulders and his eyes upon her smooth white throat were speculative, but Jayne did not notice. She was too pleased with herself and too excited by the prospect of the imminent encounter. She saw his gaze only as admiring and lustful.

He took her quickly, never for one moment, on this occasion, allowing her to gain the upper hand. Then he raised himself on one elbow, looking down at her.

'How did you come to find out, Jayne?'

The question took her by surprise; in the frantic activity of the last few minutes she had quite forgotten his secret. She stretched languorously and reached for her glass of champagne.

'I think that's my secret, don't you? Suffice it to say I *did* find out. And I'm very glad I did. I think we shall make a formidable team, don't you? It's ironic really when you come to think of it – neither of us being what we seem to be. Perhaps that's what drew us together – birds of a feather and all that. That – and, of course, our mutual liking for a love nest . . .' She laughed, low in her throat. She was enjoying herself.

Steve made no response and she set down her glass of champagne, reclining against his shoulder.

'Talk to me, darling.'

'What about?'

'Well, I know you are not Dinah's son,' she said. 'But what I would like you to tell me is who you really are.'

He reached out a hand, lazy but purposeful, talking the silk scarf from the pocket of his jacket where it lay within easy reach of the bed.

'That, my sweet,' he said softly, 'is something you will never know.'

Steve

Steve had been born in Vermont, New England, in a small town just south of the Canadian border. He was the third in a family of six children, his father was a mill-hand and they lived in a run-down street of small and badly kept houses that were all occupied by mill-workers.

As a small boy Steve was not unhappy with his lot. The woods at the edge of the town were his playground, in summer he swam naked in the nearby lake; in winter, when it was frozen over, he skated and slid or tobogganed on the steep slopes of the hills that surrounded the town. He did not care, then, that his trousers were a size too big, hand-me-downs that he had not yet grown into, or that his feet often hung out of the soles of his shoes. He had plenty to eat, his mother was a good, if plain, cook who made the most of the produce that came to hand, and it did not bother him in the least that supper was at five thirty instead of seven thirty or eight, the time more refined folks ate. In those far-off days, when happiness was a weekend or a long vacation in which he could do as he liked instead of being incarcerated in the hideous grade-school building where the children of the town had been educated since the turn of the century, it never occurred to him to look with envy at the families who lived in the pleasant tree-lined streets of the better neighbourhoods where the houses were painted so perfectly and uniformly white that they were almost hurtful to the eye when the bright summer sun blazed down on them, and the imposing red-brick houses with their wide manicured lawns which were the homes of the elite of the town might have belonged to another world. Ambition meant nothing to him then, unless it was the ambition to captain the football team or beat the other boys in the impromptu swimming races across the lake, and both of these ambitions were easily achieved. Steve was tall for his age and well built, and he had the co-ordination needed to make him good at every sport he tried. His prowess brought him the envy and adulation of his peers and Steve basked in it, accepting it as his due and spurring himself on to even greater efforts.

It was only when he entered his teens that he began to be aware that there were other areas of life where he might be found wanting. As he moved up the grades, status symbols began to matter more – the shoes, the leather jackets, the car the old man drove – and Steve began to resent the fact that his family could afford none of them.

'Be grateful we don't have to go to the Poor Board for hand-outs,' his mother said when he complained that he needed new jeans – had needed them for months. 'Be grateful for what you have.' But Steve was not grateful, not even for the fact that his old jeans had become so tight on him that the girls in his grade, beginning to be gigglingly aware of the male sex, were giving him curious – and often admiring – looks. The jeans might flatter him in an almost indecent way but they were also evidence of the fact that his family was poor, too poor to replace worn-out items of clothing, let alone follow the latest fashion craze.

To compensate for the deprivation he was beginning to feel Steve redoubled his efforts to be the best at every sport and even began to put some extra energy into his school work. He had a quick, lively intelligence which, until now, had allowed him to keep up with class lessons without really trying at all. Now he found that if he applied himself he could easily make the top half-dozen in every subject. For a little while the success was enough to satisfy him, but not for long. At fifteen Steve suffered a humiliation that reminded him all too sharply that in small-town Vermont it was not what one did that mattered, but who one was.

The humiliation came in the shape of a girl. Her name was Lisa-Marie Ford and she was, all the boys agreed, the prettiest girl in town, a petite blonde with a cute turned-up nose and shoulder-length hair that flicked at the ends. In spite of being small she was very well developed, with a tiny waist and breasts that swelled so invitingly above it that the boys' eyes stood out on stalks when she passed.

Like all the other boys Steve feasted his eyes on Lisa-Marie and imagined what he would like to do to her if he got her alone. But it was a while before he got up the courage to do anything about it. In spite of being delectably pretty Lisa-Marie had a reputation for being a little stuck-up. She delivered cutting put-downs to all those boys who dared to ask her for a date, and Steve knew that both his reputation and his ego would suffer a serious dent if he laid them on the line by making a move and being rejected.

Then one day he had seen Lisa-Marie looking at him and he had recognised in her eyes the same kind of emotion that he felt when he looked at her – the dreaming and the wanting – and it had given him the spur he needed.

It was high summer and they were down at the lake, a crowd of them, swimming and fooling in the water that was always ice-cold, even when the sun beat down on it, and lying on the shingle beach to dry off in the sunshine. As usual he had raced with the other boys to an old pontoon moored half a mile out and beaten them there and back again. He came out of the water dripping, his fair hair plastered wetly to his head, looked back to see the closest of his rivals at least twenty metres behind him, and laughed, standing there with his hands on his narrow hips and the sun turning the water droplets on his golden-tanned body to a rash of tiny diamonds. Then he had turned and walked back towards the cluster of girls who were watching him admiringly. Only Lisa-Marie was not looking, rubbing sun-oil into her arms and pretending not to notice. But when he reached them she looked up and it was there in her eyes, that unmistakable expression that needed no explanation. Steve felt a quiver of excitement dart deep inside, quickly followed by a rush of exhilaration. He returned Lisa-Marie's look, his eyes holding hers until a faint colour came up in her cheeks and she looked away. He threw himself down on the shingle then, ignoring her. But he knew, with a confidence that made him impregnable, that if he asked her for a date now she would not refuse.

Towards the end of the afternoon when they all packed their belongings together and started on the trek home he fell into step beside her. She glanced at him, that same look, half shy, half coquettish, and he came straight out with it.

'What are you doing tomorrow?'

Her pert little mouth curved up. 'Same as today, I guess. Swimming. Sunbathing.'

'But we don't have to do it with the others, do we? Why don't we go somewhere on our own?'

'Where? They'll be at the beach, won't they?'

Not for the first time Steve wished he had a car. But he hadn't and he wasn't likely to get one. He worked weekends at Ray Mallalieu's garage, washing cars and, more recently, lending a hand with simple mechanics, but on what he earned he would never be able to save enough for such a luxury. One day . . . one day . . . But for now he'd just have to do the best he could.

'I know another bay. Further round . . .' His throat felt tight now. He was less sure of himself than he had been.

She kept him waiting a full thirty seconds for her reply. Lisa-Marie might, as she had told her best friend Helen Maybury, be in love, but she had no intention of appearing easy game. Then, just as he was about to shrug and turn away in an attempt to salvage the remnants of his pride, she said: 'OK.'

He arranged to meet her on Main Street, outside the bank. It was a good central place, midway between the mill-hands' cottages and the neighbourhood where Lisa-Marie lived in a pretty white house with green gabling, Cape Cod style. She was a little late and he waited for her under the elm trees where the old men sat on wooden benches, watching the world go by. He was just beginning to wonder if she was going to stand him up when he saw her coming along the street towards him swinging a brightly coloured tote bag. She was wearing a scarlet cutaway singlet and a brief pair of shorts and looked unbelievably pretty.

'Hi.'

'Hi.'

They started the trek out to the lake, up the hill to the outskirts of town, down again, through the cool woods where last year's pine needles made a thick, soft carpet on the path. When they emerged into the sunshine again he turned towards a bay that was almost hidden from the rest of the lake. Although they could not see the others in the usual gathering place they could hear them, shouts and laughter carrying across the spit of thickly wooded land that separated them, blown on the breeze that whispered across the water.

It was a wonderful day – magical, almost, the sort of day that remains in the memory until the end of time and can be triggered and relived by a sound, a smell, a tune. For Steve that tune was the Beach Boys singing 'And we'll have fun, fun, fun, Till her daddy takes the T-Bird away!' But there was an edge of gall mixed with the sense of freedom it evoked. Lisa-Marie's daddy might have a Thunderbird (he hadn't – he drove a Buick convertible); his own certainly never would. The last six months had been worse than ever financially, for his oldest brother, Dean, whose wage packet from the mill where he now worked had eked out the family income, had got a girl into trouble and had had to marry her. At the same time his father, perhaps finally growing tired of the unequal struggle to exist, had begun to drink more heavily. There was also talk of laying off some of the mill-hands and Steve knew his mother was very much afraid that, taking age and present behaviour into account, his father might be one of them.

That day, however, the threat of worsening poverty was only a shadow on the horizon. He and Lisa-Marie swam, sunbathed and talked. Some of the talking centred on the future. Lisa-Marie was going to carry on with further education; Steve knew that although he was quite capable of doing the same he would be expected to leave school as soon as he could and find work to contribute to the family's income. Briefly the shadow threatened, then receded as he looked further into the future, concentrating on the success he was determined to be when he left the grinding poverty of Mill Street behind him for ever.

Later, much later, he kissed her for the first time, and her firm rounded little body, clad only in her polka-dot bikini, felt so good against his that he forgot his social inadequacy, forgot his embarrassment at his sun-faded swimming shorts, even forgot the doubts he had had about his ability to make love the way a real man should. For all his popularity with the girls, for all his locker-room boasting, Steve was inexperienced beyond the quick kiss-and-grope behind the gymnasium, and though he had read plenty of sex magazines of the sort that were stacked on the top shelf of the store, he had sometimes wondered how he would manage when it actually came to the point, whether he would be fumbling and ineffectual, disappointing the girl of his choice and blasting his macho image into a million humiliating fragments. With Lisa-Marie in his arms, however, the doubts melted. For today he did nothing more than kiss her – a little more deeply than any of those quick clinches behind the gymnasium, but still just a kiss – but his body was responding, all the same, in a way that told him that when the time came he would after all know instinctively what to do.

He lay on his side, face to face with her, his hands moving slowly and sensuously across her sun-warmed back, and felt the natural urges motivating his body so that it was more a question of restraining them than wondering how to proceed. He kissed her with his lips and his teeth and his tongue, holding her close, close, from the waist up but never allowing their hips or legs to touch because he thought that if they did he would be unable to control himself. That would come later, a little more, a little further each time, the next day and the next. The waiting and the wanting was a fever and Steve forgot about everything but being with Lisa-Marie and the way she made him feel.

After a week in which they went to the lake every day he made love to her because he could wait no longer. He had spent some of his precious earnings from the garage on a packet of French letters, which he had bought with some embarrassment and carried in the pocket of his shorts with enormous pride. Feeling the packet there against his hip filled him with such excitement he could scarcely breathe, but he was a little apprehensive about how Lisa-Marie would react when she knew he had been so presumptuous as to make such a purchase and nervous about the right moment to produce them. In the event it was all so much easier than he had imagined. Lisa-Marie was almost as eager as he, clinging and pressing herself close, but when he slid down her bikini pants and she felt his flesh for the first time she pulled back, whispering: 'No – we mustn't!' and he heard himself whispering back hoarsely: 'It's OK – I've got something.'

'You have?' Her voice was breathless, half admiring, half awed.

'Yes. You want me to put one on?'

'I don't know . . .'

He pressed closer to her and she moaned: 'Yes . . . oh, yes . . .'

He rolled away from her, reaching for the packet and extracting the French letter with his back towards her. He was afraid he would fumble getting it on, afraid if he took too long she might change her mind. But he managed it quickly and easily and when he rolled back her arms went around him, pulling him on top of her. She was moist with desire, so that slipping into her was easy, and though she gasped deep in her throat he was almost too excited to notice.

The worst part came afterwards, when it was over for him and he knew he had to dispose of the thing but Lisa-Marie still wanted to go on. But he did what he had to do and after a little while she stopped wriggling and lay very still, holding him close and smiling contentedly. He buried his face in her neck, enjoying the faintly salty smell of her moist skin, and she whispered something too soft for him to catch.

He raised his head. 'What d'you say?'

She opened her eyes, looking at him lazily. Her mouth seemed fuller than before, the lines of her cheek rounder.

'Do you love me?'

The words shocked him a little. Love? It wasn't a word in his vocabulary. Love? He'd never thought about it, much less talked about it. But if wanting someone as much as he wanted Lisa-Marie was love, then yes, he supposed he must love her.

'Do you?' she pressed him.

'Yeah – I guess.'

'Say it. Please say it!'

He couldn't. No matter how he tried the words refused to come.

'Steve – say it. Please!'

'Hell, Lisa, if I didn't . . . I wouldn't have . . . would I?'

Her mouth curved. For the moment the answer, incomplete as it was, seemed to satisfy her. She lay back, playing with his hair, idly running a lock of it between her fingers. He felt himself beginning to want her again.

Feeling him stir, she giggled.

'Steve! You are awful! You don't want to . . . you can't! Not again!'

I've got two more johnnies and I can! he wanted to say, but he didn't think she'd appreciate it and he did not want to push his luck.

'You see what you do to me, Lisa?' he said, levering himself up and reaching for his shorts. 'Come on, let's swim.'

Her hand grasped his thigh. 'You still didn't say it properly.'

'What?'

'That you love me.'

'I did.'

'You did not. You said you wouldn't have done it to me if you didn't love me, but I'm not sure about that. All boys want to do it. It doesn't mean . . . that.'

'Lisa, come on. Let's have that swim.'

'Not until you say you love me. You must, Steve, otherwise I'll think you just think I'm cheap and easy. You don't think that, do you, because I let you?'

'No, I don't think that.'

'And you do love me?'

'Yes.'

'And you always will?'

This was getting tiresome. If she didn't look so delectable lying there, if he didn't want her so much again already, if she had been one of the girls who lived in the mill-hands' houses as he did instead of Lisa-Marie Ford, he'd have told her to put a sock in it. But he didn't want to ruin things. Not yet.

'Yes. Now – are you going to let me put my shorts on? Because if you don't, I am going to do you again.'

And her fingers only curled more tightly around his leg. 'Oh yes please, Steve!' was all she said.

It was good – better than good – this time. It was wonderful. He felt like a king. Afterwards they swam and dried off on the shingle and the shouts and laughs echoing from the other side of the spit where the rest of the gang were fooling around seemed to come from another world. And Steve had no premonition that the moment was coming very close when he was going to be reminded with cruel suddenness who he was and where he came from.

That night, because Lisa-Marie wanted him to, he walked all the way home with her, to the leafy neighbourhood where she lived with her father, who was the chief teller in the town bank, her mother, who did not have to work at all, unless you counted looking after a home and family in such comfortable circumstances as work, and her younger sister, Jodie, who would soon be as pretty and delectable as Lisa-Marie herself.

When they reached the pleasant tree-lined street where all the houses were much like Lisa-Marie's, white, with green gables, he began to feel a little uncomfortable, a little self-conscious, without really knowing why.

At the gate he stopped. He could see Jodie sitting on the front porch with one of her friends. They were sharing a tall jug of lemonade. His feeling of discomfort increased. It was like looking in on another world, so different from his own squalid existence it made him feel like an alien. But why should he feel this way? He was as good as they were – better! One day he'd have a house and a car that would put this modest luxury to shame.

'Do you fancy going to a movie tonight?' he asked defiantly. It would take all the rest of his spare cash to pay for her as well as himself but for the moment that was unimportant.

'OK,' she said.

He wanted to kiss her again but he was all too aware of two pairs of eyes watching them from the front porch.

'I'll pick you up,' he said. 'About seven?'

'Make it half past. Mom won't be pleased if I rush dinner.'

Dinner! Christ!

'OK,' he said.

He went home. His small cramped house, with its peeling paint and the battered old chair set outside where his mother sat to peel the potatoes for supper, had never looked more squalid. He changed, and only when he removed the two-thirds empty packet of French letters from the pocket of his shorts, transferring them to his jeans, did he feel more cheerful.

There was no sign of Lisa-Marie outside her house. He slowed down. He did not want to have to go up the drive and knock on the door. He reached the gate and she still had not appeared. He stood on the sidewalk, trying to look nonchalant. The door, which was ajar, opened fully. He straightened expectantly. But it was not Lisa-Marie who came out but her father, a small portly man, balding, with a bushy moustache. He was wearing cream trousers and a cream shirt but he did not look cool. Far from it. He was red-faced and flustered and dark patches of sweat showed at the armpits of his shirt.

'Hey – you!' he called to Steve.

'Me?'

'Yes, you!' He came towards Steve. His manner was vaguely threatening. 'There's no sense you hanging round here.'

Steve swallowed. 'I'm waiting for Lisa-Marie.'

'That's what I said. No sense you waiting. She won't be out.'

'But – we're going to a movie . . .'

'Not with Lisa-Marie you're not. She's staying home tonight. And don't you come round here bothering her again.' His already highly-coloured face had turned an even deeper red.

Steve felt his own colour rising. 'I didn't bother her. She likes being with me.'

'Well I don't like it, son.' He made the familiarity sound like an insult. 'I don't like it and her mama don't like it. She's too young to be dating, especially your sort.'

'What do you mean – my sort?'

'I know where you come from, boy – Mill Street. And I don't want the likes of you hanging around my daughter. Understand?'

'No, sir, I don't understand,' Steve said. 'I come from Mill Street, sure, but I don't see . . .'

'Do I have to spell it out for you? This is a decent neighbourhood. We're decent folk. Lisa-Marie has been brought up right. I won't see her waste herself on the likes of you.'

Steve's blood was boiling now. He was so angry, so insulted, he wanted to sock the bank teller on the jaw.

'You always choose your daughter's friends?' he asked. 'What about Lisa? Don't she get no say?'

The bank teller's face worked furiously.

'Don't you talk back at me, son. If I tell you to keep away from Lisa, you'll damned well do it. And she'll keep away from you. I won't have my daughter mixing with poor white trash. So, there won't be any more sneaking off to the lake – understand? She'll spend the rest of the vacation with friends her own class.'

Steve stood his ground. 'I want to see Lisa.'

'No way. And I tell you something else, boy. I know what your sort are. One-track minds – and not in your head, either. If you've laid one finger on my Lisa-Marie, or even tried to, I'll have the law on you. Now – get!'

Steve went. The bank teller's last remark had been too close to home for comfort. He could feel the hot flush of anger turning to guilt, feel it colouring up into the roots of his hair. As he turned away he saw the curtains at the front window of the house move. He did not know if it was Lisa-Marie or her mother and he did not want to know. The packet of French letters with two missing seemed to be burning a hole in his pocket. He was fifteen years old and he felt about five, the way he'd used to feel when he'd been caught stealing apples. Except that then it had only been fear, fear of authority, fear of punishment, fear of a beating from his father's belt, and now it was also guilt – and shame.

He knew why Lisa-Marie's father had come down so hard on him and it had nothing to do with the fact that he had been alone with her for most of the week. The man might not have thought twice about that if he had considered Steve more suitable as a boyfriend for his daughter; he might have been concerned about what they had been up to, but not nearly as concerned as he was now. He might have insisted they stay with the group, not go off on their own, but he would not have banned him from seeing her altogether.

Steve burned with indignation and impotent anger. The sense of humiliation was unbelievable. Suppose Lisa-Marie should tell her father what they had done? He couldn't imagine her confessing voluntarily but perhaps the man would beat it out of her. Just because he thought he was better than the folk who lived in Mill Street didn't mean he couldn't wield a belt with the best of them. The thought of Lisa-Marie cringing and crying under the cruel bite of a strip of leather made him angry too – angry and helpless.

The day after that he went to the lake. He went alone because he was by nature a loner, though he could integrate when he had to. He had no wish to confide in any of his friends. His humiliation hurt too much and too deeply.

The crowd were at the lake and Lisa-Marie was with them. His heart began to beat very hard, a drum pounding in his throat. He went over and sat down beside her.

'Hi, Lisa-Marie.'

She turned away, not looking at him.

'Lisa . . . you all right?'

She nodded, still with her head turned away. He felt awkward, at a loss for words.

'The other night . . .'

'I'm sorry about that,' she said. Her voice was choked, her shoulders a rigid line. 'My father can be . . . pretty tight when he wants to be.'

'Yeah. He sure can.'

She turned then and her eyes were suspiciously bright.

'Was he . . . real nasty?'

'Real nasty.' He couldn't stop the indignation rising again. 'He thinks I'm not good enough for you.'

'Yeah.' A pause. 'I'm not supposed to be talking to you, even.'

'But you are. He's not going to stop us, is he, Lisa?'

'I don't know.' She let shingle drift through her fingers. 'He'd kill me if he knew we were together. And if he knew about . . .'

'But he doesn't know?' A sharp edge of apprehension.

'Shit, no! If he knew about that . . .'

'I love you, Lisa,' he said desperately. He hadn't wanted to say it when she'd asked him to, now it came out without even thinking about it. 'And you love me. Don't you?'

'I guess I have to . . . now.'

'And you'll still see me?'

'I guess so, as long as we're careful.'

'Oh sure, we'll be careful. He'll never know.'

'OK.' But she sounded nervous, uncertain.

'Coming for a walk?'

'No. Not just now. I'm OK here.'

She stretched out on the shingle. He looked at her, desire mixed in with all the other emotions.

'Tomorrow then?'

'Maybe.'

He knew then that it was over. He did not know what the bank teller had said to Lisa but he could guess – the same sort of damning things he had said to Steve himself. Now Lisa-Marie was seeing him through her father's eyes, however hard she tried not to.

Although they were alone a few more times it was never the same. Steve didn't know which hurt most, his heart or his pride. For a while he felt as if he was hurting all over. But as the weeks became months, when the trees around the town turned from green to shades of red and gold so brightly hued and so beautiful the sight of them brought an ache to the throat, his heart began to mend and by the time they had shed their leaves altogether, stretching bare bony fingers to the slate-grey winter sky, he had begun to hate Lisa-Marie for rejecting him for what he was.

Sometimes he lay awake at nights plotting what he would like to do to the Fords to gain his revenge. He thought about pushing petrol-soaked rags through the letter box of their prissy Cape Cod-style house and setting light to them and the visions he conjured up of them standing in the garden sobbing as all their possessions went up in flames gave him a kick of sharp excitement and a glow of satisfaction. Once he went so far as to bring a can of petrol home with him from the garage, and one night when there was no moon he walked over to the house and stood at the gate, fingering the box of matches in his pocket and enjoying the feeling of power that came from knowing that he could destroy not only the house, which would probably go up like a torch, but also Lisa-Marie and her family too. But for some reason he did not do it. It wasn't that he cared if the old man burned to death, trapped in his blazing home; that, he thought carelessly, did not really bother him at all. But even hating her as he now did he found he did not want to endanger Lisa-Marie.

And there was something else. If the Fords died now it would be over, there would be no more plotting of sweet revenge – and Steve did not want it to be over. He wanted to savour it again and again. One day, his chance would come. He would get the old man for sure and through him hurt Lisa-Marie. It was a much more satisfactory solution.

But Old Man Ford's treatment of him engendered more than hatred and the desire for revenge. It also fuelled Steve's determination to break out from the strait-jacket of poverty into which he had been born. One day soon, he promised himself, he would get away from this place where he was known as the son of a mill-hand from the poorest part of town, one day soon he would have a big car and wear silk shirts and suede shoes, one day soon he would have money in his pocket, eat in the best restaurants, date the classiest women. And none of them would look down on him, no father would tell him ever again to 'keep away from my daughter' – at least, not for the reason old Ford had done it.

The day Steve left high school he went home and packed his belongings together in a battered hold-all. It did not take long; his belongings were so few. The next day he set out to hitchhike south. He had only a vague idea where he was going but to him the South meant prosperity as well as endless summers. He headed for Florida, taking jobs along the way to earn money to buy food and, sometimes, a room for the night.

When he hit Florida he made for the Keys, getting casual work in the holiday trade, and for a while he forgot all about his ambitions in the pursuit of pleasure. As long as he had a few bucks to jingle in the pocket of his cut-off denims money was of no importance. Living was all that mattered – and living, here in Florida, meant sun, sea and sex. Steve was tall, strongly built and handsome, he was an excellent swimmer and he had the fierce pride that made him stand so tall he was head and shoulders above the rest. The girls who came to the Keys on vacation fell over themselves for his favours and he found he had only to wink and throw out a casual invitation to obtain almost instant gratification. These were the golden eighties, President Reagan was in the White House, promising an end to the crippling conditions of the last years, the future was there for the taking and Steve grabbed his pleasure with both hands. Here it did not matter who he was, no none knew his background, or cared less. Here he could be anything, or anyone, he wanted to be.

Steve worked a little – if you could call it work. He swam and sunbathed and when darkness fell he ate and drank and fooled and made love with the latest in a line of golden girls, all leggy and suntanned in their brief bikinis, all crazy for him.

At first he was ham-fisted, lacking in finesse, but he learned fast and soon his technique matched his promise. Practice makes perfect, they say, and here in Florida he had plenty of practice.

It was not only sexual niceties that Steve learned. Most of the girls he met were from well-to-do families and Steve made sure that the ones he selected for his adventures came from that stratum of society. The girls he consorted with had fathers who owned boats and condominiums, they were businessmen and politicians who had made their money from real estate and textiles, munitions and publishing, and cut their political teeth working for state governors and congressmen. Some of them *were* state governors and congressmen! Knowing this made Steve feel good because by comparison with them old Ford was nothing but a small-town bumpkin puffed up with his own importance.

From these girls Steve learned all about social behaviour. Occasionally he made a bloomer, always quickly forgiven, but on the whole he learned quickly and easily, soaking up like a sponge the way of talking, the way of behaving, the names of drinks and exotic dishes, the way to dress when the necessity arose – and when he could afford to do it. But at the same time he retained the hard edge that came from living on the wrong side of town and an inbred streak of callousness. The combination was a lethal one – and he knew it.

The time came when Steve began to tire of his easy-going and aimless life, unbelievable though it had once seemed. One day an ocean-going yacht owned by an international tycoon berthed nearby and word went around that the master was looking to take on extra crew. Steve, having seen, and taken a fancy to, the tycoon's twenty-year-old daughter, decided to apply, and a week later when the yacht sailed Steve sailed with her.

His job was in the engine room. It was hot, sweaty work, totally lacking in glamour, but there was compensation in the shape of the tycoon's daughter, Mary Jane. She was beautiful, amusing and bored out of her mind with the clean-cut but wimpish college boys she met socially. Soon Steve was visiting her in the luxurious stateroom she referred to, rather incongruously, as her 'cabin', and if her father knew what was going on he chose to turn a blind eye.

After two months' cruising Mary Jane left the yacht to return to her studies and Steve's interest in a life at sea went with her. Perhaps it was time, he thought, to begin making some money of his own, though he did not know, as yet, how he was going to do it. He headed for New York, took a job as a bouncer, found himself an apartment, kept his ear to the ground and began making plans. He was beginning to doubt that he could make his fortune legitimately since he had no qualifications beyond his charm and his sharp wits and no money to back him, and his thoughts were turning to the rich pickings that were there to be had from a life of crime. It was then that fate took a hand.

Though he had not been back to Vermont since the day he had packed his bags and left, Steve had kept in touch with his family, and one day he received news that his mother was sick and not expected to live more than a few months. Steve went home to see her, and the squalor of his former home and the sight of his mother, worn to a pathetic shadow of skin and bone by years of hardship and neglect, reinforced his determination to make some real money and ensure that never again would he be caught in the jaws of grinding poverty.

Talking with his sister late into the night he found himself asking about the Fords. They had moved, she told him – the old man had taken promotion and was now manager of a small town branch of the bank some forty miles south. Lisa-Marie had gone with them but, she thought, had since married.

'Imagine that old fool a bank manager!' Steve's sister said. 'They promoted him to get rid of him, I shouldn't wonder. But he's had nothing but trouble. There've been two armed hold-ups, or so I heard. I guess any bank he's in charge of would be an easy touch.'

Steve said nothing but his mind had begun working overtime. To rob a bank was almost a cliché but there could be a lot of profit in it – enough to set him up in a nice little racket like drug-dealing – and the idea of robbing Old Man Ford was an appealing one. Steve discovered all the details he could and on his way back to New York made a detour to the small town where Ford was bank manager to check things out. He was a little wary of being seen and recognised by one of the Fords but it was a risk he was prepared to take. In the event he did not run into any of them, though he checked out not only the bank itself but also the Fords' home, for he had begun to devise a plan that amused him and went some way to satisfying his desire for revenge.

The Fords lived in a small pretty house on the edge of town which was situated conveniently distant from its nearest neighbours. Clearly neither of the girls was now at home for as he watched the house Steve saw no one but old Ford and his wife, Joan, coming and going. Jodie must be away at college, he decided, and Lisa-Marie obviously had a place of her own with her husband. It surprised him how his gut could still tighten at the thought of her with someone else, but it only strengthened his desire for revenge. Steve returned to New York to make his plans.

A month later he was back. Very early in the morning he went to the Fords' house and knocked on the door. Joan Ford answered it, wearing a dressing gown over her nightdress and with no make-up to disguise the ageing of the features which had once probably been very like Lisa-Marie's. Steve, who was wearing a full-face crash helmet as an effective form of disguise, stuck a gun in her ribs and ordered her into the house. Old Ford was eating breakfast; when he realised what was happening he started shaking and blubbering and Steve experienced a surge of adrenaline and triumph.

'Go to the bank and empty the safe,' he ordered. 'Bring the money back here and give it to me. If you do, nothing will happen. If you don't – your wife gets it. And no tricks – right?'

'What – now?'

'No, you asshole – the usual time. Just make everything look normal. Do it, and your wife will be all right. But just remember I'm here with the gun looking right at her. Try any tricks and I'll blow her away.'

'All right! All right! I'll do it!' Ford was gibbering; Steve felt nothing but contempt for him. He was certain Ford had not recognised him – the crash helmet concealed his face effectively and since Ford had seen him only the once, so long ago now, he knew it would never occur to him to connect the man now threatening him with the boy he had humiliated.

At the usual time Ford left for the bank, and Steve's only worry was that someone would notice something was wrong.

'If anyone asks, say you have to come home again because your wife isn't well,' he instructed him. 'I'll be watching to make sure you are alone.' He saw Ford's eyes grow small and shifty in the sweaty face that was so reminiscent of the way he had looked that other, long-ago day.

'You'll go away then – leave us alone?'

'I'll take your wife with me and drop her off on the outskirts of town,' Steve said. 'Just to make sure you haven't got the police waiting for me around the corner.'

When Ford had gone Steve prowled around the room, looking at the photographs of Lisa-Marie and her sister as children, just the way he remembered them, but he made sure the gun he had brought with him was levelled at Mrs Ford in case she should try to get away.

'Make us some coffee,' he said after a while. Mrs Ford went into the kitchen and he went with her, glancing at his watch. He had timed Ford's journey to the bank and back; he knew exactly how long it would take.

There was still a good ten minutes to go and he was drinking coffee in the kitchen, holding the mug carefully with his gloved hands and manoeuvring it beneath his helmet, when he heard the front door open. Instantly he was alert. He slipped back the safety catch on the gun, ordered Mrs Ford to stay where she was, and looked through the door into the hall. A young woman was unwrapping a scarf from around her neck; fair hair fell around her shoulders.

'Hey, Mom!' she called. 'It's only me!'

It was Lisa-Marie. Sweat broke out on Steve's face beneath the concealing crash helmet. What the hell was she doing here? This was something he hadn't reckoned on.

At that precise moment she looked up and saw him standing there – and she knew him instantly, crash helmet or no crash helmet.

'Steve?' she said in a puzzled voice. Then her eyes fastened on the gun and widened with confusion and horror. 'What are you doing?'

He knew then that he was cornered and there was only one thing to do if he did not want to wind up in prison. He would have to shoot Lisa-Marie and her mother, kill them both, because Mrs Ford was right there behind him and she had heard what Lisa-Marie had said.

'Get in there, both of you!' he ordered, waving the gun at them.

Mrs Ford ran to Lisa-Marie, clinging to her arm and sobbing. With her dressing gown and nightdress flapping around her legs she looked pathetic and ridiculous. It would almost be a pleasure to put a bullet into her. But Lisa-Marie glared at him, her head held high.

'You've gone mad!' she said. Her voice sounded just the same as it always had. Suddenly he was remembering the way her body had felt beneath his on the shingle all those years ago, and he knew he could not do it any more than he had been able to set the house on fire with her asleep inside. Funny how a girl could do this to him, make him hate her so much and yet, with a part of him over which he had no control, love her still.

'Stay there and don't move!' he ordered. He backed along the hall, still pointing the gun at them. There was nothing for it but to get away now. The hell with the money. Then, just as he reached the door, he heard a car outside. Old Ford, back again. Perhaps he could still salvage something from this bloody fiasco! He drew back into the well of the hall and as Ford opened the door he was ready. Ford was carrying a black Gladstone bag; Steve guessed it held the contents of the safe. In one quick movement he snatched the bag from Ford and backed out through the door.

'Don't do anything!' he warned. 'The first one that moves, I'll kill you!'

But he knew he wouldn't – not if the one who moved was Lisa-Marie.

He ran down the path to where he had left his getaway car with the keys in the ignition, leapt in and brought the engine roaring to life. He was sweating all over now. He had the money, but they knew who he was. His only chance was to make his escape and disappear back into the teeming city. What a foul-up! He should have killed her – he should have! If it had been anyone but Lisa-Marie he would have. Now his plan was in ruins, his revenge soured, and he was on the run.

Steve did not get far. The Fords must have been on the telephone to the police almost before his car roared away, for he had gone only a few miles when he heard the sirens. He ducked and dived, he drove like a madman, the adrenaline honing all his natural and acquired skills, but when he saw the roadblock ahead he knew it was all over. Pointless to drive into them and probably kill himself doing it. Steve screamed to a halt, and when the patrolman came alongside he opened the door, took off his crash helmet and said, with great panache: 'Yes, Officer? Can I help you?'

He was sent for a spell to New York State Penitentiary and it proved to be the turning point in his life. There were schemes for the retraining and rehabilitation of criminals and Steve was chosen to take part in one of them. Because he had always been a good swimmer and had all the physical and mental attributes considered necessary, he was selected to train as a deep-sea diver. The training was, he found, both absorbing and challenging, covering not only the techniques of diving but also underwater engineering, and the rewards promised to be high. This, perhaps, was a way he could make enough money legitimately to put his foot on the first rung of the ladder of success, and he could do it in some far-off isolated spot where his record would not be known. Steve was not greatly ashamed of having tried to rob the bank; it was the failure to carry it off successfully that made him cringe.

On his release, because he had always fancied seeing Europe, he took up a contract with an international oil company, Excel Oil, who had massive operations in the North Sea. The bleak conditions there shocked him but the excitement of diving was still fresh and powerful and the promise of a great deal of money to be made was compensation for the biting cold, the long exhausting hours, and the absence of the three Bs – booze, broads and ballads. Ambition had resurrected itself within Steve during his time in the penitentiary – it burned now more fiercely than ever and he spent a good deal of time scheming.

Had he but known it, every one of those plans was superfluous. For in decreeing that he should find himself working on the Excel rig fate had dealt Steve a hand with a wild card in it.

That wild card's name was Mac MacIlroy.

Mac MacIlroy was one of the divers in Steve's team.

Steve's contract with Excel was for what was known in the trade as 'saturation diving', which meant working two weeks on, two weeks off, in a team of three – two divers and a bell man. During the two weeks on the hours of work were long and arduous – twelve-hour stints of diving interspersed with living in the close confines of the recompression chamber; the two weeks off were spent ashore, sleeping, partying and often generally making up for the privations of life on the rig. In these claustrophobic conditions friendships were forged and enemies made. It was rare for the divers who worked as a team on the rig to see much of one another ashore, but Steve and Mac were an exception to this rule, though to all intents and purposes they were so different that their friendship was an unlikely one.

Mac had been brought up in Gloucestershire where his father was a much-respected solicitor. He had been educated at a private day school for boys but he had opted to leave at the age of eighteen and take an HNC in engineering rather than going to university.

After a few years working for an engineering company Mac had begun to be restless. He could see little future in his present job and since he had always been a keen sport diver he had decided to try to use his aptitude professionally. He had applied, and been accepted for, a training course at Fort William, and there, in the icy, pitch-black waters of Loch Linnhe he had learned to use underwater all the engineering skills that were his on land, and more. He learned how to use a thermic lance to cut steel under water and change massive bronze valves and how to check rig equipment and repair or replace it as necessary. He trained in the use of underwater explosives and there, in the deep hole in the floor of the lake, 450 feet below the surface, he discovered the kicks that came from doing a job that was both demanding and dangerous as well as skilful.

Mac was slimly built but strong, every inch of his five-feet-nine frame lean hard sinew. His hair was light brown, his eyes several shades darker. Like Steve he was something of a loner; unlike Steve he did nothing to try to disguise it. Whilst Steve presented a deliberately laid-back approach Mac was genuinely happier with his own company or that of one or two friends. He could not be bothered with forming superficial relationships, social intercourse bored and irritated him, and he preferred reading, listening to music or walking in the wild countryside to drinking and partying in noisy, smoke-filled bars. But beneath the almost gentle exterior there ran a vein of iron and another of fire. Few people had ever seen Mac's temper but it was there all right, slow to be roused but so explosive when it erupted that those who witnessed it never forgot.

He and Steve had only one thing in common, their Christian name – though it was years since he had used it. At his school the boys had still been referred to by their surnames and his friends had soon abbreviated MacIlroy to the nickname Mac. He like the name – whilst the Snottys and the Fatsos and the Weedys could hardly wait to leave their nicknames behind Mac adopted his and took it with him into the world. Only his parents called him Stephen now. To everyone else he was simply Mac.

Perhaps he and Steve would never have crossed over the boundary between comradeship and friendship if it had not been for something which happened whilst they were diving one day.

The two of them were checking out the equipment in the fathomless ice-cold water beneath the rig whilst the third member of their team, a cheery Cockney named Des Taylor, acted as their bell man, when Steve discovered a loose nut on one of the valves. It was a routine enough occurrence and Steve began to tighten the nut, bracing himself against the pull of the water by jackknifing himself into a crouching position with his feet pressed against the foot-diameter pipe. He had done the same thing many times before without mishap but this time something went wrong. As he put his weight against the massive spanner it suddenly slipped, crashing backwards and smashing into the mask of Mac, who was just behind his left shoulder. The mask cracked and instantly ice-cold water poured in, half blinding Mac as well as totally disorientating him. Air and gases streamed out from the fractured mask in a rush of bubbles and he floundered helplessly, knowing he had to regain the bell quickly or drown, yet unable to see which way to go and too shocked to be able to think clearly.

Steve acted instantly. He grabbed Mac, dragged him back to the bell and stuffed him, choking, through the hatch. Des pulled them in, closed the hatch and signalled for an immediate return to the surface whilst Steve tried to stem the bleeding from Mac's face, which had been injured by the force of the blow. It was a routine enough accident and working as a team Mac had not been in mortal danger, but it was enough to forge a bond between the two men.

When he had arrived to begin work on the rig Steve had taken bed and breakfast accommodation in Aberdeen whilst Mac, with his longer experience and stabler financial state, had rented a house. Now, when the latest stint was completed and the team went ashore, Mac suggested to Steve that he might like to move in with him.

'Are you sure, pal?' Steve asked.

'Sure,' Mac replied. 'The place is far too damned big for me on my own.' He did not add that he had always baulked in the past at the thought of sharing with any of the other men, who were liable to run wild and go on endless benders when they escaped from the rigours of life on the rig. But he knew Steve well enough to know that he was unlikely to behave in that way – though he did not know him well enough to know the dangerous secrets that lay behind that smooth exterior.

'What the hell am I doing in a hole like this?' Steve asked irritably.

It had been a long day's diving and by the time they were through the hot water in their suits had lost its heat and they were chilled to the marrow. Not even the customary dash to the recompression chamber had done anything to warm them –

Steve's fingers had fumbled hopelessly as he removed his helmet, he had thudded awkwardly to the deck where anxious hands had peeled off his suit and when he had got to his feet again to run for the chamber in the five short minutes before the dangerous and sometimes fatal sickness known as 'the bends' began, his legs had almost given way beneath him.

His instinct for self-preservation had taken over then; somehow he had regained his balance and his numb limbs had obeyed him. He had reached the chamber with just seconds to spare and as the pressure built, returning his body to the state in which he had been working all day, he found himself wondering why he had ever thought he would enjoy diving for a living and why the hell he was sticking with it in these God-awful conditions.

Briefly he remembered his days on the Keys, the searingly hot sun on his bronzed body, and thought he must be out of his mind to ever have left it. But at least diving paid well – and didn't carry the threat of a prison sentence! A few years of this and he would have saved enough to set himself up for life – legitimately. Steve relaxed his aching limbs and waited for the 'blowdown' to be completed, letting his mind rove over the ways he could use his savings. A leisure complex, perhaps – a luxurious health hydro where he would employ well-trained specialists in diet and massage, and every sensual bodily need would be indulged. There would be weights halls, gymnasiums, treatment rooms and, of course, a swimming pool, sauna and solarium. The vision brought a little warmth back to his chilled body and he smiled briefly as he enjoyed the irony of it. Supreme comfort paid for by supreme suffering. He might, of course, decide upon something different, but whatever it was, one thing was very certain. The money he earned here on the rigs would not be squandered on wine, women and song. It had been earned too hard for that.

The blowdown procedure completed, Steve, Mac and Des returned to their quarters to change into warm dry clothing – thick Arran sweaters and heavy-duty jeans worn over longjohns and vests that reminded Steve of the ones his father had worn when the snow lay thickly over the hills and mountains of Vermont. But he was still cold; not even a hot drink and the stodgy supper of beef stew and dumplings followed by spotted dick with thick, cornfloury-tasting custard could reach the chilled core of him, and as the three men relaxed in the commissary, furtively swigging at a flask of brandy they had smuggled in – alcohol was forbidden on the rigs – the frustration bubbled to the surface once more.

'What the hell am I doing in a hole like this?' he asked of no one in particular.

A small, wiry man, universally known as 'Tiger', who was sitting at the next table overheard and laughed.

'I sure as hell know what I'm doing here – making enough bread to keep two wives and six children in the manner to which they have become accustomed!' he quipped in his thick Scottish brogue.

'You've only got yourself to blame, Tiger,' his mate, a brawny north-countryman, cracked back at him. 'You should have kept your lead in your pencil!'

Tiger grinned ruefully – it was common knowledge that a messy divorce, two wives, a girlfriend in Aberdeen and the brood of children that had resulted from his time ashore kept him penniless.

'And if you couldn't do that you should have made a sharp exit,' the northerner, a man named Derek Bradley, continued. 'God knows how many brats I've fathered – I don't, and I sure as hell don't want to know. Love 'em and leave 'em, that's what I say.'

'That's a bit rough on the women concerned, isn't it?' Des said.

'Why? Whores, most of them, anyway – as good as. They see us coming with our pay rolls bulging and they want a good time. Well, let 'em have it, I say, and if they get a bit more than they bargained for – tough!'

'So what do you reckon has happened to all your kids then, Del?' Tiger asked.

The northerner shrugged. He was enjoying himself, enjoying playing the brash hard-hearted stud.

'How should I know? Whining round their mothers' skirts, stopping them from going out and getting a bit of the other? Dumped on somebody who's fool enough to want them? Strangled at birth, for all I care!'

'For Christ's sake!' Mac said. His voice was low but full of anger and disgust. Steve glanced at him and saw a muscle working in his cheek.

'What's wrong with you, MacIlroy?' the northerner asked rudely.

'The way you are talking. It's bloody offensive.'
'Says who?'
'Says me. You've got a big mouth, Bradley . . .'
'That's not all that's big!'
'. . . and you ought to learn to keep it shut.'
'Oh yeah?' Bradley grinned. 'And are you going to make me?'
'I might – if you don't put a sock in it.'

Bradley tipped his chair on to its two back legs, grinning. Arguments, even fights, were not unknown on the rig – when a lot of red-blooded men were cooped up together for weeks on end friction was inevitable. But Mac, known for being placid and quiet, was rarely involved in any of them.

'Fuck off, Mac,' Bradley jeered. 'Go tie yourself in knots.'

'You foul-mouthed son of a bitch, Bradley!' Mac was on his feet before either Steve or Des could stop him. His fist shot out, connecting with the northerner's jaw and sending both him and his chair crashing backwards. 'Now get up and say what you just said again!' he challenged him.

For a moment Bradley was so astonished that he lay where he had fallen, then with a roar he staggered to his feet. Blood was pouring from a split lip and one of his front teeth protruded at a crazy angle.

'You bastard!' Still half dazed, yet strong as an ox, he went for Mac and the two men ricocheted around the commissary, sending furniture flying as they crashed into it. At first there were a few cheers, then, realising that this fight was going to go to its bitter end, Steve, Des, and a couple of the others intervened, separating the protagonists with some difficulty.

Mac's face was by now as bloody as Bradley's. A cut over one eye was pouring blood down his cheek and already the brow bone was swelling and darkening. His knuckles were grazed, his sweater streaked with blood, his heavy-duty jeans ripped at thigh level where he had cannoned into a corner of the self-service bar. But his expression was still one of blind fury.

'Just keep your filthy mouth shut in future!' he yelled over his shoulder as Steve and Des led him away.

'Goddamit, Mac, what did you want to do that for?' Steve asked as they bundled him into the cabin he and Mac shared. 'The bloke's a loudmouth – nobody with any sense takes notice of him.'

'Well it's about time somebody did,' was all Mac said through swollen and bloody lips.

Steve and Des exchanged glances. They were more surprised than anyone at Mac's violent reaction – it was totally alien to everything they knew about him. But for the moment the reason behind his fury was unimportant. There was a certain amount of first-aid patching up to do – fast. Unless they could work like expert corners at a bare-knuckle fist-fight, Mac was going to have cause to regret his rashness in the morning.

'I'm sorry, fellas,' Mac said.

He was quiet now, the fury spent. His face covered in iodine and plasters, he looked a sorry sight.

'Sorry? Don't be sorry – best entertainment we've had for weeks,' Des said. 'But what the hell was it all about?'

'The guy just got to me.' Mac was sitting on his bunk, head bent, knees splayed, a cup of coffee laced with some of the illicit brandy held in his hands between them. 'The way he was talking – thinking he was being so damned clever. It just got to me, that's all.'

'But why?' Steve asked. 'We all know he's got a big mouth. You've never let it bother you before.'

'It was the way he was going on about leaving bastards scattered around the country like confetti and not giving a damn that really caught me on the raw. I was adopted, you see. Stupid thing to be sensitive about, I suppose, and most of the time I'm not. But I can't say I'm sorry I hit him. He had it coming.'

'True.' Des grinned. 'It wasn't all one-sided though, was it?'

'So, if you were adopted you don't know who your real parents are, I suppose?' Steve said. The idea was fascinating him – after all, he had spent the best part of his adult life trying to lose his heritage.

'As a matter of fact I do know – or I know who my mother is, at least,' Mac said. 'I fancied finding out so I sent for my original birth certificate.'

'And?'

Mac shook his head. 'It's funny really, the way things work out. I'd always had this picture in my mind of this poor kid who had to give me up because she couldn't afford to keep me. It was the kind of story I used to tell myself to explain why she let me go. I even had some bloody romantic notion that if I could find her maybe I could make things up to her, buy her some nice things – you know what I mean. But it wasn't quite what I expected.'

He broke off. He was talking too much, he knew, but the fight and the illicit brandy were loosening his tongue, making him want to share the things he had never expected to mention to another living soul.

'Well?' Steve prompted him. 'What was the result?'

Mac shook his head. 'Bit of a fiasco, really. I'd prepared myself for finding out she was destitute, or living in a high-rise council flat or something. But the truth came as a bit of a shock. My mother – my real mother – doesn't need my help at all. She could buy and sell me several times over.'

Steve leaned forward. 'Who the hell is she, then?'

Mac sipped his drink, wincing as the hot liquid burned his cut lip, but it was nothing to the pain inside him, the irrational pain of rejection that had smouldered in his heart for years and been fanned to a fierce fire when he had finally read what was written on his original birth certificate. The shock he had felt then was just as fresh, just as new now as it had been the day he had discovered that whatever the reason his mother had abandoned him it had not been because she could not afford to keep him.

'Have you ever heard of Vandina?' he asked.

Des looked blank, but Steve knew.

'The "Touch of the Country" people, you mean?'

'The same. Then perhaps you have also heard of the woman behind it – Dinah Marshall?'

'Vaguely.'

'Dinah Marshall is my mother.'

Steve's breath came out in a soft whistle.

'Dinah Marshall is your mother?'

'That's what my birth certificate says.'

'And your father?'

'It doesn't say. Some bastard like Bradley, I shouldn't wonder.'

'Who is this Dinah Marshall?' Des asked.

Steve told him.

'Shit!' Des ran a hand through his thinning hair. 'You're having us on, aren't you, Mac?'

'Would I joke about a thing like that?' Mac put down his cup, reached in his pocket for his wallet and extracted a piece of paper. 'There it is in black and white if you don't believe me.'

He passed it to Des. Peering over his shoulder Steve also verified the details.

'Bloody hell!' he said.

Mac replaced the birth certificate in his wallet and the three men sat in silence. For the moment there was nothing else to say.

'Have you ever thought of trying to get in touch with your real mother?' Steve asked.

He and Mac were alone, sprawled on their bunks reading the newspapers and leafing idly through copies of *Playboy* and *Diving News*.

'Thought of it, yes.'

'But not done anything about it.'

'No.'

'Why not?'

'I figured she might not be too pleased, me turning up out of the blue. If she didn't want me then, why should she want me now?'

'Could be circumstances have changed. Could be she's regretted what she did. You hear of women who have their kids adopted spending their whole lives wondering what happened to them – wishing they could see them again, that sort of thing.'

Mac was silent, and Steve went on: 'She'd have no way of finding you, would she? Information like you have is a one-way traffic over here, isn't it? They wouldn't tell her who adopted you even if she asked. Any approach would have to come from you.'

'True.'

'Well – why don't you?'

'And risk getting rejected twice over?'

'It's a chance I'd take if I were in your shoes. I wouldn't be able to resist it, meeting her face to face, seeing what she's like and what she's got to say for herself. It might not have been at all the way you think. Maybe she had a damned good reason for giving you up.'

'Maybe. I can't think of one – unless it's that I was a nuisance to her.'

'But if you don't give her the chance to explain you'll never know, will you? She might fall over herself to make it up to you – and seeing who she is, that couldn't be bad. If she took you to her bosom as her long-lost son you'd never have to work again.'

Mac's eyes darkened. 'I don't want anything from her – now. She doesn't owe me a damned thing.'

'You're crazy. She's worth a mint!'

'I don't give a damn. She didn't want me then and I don't want her money now. It would choke me. Always supposing she wanted to make it up to me, which she probably doesn't.'

'You were standing up for her when you gave Bradley a beating.'

'Not necessarily. He just riled me. Leave it, Steve.'

Steve shook his head, thinking that Mac had a tile loose. He'd done a little reading up on Dinah Marshall since the night Mac had revealed she was his natural mother. The reading had confirmed what he already knew – that Dinah Marshall's company, Vandina, was very big in the business league, turning in substantial profits besides being world-renowned for style and quality. He had also learned that Dinah and her husband Van Kendrick were childless. It was his hunch that if Mac played his cards right he had a great deal to gain. But it was typical of Mac to be mulish about taking advantage of the situation. It was typical of Mac to refuse to take advantage of anything or anyone, come to that!

'Aren't you curious, though?' he asked, trying another tack.

'I guess so.'

'Well there you are then! What do you have to lose? Go and see her – or write to her at the very least. Tell her you know who you are.'

'I don't know . . .'

'For Chrissakes, Mac, I'm curious if you're not! Go see her next time you're ashore. I would!'

'I'll think about it,' was all Mac said.

He did think about it and in the end he decided there might be something in what Steve said, though for quite different reasons from those advocated by the American.

As he had said, Mac expected nothing from Dinah and he certainly had no desire to benefit financially. If she offered him money now he thought he would take it as an insult, a sop to her conscience, a bribe to try and buy back what she had given away all those years ago. But he was curious, just the same, and the desire to know that in spite of all his fears to the contrary she had had a good reason for giving him up haunted him. To Mac, that was what mattered. Not her success, not anything she could offer him in the present or the future. Simply a reassurance about the past that had filled him with uncertainty ever since his parents had told him, at the age of sixteen, that he was adopted.

Would it have been different, he sometimes wondered, if he had always known? Perhaps not, but he could still remember with almost frightening clarity the shock and disbelief he had felt when they had finally sat him down one day and confessed.

His parents had known, of course, that it was the wrong way to go about it. The social workers had all counselled that the precious baby they had wanted and prayed for for so long should be raised in the knowledge that he had been chosen, not born to them. But somehow they had been unable to bring themselves to do it. Better for him that he should not know that in this respect he was different from the other children he played with, they had told themselves. Better for him to feel utterly, completely secure. And they had scarcely admitted, even to themselves, that the reason they kept silent was more for their own sakes than for his. Soon after they had adopted Mac they had moved to a new town where no one knew Mac was not their own son, and they guarded their secret jealously, feeling somehow that it would diminish them in some way to admit they had been unable to produce a child of their own.

Sometimes they worried about the fact that he did not know the truth, sometimes they put it so completely out of their minds that they almost believed the lie themselves. But as Mac grew older they realised the day was coming when he would need his birth certificate for some reason or other, see that it was out of the ordinary and ask for an explanation.

The day they chose to tell him was his sixteenth birthday. They had bought him a ghetto blaster, a personal computer and a pair of expensive trainers he had been wanting, presents that outdid even their usual generosity, because they felt guilty about the bomb-shell they were about to deliver and hoped the gifts would be proof, if proof were needed, of how much they loved him. They let him open them, his father pulling heavily on the pipe that he did not usually smoke until the evening, his mother hovering, a jumping bean of nervous tension. And then they told him.

Mac listened to their stumbling words in stunned disbelief. At first he did not question, or in fact say anything beyond: 'Oh!' He was too shocked. The first emotion he experienced was dismay, nothing more, filtering through that haze of swirling disjointed thoughts. Then, unexpectedly, he felt horribly embarrassed, and all he wanted was to escape to his room where he could be alone.

He picked up the ghetto blaster, still in its torn wrapping paper. 'Are there batteries in this or do I need a plug?'

His mother and father exchanged glances. The need to escape became more urgent. Without waiting for an answer he grabbed the ghetto blaster and ran, taking the stairs two at a time, went to his room and slammed the door behind him. There *were* batteries in the ghetto blaster; he turned it full on and threw himself down on the bed.

Other emotions were beginning to pierce the fog of shocked disbelief now, but he was unable to identify them and he did not even try. He only knew his world had fallen apart – nothing was as it seemed. He opened his eyes, looking around the familiar room, and even that seemed subtly changed – the scarlet and black duvet and matching curtains, the ebony furniture he had been allowed to choose when he had become a teenager, the carpet, wall-to-wall gunmetal grey – *his* room, *his* den, *his* retreat, and yet somehow not his any longer because it belonged to the son of the couple downstairs and he was not that son.

He turned over, thrusting his fists against his temples to try and stop the chaotic thoughts but he could not. He did not belong here. He never had. He wasn't Stephen MacIlroy at all. So who the hell was he?

After a while he got up and went to the mirror that stood on the chest, peering at his familiar reflection but seeing it through new eyes. It had never occurred to him before that he bore no resemblance to the people he called his parents; now it seemed a total stranger looked back at him. His face, framed by light-brown hair, the dark-brown eyes, the hint of a cleft in the firm chin – where had they come from? He knew that in the days and weeks to come he would continue to wonder, yet for the moment his curiosity was almost a thing apart. It was the destruction of his world that was important, not what might take its place.

How could they have kept it from him for so long? he wondered – and felt the first sparks of anger. They should have told him, he had a right to know. But they had not told him. They had allowed him to live a lie and now, with a few well-chosen sentences, they had swept the ground from under his feet.

I hate them! Mac thought, and even as he thought it knew he could not even take comfort in that most basic defence. They had always been good to him; he had wanted for nothing. It was wrong to hate them when they had taken him in and given him a home. But they should have told him. They should have told him!

Round and round went the waves of conflicting emotions, round and round the crazy spinning thoughts, the confusion and the sense of loss akin almost to bereavement, round and round the sense of being disenfranchised, of not belonging, here – or anywhere.

There was a tap at the door. Mac barely heard it above the cacophony of heavy metal issuing from the ghetto blaster. He swung round angrily as the door was cautiously opened and his mother looked in – no, not his mother, a stranger who called herself his mother.

'Stephen . . .' Her face was crumpled, anxious, she looked as if she might have been crying. 'Stephen, are you all right?'

No! he wanted to yell. I'm not all right and I never will be again!

He did not answer.

She came into the room closing the door behind her. 'Stephen, please don't take it like this! I know it has been a shock for you, but . . .'

'Why didn't you tell me before?'

'We didn't want to upset you. And we've never thought of you in any way other than our own son.'

He let that go. He wanted to say he did not believe her, that he couldn't believe anyone could possibly forget that they had not given birth to the child they were holding, but he did not. She looked so upset that in spite of his own hurt and anger he shrank from hurting her this much. He glanced back at his image in the mirror, at the compact frame in the rugby shirt and blue denim jeans.

'So,' he said. 'Who am I?'

She shook her head, wrapping her arms around herself as if she were cold, though it was very warm, almost too warm, in the room.

'I can't tell you that.'

'Why not?'

'Because I don't know. When you adopt a baby you are not allowed to know who the real parents are. It's all highly confidential.'

He stared at her as if he did not believe her, and she went on falteringly: 'All they tell you is a little bit of background. She was a student, your real mother, an art student, I think. She was very young and she didn't have any family to support her. I suppose that's why she gave you up – she couldn't look after you all on her own. But I'm so very glad she did, Stephen. All these years I've been so very grateful to her for that . . .'

He ignored the remark. 'And my father?'

'I don't know anything at all about him. There were no details – I expect she wanted to keep his identity secret.' Her voice petered out. She did not want to express the fear that had always haunted her, that perhaps Stephen's real mother had been promiscuous – art students often were, she understood – and had not even known who the father of her baby might be.

'Stephen,' she said, going to him and trying to put her arms around him, 'you must understand none of this matters. We are your family – we have been since you were a few days old. To us, you *are* our son.'

He did not answer. He could not. Tears were choking him.

'The fact that you weren't born to us doesn't make any difference . . .'

And then he found his voice, thick and harsh with all the unshed tears.

'Oh yes it does!' he said bitterly. 'Not to you, maybe – you've always known. But I didn't know. All these years and I didn't know! To me it makes all the difference in the world!'

And of course it did.

For Mac it was the beginning of a year of rebellion, a year which began with questioning every single thing they wanted him to do and ended with him leaving school, against their wishes, to take up an engineering apprenticeship. He rebelled because he was hurt and angry, because he had lost his sense of identity and somehow needed to re-create himself. The old image would no longer do, he wasn't who he had thought he was. Even his name was not his own. For the first time he wished his friends did not call him 'Mac' – 'Mac' was short for MacIlroy and MacIlroy was *their* name, the name *they* had given him.

In his pain and confusion he hit out at them again and again.

After a while the wound began to heal. Days at a time went by when he did not think about it, then weeks, and his old easy-going nature began to reassert itself. Except that now there was a new hard edge to him that had not been there before. He papered over the rift with his parents and they thanked God that he had accepted the situation and there was no more need for lies and deceit. They honestly believed that the status quo had been resumed. And because he did love them and wanted to save them from hurt he never let them know that he still felt oddly incomplete or that he sometimes longed in the quiet hours of the night to know the identity of the mother who had given him life and the reason why she had given him away to strangers.

When the introspective mood took him he wove fantasies about her, picturing a waif-like girl, abandoned, frightened, pregnant and alone. And when he was old enough he applied for a copy of his original birth certificate.

Holding the paper containing the relevant details in his hands at last had been an emotional moment. And then he had looked at it and the blood had begun to sing in his ears.

Dinah Marshall. His mother was Dinah Marshall. Hers was a household name, as well known as any style innovator or captain of industry. Mac had no interest in fashion; well known as Dinah's name was it might have meant nothing to him except that just a few days previously he had been reading about Vandina and the huge annual profit margin it had turned in in the financial pages of the newspaper he read each day from cover to cover. He stared in disbelief, checked the newspaper article, checked again. Dinah Marshall. Could there be two? But the address on the birth certificate put her in the right part of the world, and her age fitted. Besides, *the* Dinah Marshall had once been an art student. This was more than coincidence. This was for real!

After his initial disbelief had worn off, Mac found that his overwhelming reaction was anger and a renewal of his innate sense of rejection. Dinah Marshall was no penniless waif. Yet for some reason she had willingly given him up to strangers and gone on to live her life – very successfully – as if he had never existed. Any thoughts he might have had concerning getting in touch with her were forgotten now. That sort of woman he would not want to know. That sort of life he could do without.

Now, however, some years on, lying on his bunk on the oil rig, leafing idly through the pages of *Mayfair* and thinking again of what Steve Lomax had said, he wondered if perhaps his friend was right.

Perhaps he should make himself known to Dinah, if only to satisfy his own curiosity and try to heal a deep and festering wound. Perhaps next time he was ashore he would go to see her. Then he would put her out of his mind for ever.

The last thing Mac wanted to do was to simply turn up on Dinah's doorstep and announce himself as her long-lost son. It would be too much of a shock for her, he reasoned, and might well be embarrassing for both of them. And so he sat down to write a letter, explaining who he was, how he had discovered Dinah was his real mother and asking if he could come to see her.

The reply arrived by helicopter with the rest of the mail a week later, but it was not quite what he had expected. In his wilder dreams he had hoped for some expression of joy from the woman who had given birth to him; more realistically he had prepared himself for total rejection. This was neither. Typed on company letterhead and signed not by Dinah but by her husband, Van Kendrick, the letter simply stated in formal terms that if Mr MacIlroy would contact the writer on the above telephone number he would be pleased to arrange a suitable time to meet.

Mac was surprised and puzzled, but at least it answered one of his nagging worries – that Dinah might have kept her illegitimate son a secret from even her closest family and in breaking cover he might cause her distress and upset an applecart or two. But that, it seemed, was a groundless fear. Van Kendrick clearly did know about him, and, more astonishingly, was the one who had written to ask for a meeting. That, Mac felt instinctively, did not bode well. If Dinah was keen to see him again then surely she would have been the one to write? There may be a good reason, of course – he remembered reading in a profile somewhere that whilst Dinah was the innovator Van was most definitely the organising power behind Vandina. It could be that the habit of the years was too strong to break. But he did not care for it all the same.

The next time he came ashore for his two weeks off Mac managed to hitch a lift from Aberdeen to Bristol with a commercial pilot who made the mail run five nights a week and with whom he had become friendly. It was dead of winter, bitterly cold, with snow in Aberdeen and thick heavy cloud further south. The pilot, concerned with making a safe flight in atrocious conditions, talked little and Mac was glad. Beneath his customary calm demeanour he was beginning to be apprehensive about the coming meeting and it was a relief not to have to carry on an inconsequential conversation.

The twin-engined aircraft put down at East Midlands Airport at 11 p.m. and was on its way again after a two-hour break. By 2 a.m. they were in Bristol. Mac stumbled out on to the apron where the plane had parked for unloading, muttering his thanks and wondering where he could spend what was left of the night.

'Any ideas which hotel might give me a room at this hour?' he asked.

'Any of the big ones in town, I suppose. I never use them myself. How do you plan on getting there?'

'Taxi.'

'Forget it.' His pilot friend fastened his flight bag and slung it over his shoulder. 'You'd better come home with me. You'll have to sleep on the couch, but it'll be better than nothing. Now – let's get going. I'm frozen stiff and bone tired.'

Life on an oil rig had taught Mac to be adaptable if nothing else. The sofa was barely long enough to stretch out on but when he had wrapped himself in a tartan blanket it felt like heaven. He was asleep almost before the other man's footsteps had creaked quietly upstairs and he slept without interruption until morning when the pilot's wife woke him with a cup of tea.

'Sorry to disturb you, but I have to get on.' Her tone was slightly cool – she was less than delighted to find a stranger in her front room, he guessed.

When he had drunk his tea he got dressed and folded the tartan blanket neatly. The pilot's wife, relenting a little, offered him breakfast but he refused – he did not want to impose on them any more than he already had and his friend the pilot was obviously sleeping in after his late-night flight. Mac had a quick wash and shave and left, catching a bus into town and booking into the first hotel he discovered. Then, fortified with a pot of tea and a plate of eggs and bacon, he telephoned Vandina and asked to speak to Van Kendrick.

'This is Stephen MacIlroy,' he said when the receptionist put him through. 'I wrote to you about the possibility of meeting Dinah Marshall.'

'Ah.' The man's voice was deep, less than welcoming. 'So – you came.'

'I'm in Bristol, yes,' Mac said. 'I flew down from Aberdeen last night.'

'Where are you staying?'

'The Unicorn. Just off the centre.'

'I know where it is. Do you have transport?'

'No, but I can get it. I can hire a car, no doubt.'

'Very well. We'll meet this evening. Take down this address. It's an apartment in Cotham. Do you think you'll be able to find it?'

'I expect so,' Mac said, irritated. 'What time?'

'Seven thirty.'

'I'll be there.' Mac replaced the receiver, angry with himself for allowing the man to rattle him. If they did not want to see him they had only to have said so and he would not have made the long journey from Aberdeen.

He spent the morning wandering around Bristol, bought himself lunch in a pub, and hired a car. Then he returned to his hotel and took a nap to catch up on some of last night's lost sleep.

It was already dark when he woke again, and a thick shrouding fog had dropped over the city. Mac thought briefly of the mail pilot, making the flight to Aberdeen again in this peasouper. Then he took a long bath and wondered about the coming meeting. Meeting his mother for the first time in his life was a daunting prospect and he began to wish he had left things as they were. But it was too late now to change his mind.

He had a drink in the bar before setting out for Cotham but he still managed to find the address he had been given a few minutes before seven thirty. He stood on the pavement outside looking up at it – a tall period building impressive enough, certainly, to be the home of the founders of Vandina, but Van Kendrick had said an *apartment*. Mac checked the row of bell pushes and found one labelled Kendrick, but only one. This could not be the family's main abode, then. It must be some kind of *pied-à-terre*.

Mac checked his watch, stamped his feet, and checked his watch again. Then, deciding not to wait until seven thirty on the dot, he rang the bell. After a moment Van Kendrick's unmistakable voice answered.

'Who is it?'

'Stephen MacIlroy. You are expecting me.'

A pause. Then: 'Very well. You'd better come up.' The buzzer sounded as the remote control switch unlocked the door and Mac went inside. The house oozed an atmosphere of Victorian opulence: stained-glass windows, ornate ceiling cornices, sweeping staircase. Thinking he would prefer, right now, to be embarking on a five-hundred-foot dive to doing this, he started up the stairs.

The door on the landing opened as he emerged, and for the first time Mac came face to face with Van Kendrick. His first, and overriding impression was one of power.

Van was not a big man but those meeting him rarely noticed it, and Mac did not notice it now. There was about him something which commanded immediate respect and that something was utter self-confidence. To his own surprise, however, Mac reacted to it not with awe but with an answering confidence that seemed to stem from his own quiet reserve of strength.

'Mr MacIlroy,' Van said. 'Do come in.'

'Thank you.' Mac followed him inside.

The room was surprisingly large and airy, with more stained glass, more cornices and a beautiful Adam fireplace. It was furnished sparsely but with taste; wine-coloured curtains and covers, a huge multicoloured rug covering all but a narrow border of black-varnished floorboards, lamps – all lit – in gold and pale blue, an antique swivel chair in polished mahogany with an olive-green leather seat. The immediate overall impression, however, was of masculinity. Here were none of the touches a woman might have introduced – particularly a woman noted for her stylish femininity as Dinah Marshall was – and Mac thought he had been right to suppose the apartment was a *pied-à-terre* – Van Kendrick's own city bolt-hole. Of Dinah herself there was no sign. Mac glanced around, half expecting her to appear, but she did not.

'Mr MacIlroy.' Van glanced at his watch, heavy silver Patek. 'I can spare you fifteen minutes. Can I offer you a drink?'

'No thank you,' Mac said, affronted by the other man's brusqueness. 'I'm driving.'

'Very well. Then I suggest we get straight down to business. What exactly do you want?'

Again Mac's hackles rose, but he told himself he had no right to expect his mother and her husband to kill the fatted calf.

'As I said in my letter I have recently obtained my original birth certificate and I thought I would like to make contact.'

Dark-navy eyes bored into his.

'I see.' He paused. 'Let's not beat about the bush, MacIlroy. I can't help wondering if you would have been so eager to make contact, as you put it, if you had discovered your mother was a nobody, living in a council high-rise on social security.'

Mac controlled his rising anger with difficulty. 'That has nothing whatever to do with it. I simply wanted to meet her.'

'Hmm. I wonder. Well, we'll let that pass and get to the crux of the matter, which is that although you may wish to meet your mother, your mother, I have to tell you, does not wish to meet you.'

Mac felt his stomach sink. 'You mean I've come all this way for nothing?'

'I'm afraid so. Try to see it her way, MacIlroy. What happened was unfortunate but it was all a very long time ago, when Dinah was not much more than a child. It was a most upsetting period of her life but she has put it all behind her now. She doesn't want the past dredged up, doesn't want to be reminded of her past mistakes and indiscretions. Surely if you think about it you will be able to understand that.'

'I understood right from the start she might feel that way,' Mac said. 'What I don't understand is why you have let me come all this way to tell me so.'

Van crossed to a table where a decanter and glasses stood on an antique silver tray.

'Do, please, have a Scotch, MacIlroy. I'm having one.'

He unstoppered the decanter, raised it invitingly. Mac, who felt he could certainly do with a drink, wavered.

'All right.'

'Good.' Van poured the drinks, added ice, and passed one to Mac. 'I don't wish to appear inhospitable. I merely want to make the facts clear to you. That is why I allowed you to come to Bristol, so that I could tell you myself, face to face, the way Dinah feels. I hope now you will understand that she really does not want to meet you and rake up what is best forgotten.'

Mac sipped the whisky. As yet the reality of rejection for a second time had not reached him emotionally; he had not had time to weigh it up and register hurt and disappointment.

'I hoped that by explaining it to you myself I could prevent you bothering her again,' Van said smoothly.

Mac bridled. 'I don't feel I have bothered her, Mr Van Kendrick. One letter hardly constitutes harassment – and I would remind you I am here now at your invitation.'

Van Kendrick nodded. 'That's true. But Dinah's well-being is my primary concern. She is not very strong emotionally – she never has been. Perhaps what happened to her left its scars, perhaps it is simply her nature to be highly strung, I don't know. But the fact is that Dinah simply cannot cope with this kind of stress. It makes her ill, physically and emotionally. She can't sleep, she can't eat, she can't work, and she is liable to suffer a complete nervous breakdown. I can't allow that to happen. That is why I asked you to come here – so that I could explain the situation. And why I am asking you now to go back to Scotland and forget any ideas you might have of meeting her.'

'She asked you to tell me this?'

'I am speaking to you on her behalf, yes.'

'I see.' Mac tossed back what was left of his drink. 'In that case I won't take up any more of your time.' He moved to the door, turned, looked back. 'There is one other thing I would like to know, Mr Van Kendrick. Who is my father?'

Van stiffened, setting his glass down on a small octagonal drinks table. But when he looked up his face was as pragmatic as ever.

'I am afraid I can't tell you that. It is something we have never discussed. Now I am afraid I must ask you to excuse me.'

At that precise moment the door of the apartment opened. Neither of them had heard the footsteps on the stairs; now a young woman stood there. For a brief, unthinking moment Mac wondered if it was Dinah, changed her mind and come to meet him after all, then he realised it could not be.

Dinah must be in her forties at least; this woman was much younger, probably no older than he was. He saw dark hair, sharply cut and slightly damp from the fog, a clear-featured face, and scarlet lips which gave her colour and vitality. She was wearing a bright-red swing coat with the collar turned up against the cold so that it framed that bright, alive, glowing face.

'Oh – I'm sorry!' she said. 'I didn't know there would be anyone here.'

'It's all right, Ros. My visitor was just leaving.' Van moved towards her, ushered her in, one hand lying proprietorially on her scarlet-wool-covered shoulder. 'My personal assistant, Ros Newman. We have some work to catch up on – agendas for a meeting tomorrow and some correspondence that can't wait. I did explain when you arrived that I could only spare you a few minutes.'

Work my foot! Mac thought. If she's come to his city retreat to talk about agendas, I'm the Flying Dutchman! No wonder he was so anxious to get rid of me.

'I'm sorry to have troubled you,' he said coldly. 'You need not worry that I shall do so again. I will be on the train back to Scotland in the morning. And perhaps you would tell my mother from me that the last thing I intended was to cause her distress. Though of course she might also like to know that I have made a good life for myself without her help.'

He saw Van wince, saw the girl's puzzled expression, and felt only triumph. He shouldn't have said it but he felt he owed them a parting shot.

As he went down the stairs he heard the door of the apartment shut behind him. Outside, the cold, clammy fog closed around him, making him shiver, and he realised he felt totally numb.

So – that was it. End of story. Dinah did not want to meet him and who could blame her? He was a part of her life that she wanted to forget and he must forget it too. Mac resolved to return to Aberdeen and put the whole episode out of his mind.

'Well?' Steve greeted him when he arrived back at the house they shared in Aberdeen. 'How did you get on?'

'I didn't.'

'What do you mean? What was she like?'

'I never got to meet her. Van Kendrick, her husband, summoned me to his bachelor flat and warned me off in no uncertain terms.'

'Oh.'

'Yes – oh. Completely wasted journey. So that, I guess, is the end of that.'

Steve was silent for a moment. Then he said: 'You think it came from her?'

'What do you mean?'

'Well – you think she knew that you were there?'

'Of course. Why shouldn't she?'

'The letter you had was signed by him, wasn't it? Perhaps she never got to see your letter. Perhaps he intercepted it.'

'Why should he do that?'

'I haven't a clue. But people do strange things and he could have his reasons. Could be he's the one who doesn't want the past raked up.'

'Could be, I suppose. But he definitely said she didn't want to be reminded of her indiscretions. He was very protective.'

'He would be, wouldn't he, if he was anxious to keep you from trying to make contact again?'

Mac shook his head. He was feeling depressed and fed up with the whole episode.

'Let's just forget it, Steve. Whatever the reason, the message was very clear. Dinah does not want to know. And I have not the slightest intention of forcing myself in where I'm not wanted.' He pulled out his wallet, extracted his birth certificate and looked at it for a moment. 'This might just as well go out with the rubbish.'

'Don't be so stupid!' Steve said. 'You can't do that!'

'Why not, for all the good it's done me?'

'You might need it some day.'

'I don't know what the hell for. But I suppose you're right. I'd better not destroy it.' He fished out Van's letter to him, still in its envelope, and put the birth certificate inside. Then he pulled open a drawer in the sideboard and pushed it all into the compartment out of sight. As he did so a pack of cards caught his eye. 'OK,' he said, in an effort to change the conversation. 'How do you fancy a hand of gin rummy? And the loser buys the first round when we get to the pub!'

When his contract with Excel Oil came to an end Mac decided he would like a change of scenery.

'I'm going to South America,' he told Steve and Des.

'South America? You must be bloody mad! They're a load of cowboys down there!'

'Not cowboys – gauchos!' Mac quipped.

Des looked at him blankly and Steve laughed.

'Joke. Never mind, Des, forget it. Anyway, I know what you're saying. Safety measures come pretty low down the list of priorities when you're way out on a limb like that. But the company I'm going to work for is American – Tristar US – so they should know what they're doing, and at least it should be a bit warmer than it is here.'

'Well,' Des said prophetically, 'it's your funeral.'

'Too right.' Mac couldn't explain the way he felt. He had had itchy feet ever since the episode with Van Kendrick when he had discovered once and for all that his mother had no wish to meet him, let alone try to form a relationship to make up for the lost years.

Knowing this had affected him more deeply than he would ever have imagined possible. Though he rarely thought about it consciously any more it had struck at the very core of him, aggravating the basic insecurity he had felt ever since the day his adoptive parents had told him the truth about himself. Though he still kept in touch with them, still loved them, yet he felt distanced from them by the deceit they had practised for whatever reason over the years, and that unintentional resentment refused to go away. He did not belong with them, or with anyone. He was obsessed with the need to carve out a new life for himself, re-create himself. Only then could he be at peace with himself again – and with them. He did not stop to analyse the restlessness, he only reacted to it. He wanted to see the world – and why shouldn't he do so? South America beckoned, a strange wild country where no one knew him or had any preconceived ideas about his origins. The secretive streak in his nature hated the fact that Steve and Des knew so much about him, though his visit to Bristol had only been mentioned once or twice more. In South America he could begin again, losing himself in the diving that was his life.

'They employ every blasted nationality under the sun,' Des said when he left. 'Just watch out for those bastards.'

'Don't worry, I will,' Mac said, and did not mention the fact that the word bastard now had unpleasant connotations for him.

'Why the hell won't this drawer shut properly?' Bill Tynan asked irritably. Bill was the diver who was now sharing with Steve the house which he had once rented with Mac, and he was fiddling with the top drawer in the sideboard, trying to make it run smoothly.

'I never noticed anything wrong with it,' Steve said.

'It's sticking.' Bill jerked the drawer open again and ran his fingers along the back of it. 'There's something here, that's what it is.' He straightened, an envelope in his hand. 'Looks like it's something the last fellow left behind. It's addressed to him.'

'Mac, you mean?' Steve took the envelope, recognising it at once. He opened it and drew out Van Kendrick's letter and the folded birth certificate. Mac had obviously forgotten all about it and the top drawer of the sideboard was not one they used much.

'I'll take it,' he said. 'I'll keep it for him. I expect I'll catch up with him sometime.'

'Friend of yours, was he?' Bill asked.

'You could say that,' Steve replied.

Six months later news of Mac reached the Excel rig, brought by a diver who had just returned from Rio.

'I heard there was a nasty accident down Mar del Plata way. The bloke involved used to work on this rig – Mac something, his name was.'

'Not MacIlroy?' Steve asked.

'That's it, MacIlroy. He and his partner were on the sea bed when the bell shifted, turned right over on top of their air line. The bell man couldn't do a damn thing and the crew were all bloody foreigners – you know how they mix nationalities in these outfits. The Germans and French are all right, but if you're working with the locals – forget it. This crew were Argentinian from what I heard and they didn't understand or didn't give a monkey's cuss if they did. God knows how long it was before the poor bugger of a bell man could alert them to what had happened.'

Although in the world of deep-sea diving accidents of all kinds are not uncommon Steve was shocked. One thing to hear about near-misses and violent death when one didn't know the men concerned, quite another to learn that someone as close as Mac had been involved.

'You mean they were both drowned?' he asked.

The diver shrugged. 'No air supply at six hundred feet? What do you think?'

Shit, Steve thought. Poor old Mac. Well one thing was for sure. He would never need his birth certificate now.

Six months passed. Steve rarely thought about Mac now, though when he did it was with regret. He had made few real friends in his life, and he was sorry Mac was dead. Sorry – but nothing more. The first shock had long since passed and Steve had grown used to the knowledge that Mac was no more, grown used to it and filed it away in the recesses of his mind from which it occasionally rose to surprise him again. But never with the same force, never hitting him in the guts the way it had when he had first heard it. Mac was dead and that was that – end of story.

Winter had come to the North Sea once more, intensifying the biting cold with gale-force winds that whipped the sea around the rig into mountainous waves and howled angrily around the ugly structure, testing both men and metal to their limits. Often, returning chilled to the marrow and dead tired after a dive, Steve thought about moving on, but somehow he never did and he realised he had come to look on the rig and the rented house in Aberdeen as the closest thing he had to a home.

One day he would have to move on, one day he would go back to pursuing his goal, but not yet. His bank balance was growing but it was still not enough to set himself with confidence on the road he wanted to take. Would it ever be? With the passage of time it seemed he always wanted more – and still more. Diving was a way of getting it, besides being a way of life. Yet somehow Steve never doubted that one day he would achieve his ambition, though he had no clear idea how he would do it.

And then one day he read in the newspapers of Van Kendrick's death – and he knew.

At first the idea that came to him was vague and unformed, but as he turned it over in his mind his excitement grew, driving out all the tiredness, making him forget the bone-aching cold and the depressions that came sometimes along with the isolation and the knowledge that out there in the real world he was a man with a record.

Mac had been Dinah's son but Mac was dead. Mac had been Dinah's son but no one in the world except he and Des knew it – and Des was no real threat. He never read a newspaper and he did not know that Steve was in possession of Mac's birth certificate. This was his chance, Steve thought, to start afresh with a new identity – and what an identity!

Steve had always harboured the suspicion that Van had not been speaking for Dinah when he had turned Mac away; now he turned the idea over in his mind again. Everything he had read about the partnership suggested that Van had been totally dominant, deciding the course their lives should take, manipulating and coercing. Van had been a fixer and Steve was convinced he had fixed Mac for some reason of his own. But now Van too was dead and Dinah was alone. What better moment for the reappearance of that other man in her life, her son? When Mac had gone to Bristol he had met no one but Van – if Van had told anyone about the meeting they would have no idea what the mystery son had looked like. And in Steve's possession was Mac's birth certificate – the one thing he would need to prove his identity.

It was possible, of course, that Dinah would reject him. She might refuse to see him, let alone accept him. But conversely she might welcome him with open arms. It was a gamble Steve was all too ready to take.

Steve sat down and wrote to Dinah, a carefully worded letter, and whilst he was waiting for a reply he went into Aberdeen, kitted himself out with a new wardrobe, spending lavishly from his savings and counting it an investment.

When her answer came it was everything he had hoped it would be. At her invitation he headed for Bristol – not for the impersonal flat in town where Van had interviewed Mac, but for the family home in its acres of beautiful grounds. His mouth watered as he stood on the drive looking around at what might very well be his – if only he played his cards right. Then he rang the bell.

She answered the door herself, a slim blonde, past the first flush of youth but still quite beautiful. She was pale, she was nervous, and for a moment he could not tell from her face whether she was going to laugh or cry.

'Stephen?' she said. Her voice was trembling.

'Yes,' he said.

And she opened her arms and took him into them, there on the doorstep.

'Oh Stephen, Stephen!' The tears were falling now; he could feel them wet on his cheek. 'Is it really you? I thought I'd never see you again!'

'But now I'm here,' he said.

It had been easy – so easy. He need not even have had the birth certificate – she never asked to see it. In her joy at being reunited with the son she had given up as a new born baby she accepted him completely.

There were questions, of course, later, and plenty of them, as they sat, Dinah holding tightly to his hand as if she was afraid he might disappear again if she let it go. Questions, questions and more questions – not because she doubted him but because she wanted every detail of the years between, the years she had lost.

And he gave her what she wanted. Lying had always come easily to Steve. He told her the couple who had adopted him had emigrated to Canada and that they had both been killed in a car crash when he was fifteen years old. She wept then, hugging him, saying how dreadful it must have been for him, but at least now he had *her* – at least they had each other.

And she begged him to stay.

'Don't leave me again, please. I couldn't bear to lose you again!'

He hesitated. He had no intention of going far, but he did not want her to know that.

'I have to earn a living. Diving is all I know.'

'You don't have to earn a living, not now. Look, I realise you have your pride and I don't want to patronise you, but everything I have is yours too.'

'I couldn't take it. It wouldn't feel right.'

'Work for me then! Join the company! I see how you feel, I respect you for it – only please, don't go away again!'

'I'm a diver, I'm not a businessman.'

'But you could be, I know you could! And diving is so dangerous. If someting happened to you I couldn't bear it.'

He'd almost smiled at the irony of it. He'd let her go on and on, putting up token resistance until he judged he had done enough to make her believe the whole thing was her idea, and then he had capitulated. He had moved to Somerset and everything had gone so smoothly he felt like laughing. He was Dinah's son, heir to a business that would keep him in comfort for the rest of his life. He had everything he had ever wanted. And he was safe – or so he had thought.

But when the security of his position was threatened Steve did not hesitate. The ruthless side of his nature, well hidden beneath the easy charm, came swiftly to the fore. All that mattered to him was preserving his charade.

Steve acted swiftly, unconcerned by the enormity of what he was doing. There was only one thought in his mind and that was that he had no intention of letting anything – or anyone – deprive him of the new life he had made for himself.

Chapter Eighteen

Maggie was feeling edgy though she could not have identified the reason. She finished tidying the cottage, made herself a sandwich and went outside to check on the washing she had hung out on the line. It was still not quite dry. Back in the house she looked at the clock. Liz Christopher had said that Ros's things would be ready for her in about an hour, and that was more or less up.

Maggie took her hired car and drove through the leafy country lanes to Vandina. The girl on the reception desk recognised her at once.

'You've come for Ros's belongings. Liz told me Jayne was sorting them out and would leave them with me but she hasn't done that yet.'

'Jayne. Is she about?'

'No, she's gone to lunch. Hang on, though, I'll go and look in her office and see if the things are ready for you.'

Maggie stood in the foyer waiting and a few minutes later the girl was back carrying a manila envelope, a pink cardboard file and a scarf – how Ros loved her scarves!

'These are the things, I think. They were stacked up on Jayne's desk and labelled with Ros's name. Jayne forgot to give them to me, I expect. But I'm sure it will be all right for you to take them.'

She passed them to Maggie who glanced at the meagre pile, somewhat disappointed.

'Thank you. And please thank Jayne and Liz for me, will you?'

She carried the things out to her car. The car park was deserted – obviously everyone went out at lunchtime. Maggie reversed out of the space where she had parked and took the road back to the cottage. There she put the scarf carefully away in a drawer, opened the manila envelope and the pink file, spreading the contents out on the kitchen table, and began to read.

Steve came hurrying out of Jayne's back door with something less than his usual self-restraint. As he crossed the courtyard to where he had left his car he was still buttoning his shirt and his tie hung loosely around his neck.

The keys were in the ignition – he had left everything ready for a hasty getaway – but as he revved the engine and roared away from the converted barn he turned not towards the restaurant where his alibi of lunch with Dinah awaited him, but back towards Vandina.

Christ, how could everything have gone so bloody wrong just when it had seemed he was safe, his deception unremarked, his whole future rosy and secure? Even an hour ago, when he had realised that Jayne, at least, knew the truth about him he had thought the situation was redeemable. He had had no scruples about killing her in order to silence her and though he knew he was playing a dangerous game he had been reasonably confident he could get away with it. With the supreme self-assurance that is the hallmark of the most ruthless of men, Steve had thought he could pull it off. When Jayne was found strangled who would suspect him? He would say he had been lunching with Dinah and when she backed him up he did not expect anyone to question the timing too closely. He would have liked more time in which to plan Jayne's demise, he would have preferred to dispose of her away from her home and cover his tracks more thoroughly but circumstances had been such that he had decided it would be better to silence her as quickly as possible and he imagined there would be plenty of suspects the police would look at more closely than him. Jayne had had other boyfriends, he knew, and Drew himself, with his racy background and a drug habit, would probably come under suspicion. The very fact that he had acted swiftly would work in his favour, he had reasoned. But things had not worked out the way he had expected.

He had reached for the scarf with which he intended to strangle her, there in the bedroom, and she had seen him do it. Already puzzled by his response to her question about who he really was – 'That, my sweet, is something you will never know' – alarm bells had rung for Jayne and she had sat up swiftly, moving away from him.

'What the hell do you think you are doing?'

'I'm sorry about this, darling,' he said casually. 'But I am afraid I can't let you go around spreading nasty stories about me.'

'Even if they happen to be true?'

'Especially if they happen to be true.'

'You've gone mad!' Her eyes narrowed. 'Or is this some new kind of sex game?'

He almost laughed aloud. She really was insatiable! And of course, that was the way to play it. Jayne was a big girl, she would be quite strong. If he could have slipped the scarf around her neck without her realising what he was doing it would have been one thing. As it was she would put up quite a struggle.

'Yes, that's it, a little game,' he said smoothly, though his pulses were pounding. 'You like games, don't you?'

There were high spots of colour in her cheeks and her eyes were hard and bright.

'You know I do. But not bondage – not for me. Something might go wrong. And that would be very unfortunate – for both of us.'

Something about the tone of her voice alerted him.

'What do you mean by that?' he asked sharply.

'Just that if anything was to happen to me everyone would find out your little secret.'

'Why?' The scarf felt slippery in his moist fingers.

'Because in my office is evidence to prove you are not Dinah's son.'

'Evidence? What evidence?'

She laughed. She loved it when the balance of power changed in her favour, and it had swung her way now.

'That would be telling, wouldn't it?'

'And where exactly in your office is this . . . evidence?'

She shook her head, looking at the scarf which he held in his hand.

'You really think I'd tell you that, so you could put that scarf round my neck and pull it tight and then go off and get rid of the evidence of what I know? Oh, I'm not that stupid. No, you are just going to have to trust me, darling. And stick to our little bargain.'

'What bargain?'

'Surely you haven't forgotten so soon? You keep my secret and I keep yours. I won't spill the beans, Steve. Not even about . . . this. You and I are too good together. And we're going to be better yet, now that I know what I know.'

Sweat was trickling down his face.

'How do I know you have any proof at all?' he asked.

Jayne moved lazily, reaching for her négligé and pulling it over her soft white shoulders.

'Get dressed, darling. We'll go back to the office and I'll show you.'

Steve did as she suggested. His mind was racing. He still did not know whether to believe her or not, but indisputably Jayne did know the truth about him and he could not take the risk that in her office was something that would blow his whole cover wide open.

'Come on then,' he said hoarsely. 'But for God's sake be quick. Dinah is expecting me to join her for lunch.'

'Then let's go and have lunch with her and I'll show you when we get back to the office afterwards.'

'No – we'll go now.' He couldn't wait another minute; he had to know what she had against him so that he could begin amending his plan of action.

Now, as he swung the car back towards Vandina, cold with the fear of carefully laid plans that seemed to have gone haywire, a Frankenstein's monster that was getting out of control, he looked at her sitting beside him in the passenger seat, and felt himself hating this coldly self-possessed woman who was threatening to wreck everything. Oh, he could kill her now, and enjoy every minute of it. Once he had whatever it was that could expose him as a fraud he would do it – and do it in such a way that no one would ever suspect him. But for the moment he needed her – and she knew it.

He screamed his car to a stop in the Vandina car park, composed himself and followed Jayne into the building. The girl at the reception desk was on the telephone; she waved at them as if she wanted to say something but they ignored her and went upstairs to Jayne's office.

'Now, darling . . .' Jayne turned to him, smiling that infuriatingly smug smile as she opened her door. Then, as she stepped into the room he saw her face change. She took a step forward, ran her hands over the almost empty desk top as if she could not believe what she was seeing – or not seeing – then turned back. There was alarm in her eyes.

'Well?' he said harshly. 'Where is your proof?'

'Oh Christ!' Jayne said softly. She reached for the internal telephone and buzzed the reception desk. The girl must have finished with the telephone call she had been taking, for she answered almost at once.

'The files that were on my desk,' Jayne said, her voice sharp. 'Do you happen to know what has become of them?'

Steve could not hear the receptionist's reply. Jayne put down the receiver and turned to him.

'It looks as if we're in trouble, Steve,' she said, and there was an edge of panic in her voice. 'My proof isn't here any longer. Someone has taken it.'

'Who?'

'Ros's sister, Maggie.'

He was dumbfounded. 'Maggie? But why?'

'Never mind that now.' Jayne's voice was taut with tension. 'If you don't want anyone else knowing what I know, I suggest you get those files back – and get them back quickly! They are dynamite, Steve. And Maggie Veritos has them.'

'I don't understand what can have become of Steve,' Dinah said, looking at her watch. 'I thought he would have been here ages ago.'

Don smiled at her across the table. He was enjoying the chance of being alone with her. Since Steve had arrived on the scene those occasions had been all too rare.

'I shouldn't worry, Dinah,' he said gently. 'Obviously something important has come up. I'm sure he won't mind if we begin without him.'

And Dinah smiled back at him, that lovely smile that could stop his heart beating.

'I expect you're right, Don,' she said. 'You usually are.'

Maggie sat at the kitchen table, the files and papers spread out all around her, staring into space. She could still hardly believe what she had read there, and yet already her racing thoughts were beginning to have some order to them and the pieces of the jigsaw were fitting into place.

So, this was what had been on Ros's mind in those last weeks before she disappeared – and it had nothing whatever to do with a mole at Vandina. It was more important, more far-reaching than that, and it had to do not only with the business but with Dinah's personal life. No wonder she had been so preoccupied.

Steve – an imposter! Never in her wildest dreams would such a thing have occurred to Maggie – and why should it? But somehow it had occurred to Ros and she had begun checking it out – the letters in the file, along with Ros's diary and scribbled notes proved that. For some reason Ros had been suspicious and she had set out to confirm her suspicions. But why had she told no one? And where the hell was she now?

Maggie shivered, all her fears for Ros's safety surfacing once more. She had been afraid that Brendan had been in some way responsible for Ros's disappearance but now she began to wonder if perhaps she had been on the wrong track. Could it be that it was Steve who was behind it? Had he somehow discovered that Ros knew the truth about him and set out to make sure she told no one else what she knew?

Maggie lit a cigarette and drew deeply on the smoke, but for once it did not seem to do anything to calm her – if anything it only made her head spin more and she ground it out again, trying to decide on a course of action and succeeding only in chasing around in circles. She had to tell someone what she had discovered, but who, and in what order? Should she get in touch with the police first, or speak to someone at Vandina? The revelation was obviously going to devastate Dinah and even in her present state of confusion and anxiety Maggie, with her ability to empathise, shrank from being the one to break the unwelcome news.

If only Mike were here! she thought. He would know what to do. But Mike was teaching, and it would be several hours yet before she could count on his support. But at least she could telephone and leave a message on his answering machine so that he would contact her as soon as he got home from school. He was expecting her to be there in any case and would wonder where she was. She dialled Mike's number and drew comfort from simply hearing his recorded voice at the other end of the line – even that nebulous contact seemed to help.

She left a message, simply asking him to call her at the cottage if she was not at the flat when he returned, then went back into the kitchen and packed all the papers together once more in the pink folder. She would go to the police with them, she decided. She was sorry the news would be broken to Dinah by an official rather than a close friend but she could not allow that to sway her judgement. Finding Ros was, and had always been, her priority, and this file was, she felt, vital evidence.

As she closed the folder she thought she heard a car on the lane outside, but took little notice, and a moment later the ring at the doorbell made her physically jump. She went to answer it, wondering if it might possibly be the police. But when she yanked open the door it was not a policeman on the doorstep. It was Steve.

Maggie's heart came into her mouth with a huge leap, cutting off her breath, defying her, for the moment, to speak.

'Maggie.' Steve's voice was low, as ever, yet she sensed a tension beneath the laid-back exterior, a wary alertness like that of a tiger. Or was that imagination? Had what she now knew simply made her look at him in a different light?

'Yes?' At least she had managed to speak, but it came out sounding breathless. 'What do you want?'

'Can I come in?' Even as he said it he was pushing past her. Taken by surprise she was unable to prevent him. 'I think you took some things away from the Vandina office. I'd like them back please.'

'Well I'm sorry, I'm afraid you can't have them. They belong to Ros.'

'They belong to the company. If you'll just let me . . .' He was in the kitchen now; he saw the file on the table and reached for it. 'This is what I want, I think.'

Maggie moved swiftly, snatching up the file and holding it pressed against her chest. 'Please leave, Steve.'

He froze, all that lazy power bottled up and waiting . . . for what? His eyes, ice-blue and hypnotic, seemed to bore into her.

'I'm afraid I can't do that. Not without the file. Give it to me now.'

'It's too late, Steve. It won't do any good for you to take it now. You see, I've read it. I know what's in it – and why you want it.'

His ice-cold eyes narrowed.

'Really? And have you told anyone else what you have discovered?'

'Hardly! I've only just found out myself . . .'

The moment the words were out she knew she should never have spoken them. His lips quirked into a slight satisfied smile but his eyes were still cold as chips of blue glass.

'In that case, Maggie, you leave me no option.'

Her trembling fear beame sharp, cold terror.

'What do you mean?'

But she knew, without asking. Unbelievable that this man with his clean-cut, all-American-boy good looks, throwaway elegance and easy charm should be dangerous, but dangerous he undoubtedly was – appearances had misled. This was a man who was totally ruthless in the pursuit of his aims. He had exploited, manipulated, lied and deceived those who stood in the way of his ambition. For all she knew he had already killed. And she knew, with a certainty that went beyond frightened imaginings, that he would do so again.

She was the one now who was threatening his position; rashly, stupidly, she had let him know it. And she was totally alone here, totally at his mercy. Perhaps when he returned from work Mike would find her message on the answering machine and come straight over, but it would be too late. The danger was real and it was immediate.

Almost mesmerised she saw him draw a silk scarf out of the pocket of his jacket and twist it experimentally around his fingers.

'I'm really very sorry about this, Maggie,' he said, and there was only the slightest catch of nervous excitement in his otherwise perfectly level voice. 'But at least we don't know one another very well, do we?'

'You're mad!'

'Not really. But I am very, very determined. Now, are we going to do this the easy way – or the hard way? The choice is yours.'

'You *are* mad!' Maggie's mind was running in wild circles now. Surely he did not think she was simply going to allow him to kill her without a fight? But what sort of fight? There were knives in the kitchen drawer, almost within reach, but what good would they do? She couldn't fight him, even armed with a knife; he could overpower her easily and might even turn it on her.

There was only one way to defend herself, and that was with words. Somehow she had to stay calm and delay the moment when he would twist that silk scarf around her throat and pull it tight.

But what words? What could she say? With an instinct born of terror Maggie found inspiration. Steve had not liked being called mad. Perhaps his vanity was his Achilles' heel.

'You really have been very clever,' she said. 'How did you manage it?'

He smirked and with a tiny thrill of relief she realised she had been right.

'You could say it was easy. But not everyone would have taken their chances the way I did.'

'So – tell me about it.'

'You really want to know?'

'Yes,' she said. 'I really want to know.'

He smirked again, finding himself eager, suddenly, to tell her. Jayne had asked, and he had refused, but then if he had killed Jayne time would have been of the essence. Then he had been anxious to get to Dinah and his alibi. Now that was of no importance. Jayne would provide him with his alibi, however long it took.

Jayne. The smirk became a full-blown smile. He was glad now that he had not killed her. Jayne was like him – they would make a good team. For the time being. As long as it suited him. When it suited him no longer then he would dispose of her.

A little boastfully Steve began to recount his story. As he talked Maggie's mind was running in circles as she tried to think of a way to escape. Simply to make a break and run would, she knew, be as useless as trying to defend herself with one of the kitchen knives. He was between her and the door and even if she could get past him there was no way she could escape. The other cottage in the lane would be deserted at this time of day and with his long legs and athletic frame he would catch her easily before she could reach the main road. She sat quite still, letting him talk, assessing, wondering, how to last this out, how to gain a reprieve.

It came to her quite suddenly, a thought so repellent it made her shiver with distaste yet at the same time offered a glimmer of hope. She had managed to flatter him into telling her how he had come to impersonate Dinah's son; perhaps she could flatter him into something more. He was a highly sexed man, she was sure, and he had made a pass at her once. Could she – dare she – try to interest him sexually again?

'I do admire you,' she said softly. To her own ears the words sounded insincere but Steve appeared to notice nothing. He merely continued with his tale, embellishing it with yet more details. She put down the file, which she had been hugging, on the corner of the table. Then with a supreme effort of will she forced herself to move towards him with some semblance of seduction, though her legs would hardly support her and she felt sick with apprehension.

A faintly surprised expression crossed the handsome features, then slowly he began to smile and she knew she had been right. Vanity was his weakness. Her only hope now was to play on it.

'There's something awfully attractive about someone as clever – and ruthless – as you,' she said. She stretched out a hand tentatively and laid it on his shoulder. For a moment muscle tensed beneath smooth silk then relaxed again.

'You think so? I'm glad. You are a very attractive woman yourself, Maggie.'

'Am I?' She let her fingers run on along the line of his shoulder to his neck, spreading her fingers out into a light caress beneath the hair that grew down thickly on to his collar. Then, summoning all her courage, she kissed him.

For a moment he was like alabaster, his lips unresponsive, then she felt a tremor run through his body and with a suddenness that almost shocked her he took control. He was the aggressor now, it was he who was kissing her, towering above her, crushing her, whilst his hand slid inside her blouse. His touch made her almost physically sick but somehow she forced down the nausea, responding with what she hoped was the enthusiasm he would expect. Through his silk shirt she could feel that his back was drenched with sweat – or was it her own hands that were wet and trembling?

'Maggie,' he whispered softly, like a lover. 'Oh Maggie, Maggie . . .'

And then the doorbell rang.

She felt him stiffen and knew instinctively what he was going to do. As his hand came up to cover her mouth she twisted away, kicking out at the same time as hard as she could. She felt him double up as her knee connected with his groin, pushed at him with all her remaining strength and ran, on legs that threatened to let her down, to the door. Her hands fumbled with the catch for seemingly endless moments, then the door flew open.

There were two people on the doorstep – a man and a woman. Maggie did not stop even to register that the woman was the *Western Daily Press* reporter or that the man had a camera bag slung over his shoulder. She did not speak, she scarcely even glanced at them. Her only thought was to get away . . . away . . .

They separated, startled, as she pushed past them and turned to look after her in amazement as she fled down the path. But she did not stop. Maggie turned into the lane and went on running.

Mike arrived home a little after four. He was surprised but not particularly worried to see that Maggie's car was not parked outside. She must have delayed coming over to the flat, he supposed – either that or she had been and gone out again.

He let himself in, dumped his bag and nudged the 'play' button on the answering machine which was flashing at him from the table in the tiny hallway.

First Maggie, asking him to call her at the cottage – strange, he thought; then Bryan Price, with whom he played squash sometimes, asking why he had not heard from Mike lately and suggesting a game. Mike unzipped his jacket as he listened to the messages, then clicked the machine on to 'home' and dialled the number of Ros's cottage. There was no reply, only the persistent ringing of the bell. Maggie must have already left, he decided, and would probably arrive at any moment. He went into the kitchen, put the kettle on and made a cup of tea, but as he drank it he found himself watching the clock and wondering where Maggie could be.

Mike was not an imaginative man but for some reason his intuition was working overtime now, making him uneasy. He simply could not understand what had happened to Maggie, and suddenly he was thinking of Ros, who had disappeared without trace. My God, he thought, suppose the same thing happened to Maggie? The very idea shook him to the core, colouring his usual stolidity deep black, and he realised the prospect of never seeing Maggie again was a quite unbearable one. He had been concerned about Ros – more than concerned – but the thought of Maggie disappearing from his life in the same way hit at the deepest core of him with the sickening thud of a boxer's punch, way below the belt, and brought beads of cold sweat to his forehead.

Christ, he loved her! Love was not a word much used in Mike's vocabulary; he seldom thought about it, but he thought about it now, in the same breath as Maggie, and knew without doubt that it was indeed love he felt for her.

He ran his fingers through his hair, thinking deeply. Strange really. He had, he supposed, loved Ros, in his own way, without putting a word to it. Yet now he knew that it had been but a pale shadow of the emotion he experienced with and for Maggie.

The telephone shrilled suddenly, jerking him out of his reverie, and he lunged for it.

'Maggie?' he almost said, but somehow stopped himself, and moments later he was glad he had. The voice at the other end was brisk, official.

'Mr Thompson?'

A sudden premonition of disaster tightened his throat.

'Yes.'

'This is the police station, PC Dugdale speaking. I wonder if I could ask you to come down.'

'Why? What's happened?'

'We'll explain more fully when you arrive, sir, but the crux of the matter is that we have Mrs Veritos here – Maggie Veritos. She is very upset and she asked us to contact you.'

'Has there been an accident?'

'Not exactly, sir. But I think it might be a good idea if you could get here as soon as possible.'

Mike's jaw was set. He'd been right to be worried, then.

'I'll be straight over,' he said.

'I don't believe it,' Maggie said. 'I can't bring myself to believe any of it. It's like a nightmare, this whole thing.'

She was sitting in Mike's biggest and most comfortable chair, wrapped, like an invalid, in a blanket because although the evening was warm and muggy she could not stop shivering. She was sipping whisky, the tumbler cradled between her two hands because she could not trust herself to hold it with just one, but not even the 40 per cent proof spirit could reach the icy places inside her. She was, Mike thought, suffering the classic symptoms of shock – and he didn't feel so great himself.

He had known, even before the policeman had begun to explain, that something was dreadfully wrong, yet he had still been shaken to the core when he had learned exactly what had happened.

'That bastard!' he said now. 'I just wish I could get my hands on him! I'd make him wish he'd never been born!'

'I wonder where he is?' Maggie said. She was staring into space, still reliving every traumatic moment from the time she had discovered the truth about Steve until she had dashed past the startled reporter and photographer, running and running with no clear idea except to put as much distance as possible between her and the man who had threatened her and, perhaps, murdered her sister as he had clearly intended to murder her.

'They'll catch up with him,' Mike said roughly. 'And when they do I hope they'll throw the book at him. Why the hell did they ever do away with the death penalty? But hanging would be too good for him. I know what I'd like to do with him, the bastard!'

'He's mad,' Maggie said in a small voice. 'Quite, quite mad. You should have seen his eyes, Mike.' She shivered convulsively, seeing again the expression on that handsome face, cold ruthlessness mixed with triumph and pride at what he thought of as his own cleverness.

'Of course he's mad, but that's no reason for him to get away with it.' Mike was pacing, furious in his impotence. 'When I think of what he was going to do to you . . .'

'And what he might already have done to Ros . . .' She was silent for a moment as new waves of horror overwhelmed her. 'I know we suspected that something terrible had happened to her. But I never thought . . . and I still kept hoping I was wrong. Now . . . I can't help thinking he must be behind her disappearance. She found out somehow that he was an imposter and faced him with it. And he . . . killed her to keep her quiet. Oh, why didn't we guess? Why didn't we see through him?'

'If Dinah couldn't see through him how could we be expected to?' Mike asked.

'Poor Dinah. I wonder how she's going to take it?'

'Very badly, I should think. But we can't worry about her now.'

'I should have guessed! I knew Ros had said something funny was going on at Vandina. But I was so hung up on this industrial spy thing I never looked beyond it. I suspected everyone but Steve of being involved in Ros's disappearance – even poor Brendan. He might still be alive today if I hadn't more or less accused him of having done something terrible to Ros. Now he's dead and Ros is dead and . . .'

'You can't blame yourself for Brendan's death.'

'But I do. I do!'

'Then you mustn't. He was a bastard too.'

'But he didn't deserve to die! He needed help – someone to love him. Everyone should have someone to love them, Mike. No one should be so desperate they have to jump off a bloody bridge . . .' The tears were falling now, rolling in hot rivers down her cheeks, trickling down her nose, as if somewhere deep inside her a dam had been breached.

'Oh hell, Maggie!' Mike crossed to her, kneeling down beside her, pulling her head into his chest. 'Maggie, darling Maggie, don't cry.'

The tender concern in his voice only released another wave of tears. She sobbed almost soundlessly, her breath making small tearing sounds, her body convulsed. He held her while the storm raged, not knowing how to comfort her, aware there was nothing he could say to make the nightmare go away, nothing he could do but offer her a rock to cling to.

After a while he held her away, mopping her face with his handkerchief.

'Let me get you another drink.'

She clung to him. 'No . . . don't leave me, Mike. Just hold me!'

A fresh wave of helpless anger consumed him.

'It's all right – it's all right. I won't leave you. Ssh, now, ssh, calm down . . .'

After a while the convulsive shudders and sobs began to come less often until there was only the occasional tremor, like the aftershocks of an earthquake.

'Better?'

'Mm. A bit. He won't get away, will he, Mike? He mustn't get away!'

'I'm sure they'll catch up with him. Now, sweetheart, I think you should try to get some rest.'

'Oh!' Her eyes flew open. 'My things – I haven't brought any of them! They're still at the cottage!'

'You don't need them, do you? You can borrow one of my T-shirts to sleep in if you want to.' His tone, the way he was looking at her, suggested he would rather she wore nothing; he was aching for the feel of her body close to his.

'But it's everything, Mike – underwear, toothbrush, make-up remover – I must look a fright!' Her fingers went to her face, wiping at the mascara smudges beneath her eyes. 'I might have to go to the police station tomorrow – anything! I must at least be presentable.'

'You want me to drive over and fetch your things then?'

'Oh yes, please – would you?'

'Are they all together?'

'My case is packed and ready. But I'll come with you.'

'Don't you think it would be better if you stayed here?' he suggested, thinking that to revisit the scene of her ordeal would upset her again. But to Maggie, at this moment, there was no prospect worse than being left alone.

'No, please take me with you, Mike. As long as you're with me I don't mind, really. I couldn't bear to be on my own just now.'

'Well, if you're sure . . .'

'I'm sure.'

Now that the tears had cleansed her she felt calmer, temporarily at least, though she knew the deep dark well was still there inside her, waiting to open once more and swallow her. She went to the bathroom, washed her face and combed her hair. She held tightly to his arm as they went downstairs as if to let go of it would be to let go of a lifeline, and sat as close to him in the car as the seat belt would allow. He glanced at her, saw the resolve in the tight lines of her face, and loved her all the more.

The sun was low in the sky now, bathing the cottage in a soft rosy glow. Almost impossible to believe anything bad could have happened here, in this fairy-tale setting. But beside him Maggie had begun to tremble again, almost imperceptibly but enough to remind him that the peace and tranquillity were an illusion. Anger filled him once more; if he could get hold of that bastard Lomax just now he'd throttle the life out of him!

He pulled up outside the cottage, turned off the engine and unbuckled his seat belt.

'Wait in the car.'
'No. I'll come in with you.'
'Maggie, you don't have to. Better not.'
'I'd rather come in.' Her jaw was set, controlling the chattering of her teeth. 'I want to face up to it.'
'Why? There's no need.'
'There's every need. It's like riding a horse. They say if you fall off you should get straight back on again or you never will.'
'You don't have to go into the cottage ever again.'
'Yes I do. It is . . . was . . . my sister's home.' Her voice wavered. 'I don't want strangers turning over her things, Mike. When it comes to . . . doing what has to be done I am the one who should do it. And if I don't go in now, tonight, I don't know if I'll ever find the courage. Take me with you, Mike. Only please – hold my hand . . .'
He did, searching one-handed for the cottage key and opening the door. The silence came out to meet them, unbroken as the peaceful summer evening outside, and apart from an overturned chair and the large muddy print of a policeman's boot on the pale hall carpet everything looked just as it always did.
Once inside the cottage Maggie let go of Mike's hand, wandering from room to room as if in a dream, and Mike let her go, torn between preventing her from torturing herself and allowing her to do what she had to do.
She returned at last from whatever internal journey she had been making and went to him, putting her arms around him and laying her head against his shoulder.
'All right?' he whispered against her hair.
'Yes. Shall we go, Mike?'
'Yes.'
A small scraping sound came from the hall. They both stiffened, listening and looking at one another.
'What the hell . . .?' Mike asked.
'It sounded like the door. As if someone was coming in . . .'
'Is there someone there?' a voice called from the hall.
Maggie and Mike stared at one another again in disbelief.
'My God . . .'
The door to the hall opened. A young woman stood there, a young woman in beautifully cut designer jeans and a silk shirt, a young woman whose startled expression reflected their own.

Maggie took a step forward, the blood draining from her head so that for a moment she thought she might be going to faint, and when she spoke her voice was little more than a whisper.

'Ros!'

Chapter Nineteen

'Maggie!' Ros's tone conveyed equal disbelief. 'Maggie – what are you doing here?'

Maggie ignored the question; scarcely even heard it. Joy and relief were coursing through her now, small electric shocks piercing the blanket of utter breathtaking surprise.

'We thought you were dead!'

'Dead?' Ros repeated blankly. 'Why should you think I was dead?'

'We didn't know where you were. We thought . . . and he said . . .' She broke off. Impossible to explain in the course of a few sentences all that had happened. For a moment, with Ros standing there in the flesh looking much as she always did, it seemed to Maggie as if the last days had been nothing but a nightmare, a figment of a crazed imagination. In a moment she would wake up and find herself back home in Corfu with Ari snoring beside her.

It was Mike who broke the silence and it was his voice, bewildered and a little angry, that convinced her this was no dream.

'Where the hell have you been?'

'What do you mean – where the hell have I been?' Ros flared back, responding to the accusation in his tone. 'I've been away – isn't that obvious?'

'Without telling a soul where you were going? We've been worried sick about you, Ros.'

'I don't see why. Surely I don't have to report all my movements to you? Anyway, you weren't here when I left. You were away at camp with those schoolchildren of yours. And I did try to ring you, whenever I was anywhere near a phone, but the international lines were so bad I couldn't get through.'

'International lines from where?'

'South America.' Ros banged her bag down on to a chair. 'God, I need a drink. I've been travelling since forever. And when I got back to the station I couldn't find my car. The man on duty told me it had been towed away – I ask you! You can't even leave your car in a station car park without it being towed away!'

Mike and Maggie exchanged glances. Presumably the police, taking an interest at last, had removed it for examination.

'You didn't ring the police about it?' Mike asked.

'I did not! I'll do that in the morning. Tonight all I wanted was to get home and have a bath.'

As she spoke Ros was opening her cupboard, taking out a bottle and glass.

'I'm having a vodka,' she said carelessly. 'Do either of you want one? Then Maggie can tell me what she's doing in England and you can both tell me why you are here in my home.'

'I think, Ros,' Mike said, 'that you had better make that vodka a large one. I have a feeling you are going to need it.'

She glanced at him, raising her finely arched eyebrows.

'I am?'

'Yes. And pour one for Maggie too. No – on second thoughts make that a whisky. That's what she's been drinking already.'

'And you?'

'No thanks. I have to drive. I also have to go to work in the morning. Christ, Ros, you haven't the faintest idea, have you, of the trouble you have caused?'

Ros poured whisky into a tumbler, passed it to Maggie, then raised her own glass in a half-humorous salute.

'No, but I think you are about to tell me.'

'Ros, this is not a joke. I don't know where you have been or why, but today your sister was very nearly killed.'

Ros froze, the glass halfway to her mouth.

'Maggie! How?'

'By Steve Bloody Lomax. Who, incidentally, we thought had also murdered you.'

'Me!'

'Yes, Ros, you. Look, it's one hell of a long story, but it all hinges on the fact that he is an imposter, not Dinah's son at all. Which you, of course, knew all the time, but we only learned about today.'

'How did you find out?' Ros asked sharply.

Maggie took over the explanation. 'From your files at Vandina. And when Steve discovered I knew the truth and was likely to spill the beans he was prepared to go to any lengths to silence me. I thought he'd already done the same to you, Ros. I thought you must have faced him with what you knew and he . . .' Her voice tailed away. 'Didn't he know you knew?'

Ros shook her head. 'I wanted to keep it to myself until I was a hundred per cent sure. I knew it would destroy Dinah – if she even believed me. She's so obsessed with Steve she might simply have called me a liar and dismissed the whole idea out of hand. That's why I've been haring around the world – trying to tie up the loose ends and make some sense out of what was going on, and maybe salvage something from the whole bloody mess. Look, guys, I'm really sorry if you've been worried, but I honestly didn't intend to be gone so long. I only set out to go to London, but then this other angle came up. And I have tried to telephone, truly I have. Once I actually got through – I heard you speak, Mike, and then the line just went dead.'

Mike nodded. 'The other evening. I had a funny feeling it was you. But I thought I was just kidding myself. Where were you ringing from?'

'I told you. South America. Argentina to be precise.'

'What the hell were you doing in Argentina?'

'I think I know,' Maggie said. 'That's where Dinah's real son was working when he was killed, wasn't it?'

'Yes, except that . . .' Ros broke off. 'What's happened to Steve? Where is he now?'

'We don't know,' Mike said. 'After Maggie managed to get away from him she just bolted. Presumably he did the same, knowing the game was up. As far as I can gather no one has seen him since. But you can bet your bottom dollar the police are looking for him right this minute.'

'So Dinah . . . knows?'

'I suppose she must do. Quite honestly Dinah Marshall is the least of my worries.'

Ros put down her drink. 'Oh poor Dinah! I must get over there!'

'For God's sake!' Mike exploded. 'You come waltzing back in here after causing utter mayhem and all you can think about is Dinah!'

'I have to see her. There's something I have to tell her.'

'Surely it can wait. Don't you think your own sister should be your priority just now?'

Ros cast him a narrow glance.

'It looks to me as if she has you.'

'Ros – it's not what you think . . .' Maggie began anxiously, but Mike was not going to let her off the hook so lightly.

'After what we've been through, Ros, I think you owe us a very full explanation.'

Ros grinned almost ruefully.

'That's what I love about you, Mike, you're so masterful! I arrive home after one hell of a time and all you do is order me about. All right, let's have another drink and I'll fill you in. But I warn you, it's a very long story and I'm not sure where to begin.'

'Perhaps,' Mike said, still stern, 'you could begin with what made you suspect Steve Lomax of being an imposter in the first place. And, incidentally, why you never mentioned your suspicions to me.'

Ros held his angry glare for a moment then her eyes dropped away and she sat turning the empty vodka glass between her hands, searching for the best way to answer. How could she say now that she had not wanted to tell him the truth – that to her certain knowledge two quite different young men had turned up, both claiming to be Dinah's son – because to do so would have meant admitting things she preferred to keep to herself – admitting she had been at Van's apartment one winter's night and seen the first claimant with her own eyes. Yet strangely she was unsure just why she had been so anxious to keep the long affair a secret. Perhaps, she thought, it was a habit that had become too deeply ingrained, for in his lifetime Van had insisted on complete discretion.

'I won't have Dinah hurt,' Van had said when Ros had once asked him why he never took her out to a restaurant or club, why their meetings all had to be in the utter privacy of his town apartment. 'You never know who you are going to run into, and then tongues begin wagging.'

'If you care so much for her feelings why are you having an affair with me at all?' Ros had flared.

'Because, my dear, you are young and beautiful and very, very sexy.'

'But not because you love me.'

Van had fixed her with his hypnotic, yet strangely impersonal stare.

'I have never loved anyone in my life. I don't intend to start now.'

'You seem to love Dinah.'

For a moment there had been a flicker within those navy-blue eyes, a memory touched upon, perhaps, which had been pushed aside and subjugated over the years. But Van had no intention of admitting to weakness of any sort – and to him love equated with weakness. Once, long ago, he had allowed his heart to rule his head, but not for long. He had realised his mistake in time and acted ruthlessly to ensure it did not mar the pattern of his life. Now the image he presented to the world was of a hard, if not totally ruthless man, and he had almost come to believe his own publicity.

'Dinah works best when she is happy,' he had said blandly. 'Upset the equilibrium and you impede the creative flow.'

'You bastard!' Ros had said, shocked at the heartlessness of the remark yet forced to concede that this side of him was one of the things that made him so devastatingly attractive – to her, at least. To be in the company of such a man was an aphrodisiac in itself – the challenge he presented was a constant excitement. Sometimes she despised Van, sometimes she despised herself, but it made no difference. Ros was obsessed with him as she had never been obsessed by any other man. Liking or disliking did not come into it.

But she had not been proud of herself. Sometimes, thinking of how willingly she had gone to Van's apartment, she cringed, and she shrank from admitting to anyone, least of all Mike, that someone who prided herself on her independence and fierce self-reliance could have allowed herself to become putty in the hands of a man like Van.

It had begun, their affair, soon after she had gone to work at Vandina. From the first time she had met him she had been intoxicated with him, and like an alcoholic craving another drink, she had seized upon every possible excuse to be in his company. At first she did not think he had even noticed her, but he had – he had. And he teased her along, throwing her crumbs here and there to make her more avid than ever – a look, a smile, a throwaway remark to be remembered and dissected and stored away. And when he was ready, when he knew she would not refuse him, he had made his move and she had gone to him willingly, forgetting every scruple, every loyalty, drawn by that strange power he exerted so well into a web which she knew might strangle her but from which she had no wish to escape.

At times she had felt guilt for those she was betraying – Brendan, her husband; Dinah, her employer and friend – but it made no difference. When Brendan became violent towards her she almost welcomed it, for she felt that in some way she was paying for her pleasure; as for Dinah, she worked all the harder and cared for her loyally. She came to know, better than anyone – except perhaps Van himself – that childlike side of Dinah which needed reassurance and protection, and she made it her business to minister to it in every way possible, as if by so doing she could somehow exonerate the guilt that came from knowing she was screwing Dinah's husband.

They had been together often at Van's town apartment – though perhaps not as often as Ros would have liked. And that particular winter's night when Dinah's son had come had begun no differently from all the others, except that Van had told her not to come before eight.

'I have an appointment earlier,' he had said, giving no word of explanation as to who it was he was expecting.

Ros, though she paid lip service to independence and the freedom of the individual, nevertheless was the possessor of a strongly jealous streak and it had occurred to her to wonder if the unnamed visitor might be a woman. The thought that she might have a rival had incensed her and she had made up her mind to be at Van's apartment in good time to see who left.

She remembered still, with almost startling clarity, how her face had burned as she ran up the stairs, partly from the cold, partly from a flush of apprehension for what she might find and dread of the scene that would follow. Strange, really, that it was that aspect of the evening that remained most vivid in her mind – that and the utter relief she had felt when she had opened the door with her key and come face to face not with a woman who might have usurped her, but a young man.

She had been curious – the snippet of conversation she had overheard had whetted her appetite – but she had known better than to ask there and then who he was and what he had been doing there. That had come later, after she and Van had made love.

They were lying in bed between his black silk sheets with her head nestled against his shoulder and their legs entwined, and Van was smoking one of his cigars, the smoke tickling in Ros's nostrils.

'Who was that guy who was here when I arrived?' she asked.

'No one you'd know, sweetness. Just business.'

She tugged gently at some of the greying hair that grew thickly down his breastbone, twisting it between her fingers.

'It didn't sound like business to me. It sounded very personal. "Tell my mother from me that the last thing I intended was to cause her distress . . . that I have made a good life for myself without her help." Business associates don't say things like that.'

'Don't they, sweetness?'

'No, they don't. Oh well, if you won't tell me the truth about him I shall just have to ask some questions until I find out for myself . . .'

He stiffened then. She felt a wave of anger run through him.

'You'll say nothing to anyone about him being here.'

She pretended innocence. 'Why not?'

'Because I am telling you so.'

She laughed. 'Oh Van, we are not in the office now and I don't have to do what you tell me! I shall pry all I like and . . .'

'All right,' he said suddenly, and his tone told her that this was no game to him, but deadly serious. 'I'll tell you, Ros, but you have got to realise it is confidential.'

'I can keep a secret.'

'I know you can. You wouldn't have the job you are in and you wouldn't be here with me now if you could not.' There was a tiny threatening undertone in his voice – break confidence and I'll break you, he seemed to be saying. 'That young man was, or claims to be, Dinah's son.'

'What!' In spite of what she had overheard she was still staggered. 'I didn't know Dinah had a son.'

'Nor does anyone else. That is why I don't want you shooting your mouth off. Dinah had an illegitimate child when she was very young. In those days it was still a matter for great shame. The baby was adopted at birth, Dinah and I were married and she put the whole wretched business behind her. Now, out of the blue, comes this young man claiming to be that child.' He puffed on his cigar.

'How do you know there's any truth in his claim?' Ros asked.

'He had a copy of his birth certificate. It's possible to obtain them these days, of course – God knows why the law was changed to allow it. Much better in the old days when these things were treated as utterly confidential. Anyway, I have persuaded him not to bother Dinah with any of this. He has gone back to Scotland –he's a diver on one of the offshore rigs, as far as I can make out – and I don't think he'll be back. So please, Ros, will you say nothing?'

Ros settled herself more comfortably against Van's shoulder. She could hardly believe what he had just told her; that cool, perfect, untouched Dinah had an illegitimate son. Even more unbelievable was the fact that he had been here and she had seen him with her own eyes. She found herself trying to recall what he had looked like and wishing she had taken more notice of him. He had not struck her as being particularly like Dinah, but then why should he be?

She thought again of the fragment of conversation she had overheard.

'So Dinah didn't want to see him?' she asked.

'No.'

'I can understand her being upset, but if it were me I don't think I'd be able to resist seeing how my own son had turned out.'

Van sat up abruptly, stubbing out his cigar in the huge crystal ashtray he kept on the bedside table.

'Dinah does not know he's been here. I'd be very much obliged if you would make sure she does not find out.'

'She doesn't *know*?'

'I intercepted his letter. I wrote back to him myself. I don't want Dinah upset by any of this. I will not have her upset – do you understand?'

Ros had nodded, not knowing whether to be shocked by Van's arbitrary decision or smug because she now knew something Dinah did not know and presumably never would.

It was not long, of course, before the novelty value of her newly acquired knowledge began to wear off. A 'nine-days wonder' is an old adage but one with much truth in it, and soon Ros forgot about Dinah's son. She was busy and fulfilled in her job, she had met and begun to date Mike Thompson, but her affair with Van continued nevertheless. He still fascinated her too much to allow her to end it, for Mike or anyone else.

One night when Van was making love to her something rather dreadful happened.

One minute he was lying on top of her, pumping with the ferocious vigour that seemed to be necessary to bring him to a climax these days, the next he gasped and rolled away from her, fighting for breath and clutching his chest.

'My God, Van – are you all right?' Ros raised herself on one elbow, looking down at his face, which was grey and suddenly old-looking, and his eyes, curiously distant. He did not answer her, simply lay there concentrating on getting his breath, and Ros got out of bed, slipping into a dressing gown and wondering if she should do something positive, like calling a doctor. She didn't want to do that, it would be horrendously embarrassing, but she didn't care for the look of Van at all.

She knelt down beside the bed, taking his hand.

'Van? Can you hear me?'

His eyelids blinked: Yes.

'Van – what is it? Are you in pain?'

Again, a tiny flicker. The real difficulty seemed to be his breathing. His chest heaved as he struggled with it.

'Van, I'm going to get help.'

'No!' He managed to say the word, and in spite of his condition his tone carried as much authority as ever.

She waited and gradually his breathing eased and his colour returned to normal. At last he sat up, reaching for her, and she put her arms around him.

'God, Van, you frightened me to death! What was it – your heart?'

'Could be.'

'Could be? What do you mean, could be? Have you had something like this happen to you before?'

'A few times, yes.'

'And what does the doctor say about them?'

'The doctor doesn't say anything. I haven't told him.'

'Van, you must! You looked really ill just then.'

'I don't want him to know. I don't want anyone to know. If they think there's anything wrong with me they'll revoke my p.p.l. and I don't want that.'

Van had gained his private pilot's licence soon after establishing the business, and now he had his own plane, which he flew whenever he could for pleasure. The thought of losing his licence was unbearable.

'They'll find out when you have your next medical anyway,' Ros said. 'You have to have one every year, don't you?'

'Yes – but I'll be over all this nonsense by then. For God's sake stop fussing, Ros. I've had a bit of a chesty cold and I had too heavy a dinner – that's all.'

Ros felt sure it had been much more than that but she also knew that where Van was concerned argument was useless.

The next time she saw Van clearly unwell she tried again to insist that he seek medical attention. They had been away on a business trip, and driving back along the motorway he suddenly fell silent. She glanced at him and saw beads of sweat standing out on his forehead.

'Are you all right?' she asked sharply.

'Yes.' But his voice was tight and a moment later he swung on to the hard shoulder, braking hard and sitting with his head pressed back against the headrest while his breath came in hard, shallow gasps.

'Move over,' she ordered. 'I'm taking you to a hospital.'

He moved, and she got into the driving seat and put her foot hard down, watching him anxiously out of the corner of her eye. But by the time she had taken the next exit from the motorway and was racing along the country roads trying to remember where she would find the nearest hospital he had begun to recover, and with recovery came the typical assertiveness for which Van was renowned.

'I'm all right now, Ros. Let's just go home.'

At Vandina she parked, then faced him squarely.

'Van, you have got to do something about these turns of yours. You can't just let them go on happening.'

'Don't try to tell me what to do, sweetness.'

'You are ill, Van.'

'I had too much to drink last night, that's all. If I consider there is anything seriously wrong I'll seek help. Do you understand?'

She did not argue. What was the point? And besides, what had just happened could well have been exactly what he had said – a slight case of hangover, no more, no less – while she could hardly describe to anyone what had happened on the previous occasion without admitting their illicit liaison. She was worried, but she said nothing to anyone.

A few weeks later she was bitterly regretting her decision. Flying himself in his little Cessna, Van had crashed. The moment she heard about it, long before the speculation began, Ros knew what had happened and blamed herself dreadfully. Whatever the consequences she should have told someone of her suspicions as to Van's state of health. She had not – and now he was dead. He had been wrong to ignore the warning signals – but so had she. If she had done what she had known she should have done maybe she could have saved him.

In her worst nightmares Ros asked herself how she would have felt if Van had managed to kill someone else besides himself; at other times she gratefully thanked the fates that he had not. She wept into her pillow, tears of grief for the man who had obsessed her, and guilt for her failure to do what she could have done to save him, and she salved her conscience as far as she was able by doing everything she could to comfort and support Dinah, who was devastated by Van's death.

Ros had always been fond of her mercurial boss. Everyone who knew Dinah loved her and wanted to protect her, and Ros was no exception. Sometimes it had occurred to her to wonder how this loyalty could co-exist alongside the knowledge that she was carrying on a long-term affair with Dinah's husband, but somehow it did and the fact that she not only suspected but *knew* Dinah's true vulnerability only made her more anxious to spare her any pain. After Van's death this emotion intensified. Although her own grief was sometimes insupportable, seeing Dinah's total collapse made her somehow strong and she found herself caring for Dinah, buffering her, as Van had done.

I am doing it for him, Ros told herself, and the sense of purpose helped her through the pain of her own loss.

She had long since forgotten about the young man she had met in Van's apartment. She remembered it only when she went into the office one morning to find a Dinah glowing with radiance and trembling with excitement.

The change from the gaunt and grief-stricken woman she had become since Van's death was so startling that Ros could only stare in amazement. And then Dinah had told her that she had received a letter from her son, adopted as a baby, and whom she had never expected to see again.

Ros had had to pretend surprise, of course. She could not let Dinah know she already knew she had a son, much less that she had met him. But Dinah's delight was disconcerting. Van had said he was keeping the reappearance of the boy a secret from her because he did not want to upset her – clearly the letter she had received from him now had had quite the opposite effect.

'I can't believe it!' Dinah whispered to Ros, her face glowing, her hands pressed to her cheeks like a child. 'I never thought I'd see him again, and now . . . Oh, if you knew how I've longed for him, Ros, how I have blamed myself for giving him up to strangers, wanted . . . oh, just to get a glimpse of him so that I'd know what he looked like! And now, right out of the blue, he's written to me, asking if we can meet! Isn't fate strange? They say God never shuts a door but he opens a window. I've lost Van but now suddenly my son is back. It's unbelievable really!'

Not as unbelievable as all that, Ros thought cynically. Van had sent him away before and now he had read of the great man's death he was back, trying to set up a meeting all over again. But in view of Dinah's obvious happiness it could be no bad thing.

When Steve finally arrived, however, and Ros was introduced to him, she was both startled and puzzled. For though she had seen Dinah's son only briefly at Van's apartment the young man standing before her, holding proprietorially on to Dinah's arm, was not at all the way she remembered him.

At first Ros had told herself that memory must be playing her false. Like her, that night he had been dressed for the cold winter weather – she remembered a bulky parka distorting his shape – and she told herself that in the intervening years she must have superimposed the face of someone else she had met briefly, either in the course of her work or socially. She could not, after all, picture with any clarity what the man she had met at Van's apartment had looked like, only that she did not think he had looked like this. And it wasn't only the face that was wrong, it was the voice too. She had only heard him speak one sentence but she could have sworn he had an ordinary English voice, whilst this Steve spoke with a slight but unmistakable transatlantic accent.

He had explained to Dinah that the family who had adopted him had emigrated to Canada and he had been brought up there, and she had accepted it without question. But it jarred on Ros all the same.

Carefully employing all her tact Ros had begun questioning him. The answers he gave were slick and plausible but instead of being satisfied Ros's sense of unease grew.

One day she tentatively mentioned Van's apartment.

'Lucky for him it was ground floor,' she said, almost holding her breath. 'If he'd had stairs to run up and down maybe his heart would have given out much earlier.'

And Steve, without so much as blinking an eyelid, replied: 'That's true. Though if he'd had prior warning he might be alive today.'

Ros knew then without any doubt that she was right – he had never been to Van's apartment. So – one of the young men who claimed to be Dinah's son was an imposter. But which one? With all her heart Ros hoped it was Steve who was genuine. To discover she had been duped would break Dinah's heart.

Ros puzzled and worried the facts around. With a mother like Dinah and an empire like Vandina to aspire to it was not difficult to see why an unscrupulous fortune-hunter should want to lay down a claim. But it wasn't that simple. The fact that Dinah had had an illegitimate son had been a closely guarded secret, and details of parentage would only be released to a genuine applicant after a great deal of official counselling. It did not make sense, any of it.

When Dinah began installing Steve as heir apparent Ros grew more and more worried. She was convinced something was very wrong but her loyalty to Dinah imposed an insurmountable dilemma. If Steve was an imposter then he could not be allowed to go on taking advantage of Dinah. But such a revelation would come as a terrible shock to her and would break her heart. For weeks Ros agonised, even allowing Steve to wine and dine her once or twice in an effort to get close to him and learn the truth. But she was unable to penetrate the persona he had created for himself and eventually she reached a decision. Somehow she had to find out exactly what was going on. Then, and only then, could she decide what to do about it.

Now, twisting the vodka glass between her fingers as she talked with Maggie and Mike, she faced again the dilemma that had tormented her. To explain why it was she had been suspicious of Steve meant admitting to her affair with Van. Ros, secretive and passionate by nature, was still unwilling to tell the whole truth. Yet with the knowledge now in her possession she knew that the time had come when she had to be honest about at least some of it.

'I didn't tell you because I wasn't sure,' she said. 'Can't you see, Mike, what a devastating accusation I would have been making?'

'Couldn't you have trusted me?' Mike asked.

'I should have done, I suppose. But I thought it was better to keep my suspicions to myself until I was sure.'

'I still don't see why you went off without a word. Didn't you realise how worried we would be?'

Ros sighed, shaking her head.

'Mike, please try to see it from my point of view. I thought that while you were away at school camp would be the ideal opportunity for me to follow up my investigations without you asking awkward questions. I never intended to be gone so long.'

'You couldn't have been so naive as to think you could go to Argentina and back in the same way you could go to Bournemouth.'

'I told you, I didn't set out to go to Argentina. I only intended to go to London. I had been in touch with Excel Oil – the company who employed Steve in the North Sea. They gave me the address of a man who worked closely with him on the rigs – a Londoner named Des Taylor. I decided to go and see him.'

Maggie and Mike exchanged glances. Des Taylor – the man who had rung the cottage asking for Ros.

'So – what happened?'

'This Des Taylor was away – my fault, I suppose, for not checking first to make sure I would find him at home. But I was able to talk to his parents. They showed me a photograph – their son with the two other divers who made up his team. One was Steve. The other was the young man I saw at Van's apartment.'

'What do you mean . . . you saw?' Mike queried.

Ros coloured faintly. 'I was at Van's apartment one night – working – when this young man was there. Van sent him away saying that Dinah would not want to be reminded of her past.

Anyway, I immediately recognised the man in the photograph as being that same man. Des Taylor's parents said they knew him as "Mac" and that he had gone to Argentina to dive for one of the multinationals there. They also said that soon afterwards word had got back to the Excel rig that he had been killed in a diving accident. That, I suppose, was when Steve decided to take his identity.'

'The bastard!' Mike exploded.

Tears welled unexpectedly in Maggie's eyes. The events of the day had left her raw and emotional and she was overwhelmed by a rush of pity for the woman who had been exploited so ruthlessly.

'Poor, poor Dinah.'

'Yes, poor Dinah,' Ros echoed grimly. 'She's had a pretty rotten deal from life, hasn't she? A great many people envy her, I expect, but they haven't a clue about all the traumas and heartaches she has had to endure.'

'I still don't really understand why you went straight off to Argentina without letting us know about it,' Mike said. His voice was hard, the outward manifestation of the strains of the day and the jumble of emotions he was now experiencing.

'You know me, Mike,' Ros said lightly. 'I believe in striking whilst the iron is hot, and I honestly never thought for a moment it would cause all this upset. Why should you think I was *dead*, for heaven's sake?'

'All kinds of reasons!' Maggie snapped. The relief was now beginning to turn to anger that Ros should have put them through all this anxiety and be seemingly totally unrepentant. 'Your bank statement, for one thing. You hadn't drawn any money. How did you go to Argentina without drawing any money?'

'I used my new American Express. Why the hell shouldn't I?'

'And your car – the driving seat was in the wrong position for you . . . too far back. Did someone take you to the station?' Mike asked.

'Of course not! The seat was moved back, you say? I don't understand why that should be . . . Oh yes, wait a minute. I dropped an earring. I suppose I moved the seat back to pick it up. But I don't see what you were doing poking about in my bank statements and my car anyway.'

'If you'd had a little more forethought, Ros, we wouldn't have had to.'

Ros, on the point of snapping back, changed her mind.

'I'm going to see Dinah.'

'Tonight?'

'Tonight. There's something I have to tell her which might help to soften the blow. I was going to leave it on the back burner until tomorrow, but under the circumstances I think she should know at once. Can I take your car, Mike?'

'Now – tonight? Ros, I . . .'

'If you won't let me, I suppose I'll have to call a taxi.'

'Why do you have to go and see her tonight? I shouldn't think she'd be in a fit state to see anyone. After unleashing all this, what can you tell her that will be any help at all?'

'Possibly the one thing that will give her a glimmer of hope.'

'Which is?'

But Ros shook her head. 'To be honest, I think I owe it to Dinah to tell her first before I discuss it with anyone else. But please believe me when I say it is very significant.'

Maggie and Mike said nothing. But Mike fished in the pocket of his jacket, took out his keys and handed them to Ros.

'I hope Ros won't be too long,' Mike said when she had gone. 'You look all in, Maggie, and I want to get you home and tucked up in bed with a warm drink.'

Maggie looked startled.

'But Mike, surely you realise – I'll have to stay here now.'

'What do you mean – you'll have to stay here?'

'Just that.' She felt drained, as if all the events of the day – and the past week – had suddenly come together to swamp her. There was enormous relief that Ros was alive and well, a little anger that she should have put them through so much, and also an aching regret she had not yet stopped to analyse but which she knew had to do with her and Mike. 'I must stay here with Ros. I can hardly come to your flat now, can I?'

'Why not?'

'Oh Mike, everything has changed, hasn't it? Ros is back and I'm glad . . . of course I am! Only . . .' She gestured helplessly.

He reached for her and she withdrew her hand quickly and turned away so that he would not see the tears brimming in her eyes.

'Don't, please, make it more difficult. It's over. You must see that.'

'I see that it makes it more complicated. But it doesn't necessarily mean we can't . . .'

'I couldn't do that to Ros. I couldn't let her think that I . . . that when we thought something had happened to her you and I were . . . I just couldn't!'

She was filled now with shame and confusion. The last days had been a nightmare but also a madness. It was as if the world had tilted, turned upside down, and now with Ros walking through the door it had shifted again so that everything was almost, though not quite, as it had been, like a constantly changing lava lamp.

'Ros didn't seem very concerned about anyone else's feelings when she went off without a word,' Mike said. His voice was hard.

'But she explained about that.' Maggie found herself wanting to stand up for her sister. 'Her main concern was trying to save Dinah from more hurt than was absolutely unavoidable. Oh, don't look so disapproving, Mike. I can see why she did it if you can't.'

'Then all things considered you are more understanding than I am.'

'You mustn't blame her so. Ros is . . . Ros. You know that. And she loves you, Mike. She'd be devastated if she thought you and I . . . well, did what we did. She's had a pretty tough time in the past. I don't want to upset things for her again.'

'She's made a pretty good job of upsetting them for herself.'

'Anyway,' Maggie said. 'It's not just Ros who has to be considered. There's Ari too.'

'I didn't think he made you very happy.'

'He's my husband, Mike. I owe him something, for goodness' sake. I've already betrayed him but I can't just discount him as if he didn't exist because it suits me. These last few days have been . . . well, unreal. But somehow now we know Ros is all right it's as if I can see things clearly again. And what I see is that you must forgive her for going away without telling you and I must go home to Corfu and try to make up to Ari for what I've done.'

Her voice choked off in a sob. Mike made a half-move towards her, then checked.

'All right, Maggie, have it your way. To be honest I think you're overemotional and getting everything out of perspective.'

'No, Mike, I'm seeing it straight. For the first time for days I'm seeing things the way they are.'

'All right,' he said wearily. 'I won't argue with you. I've had enough for one day.'

'*You* have had enough!'

'Yes, me. I have feelings too. And I've had quite enough of women and their fickle-mindedness to last me for some time. I'm going home.'

'You can't . . . Ros has your car.'

'Dammit, so she does. Well, Maggie, if you insist on staying here I suggest you get yourself to bed and I'll wait here for Ros to come back. Alone.'

His voice was cold and final. Maggie felt the tears springing to her eyes. It would be easy, so easy, to put her arms around him and tell him what was in her heart – that she loved him desperately and wanted nothing more than to be with him tonight and for the rest of her life. But it would achieve nothing. She loved him – but she had met him too late. To be with him now she would have to hurt two people she cared for, and she knew instinctively that happiness taken at the expense of others would be happiness paid for too dear. Better to leave things as they were, leave him while he was angry and while she still had the strength to do so.

'Goodnight, Mike,' she said. And turned and went upstairs.

Chapter Twenty

Don Kennedy was hovering anxiously outside the door of what had once been Van's study. His smooth pink face was flushed with anxiety and there was a strained look about his eyes. It had, he thought, been one hell of a day – and it was not over yet.

He hesitated, listening out for any sound from within the study, but heard nothing.

'Dinah!' he called urgently. 'Dinah – it's me, Don. Are you all right in there?'

Still no reply. It was almost an hour now since Mrs Brunt, Dinah's housekeeper, had called him on his car phone and asked him to come at once, and apparently almost three hours since Dinah had arrived home from the factory and locked herself in Van's study.

'I'm frantic about her, Mr Kennedy,' the housekeeper had said when he had arrived, parking his BMW untidily on the gravel drive and hurrying into the house. 'I don't know what it is that's the matter with her, but something is, and if you ask me it's pretty serious. I've never seen her like this before – leastways, not since Mr Van got killed.'

'Yes, I think it is serious,' Don said. After lunching with Dinah he had not returned to the office but had gone into the city for a series of business meetings, and he had been on his way home when Mrs Brunt had finally reached him. He had immediately pulled into a lay-by – Don never used the telephone whilst he was actually at the wheel – and called Vandina to see if he could find out what was going on. A distraught Liz had told him the events of the afternoon and at once he had headed for Luscombe Manor, driving with a reckless speed that was totally foreign to his cautious nature and cursing himself for not having been there when Dinah had most needed him.

Dammit, he'd known there was something about Steve he didn't like – why hadn't he acted upon his intuition and had the guy checked out? But it was easy to be wise with hindsight – until this moment he'd thought that perhaps his dislike was founded on jealousy for the man who had walked in and monopolised Dinah's affections, and this brutal self-honesty had made him ashamed. Don loathed selfishness, in himself as in others, and he had not been proud of the fact that he should feel such burning resentment towards a young man who had patently made Dinah so happy.

That, of course, was the other reason he had stood by and done nothing. He hadn't wanted to destroy her happiness. Now, staring disaster in the face, he wished wholeheartedly that he had been more circumspect.

What the hell next? he had wondered, putting his foot flat to the floor of his BMW in his anxiety to get to Dinah. Her whole world, once so secure, seemed to be caving in around her. First Van's death, then Ros's disappearance, then the 'mole' – a mystery still not satisfactorily solved – and now this. All devastating, all quite enough to rock Dinah off her fragile base.

'Fill me in, Mrs Brunt,' he had said as the housekeeper stood wringing her hands nervously. 'Where is Miss Marshall now?'

'Still in the study. She came in looking like she'd seen a ghost – white as a sheet, she was. "Miss Marshall, whatever is the matter?" I said to her, but she wouldn't answer me. She was like in a daze – her eyes were all . . . dead. I don't know if she even heard me, Mr Kennedy, and that's the truth. Then: "I'm going to be with Van," she said. "Whatever do you mean, Miss Marshall?" I said. She gave me quite a turn, the way she said it. But no, she still didn't take any notice of me. She went past me like I wasn't there, straight into his study, and she's been there ever since. Whatever is it, Mr Kennedy? Whatever is the matter, for her to take on like it?'

'It's to do with Steve,' Don said. 'You'll hear all about it before long. But just now the most important thing is Miss Marshall's welfare, don't you think? I'll talk to her.'

'Oh I wish you would, Mr Kennedy. That's why I called you. You're the only one she's likely to take notice of. Except for Steve, of course, but when I rang the factory they said he wasn't there . . .'

She was following Don along the passage, talking all the while, obviously hoping to discover what was going on. Don did not answer her. The last thing he wanted just now was to have to go through the story as he knew it – and he was uncertain at the moment as to whether he was in full possession of the facts in any case. The garbled explanation he had had from Liz at Vandina had been that Steve had made some sort of attack on Ros's sister and then disappeared, but there was also some suggestion that doubt had been cast on Steve's identity. Well, for the moment both his and Mrs Brunt's curiosity would have to wait. The most important thing, as he had pointed out, was Dinah's welfare.

He knocked on the door, called out, waited and knocked again. His anxiety was a tight knot in his stomach now and unwillingly he acknowledged the fear that had assailed him when Mrs Brunt had reported Dinah's words – 'I'm going to be with Van.'

Surely – *surely* – she hadn't done something really stupid? Could it be that what had happened had finally tipped the balance of her precarious mental stability? She took sedatives, he knew – the doctor had prescribed them for her when Van had been killed – and she had been unable to give them up completely, even during the happier times after Steve's arrival. When she had said she was going to be with Van had she meant that she simply wanted to be there in the room where she felt his presence most strongly – or had she been thinking of going to him in a more literal sense? Don felt the beads of sweat begin on his forehead. He pulled out a handkerchief to mop them away and banged on the door again.

'Dinah! For God's sake, answer me!'

Still there was only silence from the study.

'Dinah!' he called again. 'If you won't open this door I am going to have to break it down!'

'No!' The voice from behind the closed door was so tiny, so soft, that at first he thought he had imagined it. Then, as he pressed his face against the wood panelling, he heard it again. 'Please . . . just leave me alone!'

Relief coursed through him, followed almost immediately by a fresh bout of anxiety. She was alive but her voice had sounded muffled. By tears? Or because she was drowsy?

'You can't stay in there forever,' he called, trying to make his voice authoritative and comforting at the same time. 'Now open the door for me, Dinah, there's a good girl.'

He waited, mopping the beads of sweat from his forehead again.

'I suppose you could break a window,' Mrs Brunt said behind him. 'It would be easier than the door.'

He ignored her. 'Dinah, can you hear me?' he called. 'If you don't come out on your own I'm going to have to come in there and get you.'

And to his intense relief he heard the sound of the key being turned in the lock.

'All right, Mrs Brunt, I'll deal with this,' he said hastily, knowing that the last thing Dinah would want would be to have the two of them fussing over her, and unwillingly the housekeeper backed away a few steps, standing arms akimbo, head poked forward on her ample shoulders to gain the best possible view of proceedings.

He waited for Dinah to open the door. She did not, but when he tried the handle it turned. Dinah had retreated back into the room, standing beneath Van's portrait and staring up at it without moving.

Don went into the study, closing the door behind him. After a moment Dinah turned round, and although he had expected something of the sort he was still shocked by her appearance.

She had aged ten years, he thought, in the hours since he had last seen her. Her fine features were pale and drawn, her eyes huge and haunted. She looked almost unbelievably fragile, her slim figure in its perpetual black appearing more waif-like than elegant.

'Oh Don!' she said. It was half sigh, half sob. 'You've heard, I suppose, what has happened?'

'Only that Steve has disappeared. The details are very sketchy.'

'He has disappeared because the police want to talk to him. It seems he attacked Ros's sister and they think he might have something to do with Ros's disappearance too. And you know what is behind it? Ros had found out that he has been deceiving all of us. All the time. He's not my son at all. He's an American, who knew my son – my real son. They worked together on an oil rig in the North Sea. And when my son was killed . . .' Her voice cracked. '. . . he took his birth certificate and his identity. It's so awful I just can't believe it. Can you?'

'Dinah, my darling . . .' The endearment slipped out unintentionally, but now that he had gained access to the study he honestly did not know what to say to her that would not sound false or contrived. 'Dinah – I am so sorry.'

'Oh, don't be sorry!' There was an edge to her voice that might almost have been hysteria. 'I've got no one to blame but myself. What a fool I've been! What a bloody fool!'

'You weren't to know, Dinah,' Don said gently. 'We were all taken in. He was very plausible.'

Her hands clenched and unclenched.

'I wanted him to be my son so much! All these years I've longed for him so! But I should have known it wasn't him – surely, surely I should have known!' Her voice tailed away and he searched for words of comfort, but before he could begin she went on in the same flat, distant voice: 'The funny thing is I think I did know really. There was a little voice inside me saying it was too good to be true. And I couldn't see anything of us in him, no matter how hard I looked. Nothing of me and nothing of Van. That was what I couldn't understand really. I thought there would have to be something of Van. A man like him, so vital, so . . . powerful . . . surely he would have passed something on to his son?'

Dear God, she has taken leave of her senses, Don thought.

'Dinah,' he said aloud, 'I think you are letting your imagination run away with you.'

'No,' she said, 'not now – not any more. It was when *he* came that I did that. It wasn't just that I thought he was my son, my darling baby, who I'd never expected to see again. It was as if Van had come back to me – or that was what I wanted to think. And now I know it was all a lie. Van is dead and our son is dead and I'll never see either of them again.'

She leaned against the wall rocking back and forth in an agonised frenzy.

'Dinah . . .' Don felt helpless in the face of such overwhelming emotion. 'Darling, please don't do this to yourself.'

'He made me do it, you know,' Dinah wept. 'He made me give up our child and pretend it had been stillborn. He didn't want to share me. He loved me so much – and I loved him. But he shouldn't have made me do it! How could he do that to me – and to his own child?'

Don realised then, with a sense of shock, just how far Dinah had been deluding herself. When had she begun to believe that

Steve was not just her own son but also a part of Van come back to her?

'Van was not the father of your child, Dinah,' he said gently. 'You know that as well as I do. He only did what he thought was best, for both of you.'

Dinah's eyes were blank, questioning. 'Did he?'

'Yes, he did. I know things haven't turned out the way you hoped but you are just going to have to try to come to terms with that. You still have your work and you have a lot of friends who care a great deal for you.'

For a moment longer Dinah stared blankly, then suddenly her head jerked back, her features contorting into a soundless scream, and her arms clutched wildly at empty air.

'I don't want my work!' she sobbed. 'I don't want my friends. Don't you understand . . . I just want my son!'

He waited helplessly until the spasm passed and she folded her arms around herself, weeping.

'Oh Don – Don – nobody will ever understand what it's been like. You go on, everyone thinks you have forgotten, but you haven't – oh no. Inside, inside it never goes away. When he came back I thought . . . I thought . . .' Her voice tailed away to a whisper. 'I don't want to go on living. Oh Don, what am I going to do?'

Her pain tore at him and he did the only thing he could do, the one thing he had wanted to do through all the years he had known her. He went to her, taking her in his arms, holding her face into his shoulder while she sobbed her hurt, her grief, her longing.

'Dinah, dear Dinah, let me take care of you.'

And to his disbelief, to his joy in the midst of utter confusion, he heard her whisper: 'Oh please, Don. Please – yes.'

The headlights of Mike's car cut a swathe through the darkness as Ros turned into the drive leading to Luscombe Manor, a darkness made more complete by the thick overhanging trees and the fact that there was no moon. But when the house came into view there was suddenly light in abundance, blazing from every window since no one had bothered to draw the curtains, and Ros thought it looked a little like an empty stage with the spotlights full on, waiting for the players.

The sick dread of the coming interview weighed heavily within her along with the tiredness that comes from a long, wearisome journey. Ros felt as if she had been travelling forever. First the coach from the coast back to the village in company with the divers and roughnecks, then the light aircraft, the internal flight and finally the international airliner, only to be followed by the train journey from Heathrow and the taxi from Bristol. Exhausting both physically and mentally, and she had wanted nothing more than to get home, make herself a hot drink, run a deep bath with at least a bottle of scented oil in it – oh, the luxury after the spartan existence of the past week! – and go to bed in her own comfortable bed. But when she had been confronted by Mike and Maggie – what in the world had Mike been thinking of to drag Maggie all the way from Corfu? – she had realised that such a course of action was completely out of the question.

Ironic, really, that all this mayhem should have blown up just when she was away trying to sort things out with as little fuss as possible. Now she must do her best to make amends for a situation she could not help feeling had been of her making. For after all, if it had not been for her Steve would probably never have been exposed as an imposter. He was a liar and a cheat, possibly worse, and knowing what she had known there was no way she could stand idly by and let the situation continue. But if she hadn't known, if she hadn't been at Van's apartment that day and seen the real son, would it have mattered so much? For Dinah, presumably, ignorance had been bliss, and now that had been shattered in a way that could hardly have been more shocking.

Ros got out of the car, heels scrunching on the gravel. Mrs Brunt opened the door when she rang the bell.

'Ros, isn't it?' she said, peering out into the darkness. 'I thought you'd been away.'

'I have but I'm here now and I want to see Dinah.'

'She's with Mr Kennedy – in there.' She gesticulated towards the library. 'She's been in a terrible way, but I think he's calming her down.'

Ros tapped at the door and opened it. Don and Dinah were standing by the window and he was holding her in his arms. As the door opened he looked up, flushing slightly, but not letting go of her, then registered utter surprise as he saw who it was that had come in.

'Ros! What are you doing here? And where have you been?'

Dinah lifted her face from Don's shoulder. Ros could see she had been crying.

'Ros! Oh Ros, I'm sorry . . . but you have no idea of the terrible things that have been happening here . . .'

'Is this intrusion absolutely necessary, Ros?' Don asked curtly.

Ros ignored him.

'Dinah, I have something to tell you,' she said gently. 'I know what's happened here and I know you have had a terrible shock. But it's not quite what you think. Steve took the identity of your real son because he believed that he had been killed in a diving accident in South America. That was the story that got back to this country. But it had got a little distorted. There was an accident, and a man was killed. But it was not your son who died. It was his partner, the other diver in his team. Your son is alive and well and working on a rig off the coast of Argentina. That's where I've been this last week. I managed to trace him. And he has promised me that if you want to see him he will come back to England as soon as his contract is completed.'

Dinah's hands flew to her mouth.

'You're just saying that! I don't believe it! It can't be true!'

'It is true, Dinah. He is the reason I have been away from the office. I'm sorry about that – it was all a little beyond my control. Look – I know you must feel terribly betrayed and perhaps after this experience you won't want to see him but . . .'

'Not see him? Not see my son? Don't be silly! Oh, Ros, what is he like?'

Ros smiled. In spite of everything it was impossible not to smile. She found herself remembering with pleasure the man she had met in Argentina – the man who was really Dinah's son. She had liked him instantly and during the long conversations they had shared she had come to like him more and more. Perhaps more than just liking, she thought, allowing herself an echo of the warmth and attraction that had sparked between them. She had felt then that Mac was someone very special and she felt it again now, a teasing excitement deep inside. There had not been the time or the opportunity on her brief visit to discover whether that attraction could blossom into something deeper, but she had found herself hoping that the chance might yet present itself. Brendan had been her first love, wild and destructive, Van had been something of an obsession – what was it about Van that had been so compelling to women? – and with Mike she had found a relationship she had thought she could live with but which had never really sparked her on a deeply emotional level. Mac had reawakened emotions she had almost forgotten and certainly not sought, given her past experiences. But he also had about him the kind of strength that made her feel she could trust him and perhaps let down the defences she had erected and truly love again. It was a good feeling.

'He's not a bit like Steve,' she said now to Dinah. 'He is much quieter but also a great deal more genuine.'

'Oh. I see.' Dinah stood thinking, hands pressed against her mouth. Then: 'What colour are his eyes?' she asked.

'His eyes?' Ros was startled. 'Brown, I think.'

'Brown. Yes, brown.' They both looked at her, puzzled, but it was obvious she was seeing, remembering something which they could not.

Don took her hand. 'I'm very glad about this, Dinah, but I will tell you here and now that I shall not stand on the sidelines again whilst someone else takes you for a ride. I've done that for too long.'

He glanced at Ros and something in the look told her he knew, had always known about her and Van. She shifted impatiently.

'I wanted to tell you immediately about your son, Dinah, but maybe it would be best if the details waited for the morning.'

But Dinah shook her head, tremulous joy shining through what had been her tears.

'Oh no, Ros, please! I want to know all about it right now!'

Ros sighed. She rather thought it was going to be a long night.

'I have been thinking, darling,' Jayne said to Drew, 'I am going to leave Vandina and work for Reubens full time. If they'll have me.'

'If they'll have you! You know damned well how much they wanted you!' Drew stretched back lazily on his leather lounger, puffing casually on a reefer.

Jayne smiled. Drew was in total ignorance about the role she had been playing; that had all been ironed out between his father and herself, and she had not considered it wise to allow Drew in on the plan. When he had had too much to drink he was all too likely to let something slip which could have ruined everything.

'You'll do well at Reubens,' he said now. 'You won't be in the shadow of that damned woman.'

'True.'

And it was, she thought. Stealing ideas from someone else meant only a poverty of inspiration in the person doing the stealing. Jayne had begun to believe she was worth more than that. And besides, she never wanted to see Steve again as long as she lived.

When he had left this afternoon it had taken an hour before she had stopped shaking. All very well to have given the impression of being totally in control; Jayne was nothing if not an actress and she had given the performance of her life.

I have played with fire a good many times, Jayne thought, but never have I been closer to being incinerated! The flippancy of the sentiment did nothing to detract from the seriousness of the situation. Steve was prepared to go to any lengths to keep his secret and she had alerted him to the fact that she knew what it was. This time she had been lucky, this time she had talked her way out of danger, but she was not sure how long her luck would hold. Sooner or later Steve would decide he could not take the chance that she might spill the beans, and Jayne did not think that then he would give her any warning. She did not want to be around to suffer the consequences – and quite honestly there was no reason why she should be. Time to leave Vandina, time to go to Reubens not only with the tips and ideas she had picked up from Vandina but also with her own raw talent.

Jayne had given herself the afternoon off to give herself a chance to recover from her fright, but she had not wasted it. When the trembling had eventually stopped she had begun to plan – and now she put her plans to Drew.

'So you agree with me then?'

'I certainly do, babe. We've been here long enough – I'm ready to move on.'

She felt a small shadow of dismay. Would Drew ever settle anywhere? But that was a problem for the future and she would face it when the time came.

'It's lucky this place is only rented,' she said. 'I'll speak to the agents in the morning and get the contract terminated. Then I'll take a couple of days' holiday that's due to me and we'll go and look for something suitable in the right area for Reubens. Agreed?'

'Agreed.'

She smiled. The nerves had almost completely gone now, the supreme confidence returning.

'We make a pretty good team, Drew, you and I. Unconventional but very well matched.'

And he puffed his reefer and smiled lazily back at her.

Steve was on the motorway, heading north but without any really clear idea yet of where he was going to go and what he was going to do.

What a fiasco! he thought. What a waste of the most perfect set-up he was ever likely to find! But it was useless to waste time crying now over what could not be altered. He'd given it his best shot and it had all fallen apart. The only thing he could do now was get the hell out of it and start again somewhere.

When the press had arrived at the cottage and Maggie had made a run for it he had made a run too, realising that to stay would be to invite certain arrest. He had driven at speed to Luscombe Manor, packed what he could of his belongings and any small items of value that he could lay his hands on – some pieces of Dinah's jewellery, Van's gold watch and an antique hip flask, some original miniatures and a few other easily portable pieces which Dinah had told him had been highly valued. He did not suppose she would readily miss any of it and if she did he could not imagine her accusing him of stealing them. In fact he rather thought Dinah would refuse to believe any of the stories about him, so confident was he of the hold he had over her. But it was no use relying on that now. He had to get out of it and lie low for a few days while he decided what to do next. Something would come up. And at least he now knew he had a way with him that would serve him well as a con man. Perhaps that was the way his mind should be running. But whatever he did it had to be big. He had tasted a way of life he liked. He had no intention of settling for less.

Steve positioned his car in the fast lane and put his foot down.

Best to put as much distance as he could between himself and Somerset before he looked for somewhere to put up for the night. The cars ahead of him on the motorway mutated from glowing red tail lights to indistinct blurs to recognisable shapes as he sped past them; the headlights of traffic on the southbound carriageway rushed past him in a never-ending series of bright flares.

He became aware of the flashing blue light as something alien in this pattern, and glancing in his rear-view mirror saw it bearing down on him from behind. Too late he realised he should have stayed in the slow lane and done nothing to draw attention to himself. They might only be after him for exceeding the speed limit now, but if they caught him they would very soon realise – if his description had been circulated – that he was a wanted man. His car was distinctive – he was distinctive.

Oh shit! Steve thought. He put his foot flat to the boards and the car surged forward. Faster, faster, as fast as he could go, with the needle creeping up and the lights zooming past at such a rate that they almost made him dizzy. But still the police car was there on his tail.

Steve's mind was racing almost as fast as the car and he found himself remembering another chase, years ago and thousands of miles away. The car that was on his tail would be in radio contact with their headquarters, they would be asking for assistance, maybe setting up a roadblock. His only chance was to get off the motorway. He kept his foot down until he saw the signs for the next exit, screamed past the traffic in the centre lane and swerved left. The exit lane came up to meet him, too fast. He braked hard and felt the car getting away from him. For timeless seconds he fought with the steering wheel but he was skidding sideways. The front end of the car ran off the road and suddenly the world was turning topsy-turvy, over and over, the lights making crazy patterns in his head, his ears resounding to the sounds of tortured metal and splintering glass. The car came to rest on its roof. For a moment Steve was too stunned for thought, then desperately he tried to free himself. Useless. Almost unhurt but effectively trapped upside down by his seat belt Steve could do nothing but struggle helplessly and watch the blue flashing lights of the police car draw up alongside him, portents of a fate he could no longer escape.

Epilogue

Maggie sat on the low wall at the edge of the ocean, watching the sun dip into the darkening water. On the horizon sea merged with sky in a faint blue haze which marked the coast of Albania, and the peace was broken only by the distant barking of a dog and the first mournful cry of a skops owl in an olive grove above the house.

Peace, perfect peace – the end of yet another Corfu day. If only she could take just a small measure of that peace into her heart. But she could not. She had come home and everything was the same as it had always been yet also subtly different. And the difference put a turmoil where once there had been acceptance, and the sameness made the future stretching ahead of her almost unbearable.

She had left England the day after Ros's reappearance. Ros had begged her to stay a while longer but she had refused. She didn't want to have to face Mike again, didn't want to have to be strong for a moment longer than was absolutely necessary. She had booked a flight and left without seeing him again and the leaving had been a pain inside her that was both sharp and also heavy and dull with hopelessness.

She had thought that perhaps once she was back in Corfu the memory of the way she had felt with Mike would dull a little, blur around the edges until it could be assimilated into everyday life as nothing but a sweet ache for what might have been. Perhaps she would be able to transfer some of the energy she had felt in England into making her marriage to Ari work. She had to make it work! – the commitment was there just as it had always been and in it was her future. But the reality had not been easy.

'So, you have decided to come home then,' Ari had said, cool and sarcastic. 'What have I done to deserve this?'

What have you done? she felt like asking. Have you spent your nights in my absence with Melina? But she had said nothing. What right did she have now to question his fidelity? Hadn't she behaved just as badly?

'Ari, please, couldn't we try to make this work?' she had pleaded.

But his reply had not been encouraging.

'I have always tried, Maggie. I shall continue to try. What you do is up to you.'

The distance between them had chilled her and she found herself comparing it all too readily with the closeness she had felt with Mike, then blaming herself for this further betrayal.

Life had quickly returned to the old pattern, the days when she wandered aimlessly about the house, the late nights when he did not come home, and always, always the claustrophobic web of his family drawing her in. Sometimes Maggie caught herself waiting, waiting for something, and though she could not consciously put her finger on what it was she wondered if it might be that subconsciously she was hoping for some word from Mike.

He wouldn't get in touch, of course, she knew that. She had made her position clear and he was too proud to try to persuade her to change her mind – even if he wanted to, which was doubtful. She had heard from Ros and it sounded as if she had been seeing Mike. The mention of his name in Ros's letter was painful, yet Maggie read and reread it, savouring it in a way that gave her a strangely masochistic pleasure.

Ros's letter told her other things, too. Steve had been arrested – he had crashed his car after a motorway chase and been found to be in possession of a number of items which he had stolen from Luscombe Manor. There could be other charges, too, if Maggie was to come home and press them. Maggie set her jaw at that. She had no intention of going home to give evidence about what had happened at the cottage on that last day.

The letter contained other pieces of news – Dinah was bearing up well, and there was talk that she was going to marry Don Kennedy. Ros hoped that when Mac came home from South America and came to see her some of the horror of what she had suffered would be erased for ever. Oh yes, and Jayne Peters-Browne had left Vandina very suddenly and gone to work for the rival firm of Reubens.

'I suspect she might have had something to do with the leaks of security we had here,' Ros had written. 'But if anything I think she did Vandina a favour. There is enormous enthusiasm for Dinah's new line in luggage and working for it has given Dinah something else to think about in these trying times.'

Maggie had been glad for Dinah but it was only a thin veneer to cover the well of constant sadness she was experiencing herself.

Now, sitting and watching the sun dip into the sea, the confusion within her made tight knots of indecision. If only I could have a cigarette! Maggie thought with longing. But she knew she must not. She had been meaning to give up for ages and now she had to – it was not only her own health that was at stake. For Maggie had found out that she was pregnant.

The discovery had been a complete shock to her. Preoccupied as she had been it had not even occurred to her that her period was late until one morning she had woken up with a little niggle in her stomach that had reminded her. She hadn't had a period since she had been to England! She had got up, then, and fetched her diary so as to make some calculations. Yes – it should definitely have started ten days earlier. Maggie was alarmed. She was usually extremely regular. Perhaps all the traumas of the last weeks had caused her to be late, she thought – she had heard that flying could cause an upset in the hormones, and goodness knows she had run the gamut of all kinds of emotional storms besides. But somehow, however she tried to rationalise, the suspicion was there lurking just below the surface, and a visit to the doctor confirmed it. The lateness of her period was no hormonal fluke. She was, the doctor told her, pregnant.

At first Maggie could scarcely believe it. For so long she had believed herself unable to conceive that she had almost stopped thinking about it. Now she found herself experiencing a cocktail of confusion, joy and something not unlike panic. For instinctively she knew the child she was carrying was not Ari's, but Mike's.

What the hell was she going to do? she asked herself now, sitting on the wall and looking out to sea. As yet she had not told Ari the news and she did not know how she was going to bring herself to do it. He would be delighted and so would his family. Wasn't this what they had wanted for so long? But the thought of accepting their congratulations was anathema to her; pretending the baby was Ari's was a deceit she could not countenance. Yet to tell the truth would mean the end of her marriage.

There is no way out, no way at all, Maggie thought, and found herself thinking of Dinah, faced all those years ago with a similar dilemma. Dinah had solved her problem by having her baby adopted and Maggie supposed her own parallel solution would be an abortion. But it was something that she could not consider for even a moment. She wanted her baby, wanted it desperately, not only for herself, but also because it was a part of Mike.

The breeze whispered in from the sea and Maggie shivered. She got up from the low wall and started back towards the house; halfway there she heard the telephone ringing.

The sense of *déjà vu* was immediate, whisking her back to that other evening when Mike had telephoned to say Ros was missing and it had all begun. Could it be . . .? Would she lift the receiver and hear Mike's voice at the other end of the line? The longing was a sharp pain deep inside her. She ran into the house and snatched up the receiver, and when she heard the crackles on the line signifying a long-distance call she began to tremble.

'Hello?'

'Maggie! Is that you? Can you hear me?'

Not Mike, but Ros. Maggie felt the disappointment like a physical blow.

'Ros! Hi! What a surprise!'

'A surprise to be able to get through!' Ros quipped. 'How are you anyway?'

'Fine.' But it was a lie. 'And you?'

'Yes. Look, Maggie, I don't think we should waste time on small talk in case we get cut off. The reason I'm ringing is to let you know that Mike and I have broken up – gone our separate ways.'

Maggie felt her stomach fall away.

'You and Mike? Why?'

'Lots of reasons. For one, I think I'm in love with someone else.'

'Who?'

'Dinah's son – her *real* son, Mac. I can't seem to get him out of my mind, Maggie. I can't stop thinking about him.' In spite of the poor quality of the international line Maggie could hear the glow of pride and pleasure in Ros's voice, a nuance that had been missing through the turbulent years.

'I see. And what about Mike?'

'Well to be honest, that's the reason I'm ringing. I think Mike is in love, too. With you.'

Maggie's heart had begun to beat very fast and very irregularly. 'Why? What has he said?'

'It's not so much what he's said as the way he looks whenever your name is mentioned. What did you do to him, I'd like to know?'

'Nothing. I'm sure you're wrong . . .'

'I'm sure I'm right! You can't pretend nothing happened while you were here. I just don't believe you. You haven't been happy with Ari for ages – admit it. And if you feel the same way about Mike that I feel about Mac you'll get on and do something about it. He hasn't been in touch, I suppose?'

'No.'

'No, he wouldn't. Wife-snatching isn't his style. Well, darling, I guess it's up to you now. Don't let him slip away, Maggie, if it's as special as I think it is. That sort of thing only happens once or twice in a lifetime, believe me.' The line crackled. 'Look, I'd better go now. Maybe see you soon.'

'Yes – and thanks for ringing, Ros.'

'No problems.' And she was gone.

Maggie replaced the receiver and stood with her hands pressed to her mouth. All kinds of emotions were darting inside her – surprise that Ros and Mike had broken up, in spite of what had happened between them, pleasure for Ros that she seemed to have allowed herself to fall in love again at last, and a crazy spiralling excitement that maybe, now that the coast was clear, there could be something between her and Mike. But the sense of euphoria that Ros's call had evoked lasted only briefly – and then reality was rushing in. There was no getting away from the fact that the telephone call had come from Ros – Mike had made no effort to contact her and try to persuade her to return to England, and she didn't think he would. And even if he did, there was still Ari to consider. Maybe theirs was not a happy marriage but to Maggie it was still a binding one.

The hell with it, Maggie thought, I am going to have a cigarette. Just one can't possibly hurt.

She fetched her wrap, lit that one forbidden cigarette, and went back outside to sit on the patio. She was still there, an hour later, when she heard Ari's car on the track.

He came swaggering around the corner of the house and she

knew at once that he had been drinking. When he saw her sitting there he checked, adopting a hectoring tone.

'What are you doing sitting out here for? Why aren't you ready for bed?'

'Why shouldn't I sit out here as long as I like?' Maggie flashed back. 'And talking of time, where have you been? If it's too late for me to sit on the patio, surely you should have been home hours ago.'

'Maggie, we are not going to go all over this again, I hope. What's the matter with you, always nagging?'

He made to walk past her and as he did so she caught a whiff of that unmistakable, elusive perfume.

'You've been with *her*, haven't you? Melina! Don't deny it, Ari. I can smell her from here.'

'What if I have? At least she doesn't nag me all the time.'

'I don't suppose she does – she's not your wife!'

'More's the pity.' He muttered it under his breath, but she heard.

'*What* did you say?'

'I said "more's the pity",' he returned defiantly. 'The trouble with you, Maggie, is that you are too damned English. Greek girls know how to treat their men. They don't nag all the time and they don't go flying off home at a moment's notice. My family warned me, did you know that? They wanted me to marry someone like Melina. But oh no, I knew best. I thought I was a modern man and we would have a modern marriage.'

'But we haven't, have we?' Maggie said. Suddenly she was not angry any more, but sad. 'This isn't a modern marriage. It's a Corfiote one. In the end your traditions were too strong for you to break. And I don't think I can cope with them, Ari.'

He shrugged. 'Oh come on, this is getting us nowhere. Let's go to bed.'

'No,' she said. 'We can't sweep it under the carpet yet again. Tell me the truth – would you rather be married to Melina than to me?'

'What sort of a question is that?'

'An honest one. I am asking you a simple question and I want a straightforward answer. Would you be happier married to Melina?'

'How should I know?' he blustered. '*You* are my wife.'

'But if I wasn't – would you go to her? Your family would like it, wouldn't they? A nice Corfiote girl who behaved the way they expected. Could she bring you a dowry, Ari? A few olive groves, perhaps? And I'm quite sure she could give you . . .' She broke off, her hands flying automatically to her stomach. Ari had always insisted that the fact they had not had a baby before now was her fault, but obviously that was untrue. She had made love with Mike on just one occasion and she was pregnant. That meant, surely, that the fault must lie elsewhere. She hesitated, torn yet again with indecision as to what she could do about her situation – and Ari's. But as she hesitated his black eyes flashed angrily. He had seen the small instinctive gesture – and misunderstood it.

'Yes,' he grated. 'If you were going to say she could give me a son I am quite sure you are right. I don't know what's the matter with you, Maggie. Haven't I done enough to make you pregnant? Yet nothing happens. You know what I think? That you are a barren woman! You will never give me a child. I am ashamed to face my parents and tell them there is no little one. You have failed me in this, Maggie, and it is worse than the nagging, worse than all your stupid English ways. I am a man – I deserve a son. And yes, I think Melina could give me one, since you ask. And my parents would be pleased to know their grandchild was pure-born Corfiote!'

His outburst had shocked Maggie to the core. She had been on the point of trying to tell him gently that perhaps he really should seek medical advice; now suddenly she saw his blindness for what it was and it made her furiously angry. How dare he blame her for his childlessness? How dare he patronise and chastise her? And how dare he treat her – and their marriage – with such disdain? Perhaps he was Greek, but he had been in England long enough to see things from her point of view if he only had the sensitivity. But he did not.

'Well, if you want a child with Melina I suggest you do something about it!' she said.

She saw the shock on his face. 'Maggie . . .'

'No, I mean it,' she said. 'You have obviously regretted your rashness in marrying me for a very long time. And to be honest I have regretted it too. I have tried, I really have tried to make this marriage work because I didn't want to admit defeat, didn't want all the prophets of doom to be proved right. But I'm afraid they were right. It's never going to work, Ari, it's never going to make either of us really happy. And I suggest we end it here and now before either of us gets hurt any more.'

Ari made to speak, then gesticulated impatiently.

'Maggie, I am going to bed. We will talk about this again in the morning.'

'Yes,' she said. 'But I already know what the outcome will be.'

He threw her a black glance and went into the house. By the time she followed he was already in the bedroom, banging about.

Maggie crossed the living room, looking around and wondering why the house that had been her home ever since she had come to Corfu suddenly looked so alien to her. There was really nothing of herself here, she thought; she had tried so hard to adapt to the Greek way of life, but it had not worked out. But suddenly it was almost unimportant, a mere curtain-raiser to the rest of her life. Only one thing was important now, and that was being with Mike.

She crossed to the telephone, picked up the receiver and dialled the international code for England. The bell at the other end seemed to ring for ever and she began to think he was not there. But with a sort of desperate optimism she waited and waited, praying that the line would not break up, praying that he would answer.

When she heard his voice her knees went weak. Dear God, she loved him!

'Mike?' she said. 'Mike – it's me, Maggie. I've just decided. I'm coming home.'

She held her breath then, half afraid of what he would say. When he replied his words were typically phlegmatic, but even across the thousands of miles of telephone wires she heard the genuine emotion in his voice.

'Thank God for that, Maggie. I'll be waiting.'